KNOCKDOWN

KNOCKDOWN
A RIG WARRIOR NOVEL

WILLIAM W. JOHNSTONE

AND J. A. JOHNSTONE

PINNACLE BOOKS
KENSINGTON PUBLISHING CORP.

www.kensingtonbooks.com

PINNACLE BOOKS are published by

Kensington Publishing Corp.
119 West 40th Street
New York, NY 10018

PUBLISHER'S NOTE

Following the death of William W. Johnstone, the Johnstone family is working with a carefully selected writer to organize and complete Mr. Johnstone's outlines and many unfinished manuscripts to create additional novels in all of his series like The Last Gunfighter, Mountain Man, and Eagles, among others. This novel was inspired by Mr. Johnstone's superb storytelling.

All Kensington titles, imprints, and distributed lines are available at special quantity discounts for bulk purchases for sales promotions, premiums, fund-raising, educational, or institutional use. Special book excerpts or customized printings can also be created to fit specific needs. For details, write or phone the office of the Kensington sales manager: Kensington Publishing Corp., 119 West 40th Street, New York, NY 10018, attn: Sales Department; phone 1-800-221-2647.

PINNACLE BOOKS, the Pinnacle logo, and the WWJ steer head logo are Reg. U.S. Pat. & TM Off.

ISBN-13: 978-0-7860-4428-3
ISBN-10: 0-7860-44428-4

First printing: September 2020

10 9 8 7 6 5 4 3 2 1

Printed in the United States of America

Electronic edition:

ISBN-13: 978-0-7860-4429-0 (e-book)
ISBN-10: 0-7860-44429-2 (e-book)

CHAPTER 1

The fat man ran the keen edge of the blade across the ball of his thumb, studied the bead of dark red blood that was the result, and then licked it off.

"You see, my machete is very sharp, *gringo*. You will barely feel a thing when I cut your head off with it."

"Yeah, well, I guarantee you'll feel it when I shove that pigsticker up your *culo* and start twisting it, Pancho."

The man sitting at the table in the corner of the little cantina slurred his words. The mostly empty bottle of tequila in front of him explained why. The fiery liquor he had guzzled down also explained the boldness of his response.

The fat man scowled and stepped closer to the table.

The three men who had been at the bar with him started in that direction as well, as if they sensed that the situation had just become more serious. They couldn't have actually heard the words—not with *Tejano* music blaring in the cantina, mixing with the breathless drone of the announcer calling the soccer game on the TV mounted above the bar and trying to make it more exciting than it really was. No, it was far too loud.

Maybe they smelled the blood.

A big man sitting at the bar turned his head to watch the three *amigos* headed for the table in the corner. He swiveled on the chair and stood up. He towered over everybody else in here, and his shoulders were as wide as an axe handle. Thick slabs of muscle on his arms and shoulders bulged in the fabric of his black T-shirt.

"*Señor*," the bartender said behind him. The big man looked around. The bartender shook his head worriedly and went on in English, "You should not interfere, *señor*. Those men, they are . . . Zaragosa."

The big man frowned.

The bartender lowered his voice even more. The big man could barely hear him as he half-whispered, "Cartel. *Comprende?* Look around."

The big man looked and got what the bartender was talking about. Everybody else in the cantina was doing their best not to even glance in the direction of the looming confrontation in the corner. Nobody wanted to get involved and risk offending the cartel.

"That guy's an American," the big man said. "I'm not gonna just stand by and let him get hurt."

An eloquent shrug from the bartender. He had tried to prevent trouble. No one could blame him now for what might happen.

Over in the corner, the fat man with the machete said, "What did you call me?"

"Are you deaf as well as stupid, Pancho?"

The man at the table reached for the bottle. He had lean, weathered features under close-cropped gray hair. It was difficult to tell how old he was. Anywhere from fifty to seventy would be a good guess.

His hand trembled a little as it closed around the neck of the bottle. Whether the tremor was from age, a neurological condition, or too much to drink was also impossible to say.

The fat man spat a few curses in Spanish, lifted the machete, and slammed it down on the table in front of the *gringo*. The blade bit deeply into the old, scarred wood. The fat man's lips drew back from his teeth in a snarl as he leaned forward.

"I will not cut off your head," he said. "The next time, my blade will cleave your skull down to your shoulders, *viejo*!"

"Ain't gonna be no next time. You really are stupid. Your little knife's stuck, *gordo*!"

At the same time, the big man moved up behind the fat man's three *compadres* and said in a loud voice, "Hey! What're you doing to that old geezer?"

The fat man wrenched at the machete. The old man was right. The blade had embedded itself so deeply in the tabletop that it was stuck.

The old man came up out of his chair like a rattlesnake uncoiling and swung the tequila bottle he held by the neck.

The fat man tried to jerk back out of the way. The old man was too fast. The bottle smacked hard against the side of the fat man's head but didn't break. The impact made the fat man take a quick step to his right, but he caught himself and grinned.

"I'm gonna mess you up, *viejo*."

The old man said, "Oh, crap."

The fat man's three buddies turned toward the big *hombre* who had challenged them. He didn't give them a chance to set themselves. Throwing his arms out wide, he charged them, grabbing the two on the flanks and bulling his shoulder right into the one in the middle.

That bull rush swept them all backward into the fat man, who was trying to wrench the machete loose from the table.

It was like a tidal wave of flesh washing over the fat man and knocking him forward into the table. The old man hopped out of the way with a nimbleness that belied his age.

The weight of all four men came down on the table. Its spindly legs snapped, and the whole thing crashed to the floor. The fat man and his *amigos* sprawled on the wreckage. One of the men howled in pain as he got pushed against the edge of the machete and the blade sliced into his leg.

With an athletic grace uncommon in a man of his size, the big *hombre* had caught his balance before he could fall on top of the others. He took a step back and looked at the old man. "We'd better get out of here."

"Not yet," the old man said with a gleam in his eyes. "Pancho and me still got to settle up."

CHAPTER 2

The big man rolled his eyes and then swung around to face the rest of the customers in the dim, smoke-hazed cantina. They were watching with a mixture of keen interest and trepidation, but none of them seemed eager to mix in.

According to the bartender, the fat man and his friends worked for the Zaragosa drug cartel, and nobody wanted to mess in cartel business.

The old man leaned over, caught hold of the fat man's dirty shirtfront with his left hand, pulled him up a little, and used his right hand to slap him hard, back and forth. Before that, the fat man had appeared a little stunned from being knocked down, but the sharp blows knocked his wits back into him.

He roared in anger and used a foot to hook one of the old man's legs out from under him. The two of them grappled together and rolled across the filthy floor.

Two of the other three tried to get up and rejoin the fight. The third man was still yelling as he clamped both hands around his leg, which was bleeding heavily from the machete wound. It looked like he might have nicked an artery.

As the two cartel members scrambled to their feet, the big *hombre* caught them by the neck from behind. The muscles in his arms and shoulders bunched as he slammed the two men together. Their heads *clunked* loudly. Both men came unhinged at the knees and crumpled to the floor again.

The big man gestured toward the bleeder and addressed the room at large in decent Spanish: "Somebody better help him before he bleeds to death."

When he turned his head, he saw that the old man somehow was getting the best of his overweight opponent. The wiry old codger knelt on the fat man's chest and punched him in the face again and again. Blood blurred the fat man's features. The big *hombre* stepped up behind the old man and hooked his hands under his arms.

"Come on," he said. "He's out of it. And we need to be out of here."

The old man was breathing hard. He glared down at the fat man. But after a few seconds, he said, "Yeah, you're right." He shook free of the big man's grip. "Let's go."

With the four cartel members out of action, no one else in the cantina made a move to stop the two *gringos* as they headed for the door. They stepped out into the hot night air. Gravel crunched under their feet as they crossed the parking lot.

The door of the squalid cinder-block building slammed open behind them. The big *hombre* looked back and muttered, "Oh, crap."

The fat man stumbled out of the cantina and waved his hand, which was holding a pistol. It spurted flame and thundered in the night. The big man sprinted toward the pickup he had driven across the international bridge from Texas earlier in the evening. The old man followed him.

"Where's your car?" the big *hombre* flung over his shoulder.

"Don't have one! I walked across the bridge!"

That could actually be smarter than driving in Mexico, but wandering around a border town at night wasn't a very bright thing to do these days. Such places had always been hotbeds of crime, but now, with the so-called authorities virtually powerless when compared to the cartels, *norteamericanos* risked their lives being anywhere near the border, let alone across it.

At the moment, however, the big *hombre* was glad he had transportation out of here. The fat man was shooting wild, but there was no telling when he might get the range.

"Come with me!" the big man yelled to his newfound companion. He hoped nobody had stolen or slashed his tires while he was in the cantina, or damaged the engine in some way.

The big man unlocked both doors of the pickup with the remote key as they ran toward it. The old man yanked the passenger door open and piled in while the big *hombre* threw himself behind the wheel.

Gravel kicked up not far from the pickup as the bullets came closer. The engine cranked, caught. The big man slammed the truck into gear and peeled out, spraying gravel behind him. A wild turn onto the potholed highway, and he was speeding toward the cluster of high-intensity lights that marked the international bridge a quarter of a mile away.

The big man watched the rearview mirror. No headlights popped into view. That was good. Even if the bridge wasn't busy, crossing would take long enough that the fat man and his friends could catch up if they wanted to. Maybe they were back there attending to the guy who'd sliced his leg open.

"Well, that was a mite exciting," the old man said. He didn't sound drunk anymore.

The big man just glanced over at him and didn't say anything. At the bridge, he guided the pickup into the Ready Lane line behind two other vehicles. The American border guards passed those through fairly quickly. Still no headlights coming up behind the pickup. The old man handed the big *hombre* his driver's license. He put it with his own and handed them to the guard as he pulled up to the now-lowered barrier.

The guard scanned the RFID chips on the licenses and then nodded at the results that came up on his scanner. He asked the usual customs questions about regulated goods they might have with them.

The big man said, "Nope, not a thing."

The guard handed the licenses back, then nodded at his cohort in the control booth, who pushed buttons and started the barrier lifting. The big man waited for it to clear and drove through at an unhurried pace, back onto Texas soil.

He drove through the border city, a garish oasis of lights in the vast darkness of the border country, and pulled into the parking lot of a nondescript motel on the north side of town, away from the border.

He brought the pickup to a stop beside an eighteen-wheeler parked at the edge of the lot, a Kenworth long-hood conventional with an extra-large sleeper behind the cab.

The big *hombre* killed the lights and engine, then sat there in the darkness for a long moment before he turned to the old man and said, "All right, Barry, what the hell was all *that* about?"

CHAPTER 3

"Take it easy, Jake. It was all under control."

"It didn't look under control to me," Jake Rivers said. "Especially when blood started spurting out of that guy's leg. He may have bled out by now."

Barry Rivers shrugged. "That wasn't supposed to happen. Just bad luck the guy fell on the machete and cut himself. But I imagine Pancho got the bleeding stopped in time. If he didn't . . . well, that's one more Zaragosa foot soldier the good guys won't have to worry about in the future."

He paused, then added dryly, "Anyway, what happens on the other side of the river isn't your worry. You were a little outside of your jurisdiction, after all."

Jake leaned back against the pickup seat and sighed. "So were you."

"Nope, not really." Barry shook his head. "I don't have any jurisdiction. I just go where I need to go and do what needs to be done."

Jake might have argued with him out of habit, but deep down, he knew his uncle was right. Sometimes the good guys had to bend the rules a little.

The trick was to not bend them so much that you became one of the bad guys.

Unfortunately, that distinction was a pretty murky one sometimes.

He pushed that thought aside and said, "What I want to know is what we were doing there in the first place. Why'd you ask me to meet you there? And why, in the name of all that's holy, would you pretend to be drunk and pick a fight with a bunch of cartel enforcers?"

"How do you know I wasn't really drunk?"

Jake made a skeptical noise. "You wouldn't have sobered up this fast if you were. Anyway, in the five years I've known you, I've never seen you drunk. I doubt if you'd start now."

Barry chuckled. "You don't know everything about me, kid. I've done some things I'm not proud of. I was pretty close to being a drunk for a while. But that was a long time ago." Barry shook his head. "A whole other life, it seems like sometimes."

Silence lay between them for several moments. It was true that quite a bit of Barry's shadowy existence was still shrouded in mystery to Jake. Up until a few years earlier, Jake had believed that his uncle was long dead, killed in an explosion when Jake was just a child.

Barry had survived that murder attempt, though. Plastic surgery had turned him into the top-secret operative code-named Dog.

He had worked for those at the highest levels of government. Sometimes, he had worked *against* those at the highest level of government when they didn't have the best interests of the country and its citizens at heart.

Over time, Dog, or the Rig Warrior, as he was sometimes called, had become part legend, part boogeyman in the intelligence community. Some people didn't believe he even existed, or at least professed not to believe.

There was a good chance they just didn't want to draw his attention to them.

Because where Dog went, death often followed.

Jake might not ever have known any of that if a gang of vicious criminals and terrorists hadn't taken over the university campus where he was taking postgraduate courses and trying to figure out what to do with his life.

A decorated veteran, deadly with fists, blades, and guns, Jake hadn't taken that atrocity lying down. He had fought back with everything he had, and along the way he had gotten some vital help from a mysterious figure who had turned out to be his long-lost uncle.

Discovering the truth about Barry had led Jake to take up a similar mission of his own to right the wrongs in the world, only these days Jake was doing it through more established channels. With the backing of a special agent named Walt Graham he had met during that crisis at the university, Jake had joined the FBI, graduating at the top of his training class at Quantico.

So far, it had been the best decision of his life. He enjoyed the work, liked the idea of taking down low-life scum in all walks of life. The power struggles and manipulation in the upper echelons of the bureau sometimes bothered him, but he ignored that aspect as much as he could and focused on catching the bad guys.

He was good at catching them, too. He could have risen in the bureau's hierarchy—if he had wanted to. But that would have meant playing those political games, and Jake was having no part of that.

He had stayed in touch with Barry, though, and even helped him out now and then, when he could without straying too far from FBI protocols. He was a straight arrow, to use an old-fashioned, out-of-fashion term. He knew it. Couldn't help it.

So he hadn't been surprised when Barry had contacted him through the usual back channels and requested a meet in that cantina on the Mexican side of the border.

Jake, who was working out of the Dallas field office these days, had been able to take a few personal days to make the trip down here. Barry had told Jake to pretend not to know him, at least until Barry gave him a sign that it was all right, so that was what Jake had done.

"You could have gotten us killed, you know," he said now, not liking how irritable he sounded but unable to do anything about that, either. "Those cartel guys aren't known for their tender mercy. That fat one wanted to cut your head off."

"Nah, I don't think he really did. He was just fooling, showing off for his *amigos*."

"Are you crazy? After that he tried to shoot us."

"Believe me, Jake," Barry said, "if Pancho really wanted to shoot us, we'd be dead now."

"You can't know—" Jake stopped abruptly. He looked over at his uncle. The light from the motel's neon sign painted Barry's lean face in green, red, and yellow shades.

"You *do* know, don't you?" Jake went on. "You know what kind of shot that cartel enforcer is."

"Pancho gets top marks on the range," Barry said. "He's one of the best shots in the DEA."

CHAPTER 4

Jake closed his eyes, shook his head, and muttered something under his breath. Then he asked, "Is Pancho his real name?"

Barry nodded. "Pancho Gonzalez Gutierrez. Named after an old tennis player you've probably never heard of. Pretty clichéd, isn't it? But I've known more than one guy whose real name was John Smith."

"And he's an agent with the Drug Enforcement Administration?"

"Yeah. Known him for years. We worked on a few ops together, a long time ago."

"And here I thought you were just being politically incorrect, as usual, when you called him Pancho."

"That's what his friends thought, too. I don't think anything that happened tonight will give them any cause to suspect him, do you?"

Jake didn't answer that. Instead he asked, "How long has he been undercover?"

"I'm not sure. Two years, at least."

"Did he get hold of you and request a meet?"

"That's right. He said he had some intel for me. He

passed it along while we were rolling around the floor, fighting."

"Why you and not his bosses at the DEA?"

Barry's voice took on a slightly more serious note as he said, "Now that, I can't tell you. Unless . . . and I'm just shooting from the hip here . . . he has some reason not to trust them completely."

Jake leaned back against the pickup seat again. "That's a pretty serious accusation."

"I'm not accusing anybody. I'm just saying that would explain why Pancho reached out to me. He knows I'd always have his back."

Jake thought that over and nodded. "So what did he tell you?"

"The Zaragosa cartel doesn't just smuggle drugs into this country. I already knew that. They'll bring in anything as long as the price is right, including people."

"Human trafficking," Jake said. The revulsion and anger in his voice made it clear what he thought of that. "The bureau is aware of it."

"No, I'm not talking about coyotes running truckloads of illegals across the border."

"You mean undocumented immigrants."

"No, I mean illegals, blast it," Barry said. "They're criminals. Don't think the fact that I recognize that means I don't have any compassion for them. I do . . . most of them. Not for the drug addicts and thieves and rapists and murderers, though."

He slashed the air with his hand. "We're getting off the subject here. What I'm talking about is how the Zaragosa cartel will also bring in high-profile clients who are willing to pay a lot of money to ensure that they get into this country without anybody knowing. Pancho's heard rumors that a job like that is in the works."

"Who's the client?"

"He hasn't been able to find out yet. Whoever it is, though, must be somebody with plenty of financial backing who doesn't mean well. Otherwise, he wouldn't hire the Zaragosas to get him across the border."

Jake cocked his head to the side and said, "Your friend was able to tell you all this while you were rolling around on the floor, pretending to be trying to kill each other?"

"He's pretty good at boiling things down to their essentials."

"Wait a minute. If the whole thing was a ruse so he could pass on that intel to you, why'd you beat him up so bad? He had blood all over his face."

"Had to make it look good," Barry said. "Pancho understood that. Shoot, if I hadn't roughed him up, *that* would have looked suspicious. As deep cover as he is, he couldn't afford that."

He laughed and went on, "Of course, now his *amigos* are going to give him trouble about getting his butt kicked by an old *gringo*. Speaking of which . . . Don't think I didn't hear you call me an old geezer back there. You should be showing more respect to your elders, boy."

"Maybe I would have if I'd known what was going on. As far as I could tell, you'd gone loco." Jake shrugged. "But I guess I understand now. What's the next step?"

"Pancho's going to keep trying to turn up more intel on his side. We'll work the case from this side."

"We?" Jake repeated. "I'm on my own time here, not the bureau's."

"Well, you've got more personal time coming, don't you?"

"And cases of my own to work!"

Barry waved that away. "Nothing as big as this is going to turn out to be."

"How can you possibly know that?"

"That's what my gut tells me, and I've learned to trust my gut. I wouldn't still be alive without it."

For a moment, Jake didn't say anything, then, "You're going to get me kicked out of the bureau, that's what you're going to do. You know that, don't you?"

Barry grinned in the neon glare. "What's more important, being a bureaucrat . . . or saving the world?"

"Your gut says this case is that big?"

Barry sniffed. "Says it could be."

Jake drew in a deep breath, blew it out. "I guess you've got yourself a partner . . . for now. I'll work it out. On one condition. I don't go into any more situations blind. You tell me what's going on ahead of time . . . you old geezer."

"I've killed men for less than that."

The bad part was, Jake wasn't sure if his uncle was joking or not.

CHAPTER 5

Western Nevada

The train was a short one, only six tank cars behind a huge GE AC6000CW locomotive with six thousand horses—very overpowered for the current job. It was available, though, and the bosses wanted to get that goop to the containment site as soon as possible, so Rudy Hendrickson wasn't going to complain.

He wasn't going to ask too many questions about what was in the tank cars back there behind the short-hood puller, either. He knew it was hazardous. The train's destination was a hazardous waste containment facility in middle-of-nowhere Nevada, and places didn't get any more middle of nowhere than that. He and his fireman, Daryl Marshall, would get there and stay out of the way while guys in protective suits hooked up thick hoses and drained the tankers into underground containment trenches. Then they'd decontaminate the tankers, inside and out, and once that was done, Rudy and Daryl would be on their way back to Reno. They had made this run before, so it was nothing new to them.

The train was making good speed south toward the containment facility. Rudy sat on the right-hand side of the cab and checked all the display screens and gauges and dials on the control stand spread out in front of him in an abbreviated U-shape. He performed those checks diligently, because he was a professional engineer and that was his job.

At the same time, he'd been at this long enough that he could tell by the sound and feel of the train that it was moving along just as it was supposed to. The big engine was in good shape and didn't miss a beat.

From the fireman's seat on the left side of the cab, Daryl pointed through the windshield and said, "Look up yonder. Is that a roadrunner goin' across the tracks?"

"No, and we're not gonna find any tunnel mouths painted on the sides of cliffs, either," Rudy replied. "You're such a kid. Grow up, Daryl."

"Hey, there's nothin' wrong with likin' them cartoons. I read some article online that said they was masterpieces of animated cinema."

"Yeah, they are pretty funny, I suppose," Rudy admitted. "But they're still kid stuff."

The tracks ran straight and mostly level through this area. A few slight rises, but nothing you could even remotely call a hill. To the left, about five miles east of the rail line, a range of small mountains jutted up abruptly without any foothills. To the west were sandy flats dotted with scrub brush stretching as far as the eye could see.

Rudy knew every foot of the route. Three miles ahead, the tracks descended into a broad, shallow valley known as Rattlesnake Wash. In that valley was the Rattlesnake Wash Industrial Containment Facility, owned by Sherman Global Enterprises. Rudy knew that because he'd seen the name on the sign attached to the outer fence. He didn't know anything else about the place and didn't care. One destination was pretty much like any other, as far as he was concerned.

Daryl leaned forward in the fireman's chair and squinted against the sun glare coming through the windshield.

"What's that?" he asked, pointing down the tracks.

"Don't go tellin' me you've spotted a coyote now."

"No, it's something flying above the tracks."

"A bird?" Rudy leaned forward to peer through the glass, too. "Maybe a big buzzard?"

"Naw, not flyin' like that. I know! It's a drone."

Rudy had spotted the thing by now, swooping and flitting back and forth through the air not far above the tracks a couple hundred yards in front of the train.

"That doesn't make any sense! Those things are radio controlled and have a fairly short range, and there's nobody around here to be guiding it."

Or maybe there was, he realized as he spotted a reflection off something to the right of the tracks. He looked closer and saw the front end of a van parked behind a sandy swell. Somebody in the van could be controlling the drone.

Rudy started to curse under his breath as he reached quickly for the brake.

"It's landing on the tracks!" Daryl said excitedly. "Dang, somebody's about to lose their drone! Little thing's no match for a big ol' locomo—"

The drone disintegrated in a ball of flame. The explosion filled the air with smoke and dust, making it impossible to see how much damage it had done to the rails. The engine lurched as the brakes caught hold and the sand nozzles sprayed sand in front of the drivers to increase traction.

But it wasn't enough, not nearly enough, and Rudy knew it. At the speed they'd been making, he would have needed close to a mile to come to a complete stop.

He flung himself out of his seat and yanked up the latch on the cab door. "Come on!" he shouted to Daryl. The two of them were the only crew. They still had a slim chance of getting off the train before it derailed. That window was only a couple of seconds, though.

The two men rushed onto the platform at the front of the locomotive. Rudy was closer to the steps. He went down them and dived, throwing himself as far away from the rails as he could. He hit the ground hard and rolled. Out here, the rumble of the train only a few yards away was deafening. He didn't know if Daryl had made it or not, but as he came to a stop on his belly, he raised his head and looked around for his friend and coworker.

Daryl lay about twenty yards ahead of him. The fireman pushed himself to hands and knees but stayed there like that, shaking his head groggily. Rudy struggled against the sand as he clambered to his feet.

"Daryl!" he screamed, trying to be heard. "Daryl, come—"

The front end of the locomotive disappeared into the cloud of dust and smoke. Rudy had just been thinking the racket was loud before. Now, as the massive engine derailed, the roar seemed loud enough to shake a man's teeth right out of his head, pulp his bones, and turn his brain to jelly. As the tank cars began to tip, Rudy turned and ran.

From the corner of his eye, he saw Daryl finally leap

to his feet, but it was too late. Daryl ran a couple of steps, tripped, fell, and rolled over to stare up in horror at the tank car toppling right toward him. His mouth was wide open, but nobody ever heard his scream. He probably couldn't even hear it himself.

Then the overturning car obliterated him.

CHAPTER 6

Rudy had nothing in front of him except open ground, so he squeezed his eyes shut, put his head down, pumped his arms at his sides, and ran like the devil himself was after him.

Which was a pretty apt comparison, because a couple of the tank cars ruptured, and whatever the noxious stuff inside them was flooded out and encountered sparks flying from the wheels as they skidded along the tracks, causing another explosion. The shock wave from the blast slapped Rudy off his feet like a giant hand.

He yelled instinctively as he flew through the air before his face plowing into the sandy ground shut him up. Dirt went down his throat and choked him. He came up coughing and shuddering.

It felt like the hair was singed off the back of his neck and the skin was blistered, but he was alive, and it didn't seem like anything was broken. He forced himself to his feet and stumbled onward.

If the stuff in the tankers was bad enough that it had to be sealed away in underground trenches, he sure didn't want to be breathing any of the smoke from it as it burned.

He looked back, though. All the cars were off the

rails now, lying on their sides. Huge clouds of black smoke from the burning diesel fuel shrouded the locomotive, and two other fires from the spilled chemicals were sending gray smoke into the air. It was a horrible catastrophe.

Rudy's brain was stunned. He tried to force himself to think.

He hadn't had time to grab the radio and let the control center at the yard back in Reno know what was happening. When the shipment didn't show up on time at the Rattlesnake Wash facility, they would probably get in touch with Reno to find out what was going on, but that might be the first anybody would know that something was wrong. No telling how long it would take to get somebody out here to check on things.

No, wait, he told himself. The smoke. They would see the smoke. With that much of it billowing up into the sky, they would know something really bad had happened. At a place like that, they were bound to have some firefighting equipment. They might even have an emergency vehicle on the way out here already.

All he had to do was wait right where he was, and when they arrived, he could get some help.

But help for what, he asked himself. Nobody could do anything for poor Daryl now. He was gone. Rudy didn't think he was hurt other than some bumps and bruises, but it was probably a good idea to have himself checked out medically.

Most importantly, he could raise the alarm, he thought as he finally stopped running and bent over to rest his hands on his knees as he tried to catch his breath. Somebody had flown that drone in and blown up the tracks to cause the derailment.

Why hadn't they just planted a bomb on the tracks with, say, a pressure trigger? Surely it had to be trickier to attach explosives to a drone, fly it in to the right place, and then set them off, probably with a radio signal.

The only reason Rudy could think of why anybody would do that would be just to show off. Which meant the guys in that van were arrogant sons of—

He caught his breath. *The van.* He had forgotten all about spotting it just before all hell broke loose.

The roar of a racing motor brought it all back to him.

Rudy's head jerked up. He saw the van speeding toward him, throwing up a cloud of dust behind it. Rudy sobbed and turned to run.

Whoever had derailed the train probably didn't want to leave any witnesses behind. They must have spotted him running away from the scene of the disaster. If they were smart enough to pull off an attack like this, they would probably figure out that they didn't have much time before a response team from the containment facility arrived on the scene.

He couldn't outrun the van on open ground, but there were some sand dunes off to his left. If he could reach them, the van wouldn't be able to follow him. It wasn't a dune buggy. Its tires would bog down in the soft sand.

Of course, the people in the vehicle could still chase him on foot, but he might have a chance of giving them the slip. That was the only way he would come out of this alive.

So he was running for his life again, and he knew it.

Unfortunately, he was gasping by the time he'd gone a hundred yards. A stitch in his side threatened to double him over. Maybe jumping off the train and then being tossed around by the explosion had injured him after all, because every time his weight came down on his left leg, it felt like somebody was carving into his knee with a dull knife.

And with every step, the sound of the van closing in on him got louder.

He couldn't make it to the sand dunes. He stopped and bent over again, staying that way until the van went past him and slewed to a sideways stop.

The passenger door opened. So did the sliding door on that side. Two men got out and walked toward Rudy. The man behind the wheel stayed where he was.

He lifted his head to stare at the men approaching him at a deliberate, inexorable pace. Might as well get a good look at the ones who were going to end his life, he thought bleakly.

With their dark skin and dark hair, they might be Hispanic or Middle Eastern. Rudy couldn't tell. One of them had a mustache, but that didn't help. He leaned toward thinking they were Middle Eastern, because this had all the trappings of a terrorist attack.

Of course, it didn't matter where the men came from or why they had derailed the train. Nothing mattered now.

The one with the mustache held a pistol. The other man had a gun stuck behind his belt, but he didn't take it out.

Rudy was still breathing hard, but as he straightened, he had enough air to say, "You boys can just go to—"

The gun in the man's hand came up, spurted flame, and put an end to it for Rudy. He flung his arms out to the sides and went over backward, landing on his back. His eyes were wide open but unseeing.

The bullet had made just a small hole in the center of

his forehead as it went in. The much bigger hole in the back of his head where it came out leaked a lot of blood, but the thirsty ground soaked it up before it could spread.

The smoke from the burning tank cars continued to rise and spread. The flames reached the cars that hadn't ruptured, and within minutes, they exploded, too.

The men in the van were long gone by then.

CHAPTER 7

"The two members of the train's crew are the only known fatalities at this time. We're also getting reports that a number of people in Antioch Crossing, a small town downwind of the derailment and fire, have sought medical help for respiratory difficulties after the smoke blew through the area where they live. It's unknown at this time how serious these problems may be, or how widespread, but it's one more indication that this is a serious disaster with the potential to get even worse."

The news anchor paused and put his best look of gravitas on his face, so the viewers would know that this was a serious situation and they had better sit up and pay attention, by golly, and most of all, they shouldn't change the channel to something else.

Jake Rivers picked up the TV remote to do just that, but his uncle Barry said, "Hold on a minute. I'm watching this."

Jake stretched his legs out on the motel room bed and adjusted the pillows he had propped behind him. "You think there's something fishy about that train accident?"

"I think there's something fishy about *everything*, until I know better."

Barry was sitting on the other queen-size bed, eating a hamburger he had brought back to the motel in a to-go box from the café where they'd had lunch a few hours earlier. Barry ate more than anybody Jake had ever seen, especially considering that he stayed so lean. He had to have one heck of a metabolism to burn it all up.

The news anchor went on, "A spokesman for the railroad has issued a statement saying that the rails in the area of the accident were inspected within the past month and found to be in good shape. The locomotive was in top working order, according to the railroad, and both members of the crew were experienced and considered fine employees. At this point, it's impossible to rule out either human error or mechanical failure, but it's safe to say that right now, we just don't know what caused this tragedy."

"Or who," Barry responded to the image on the screen.

Jake frowned over at his uncle. "You think the derailment was deliberate?"

"More than twenty years ago, I started warning people that the railroads in this country were vulnerable to terrorism," Barry said. "A few of them listened, but nobody really did much. The first bombing at the World Trade Center in '93 and then the attack on the *Cole* in 2000 made people more aware of the threat of terrorism, but a lot of them still had the old it-can't-happen-here attitude. Then 9/11 happened, and they damn well *knew* it could happen here, but the focus then was on air safety. Only a fraction of Homeland Security's efforts . . . and more importantly, only a fraction of the *budget*— was directed at improving the security of the nation's railroads." Barry stopped, grunted, and shook his head. "I sound like a professor lecturing, don't I?"

"Well, you've gotta remember, I wasn't even born in '93, and I was too little to remember anything firsthand about the *Cole*. It wasn't as big of news. I remember 9/11, though. Really well." Jake shrugged. "It was all about the airplanes, all right."

The news broadcast had taken a break, but the anchor was back now and had two women and another man at the desk with him. When Jake started paying attention again, the anchor was in the middle of asking one of the men a question. ". . . too soon to start thinking about this as an act of terrorism, Charles?"

"Oh, yes, it certainly is too soon," the man replied. "We have no reason to believe that this incident was anything except a tragic accident, and yet another reminder that we should not be transporting these terrible toxic wastes or even continuing any industries that produce them. We've done so much damage to our poor planet . . . so much that by now it's irreversible—"

"It doesn't matter what climate change and environmental damage are doing down the road if we're dealing with a problem *right now*," one woman at the desk broke in. "What we're facing here may well be an attack on our country that left two men dead and who knows how many innocent people injured. In the long run, there's no telling how high the death toll may rise—"

The second woman interrupted her. "But that's still no reason to go throwing around wild accusations of terrorism directed at people who probably didn't have anything to do with it."

"I didn't accuse anybody," the first woman said.

The man said in a voice tinged with acid, "Yes, but

we all know who you were about to blame for it, Helen. No matter what happens, you're always quick to lay the blame at the feet of people who more often than not have been proven to be more peaceful and tolerant—"

The anchor was holding a finger against his ear, obviously listening to someone on his earpiece. He leaned forward and said, "I'm sorry to break in here, Charles, but we've just received more information on this."

Jake smiled bitterly and said from the bed, "Annnnd . . . it's Islamic terrorists."

Barry finished the last bite of his hamburger and wiped mustard from his lips with a napkin from the to-go box. "I hate to agree with anything those talking head morons say, but don't jump to conclusions. There are some radical environmentalist groups crazy enough to believe that spilling a bunch of hazardous waste is an appropriate way to protest what they think is being done to the planet."

"Not white supremacists, you mean?"

Barry looked disgusted and made a scoffing noise. "You could fit most of the true white supremacists in this country in a high school football stadium. The left just got used to throwing around that term, and other hot-button words, for anybody they disagree with."

"Terms like 'literally Hitler,'" Jake said with a smile.

"Yeah."

On the TV, the anchor said, "Apparently, a group calling themselves Lashkar-e-Islami is claiming responsibility for the train derailment in Nevada and warning that this will be the first of many such attacks. We have footage of a spokesman for this group making this claim, footage that was sent to news organizations across the country, but we're not going to air it until we have more verification."

"Restraint on the part of TV news," Jake said dryly. "Will the proverbial wonders never cease?" He grinned at his uncle. "And it *was* Islamic terrorists, see?"

"This time," Barry acknowledged.

The news anchor continued, "I'm told that the name, Lashkar-e-Islami, translates as Army of Islam and that several terrorist organizations in Afghanistan and Pakistan have used similar names in the past. Helen, do you believe this group is an offshoot of those, or something totally new?"

"There's no way to tell, Ross, but I'm sure if we're patient, they'll tell us, since all these terrorists love to talk about themselves."

The man called Charles looked like he had just bitten into a lemon. "That's a very unfair statement," he declared. "So many of these people have been forced into taking extreme measures by the overpowering oppression they've been forced to live under for decades now. Of course they want the world to understand what they've endured."

"So you're saying that you sympathize with terrorists?"

"I'm saying that at the very least, we ought to try to understand why they do the things they do and adjust our own behavior so that in the future, they won't feel like they have to strike back against us any way they can."

"That sounds to me an awful lot like sympathizing with terrorists."

Barry said, "You can turn it off now. They're just going to bicker for a while."

Jake pressed the button on the remote. "What now?"

"We wait," Barry said. "We'll give those feelers we put out a chance to turn up anything."

As if on cue, the burner phone lying on the bed beside him chimed with an incoming text message.

In more than three decades of operating in a world of dangerous shadows as he battled evil and corruption wherever he found it, Barry "Dog" Rivers had made contacts with people in all walks of life, from the highest to the lowest. He was the worst enemy any criminal or crooked politician or terrorist could have, but when he was your friend, he was loyal to the end and would risk anything to help someone who deserved his help. Those he encountered knew that, and so whenever he needed a favor or just some information in return, there was usually someone out there, somewhere, who could provide it.

The previous night, after returning to the motel following the brawl at the cantina, Barry had put the word out on his own personal grapevine, stretching all along the border from Texas to California, that he was interested in any "special" shipments about to be made by the Zaragosa cartel.

Now, both Barry and Jake hoped that effort was about to bear fruit.

"This is from a friend of mine in New Mexico, over in the bootheel," Barry said as he read the message. "He runs a guide service for hunting and hiking in the Big Hatchet Mountains. It's about as isolated an area as you can find along the border, and the drug and illegal immigrant traffic is pretty high there at times. Chet says he's seen an unusual level of activity in the past few weeks, though. More suspicious characters than normal moving around the mountains, as if somebody's checking everything out . . . which the cartel might do if they were planning to move something even more important across there."

"Think it's worth checking out?" Jake asked.

Barry was thumbing a reply on the burner. He sent it and said, "I told him we'd be there tomorrow. It's a long drive. We'll make it as far as El Paso today."

"I guess I'd better let the office know I'll be taking some more time off."

"That's a good idea," Barry said. "I've got a hunch this could turn into something bigger than either of us have considered so far."

CHAPTER 8

Barry had been a long-haul trucker in his younger days, working for his father's company out of New Orleans. That was before he had gotten involved in the arms business—and a long time before a series of violent tragedies had forged him into the man known as Dog.

After that, he had driven secure delivery runs for the government, and those assignments had led to him becoming an unofficial agent for those high in the halls of power, as long as they deserved his allegiance.

And despite all the decades that had passed, he still felt most comfortable behind the wheel of a big rig as it rolled along the highway. The road was his home.

He was well-equipped to live there in the truck that now moved across the vast, mostly empty landscape of southern New Mexico.

The rig was a top-of-the-line Kenworth long-hood conventional, a model designated Z1000 that wasn't for sale to the public yet. This was a prototype that Barry's influential contacts had allowed him to get his hands on, and once he had, he'd made even more modifications to it.

Armor plating all around that would withstand even an RPG blast. Bulletproof glass for the windshield and all the windows. The average trucker didn't need those additions, but they were vital in Barry's line of work.

Under that hood was one of the most powerful truck engines ever built: a PACCAR MX-15, an 8-cylinder, 14.7-liter monster, also a prototype. Barry could have hauled just about anything with an engine like that at his command, but for his purposes, the MX-15 and the armored front end of the big rig turned it into a very effective battering ram.

Inside, the cab was as comfortable and full of bells and whistles as any top-of-the-line Kenworth. The navigation system was state of the art, paired with a powerful computer and satellite phone linked to a pop-up dish antenna that kept Barry in constant communication with the rest of the world no matter where he was or what the conditions might be. The air conditioner would freeze a guy out in the summer; the heater would keep him warm in the worst blizzard. The sound system could make him feel like he was in the front row of a rocking country concert or in a smoky midnight jazz club, depending on what kind of mood he was in.

The truck was also equipped with radar, sonar, and infrared sensors, and with the flick of a switch on the console, Barry could lower a filter over the windshield that effectively transformed it into a giant night-vision scope so that he could drive in almost total darkness if he needed to.

Behind the cab, the normal Kenworth sleeper would have been comfortable enough for most people, but

Barry needed more storage space, so he had opted for an enlarged sleeper that included a small kitchen and bathroom, queen-size bed, flatscreen TV, second computer workstation, and closet. One of the walls swung out, though, to reveal the sleeper's most important feature.

The weapons locker.

Inside were four semi-automatic rifles with 30-round magazines; two semi-auto shotguns; two sniper rifles with high-powered scopes; a vintage Winchester lever-action in .44-40; more than a dozen handguns in various calibers ranging from .22 to .45, including a couple of vintage 1911s in perfect working order, a Browning Hi-Power, an S&W MP Shield in 9mm, and a Colt Single Action Army revolver; and, in a drawer underneath the gun racks, thousands of rounds of ammunition. In a rack attached to the inside of the door hung an assortment of knives, all the way from a small switchblade to a heavy bowie with a beautiful bone handle that had a brass ball on the end. Weaponry, like everything else, had made enormous technological advances over the years—but sometimes the old ways of killing were just as good . . . or better.

For all the improvements Barry had made to an already impressive piece of machinery when he got his hands on it, the Z1000 wasn't flashy on the outside. It was painted a deep, rich red with plenty of chrome, including its twin stacks, but despite being a very nice-looking truck, it didn't stand out *that* much from hundreds of other trucks on the road. A lot of them had fancier paint jobs and more chrome.

When Barry had shown it to Jake during one of his visits after Barry had finished modifying the truck, the younger man had said, "You know what you really ought to do? You ought to have flames painted on it. Or maybe a mural on the sides with, like, mountains and an American eagle—"

"So what you're saying is that I should make it stand out so much that anybody who sees it will have a hard time forgetting it," Barry had interrupted his nephew.

Jake had stood there frowning for a long moment before saying, "Yeah, I guess that's probably *not* the best idea, is it? In our line of work, you don't want to draw a lot of extra attention to yourself."

"We're not exactly *in* the same line of work," Barry had pointed out. "Yours has a lot more rules and regulations than mine does. But you're right. This baby's going to get some second looks, especially from people who know trucks, but they'll forget about it fairly quickly. And there are no readily visible distinctive features to include in a description later, except for the oversized sleeper, and most people won't remember that. To the civilians, it's just a big truck. That's all."

"You need to give it a name," Jake had suggested. "Like . . . the Dog Pound."

Barry just stared coldly at him.

"Okay, maybe not the Dog Pound," Jake had said. "But I'm sure you can come up with something."

So far, though, in the six months that Barry had been driving the truck, he hadn't. It didn't have a name, and that was all right with him.

He glanced in the big side mirror and saw Jake's pickup tooling along behind him. They were almost the only traffic on this lonely stretch of highway heading down into the bootheel, the southernmost part of New

Mexico. Up ahead, Barry could see a dark, irregular line on the horizon to the southwest. That was the Big Hatchet Mountain range.

An hour later, they pulled into the little town of Hachita. There wasn't much to the place—half a dozen businesses on one side of the highway, a scattering of trailers, cinder-block houses, and old-fashioned adobes, complete with wooden *vigas* sticking out along the flat roofs. Those dwellings looked ready for John Wayne to come sauntering through the front door at any moment, Barry thought.

Some of them had satellite dishes on the roof, though, something you never saw in any of "the Duke's" movies.

Barry turned off the highway and drove along a narrow dirt lane toward an old mobile home that looked like it had been there for twenty years or more. As he came closer, he saw a faded metal sign stuck in the ground that read BIG HATCHET TOURS – HUNTING – HIKING – CAMPING. There was a phone number below the name.

An old pickup that had seen better days was parked to one side next to a vintage Mustang. Barry tried not to wince as he saw how dust covered the faded paint on the Mustang was. The car could have been a beauty if it had been taken care of and kept out of the weather. That wasn't the case. But he still liked what he could see under the dust.

Even with the big swamp cooler running, the truck's approach could have been heard inside the mobile home. So Barry wasn't surprised when the door opened and a tall, rangy man stepped out onto the wooden deck built on the old trailer. He wore boots, jeans, and a flannel shirt with the sleeves rolled up over deeply tanned forearms. The battered Stetson on his white-haired head had the brim pulled down to shade his eyes. He cradled a gun in his hands.

The weapon wasn't an old-fashioned Winchester like the one in the hidden compartment behind Barry. That was what most people would expect an obvious Westerner like this to be carrying, just going by looks.

No, the man was carrying what appeared to be a fully automatic World War II–era Thompson submachine gun.

Barry turned off the truck's motor and opened the door. As he stepped down from the cab, Jake pulled up behind the truck in his pickup. Barry motioned for him to stay where he was, for the moment, and then walked casually toward the mobile home. He wasn't sure just how touchy Chet was, but it was a good idea to walk soft around anybody toting a Thompson.

Raising his left hand in greeting, Barry called, "Hello, Chet. How you doin', old son?"

"Barry?" Chet Taylor asked in a deep, gravelly voice. "Is that you? Figured it was, since nobody else I know would drive up in a big hoss of a truck like that. But then this decrepit codger climbed out, and I wasn't sure anymore. You got old!"

"You're not exactly a spring chicken anymore yourself, are you?"

Chet laughed and lowered the Thompson's muzzle so it pointed at the ground. "Shoot, I was born old," he said. "Fellas like you and me, that's how we tend to be."

"Not so old that we can't take advantage of modern technology, though," Barry said as he came to a stop in front of the deck. "I'm glad you got my message. Even more glad to see that you're still alive and kicking."

Chet grunted. "I'll be kicking as long as I'm drawing breath."

"I believe it."

"Who's that who followed you in here?" Chet nodded toward the pickup as he asked the question.

"My nephew Jake. We work together sometimes."

"I didn't know you had a nephew. Of course, you never were much of one to talk about family."

A grim look came over Barry's features for a moment. "That's because, other than my dad and now Jake, most of 'em were on the sorry side. But he's a good kid, you can count on that. Doesn't really like it when I call him a kid, though."

"Most kids don't." Chet leaned his head toward the door behind him. "Tell him to come on, and we'll all get inside outta this sun."

Chapter 9

Chet Taylor was about the same age as Barry. His seamed, weathered face was the color of old saddle leather, making it very evident that he had spent most of his life outdoors.

After introductions were made, he led Barry and Jake into the mobile home, which was comfortably cool, especially after the heat outside. With the bone-dry humidity around here, a swamp cooler worked just fine. The big unit attached to the mobile home looked like it might be fifty years old, but judging by the quiet humming sound of its motor and the cool air it was putting out, it still worked like a top.

Taylor hung his hat on a hook, set the machine gun on the kitchen table, and went to the refrigerator. "Get you boys a beer?" he asked.

"A cold beer would be mighty tasty about now," Barry agreed.

Jake was staring at the Thompson. He frowned, pointed at it, and asked, "Is that real?"

"Of course it is," Taylor replied.

"Federal law—"

"Federal law says this fully automatic machine gun is completely legal as long as it was manufactured and registered before 1986," Taylor said. "I've owned it since 1975, so I guess that answers *that* question."

"You use it on those hunting trips you make into the Big Hatchets?" Barry asked. "That doesn't seem very sporting."

Taylor grunted. "I don't do much hunting myself. I hire out as a guide to folks who want to get themselves a bighorn sheep or a mountain lion. No, I keep that Tommy gun around for humans."

He popped the caps off three beer bottles and set two of them on the table next to the machine gun.

"You may have to explain that," Jake said.

Taylor sat down in an old recliner with his own beer and regarded Jake coolly.

"No offense, son," he said, "but why do you reckon I owe you an explanation for anything?"

"Jake works for the FBI," Barry said. "He's picked up the habit of asking questions."

"And it sounded to me like you just admitted to shooting people with that thing," Jake said.

Taylor said, "I've shot in their general direction, but to the best of my knowledge I've never hit any of 'em, and nobody's ever accused me of it. But if you've got a bunch of coyotes hanging around, a burst or two from that old Tommy gun is usually enough to scare 'em off."

"Coyotes," Jake repeated. "You mean people who bring in illegal immigrants from Mexico?"

"Well, actually I was talkin' about the four-legged kind," Taylor replied dryly, "but I reckon the other description might apply, too. Since the Feds cut back on their funding and manpower and patrolling, the whole bootheel down here is like a smuggler's highway. Plenty of illegals coming through. Some of them pay their way by toting packs full of marijuana or other drugs across the border for the cartel. There are plenty of full-time mules, too, who make their living carrying drugs through the mountains and then walking back across the border."

"They work for the Zaragosas?" Barry asked.

Taylor's shoulders rose and fell. "Whichever bunch is running things that week. The way they fuss and feud, you don't hardly know which cartel's in charge from one day to the next. The thing of it is, it doesn't really matter. No matter what they call themselves, each cartel is the same thing: vicious."

Jake pulled out a chair at the table, sat down, and picked up one of the beers. "If it's that bad," he said, "why do you stay here?"

"Because I've been here for a long damn time, and I'm a stubborn old man. I'm not gonna let scum like that run me off my own place."

Barry snagged his beer from the table and sat down across from Jake. "I hear you," he said. "I'd feel the same way. And I'd still be squatting here, too."

Taylor snorted. "No, you wouldn't. As long as that bunch leaves me alone, I leave them alone. If it was *you*, you'd be out there in the brush at night, lying in wait for them and making them pay a toll in blood for every shipment of drugs they bring across." He waved a hand. "I'm not sayin' you'd gun down the mules or the migrants. Some of them are decent *hombres* who just want a better life for themselves. But you'd soon figure out who was running things and go after them."

Jake took a swig of the beer and said, "Don't give him any ideas, Mr. Taylor. He's liable to retire one of these days, and that sounds just like how he'd spend his golden years."

Barry laughed. "You don't think I'll be sitting in a rocking chair, taking life easy?"

"Not hardly," Jake said.

"Well, there's probably some truth to that," Barry admitted. "But what's been going on around here lately that made you respond to my message, Chet? Something worse than usual?"

"Not worse, necessarily. Just more of the same. Enough more to notice it." Taylor pushed back in the recliner, stretched his legs in front of him, and crossed his ankles. "I'm up in the mountains nearly every day, and I've seen more strangers in the area than have ever been there. The cartels check out their smuggling routes and make sure there are no Border Patrol or sheriff's department units in the area, but normally they wouldn't be there more than twice a week. Like I said, now it's every day."

"Have they given you any trouble?" Barry asked.

"No, because I steer well clear of them," Taylor replied. "I know how to keep my head down. I see them, but they don't see me."

"Doesn't the Border Patrol use planes to patrol the area?" Jake asked.

"They did, but all their crates have been grounded for a while. Mechanical difficulties, I hear. Could be the government just doesn't want to pay for the fuel. So what you have are some hardworking agents in jeeps and pickups, living in what are called forward operating bases, mostly travel trailers. They go out at night with thermal imaging cameras to hunt for folks who shouldn't be out there."

Taylor sipped his beer and continued. "What they're really doing is taking their lives in their hands, because they're liable to run into cartel soldiers protecting the routes. There was a time those old boys would hesitate to shoot at American lawmen because they didn't want to call too much attention to their operations. Now they don't care. They know they can get away with it."

"That retirement project's starting to sound better and better," Barry said. "But right now, our main goal is to find out *why* the cartel activity has increased. We have intel saying that they're moving a special shipment across the border sometime in the near future."

Taylor nodded and said, "I can believe it. That'd explain why you can't hardly turn over a rock out there without some two-legged varmint scurrying out from under it." He looked at Jake. "This is an FBI operation?"

"No, I'm here on my own time," Jake said. "Just giving my uncle a hand with it."

Taylor nodded knowingly. "So this is Dog pokin' into it. Well, that ought to make it interesting."

Jake looked at Barry and said, "He knows about Dog?"

Barry shrugged. "Chet's given me a hand a time or two in the past. I'm a good tracker, but he's probably the best I've ever seen."

"Flattery'll get you another beer," Taylor said with a smile. "But what you really want is for me to take you into the Big Hatchets so you can have a look around for yourself. Isn't that right?"

"That's what I was thinking," Barry agreed. "We can pay for your services as a guide, too."

"You don't have to offer me money—"

Barry held up a hand to stop his old friend. "It's not

coming from me," he said. "I know that'd offend you. This comes from higher up."

"Those mysterious people you work for but can't talk about."

"That's right."

"In that case," Taylor said, "I'd be happy to take the money. But it's too late to start today. Why don't we head out first thing in the morning?"

"That'll work."

"You'll have to leave that behemoth of yours here, though. We'll take my truck and Jake's, and there'll probably come a point where we have to walk. It's pretty rugged country down there. A fella's got to know what he's doing."

He looked pointedly at Jake.

"I was an Army Ranger."

"Good enough," Taylor said with a nod.

CHAPTER 10

"What's the story on him?" Jake asked that evening as he and Barry were sitting in the sleeper/living compartment of the Kenworth.

Earlier, the two of them had gone with Taylor to have supper at one of the two cafés in Hachita, where Taylor had mentioned casually to the friendly waitress that he was taking the visitors into the mountains in the morning to hunt bighorn sheep.

Later, when they were back at the mobile home, Taylor had explained that while the waitress had laughed and joked around with them, she couldn't be trusted. Not fully, anyway.

"Most of the people who live around here have relatives on the other side of the border, and they're all afraid of the cartel. Even the ones who *work* for the cartel are afraid. So they keep a pretty close eye on me and everybody else in these parts who's not part of the operation. They see anything suspicious, they're gonna pass it on. There's a pretty good grapevine between here and Janos and Colonia el Camello, the closest towns on the other side of the line in Chihuahua."

"So you're saying they spy on you," Jake said. "Even that pretty little waitress."

"Yeah. Elena has a brother I'm pretty sure works for the Zaragosas. They won't think anything of me taking a couple of clients up into the mountains to hunt, though. That's pretty common."

"I'm surprised they leave you alone," Jake had said.

"I guess they know I'm a tough old buzzard who wouldn't be that easy to kill. But I mind my own business, so it's easier for them to just ignore me."

Barry had pointed out, "Except you're not minding your own business now."

"Yeah, but they don't know that."

Now, in the truck, Barry said in answer to Jake's question, "Chet was a legend in Special Forces. Was an operator in all the world's hot spots for ten years. But then he'd had enough, and he walked away from it. Came back here to the area where he grew up."

"Not everybody can walk away."

Barry nodded. "I know. Some men get it in their blood and can't go back to living a normal life." His mouth tightened. "I tried. I did it for a while. But it didn't pan out. Chet managed to make it work, though. Maybe because he's still outdoors most of the time, still makes his living with a gun in his hand."

"Bighorn sheep don't shoot back, though," Jake said.

"That doesn't mean what he does is easy—or without its dangers. And since the cartel moved in, it's worse than ever. He's too stubborn to give up, though, like he said."

"You think this is where they're going to move whatever the shipment is?"

"I haven't heard anything from my other contacts that sounds more promising." Barry was sitting in a swivel chair in front of the computer workstation. He swung around to face the computer and moved the mouse to wake it up. "Let's take a look and see what we're working with."

The powerful satellite uplink allowed Barry to call up a detailed map of the area. Jake looked over his shoulder as he pointed out the little settlement of Hachita, where they were, as well as the rugged Big Hatchet Mountains stretching to the south and the thin line of the highway to the west, running down to the border.

The bootheel shape of this corner of New Mexico meant that directly east of the Big Hatchets was the uppermost part of the Mexican state of Chihuahua. Barry pointed to a spot just east of the border and said, "See that?"

Jake leaned closer and frowned at the concentration of large, dark circles visible on the satellite image. "What is it? Looks like a bunch of oil tanks or something."

'No, those aren't tanks at all. They're fields. They're cultivated and irrigated in those circular shapes. The system's called center-pivot. The irrigation equipment rotates around a hub. As dry as it is around here, you have to drill deep wells and irrigate if you're going to grow anything, and that system's proven to be efficient. But that's not really what I'm talking about." Barry's fingertip almost touched the monitor screen. "Right there next to those fields."

"Oh. Yeah. It's a little town, isn't it?"

"Colonia el Camello. Chet mentioned it. I don't know how heavy the cartel presence is there, but it's really close to the border, about two miles away. If you were to cross there, go through the southern end of the Big Hatchets, and angle northwest, you'd eventually come to State Highway 81. From there, it's less than a two-hour drive to Interstate 10, and once you hit the interstate . . ." Barry shrugged. "The whole country's wide open to you from there."

Jake nodded slowly. "Sounds like it would work, all right. But they're already bringing in drugs and illegal immigrants, according to Chet, and having plenty of success at it. Why all this added attention?"

"Because this is something else," Barry said. "Or some*body* else."

Jake frowned. "They'd go to all that trouble just to bring in a person?"

"If it was somebody important enough."

"Sounds important enough to find out."

Barry nodded. "That's just what we're going to do."

The truck's sleeper had a pull-down bed as well as the queen-size bed. Jake used it and slept well. They had breakfast before dawn the next morning in Chet Taylor's mobile home, surprisingly good flapjacks and bacon cooked by the guide and washed down with strong black coffee. The sun hadn't quite come up, but the eastern sky was awash with red and gold when the three men set out toward the Big Hatchet Mountains, Taylor leading the way in his old pickup while Jake and Barry followed in Jake's pickup.

The air had a definite chill to it that made Jake's denim jacket feel good. The days might be blistering hot, but the nights in this high desert country got pretty cold year-round.

They had semi-automatic rifles behind the seat, and each of them carried a pair of 9mm pistols. Each had a sheathed knife strapped to his belt, too. The packs that rode on the seat between them contained several bottles of water each, along with emergency rations, blankets, matches, and other survival gear. Jake and Barry, as well as Chet Taylor, too, of course, were perfectly capable of living off the land for a while if they had to. They didn't expect that to be necessary, but only a fool was unprepared.

They followed the highway south toward the border for several miles before Taylor turned east onto a narrow dirt track that led toward the mountains. The wheels of Jake's pickup bumped over a cattle guard across the gap in the barbed wire fence where the dirt trail started. Taylor's pickup was already kicking up a plume of dust behind it. Jake drove into it, being careful not to go too fast.

The sun poked above the peaks, causing Jake to lower the visor on his side and put on his sunglasses. Barry did likewise. Jake mused, "You know, it would be fun if we were going out here hunting for real. All those years when I didn't even know you were still alive, we didn't get to do anything like that." He paused. "You ever miss living a normal life, Barry?"

"I was able to give it a try, here and there," Barry replied as he kept his gaze centered straight forward through the windshield. "Somehow, it never worked out well in the end, even when I thought it was going to. Why haven't *you* settled down, gotten married and started a family?"

"Well, there's my work for the FBI—"

"Don't give me that. Plenty of agents are married. They get up and go to work in the morning, come home in the evening. Sure, there are risks, but that's true for cops, firefighters, and anybody else who deals with the rough edges of life. Being in the FBI isn't keeping you from doing anything."

Jake grimaced and said, "Well, it just seems like there's never time. I've been in a few relationships, but I can't seem to concentrate on 'em—"

"Because you spend so much time thinking about catching the bad guys." Barry laughed. "You ever hear guys in our line of work call themselves sheepdogs? We spend our time looking after the flock and don't think about ourselves, only the ones we're charged with taking care of. There's nothing wrong with that. You just have to accept that you're probably not going to have some of the things that regular guys do."

"But we get to do things that they can only dream about," Jake pointed out.

"Yeah . . . like risking our lives in some of the most miserable conditions in the world, while hunting down some of the worst humans out there."

"Well, somebody's got to do it, or else the world would be even more overrun with evil than it already is."

"That's true," Barry said. "Better slow down. We're about to get into some rough country."

CHAPTER 11

Colonia el Camello, Chihuahua, Mexico

In the early morning darkness, Francisco Zaragosa looked around this pesthole of a hamlet, turned his head to the side, and spat into the dust of the dirt street.

Behind him, his brother Angel giggled. "Look," Angel said. "You hit a bug."

It was true. The gob of spittle had landed on a scorpion. The creature was scuttling around, evidently perturbed by being drenched in Francisco's spit. Francisco watched the scorpion for a second, then lifted his foot and brought his boot's heel down on it. The dust was so thick that he didn't feel a crunch, so he ground his heel back and forth to be sure he had crushed the scorpion.

"Oh," Angel said. "You killed it."

Francisco patted his brother's cheek. "It was a stinging bug, Angel. I didn't want it to hurt you."

Angel thought about that and nodded. He said, "I don't like stinging bugs. Thank you for killing it, Francisco."

"Anything for you, brother."

They were a mismatched pair, Angel the older of the two in years but with the mind of a child. Somehow, that made him look more youthful. He was tall and slender, with a ready smile and a shock of raven-black hair.

Francisco was three years younger, half a head shorter, and much thicker. He had lost a lot of his hair, and what was left was shot through with gray, like the mustache that grew under his hawklike nose. He wore khaki trousers and a short-sleeved shirt that revealed brawny, heavily furred forearms.

He looked back toward the three white SUVs that had rolled into the tiny farming community a short time earlier. The heavy tint on the vehicles' windows kept anybody from seeing into them. The windows were bulletproof, too. Francisco and Angel had ridden in the middle one with their guest. His nephews Juan Carlos and Javier, his sister Yolanda's boys, had ridden in the lead SUV. His other nephews, Gerardo and Miguel, sons of his other sister, Isabel, had been in the SUV bringing up the rear. They had half a dozen cartel soldiers in the group, too.

The cousins didn't like each other, which was no surprise considering that their mothers had grown up clawing and spitting at each other like a couple of wild-cats, but they got along, especially when they were working, because they all feared their *tío* Francisco. And they treated Angel well, which was another reason, besides the blood tie, that Francisco put up with them. He had promised his *madre* that he would look after his poor, broken brother, and he was a man of his word.

Of course, sometimes he wasn't sure just how *broken* Angel was. With his good looks and sweet, shy nature, beautiful women flocked to him. Francisco had plenty of women, too, but in his case, it was money and power that attracted them.

Well, he was about to be richer, which meant he would also be more powerful, so that was one thing to be pleased about, even in this squalid, ugly village in the middle of nowhere.

Their special guest, the man who was paying the cartel an unholy amount of money to get him into the United States, was a handsome man, too, with his dark eyes and fashionable stubble. Francisco had no idea how he did with women and didn't care. All that mattered was the money.

Bandar al-Saddiq got out of the second SUV and walked briskly toward Francisco and Angel. His expensive clothes made him look like he was about to go on a safari rather than trekking across a mountain range. He put his hands in the pockets of his sharply creased trousers and asked in perfect Spanish, "What is the delay?"

"A problem with our men who are supposed to pick you up on the other side of the border," Francisco said. "We've been in touch with them on the radio. They say there is some unexpected . . . what is the word? . . . glitch."

"Glitch?" Saddiq repeated. "I am not paying for glitches, *Señor* Zaragosa."

"Of course not," Francisco replied, making an effort to hang on to his temper. He didn't like being spoken to that way. Saddiq was not showing the proper respect. None of his kind did. Fanatics. All they cared about was their so-called religion and hurting anybody they deemed an infidel.

Francisco went on, "You must admit, the operation has run very smoothly so far. The test run your people made in Nevada—"

"You had nothing to do with that," Saddiq snapped.

"They bought the explosives from associates of mine," Francisco replied. This time, he allowed a little edge to creep into his voice. Big payday or not, he would take only so much from this Middle Eastern dog.

"But it was my people who ran all the risks," Saddiq replied. "My people who wreaked havoc on the Americans in the name of Allah."

Francisco shrugged. "They wrecked a train. It's only half as big a story today as it was yesterday. Tomorrow it will be forgotten."

"That was just the beginning—"

The radio in Francisco's pocket crackled, interrupting Saddiq's fervent response. Francisco held up a hand, used his other hand to take the radio out, and keyed the mike.

"What is it? Will you be ready?"

"We will, Francisco. You can send the package any time you like." That was Daniel Colón's voice on the other end of the connection. He was one of Francisco's most trusted lieutenants. "I have sent men to take care of the problem."

"You split your group?" Francisco wasn't sure he liked the sound of that.

"It won't be a problem, you can count on that," Daniel assured him. "I sent only four men to deal with some . . . interlopers . . . and that will be plenty to dispose of them."

CHAPTER 12

The Big Hatchet Mountains

Taylor had been right. They reached a point at the base of the mountains where they had to leave the pickups and go ahead on foot.

The sun was well above the peaks, and the temperature was starting to rise along with it. Jake had taken off his jacket and left it in the pickup before he put on his pack, and he was glad he did. The sun and the effort involved in swinging along the mountain trails loosened his muscles and felt good.

Taylor was in the lead. He had the Thompson slung on his back and carried a high-powered rifle. A Colt 1911 was holstered on his hip. It looked vintage, too, like the Tommy gun. Jake hadn't asked him if it was the genuine article, but he suspected it was.

As they walked, Taylor pointed out various plants and geographic features. After he'd done that several times, he started to again but stopped himself.

"Dang it, I'm so used to bein' a guide, I just let the usual spiel come out. You fellas shoulda told me to shut up."

"Not at all," Jake said. "I like learning new things."

"Yeah, but that's not why we're here." Taylor had stopped at a bend in the trail. The rugged landscape fell away sharply on two sides, to their right and ahead of them. The slope wasn't sheer, but it was steep enough that a tumble down it wouldn't be a good thing. They were high enough now that they could see for several miles. The view from up here was a sweeping vista of gray and different shades of brown, broken up here and there by blotches of dark green marking the location of stubborn clumps of vegetation.

Jake saw scattered points of sun reflection, too, and said, "Those glints are worrisome."

"Not really," Taylor said. "That's not the sun shining on gun barrels, like you're thinking. There are out-croppings of quartz all through these mountains, enough that a hundred and forty years ago, prospectors flocked all through them, looking for gold and silver. They never found enough to make it worthwhile. No, the Big Hatchets are pretty much worthless . . . except for that."

He lifted an arm and pointed. Jake and Barry looked and caught their breaths as they spotted a pair of big-horn sheep standing on a tiny ledge a couple of hundred yards above them.

"Beautiful," Barry murmured, while Jake said, "How in the world did they get up there? Fly? I don't see any sign of a trail."

"They don't need much of one," Taylor said. "I've seen 'em go up slopes you wouldn't think an insect could crawl up, let alone a big critter like that."

The sheep were very picturesque with their massive horns curling around their heads. They stood so utterly still they might have been statues carved out of the mountainside. Then, without warning, they bounded away, their hooves finding near-imperceptible rock ledges to land on, and with flicks of their tails, they were gone.

"Man," Jake said, "they'll take your breath away, won't they?"

Taylor nodded. "When you're out here, surrounded by all this"—he waved a hand at the rugged but starkly beautiful terrain—"and you see something like that, it sort of makes the rest of the world go away for a while. You can forget about all the hating and the fighting and just think that maybe this is the way the world was intended to be all along." He shrugged. "But then you remember that there are mountain lions up here, too. No matter where you go in the world or how pretty it is, there are always predators lurking somewhere not too far away, just waiting for a chance to strike."

Barry said, "Yeah, but the kind of predators you're talking about kill to eat, not because of politics or religion or some sort of twisted fanaticism. A mountain lion won't come after you because of who you voted for or what god you pray to."

"But if you run afoul of them, you're just as dead no matter what the reason," Jake said.

"You boys can stand around and philosophize about it if you want to," Taylor said. "I just figured I'd show you those sheep." He frowned and shook his head. "We came looking for those fellas who've been prowling around out here, and I'm surprised we haven't seen any of them so far."

As a matter of fact, other than the people in the few cars they had seen while still on the highway, they hadn't encountered anyone. Taylor had explained that at the end of that road was the Antelope Wells border crossing, the least used of any official border crossings between the U.S. and Mexico. It consisted of a low concrete wall with a gate in it, a small office, and a travel trailer where the two officers posted there lived. It was probably the most isolated outpost of civilization anywhere in the continental United States.

Only a few cars a day used the crossing. Anybody who didn't want to go through the gate, for whatever reason, could try to drive around the wall, but if they did, there was a very high probability their vehicle would get bogged down in the soft, sandy ground.

Now, as the three men stood on this high trail, Barry asked, "Is it normal not to run into anybody down here?"

"Sure," Taylor replied. "As the cartels have tightened their grip on this area, fewer and fewer people come to hunt and hike, and it's been a long time since I brought anybody out here who wanted to camp. It's just too dangerous. If I spot somebody else moving around and I don't know who they are, I lie low and wait until they're gone. Mostly, smugglers are like rattlesnakes: Leave them alone, and they'll leave you alone. There's no way of knowing when they'll get proddy, though, and start to worry about somebody seeing them. *That's* when it can get dangerous."

They moved on, climbing higher. The view got even more spectacular, if that was possible.

After a while, Jake said, "What if we don't see anything suspicious? Do we just keep coming out here?"

"Well, what Chet's told us is the only lead we have right now," Barry replied. "So I suppose—"

"Fellas," Taylor said, "I just saw the sun reflect off

something over there on that ridge, and I don't think it was quartz this time. Three o'clock."

He didn't point, but his words told Jake and Barry where to look. They did so, not moving too quickly so if anybody was watching them, their actions wouldn't alert whoever it was that he'd been made. Jake turned his head deliberately, as if he were just scanning his surroundings as a man might do in country like this. His gaze reached a long, hogback ridge about three hundred yards away, with a deep valley between it and the trail where the three men stood now.

Jake looked around just in time to see a flash over there on the ridge. At that same instant, Chet Taylor grunted. He took a quick step back that brought him against the rock wall rising on that side of the trail. Eyes wide, he leaned against it and stared down at his chest, where a bloodstain was starting to spread on the thick flannel shirt he wore.

CHAPTER 13

Barry lunged toward Taylor and got an arm around him as he started to slide down the rock wall toward the trail. That sudden move probably saved Barry's life, because rock chips exploded from the wall just behind him as another bullet smacked into it.

Jake had seen the muzzle flash from the first shot. He brought the rifle to his shoulder in one swift, smooth move and started firing. At this range, without a scope or time to draw a bead, he didn't hope to hit the sniper on the ridge, but with any luck he could distract the man and make him keep his head down while Barry and Taylor made it to cover.

Barry half-dragged, half-carried Taylor along the trail toward some rocks a little higher up. They weren't big enough to provide complete shelter, but they were the closest cover and better than nothing. Jake moved after them, continuing to fire toward the ridge across the valley as he did so.

Taylor wasn't dead. His legs were moving, although they seemed too weak to hold him up if Barry hadn't been taking most of his weight. Barry was tremendously strong for his lean build. He reached the rocks, stretched Taylor out on the ground behind them, and dropped to his belly behind another of the stone slabs. He had kept his rifle in his right hand while supporting his old friend with his left arm. Now that he had the chance to fight back, he thrust the rifle over the rock in front of him and called to Jake, "Covering!"

Jake ceased fire and concentrated on running up the trail. He covered the twenty feet to the rocks in three long strides and bellied down so that Tayler was between him and Barry.

"How bad is he hit?" Jake asked, raising his voice to be heard over the sharp cracks from Barry's weapon.

"You saw the blood. Plenty bad enough. But the bullet must have missed his heart or he would be dead by now. I'll keep up covering fire while you check."

Being careful to keep his head down, Jake slid over closer to Taylor and snaked an arm out to unbutton the man's shirt and pull it aside. That revealed the bullet hole in Taylor's chest. Jake heard the faint whistling sound as Taylor struggled to pull in feeble breaths.

"Got a lung," he told Barry. He wriggled around so he could take off his pack without exposing himself to the sniper on the ridge. The first aid kit inside the pack held several sterile dressings. He fished it out, dumped a little packet of antiseptic powder into the wound, then tore open one of the dressings and stuffed it into the bullet hole. Taylor immediately started to breathe a little easier.

Jake put a pressure bandage over the wound and the makeshift plug. He used his teeth to pull the cap off an ampule of painkiller and pushed that into Taylor's neck.

"He might pull through . . . if we can get him some medical attention in a hurry," he said to Barry.

"That might be a problem," Barry said as he dropped

the empty magazine from the rifle and snapped a new one into place. "That fella over there doesn't want us to go anywhere."

A rattle of rocks from somewhere back to Jake's right made him twist his head in that direction. Two men were coming up the trail toward them, each carrying a Heckler & Koch MP5K machine pistol. When they realized that Jake had seen them, they jerked the weapons up and opened fire.

Unfortunately for them, they rushed their shots. One man's bullets sprayed well above the rocks where Jake, Barry, and Taylor had taken cover, while the other put his rounds into the trail well short of them. Some of those bullets ricocheted in their direction but missed.

Jake didn't miss. He pulled the Browning Hi-Power from the holster on his belt and put two 9mm rounds into the chest of the man closest to the edge of the trail. Only an inch separated the bullet holes that appeared on the man's shirt pocket. He didn't even yell as he went backward off the trail and tumbled over and over down the steep slope.

The second gunner had controlled the recoil of his HK and brought it back down, but before he could squeeze off another burst, a shot from Jake's Browning shattered his right kneecap. The man screamed as that leg folded up under him and pitched him toward the brink. He let go of the machine pistol to catch himself. The HK skittered over the edge and clattered away.

The man clutched his ruined knee with his left hand while trying to fish out a handgun with his right. Jake shot him in that shoulder, then drilled the left shoulder for good measure. The man slumped back, helpless to do anything except lie there and whimper.

Barry paused in his shots aimed at the ridge and asked, "Any more bogies in that direction?"

"Negative," Jake said, "but I'm keeping an eye out for them."

"How's Chet?"

Jake glanced at the unconscious Taylor. "Breathing."

"Probably the best we can hope for right now." Barry raised himself up and opened fire again. He squeezed off two rounds and said, "Ha!"

"What?" Jake asked. "Don't tell me you hit him! At that range, with no scope?"

"Not all of us grew up shooting with a scope . . . Some of us needed to be good enough without one to stay alive sometimes."

Jake had field glasses in his pack. He found them, held them to his eyes, and searched for a moment before finding a narrow view of part of a man's body stretched out between two boulders.

"He's not moving, that's for sure," Jake said after a minute or so. "Are there any more of them over there?"

"I haven't seen anybody move—Wait! There he goes! To the left!"

Jake moved the glasses in that direction. He picked up the running figure of a man who was angling away from the ridge crest. Barry fired twice. Both bullets kicked up dust right behind the fleeing man.

"Lead him a little more!" Jake called.

Barry fired again, but just as his rifle cracked, the man on the ridge dipped down out of sight.

"He's gone," Jake said. "Must've made it to a trail on the far side."

"I didn't wing him with that last shot?"

"Didn't look like it."

Barry muttered something disappointed sounding, then said, "Are both of yours dead?"

"I don't think so." The second man Jake had shot had stopped wailing, but he moved a little now and then, as if in too much pain to stay still. "One fell off the trail, but the other's alive."

"Good. I've got some questions for him."

"What about Taylor?"

"He's not going to make it," Barry said flatly. "Look at him."

Jake looked, saw how gray Taylor's face had become, and knew his uncle was right. There had been no exit wound on Taylor's back; Jake had seen that when Barry was helping him to cover. Taylor might have been better off with a through-and-through, even if it nicked a lung. More than likely, the slug had bounced around in there, doing who knows how much damage. Chances were, Taylor was bleeding to death internally—and quickly.

"Go get him and drag him up here," Barry went on. "You don't have to be gentle about it, either."

"You sure all those snipers are gone over there?"

"Well, if they're not," Barry replied with a grim little chuckle, "when they take a shot at you, it'll give me something to aim at."

Jake grunted, then allowed himself a slight smile. He supposed it *was* a little funny.

Then he was up, moving quickly down the trail toward the man he had shot. The man had bled quite a bit. He was twitching in pain and let out a low moan as Jake approached him. His eyelids fluttered in fear as he recognized the man who had shot him full of holes.

Jake reached down, got hold of the man's ankle on the uninjured left leg, and dragged him up the trail. As

Barry had suggested, he wasn't gentle about it. The wounded man grunted every time his head bounced on the hard ground of the trail.

Nobody had taken any more shots at Jake from the ridge on the other side of the canyon while he was carrying out this grim errand. That made it seem likely only four men had been bent on this mission of murder, two over here on the trail and two on the ridge.

And one of them had fled, which meant whoever had sent them out to kill would soon know they had failed, at least partially. Jake thought it very unlikely that Chet Taylor was going to survive his wound.

Barry got to his feet as Jake hauled the prisoner behind the rocks. Barry's rifle was ready to open fire on the ridge again if need be, but an echoing silence continued to hang over the mountain landscape.

"Taylor?" Jake asked.

"Still breathing, but I don't know for how much longer." Barry's mouth twisted. "At least he's as comfortable as he can be in this situation." He turned toward the prisoner. "Let's have a look at this fella."

The wounded man was Hispanic, stocky, in his thirties. His features were coarse. If he hadn't been in such pain, they probably would have had a brutal cast to them. Now he just looked like he was hurting. His eyes were almost closed, and he seemed only semiconscious.

Those eyes opened all the way, and a wide-awake scream ripped from him as Barry rested a boot on his shattered kneecap. He tried to jackknife into a sitting position but couldn't manage it with his wounded shoulders. Instead, he slumped back and whimpered.

"I don't take any pleasure in hurting people," Barry said as he pointed the rifle in his hands at the man's face. "But you just tried to kill us, and I'm not inclined to feel merciful right now. So you're going to tell me who sent you after us and whether there are any more like you out there. Otherwise, you're no use to me." He rested the rifle's muzzle on the man's forehead. "And I think you know what that means."

CHAPTER 14

The man started speaking agitatedly in Spanish. Barry bore down on his ruined knee again and prompted another scream.

"Don't start telling me about how you don't dare talk," Barry said in an icy voice. "You really think anybody else can do anything worse to you than what I'm about to do?"

The prisoner subsided into incoherent whining again. Barry looked over at his nephew, saw the troubled frown on Jake's face, and asked, "Does this bother you?"

Jake grimaced. "No, not really. Like you said, he tried to kill us. His friends shot Mr. Taylor. It just takes a little getting used to, that's all."

"Maybe you had better go check on Chet," Barry suggested, motioning toward Taylor with his head.

Jake considered that for a second, then shrugged and turned away.

He stopped, though, and turned right back. Barry asked, "Change your mind?"

"Mr. Taylor's not breathing anymore," Jake said.

He stepped closer to the prisoner, pulled the knife from the sheath on his belt, and rested the blade on the man's left shoulder where the bullet had gone in. As he began to put pressure on it and the prisoner shrieked, Jake said, "Talk."

Barry looked over his shoulder, saw that Jake was right about Taylor, and muttered a curse under his breath.

"He went out in the country he loved, but not the way he would have wanted. I can give you a hand there, Jake."

"I got this," Jake said over the fading sobs of the prisoner as he let up on the knife.

Then, after letting the man catch his breath for a moment, he bore down on it again.

Five minutes later, they knew that the man and his companions had worked for Francisco Zaragosa, head of the Zaragosa cartel, just as Barry and Jake had supposed. The men had been with a larger party that was supposed to meet and escort a special shipment crossing the border from Colonia el Camello in Chihuahua.

That speculation on Barry's part had been right. Once the cartel soldiers had the shipment, they would take it through the Big Hatchets and rendezvous with a convoy of SUVs on the highway to the west.

"What kind of shipment are we talking about?" Jake asked. "Goods . . . or people?"

"Blessed Mother," the prisoner gasped. "I do not know. I think . . . I think it must be . . . a man . . . a very important man. We have been watching these trails . . . for weeks now . . . Watching everyone . . . who comes and goes . . . The old *gringo* . . . he is too nosy . . . He thought we did not . . . know he was there . . . but the Zaragosas . . . know everything . . ."

That jibed with what Barry had speculated after talking to Pancho Gonzalez Gutierrez, too.

"This VIP, they're bringing him in today?"

"They should be . . . on the way . . . now." The prisoner sobbed. His face was wet with tears and sweat and pale under its olive tint. "Please . . . Mother of Mercy, please . . . help me. I need . . . a doctor."

"What you need," Barry said in fluent Spanish, "is to tell us exactly where that rendezvous will be."

"If . . . if I tell . . . you will help me?" The wide, pain-filled dark eyes flicked toward Jake. "You will not let this one . . . hurt me again?"

Jake moved his bloody knife closer to the shoulder wound again. "That man you and your friends killed was an old friend of my uncle's. I met him yesterday. Who do you think is more likely to hurt you? I can let him finish this job—"

"No! *Madre Dios*, no! They will meet the convoy . . . eighteen miles south of . . . Hachita. Our men . . . delivering the package . . . have the coordinates . . ."

Jake and Barry glanced at each other. "What time is the meet set for?" Jake asked.

"Between noon . . . and one . . . Please, *señores* . . . this is all I know—"

"Who's in charge?" Barry broke in. "Who's running the operation for Zaragosa?"

"D-Daniel . . . Daniel Colón."

Barry nodded. "I know the name. One of Francisco's top men. If he's taking charge of this personally, it's got to be somebody important who's coming over the border."

"And we're losing time now," Jake said as he straightened. "If we're going to find them, we need to get moving."

"We're not *going* to find them," Barry said. "These mountains cover too big an area for that, and we don't know the terrain. We don't have any idea which trail they're going to use, and we wouldn't know where it was if we did."

"Then what are we going to do?" Jake asked, frustration and anger creeping into his voice.

"If we can get back to my truck in time, we can intercept them . . . and stop them . . . in Hachita. That's our best bet of finding out what this is all about."

Jake thought about it and nodded. "All right. We need to take Mr. Taylor back with us, though."

"Never figured on doing any different."

"*Señores!*" the prisoner said. "You must help me! You promised!"

"I don't believe we actually ever did promise that," Jake said.

"But we won't hurt you any more, since you told us what we need to know," Barry added. "Jake, you mind carrying Chet's body?"

"Of course not."

Jake went to Taylor's side, got down on one knee, and got his arms around the man. He lifted Taylor as carefully as possible and got to his feet, grunting a little from the strain. Carrying Taylor back down the mountain to the pickups would be quite a chore, but Jake was massively strong.

"*Señor,*" the prisoner said, "you will carry me? I . . . I do not think I can walk."

"Don't believe we ever said that, either," Barry replied.

He picked up Jake's rifle and Taylor's Thompson submachine gun and carried both those weapons as well as his own as he started along the trail behind his nephew.

"*Señor!*" the man screeched.

He continued yelling as Jake and Barry headed down

the trail. Curses spewed from his lips in English and Spanish. As badly wounded as he was, there was no way he could survive out here in this wilderness, dozens of miles from anywhere.

Buzzards were already starting to circle in the sky overhead, swooping lazily but ominously through the hot, dry air.

Barry glanced back when the yelling stopped. The wounded man couldn't use either arm. They flopped around limply as he dug at the ground with his one good leg, grunting with the effort as he pushed himself toward the edge of the trail.

Barry paused to watch. The cartel soldier used his leg to lever himself into another roll, then another. He was very near the edge now. One more good push sent him over it, and he cried out involuntarily as he began to slide, bounce, and roll down the steep, rock-studded slope.

By the time he reached the bottom, a couple of hundred yards later, his brains would be bashed out several times over—but Barry supposed the guy preferred that to waiting for the buzzards to get brave enough to come down and start pecking at his eyes while he was still alive.

"Down you go," Barry muttered as he turned away. His long legs allowed him to catch up quickly with Jake.

"What happened back there? You didn't go back to help him, did you?"

"No, he helped himself," Barry said.

CHAPTER 15

"Are you certain you know where you're going?" Bandar al-Saddiq asked irritably as he used his handkerchief to mop sweat off his face for what seemed like the thousandth time since he had started tramping through these ugly mountains.

Burly, bullet-headed Daniel Colón replied, "Of course. I know exactly where we are and what our route should be."

"How can you possibly know that, here in the middle of this"—he waved a hand at their bleak surroundings—"this absolute wilderness?"

"'S'okay," Colón said with what was meant to be a reassuring shrug of his shoulders. "I got GPS."

He showed Saddiq the handheld unit and waggled it back and forth.

They had been trudging through the mountains for more than an hour since crossing the border just west of Colonia el Camello. There was no fence or any other kind of barrier, and honestly, unless you *knew* where you were, no way of knowing when you entered the United States. The white SUVs had driven to a particular spot and then stopped. Saddiq assumed Zaragosa's drivers knew where they were going.

Once there, they had waited—inside the vehicles, with the engines running for the air-conditioning—until four all-terrain vehicles had roared up from the west.

"Your ride," Francisco Zaragosa had said dryly, and his idiot brother giggled at that. Saddiq found both of them repulsive, as well as the rest of the men who worked for the cartel. They were all infidels.

Sometimes, though, in order to do the will of Allah, a warrior had to associate with lesser men. Part of the holy task was to use those men to further the aims of the Prophet without being dragged down to their degenerate level.

They had climbed out of the SUVs. Zaragosa introduced him to Daniel Colón, one of the men on the ATVs. There were two on each all-terrain vehicle, all of them bristling with weapons. That was good to see, anyway.

Zaragosa and Colón talked briefly in low voices that Saddiq couldn't make out. Zaragosa looked unhappy. Clearly, Colón was trying to convince him that all would be well.

Finally, Zaragosa turned to Saddiq and said, "The operation will proceed."

"There is trouble in the mountains?"

"No, no trouble," Zaragosa said quickly, shaking his head. "Some potential witnesses to be taken care of."

"You mean killed?"

"The death of some *gringos* bothers you?"

Saddiq laughed. "Hardly. The more dead Americans, the better."

"Just leave enough of them alive to buy our cocaine and heroin, eh?" Zaragosa joined in the laughter, and so did the feebleminded one.

After that, Saddiq climbed onto one of the ATVs with Colón, and they set off toward the mountains that lay within the boundaries of the United States.

The Americans were fools to leave their borders so unprotected, Saddiq thought. Some of their politicians had tried mightily to improve the nation's security. But with a political system that allowed just about anybody to vote and politicians who traded giveaways for support, no one managed to make any conclusive decisions. All to Saddiq's benefit.

But if the infidels wanted to pave the way to their own destruction, who was Saddiq to stop them . . . ?

The ATVs had been able to travel only so far before Saddiq and his escort had to abandon them and proceed on foot. That was when the ordeal truly began.

Saddiq had brought along a straw hat—like an American cowboy hat—that he thought looked ludicrous, but at least it kept the sun off his head. He felt his suit soaking through and wilting from his sweat, though.

This discomfort was just one more thing the infidels would pay for, he told himself.

More cartel men were waiting for them in the mountains. Saddiq expected Colón and the others to turn him over to them and head back to Colonia el Camello, but Colón said, "Francisco told me to stay with you and make sure you are safe until we rendezvous with the men who will take you north." He waved at the heavily armed men in both groups, who now numbered fifteen. "Nothing will happen to you, *Señor* al-Saddiq."

"Of course not," Saddiq said. "Allah protects those who wage jihad in his name. We die only when we are ready, and then only in the service of Allah."

Colón nodded solemnly, but it was clear he was just an infidel, too.

A useful idiot, like the incompetent American politicians who were weakening their country.

Saddiq took frequent drinks from a jug of water carried by one of the men. Finally, just as he thought he would not be able to go on, they reached the western edge of the mountains and walked down a slope to where half a dozen jeeps waited. Saddiq saw a silvery line in the distance, several miles away across the flats that stretched to the west.

Colón saw what he was looking at and said, "That's the highway. That's where more of our men will meet us in SUVs."

"Air-conditioned, I hope."

"Of course!" Colón laughed. "Only fools would have a car without air-conditioning."

They all climbed into the jeeps and set off toward the highway. After the long walk through the mountains, it seemed that they covered the remaining distance in little more than the blink of an eye.

The jeeps pulled up on the gravel shoulder next to the two-lane highway, pointing north. "Everything is on schedule," one of the men told Colón after talking quietly on a satellite phone. "The convoy will be here in ten minutes."

"I wish you good fortune, my friend," Colón said to Saddiq.

"And you as well," Saddiq replied. He searched for the word he wanted. "*Amigo.*"

That brought a smile to Colón's face. Inwardly, Saddiq shook his head.

Did these degenerates truly believe that their squalid

country, with its filthy, disease-ridden habits, would be allowed a continued existence once the United States was conquered? No, as the holy, divinely ordained caliphate spread worldwide, Mexico would be swallowed up, too. Swallowed up and spit out, remade by the glories of Islam.

More SUVs—four of them, all gleaming black this time—rolled up precisely ten minutes later, making precise turns so that they were facing back north. Armed men swarmed out of them as they stopped.

"These *hombres* will take you to your next destination," Colón told him. "Welcome to the United States, *Señor* al-Saddiq."

Chapter 16

It seemed sort of disrespectful to Jake for him to sling Chet Taylor's body over his shoulder like a big bag of potatoes, but even with his massive strength, that was the only way he could carry the man as far as he needed to. A couple of times along the way, he had to have Barry help him shift Taylor from one shoulder to the other to relieve the strain.

By the time they reached the pickups parked at the edge of the mountains, Jake was red-faced, drenched with sweat, and puffing from the effort of carrying Taylor that far. He was sure Barry would never have left his old friend's body for the scavengers, though. Jake had known Taylor for less than twenty-four hours, but he felt the same way about the man.

"Put him in the back of your truck," Barry said. "We can leave his pickup here and send somebody back for it later. If anything happens to it in the meantime, Chet's not going to care."

"There's a blanket in the truck box," Jake said. "If you'll get it out, we can wrap him in it."

Barry did that, and within minutes they had Taylor's

body secured in the back. They piled into the pickup's cab with Jake taking the wheel.

He took the rough dirt road leading back to the highway as fast as he could without running the risk of breaking an axle from all the bouncing and jolting. As he held the wheel tightly, he said, "What if that cartel convoy has already picked up whoever or whatever it is and gets to Hachita ahead of us?"

"The rendezvous was supposed to be eighteen miles south of Hachita between noon and one o'clock." Barry looked at the watch on his wrist. "It's 12:09 right now. This trail veered off from the highway fourteen and a half miles south of town."

Jake narrowed his eyes. "How do you know that?"

"Because I pay attention to things," Barry said. "It's a good habit to get into."

Jake grunted and shook his head. "So you're saying it's not likely they've picked him up yet."

"And if they have . . . if they're ahead of us . . . we ought to catch up to them before they get to Hachita."

"Because once we're on the highway I'm going to drive like a bat out of hell?"

"Now you're getting it." Barry started putting fresh magazines in each of the semi-automatic rifles. "If we don't see them on the way, we can be pretty sure they're behind us."

What his uncle said made sense to Jake, but he knew how odd, unexpected things could happen. Still, right now there was no point in borrowing trouble. They would get back to Hachita as quickly as they could and see what happened from there.

Barry's idea of blocking the road with his truck

seemed workable. The highway was just two lanes plus shoulders, so while the truck wouldn't stretch all the way across it, it would take up most of the room.

If Barry was at the wheel and the lead SUV in the convoy tried to swerve around it, he could pull forward or back up to get in the way. Jake would bet on Barry's reflexes and reactions against those of any drug smuggler out there.

Out here on the flats, the line of telephone poles that lined the highway were visible from several miles away. Jake supposed the phone line ran south because of that border crossing Chet Taylor had mentioned. There were probably also some isolated ranches down in this area.

Because of that visibility, they were able to see the vehicles moving swiftly northward along the highway before they got there. Although the distance was still too great to make out details, Jake could tell there were four vehicles in a fairly close group.

"Don't know what else you could call that except a convoy," Barry drawled.

"Yeah, and they're speeding up," Jake said. "They're bound to see all the dust we're kicking up. It's such a big cloud I don't think they could miss it."

"And by now, the one ambusher who got away probably alerted everybody else involved in the operation that he and his friends weren't able to kill all of us." Barry's voice took on a grim note now. "Just one." He paused, then went on, "So they probably have a pretty good idea who we are, and they won't want us bothering them."

Jake calculated angles and speed in his head. "I don't think I can make it to the highway ahead of them. We won't be far behind them when we get there, though."

He didn't take his eyes off the dirt trail as he added, "You know, they might *not* be the ones we're looking for."

"My gut says they are." Barry snapped a fresh magazine into the butt of his 9mm pistol. "I guess what they do next will tell us one way or the other, won't it?"

Jake kept a heavy foot on the accelerator as they approached the highway, but he was right—the tight group of SUVs raced past, heading north, before the pickup could get there. By the time Jake hauled the wheel over and the pickup skidded onto the asphalt, the convoy was two hundred yards ahead of them.

No other vehicles were in sight in either direction. To say this wasn't a heavily traveled highway was an understatement. But that was good, Jake thought, because that way they didn't have to worry about innocent bystanders.

Jake had barely gotten the pickup straightened out when the brake lights on the rear vehicle in the convoy suddenly flared bright red. The SUV slewed sideways. Its brakes and tires had to be screaming, but Jake couldn't hear any of that over the roar of the pickup's engine.

The back door on the side of the SUV facing toward the pickup flew open. "Evasive action!" Barry yelled as a man sitting in the SUV's back seat lifted a heavy automatic rifle and opened fire on them.

Jake jerked the wheel to the left. The pickup whipped completely into the left lane. Ahead of them, little chunks of asphalt sprayed into the air as the slugs from the automatic rifle chewed up the road.

Those little explosions allowed Jake to track the burst as it came toward the pickup. He juked the vehicle back hard to the right.

The crazy thought crossed his mind that he was glad he and Barry had wrapped Chet Taylor's body in the blanket and then tied it down so that it couldn't roll around back there.

Now that the SUV was stopped, Jake's pickup was closing in on it in a hurry. Barry leaned out the passenger window, snugged the rifle's stock against his shoulder, and started shooting. The way Jake had the pickup weaving back and forth made it difficult to aim, but Barry had an uncanny knack with firearms, an ability that bordered on the supernatural.

The man in the SUV's back seat suddenly slumped. The auto-firer slipped from his hands and fell to the pavement. The gunner doubled over and toppled out after it.

The driver had rolled his window down. He poked a handgun out and triggered several shots toward the pickup. The other passengers threw open the doors on the far side of the vehicle, jumped out, and split up to hurry to the front and back of the SUV. They opened fire with pistols as well.

Jake's pickup wasn't custom-made like Barry's rig was, but it was heavy enough to absorb a few hits. The windshield on the passenger side starred from a bullet's impact but didn't shatter.

Barry stopped shooting long enough to shout, "Go around them!"

Jake responded instantly. He swerved onto the right shoulder, overshooting slightly so that both tires on that side strayed off the gravel and onto the dirt. That made the pickup tilt more, but with four-wheel drive and the left-hand tires still on the road, the truck slowed down a little but kept going.

Jake tightened the grip of his right hand on the wheel and used his left to pluck the Browning Hi-Power from the holster at his waist. He squeezed off three rounds at the SUV as the pickup roared past.

The man who'd been standing at the back of the vehicle, using it for cover as he took potshots at Jake and Barry, was now exposed. One of his bullets whined off the pickup's body somewhere not far from Jake.

That was the last shot the cartel soldier ever fired, however, because one of Jake's rounds had caught him in the temple and blown a fist-sized chunk of bone out of his skull.

The pickup shot past the SUV on the shoulder. With a bump of the tires, all four wheels got back on the pavement and the pickup leaped forward, its speed increasing again. Barry twisted around in the window again and emptied his rifle's magazine at the vehicle they had just passed.

The man who had been firing over the hood tried to dive back into the front seat, but a couple of bullets struck him between the shoulder blades and drove him through the open door, all the way against the driver.

Barry pulled himself back inside the pickup's cab. "How much did they gain on us?"

"They're a quarter of a mile ahead now," Jake said.

"Can you catch them?"

"You're blasted right I can," Jake said through gritted teeth as he again tightened his hands on the steering wheel and leaned forward to peer through the dusty windshield.

CHAPTER 17

"The package will be in the second vehicle," Barry mused as the pickup raced after the SUVs. "The other one bringing up the rear will drop off any time now to try to stop us, or at least slow us down."

"And the other two will switch places so there's another vehicle between us and the package," Jake said. "I've been mixed up in a few chases like this. Even if we can fight our way through them, I'm not sure we can catch up before we get to Hachita. And if they beat us there, we won't be able to block the highway with your truck."

"Then we're gonna have to beat them there."

Jake shook his head. "I don't see how."

"We go around them."

A frown creased Jake's forehead as he said, "We can't. You saw how the pickup slowed down once we got even partway off the shoulder back there. The ground's just too soft—"

"Not up ahead, it's not," Barry interrupted. "There's a salt flat off to the west that runs for several miles. It comes pretty close to the highway up here before too much longer. I noticed that earlier, too. If we get out on that stretch, we can go a lot faster. You may not remember this, but guys used to set land speed records at Bonneville Salt Flats in Utah."

"This ain't Utah!" Jake grinned humorlessly as he spotted the long stretch of white, absolutely level ground up ahead to the left. "But I guess it'll have to do."

He picked out what looked like a feasible route to the salt flats without any gullies or giant holes or sand dunes and twisted the wheel again.

Despite his still-raging anger at Chet Taylor's murder and the seriousness of the situation, Jake couldn't stop himself from letting out an exuberant whoop when the pickup actually left the ground for a second as it charged off the road and headed across the countryside.

Dust, dirt, and gravel spewed in the air from the pickup's tires. Jake had to fight the wheel a little, but he kept the vehicle moving in the right direction.

The slowdown was inevitable, however. He twisted his head to look toward the highway and saw the three SUVs pulling farther ahead.

"Keep it floored!" Barry said. "You need to get across the outer edge of the salt flat as fast as you can so we don't break through the crust."

"Got it," Jake said.

The long, white flat was coming up quickly. He pressed the gas harder, and the pickup shot out onto the smoother surface. It was moving too fast for the salt crust to crack under its weight. Just the opposite of a frozen pond, this dried-up salt lake was thicker and sturdier in the center, rather than along the edges.

And the farther out onto it the pickup went, the more the vehicle's speed increased. Jake kept the pickup in top shape. He watched the gauges on the dash, but there were no warning lights, no needles edging too far toward the red. The heavy-duty engine was operating perfectly.

The speedometer reached 100 mph and continued its steady climb to 110. Jake said, "Can't get much more speed out of it than that, Barry."

"That's all right," Barry said. "Unless those SUVs have been modified . . . which is always possible, I suppose . . . they can't maintain speeds like this for very long. In fact, I think we've already closed up the gap some."

Jake took his eyes off where they were going for a split second and checked their position relative to their quarry. His uncle was right: They hadn't drawn even with the convoy yet, but they were getting closer.

"We'll lose some ground when this flat runs out and we have to get back onto the highway," he cautioned.

"I know. You'll just have to get far enough ahead of them that it won't matter before then."

"Yeah, that's all," Jake muttered. He concentrated on his driving for a few moments, then said, "They're bound to have seen us over here and figured out what we're doing by now. Do you think they'll try to stop us?"

"Oh, I imagine you can count on that," Barry said.

CHAPTER 18

The man in charge of the group that had picked up Saddiq had introduced himself as Enrique Galvez. He sat beside Saddiq in the rear seat of what was now the middle SUV in the group of three and spoke over a radio in Spanish too fast for Saddiq to follow. Saddiq could read quite a bit of Spanish and follow along when it wasn't spoken too quickly, but he had no hope of understanding what was coming out of Galvez's mouth.

They both spoke English, though, and that was the language Galvez used as he lowered the handheld radio and grimaced.

"Only one of the men Colón sent to eliminate those *gringos* survived," Galvez reported. "So that must be them chasing us. The *gringos*, I mean."

"Do you know who they are?" Saddiq demanded.

"We believe one of them is a man named Taylor who lives in Hachita. He guides hunting parties into the Big Hatchets . . . and snoops in things that are none of his business. The other two . . ." Galvez shrugged. "*Quién sabe?* Who knows? Friends or clients of his, perhaps."

Saddiq's voice was scathing as he said, "So ordinary American hunters, with their beer bellies and small endowments, are capable of disposing of half a dozen or more of your best men, seemingly with little effort?"

Anger hardened Galvez's face. "They may not be ordinary," he admitted. "But they will die like anyone else."

He lifted the radio to his mouth, keyed the mike, and snapped an order in Spanish. Saddiq asked, "What are you going to do?"

Galvez pointed to the vast salt flat stretching across the landscape to the left of the highway. Out there, a quarter of a mile away, was the speeding pickup containing their enemies. It had almost drawn even with the car in which Galvez and Saddiq rose.

"They will never get off that salt flat alive," Galvez said confidently.

"Oh, crap!" Barry yelled.

Jake knew from experience that when men were under fire, they seldom shouted, "Incoming!" like in TV and the movies. They were more likely to let out some other startled exclamation—usually a curse or obscenity.

He could tell from Barry's voice that something bad was about to happen. When he jerked his eyes in that direction, he saw an object trailing smoke and fire sizzling through the air toward them. Jake's reaction took only a shaved fraction of a second. By the time Barry added, "RPG!," Jake had already wrenched the wheel to the left.

Whoever had fired the rocket-propelled grenade from the convoy had good aim. If Jake had continued straight ahead, the grenade would have struck Barry's door and blown them both into little pieces.

Instead, by juking to the left, Jake caused the RPG to fall a few yards short. It hit the ground and exploded in a ball of fire.

The blast was close enough that the force of it tipped the pickup onto its left wheels for a second, chunks of crystallized salt pelting the right-hand side of the vehicle. The pickup didn't turn over. The right wheels slammed back down, spinning on the salt for a heartbeat and causing the pickup to slew a little before catching. The pickup leaped ahead again as it gained traction.

"If they have one of those, they probably have another!" Jake called to his uncle as he pressed the accelerator to the floor again.

"Or more!" Barry replied. "I'm keeping an eye on them. I'll sing out if they—Here comes another one! Brake!"

That was some quick reloading, Jake had time to think as he moved his foot from the gas to the brake and stomped hard. The back end fishtailed, drifting right. Jake let it go. The pickup spun crazily as the RPG sizzled through the air and detonated in front of them this time. The explosion blew a hole in the salt flat big enough to overturn the pickup if a wheel went into it. Jake hauled hard on the wheel, desperately trying to keep the pickup out of the hole.

Still turning around and around, the pickup went over the hole, narrowly missing it with both front and back wheels. A few yards later, Jake regained control of the vehicle.

"They slowed us down, blast it!" Jake said as he saw that the convoy had pulled slightly ahead again.

"Give it the gas!" Barry told him. "I saw which SUV

that last grenade came from. The one in the back. I don't intend to let them draw a bead on us again!"

As he said that, he thrust the barrel of his rifle out the window and opened fire. Whatever—or whoever— the package was, they wanted it safe and sound so they could figure out what was going on, but Barry was convinced the special shipment was in the middle vehicle. He raked the side of the third SUV with 5.62mm rounds. The range was a little too long for really accurate shooting, but he put as many bullets as he could in the vicinity of the rear window on the driver's side, figuring that was where the man with the grenade launcher was.

Muzzle flashes flickered from the windows of the other vehicles. A few bullets whammed against the side of Jake's pickup but didn't penetrate. Jake had regained the ground he had lost, and he was about to start pulling ahead again.

Something hummed from right to left in front of him. That was a bullet, he realized with a somewhat detached air. It had come in through Barry's open window, passed in front of both of them, and exited through the open driver's window. Avoiding death by a matter of inches was kind of a big deal, but neither of them had time to think about that now.

Barry had sat back to reload again. He shoved his rifle back out the window and resumed shooting. He targeted the first and third SUVs, avoided the one in the middle.

"We'd better be right about where the package is," Jake called.

"I usually am," Barry replied. That would have sounded arrogant coming from a lot of people. From Dog, it was just a statement of fact.

The pickup was even with the lead vehicle in the convoy. Jake mentally asked the engine for all it had. As if that creation of metal and rubber had heard him, the pickup seemed to go a little faster. It edged ahead of the convoy, then slowly gained more and more ground.

Barry leaned out the window to fire back at the lead vehicle. When the magazine ran dry, he dropped back into the seat.

"I thought maybe I'd get lucky and blow a tire, maybe flip that SUV and stop the others," he said. "Didn't work, though. They've probably got solid tires on those things."

Jake turned his head. He had to look through the pickup's back window to see the convoy now. He glanced into the pickup bed. Chet Taylor's blanket-wrapped body was still there, despite all the explosions and bouncing and flying around. He was glad they had tied it down securely.

"We'll stop them in Hachita," he said.

CHAPTER 19

In the middle SUV, Bandar al-Saddiq was livid.

"Who are those . . . those . . ." He added every American obscenity he could think of, plus a few that probably didn't exist but should.

Then he stabbed a finger, shaking with anger, toward the pickup that was now well ahead of the convoy and angling back toward the highway.

"Kill them!" he shouted at Enrique Galvez.

The Mexican looked angry, too, as if he didn't like being yelled at that way. Saddiq didn't care. Clearly, those men in the pickup—whoever they were—meant to interfere with the mission that had brought him to the United States.

That couldn't be allowed to happen. The stakes were too high. Too many people had invested their wealth, their honor, their very lives in this plan to finally bring the Great Satan to its knees and teach the infidels their proper place in this world—under the boot of Islam.

Lashkar-e-Islami would succeed where al-Qaeda, ISIS, and all the others had failed. They would strike where the Americans' hearts were truly located.

But only if Saddiq, who had contrived the scheme with the aid of a few others, was on hand to supervise the operation. He knew it was vainglorious, even sinful, to believe that he was so vital to its success, but when you came right down to the facts, it was true. This was, as the infidels would say, his baby.

And he would not allow it to come to nothing now.

"They are too far ahead of us now for the rocket grenades," Galvez said gloomily. "They are out of effective range for our rifles, too." He shook his head. "There is nothing more we can do, *Señor* al-Saddiq. But I give you my word . . . if they try to stop us, they will not succeed. There are only two men in the cab of that pickup. They cannot fight us and win."

"They seem to have done a good job of staying alive so far, against superior odds."

Galvez shrugged. "Clearly, the *gringos* are not ordinary hunters after bighorn sheep, as we thought they might be."

Saddiq sat back and blew out an exasperated breath. "I believe they *are* hunters," he said. "But *I* am their prey." He leaned sharply toward Galvez, and his lips drew back from his teeth. "They knew I was being brought across the border today, or else they would not be here. They *knew*!"

"They could not have," Galvez insisted. "No one would dare betray the Zaragosas. Anyone who did such a thing would die screaming, and his entire family with him."

"Someone dared. Those men"—Saddiq gestured toward the speeding pickup, which had pulled well ahead now—"are professionals. The way they drive, the way they shoot . . . Only men who fight for a living would be capable of doing what they have done. And there had to be a good reason they were here today, in this place."

Saddiq folded his arms over his chest and sat back again, indicating beyond any doubt that he believed himself to be that reason.

Galvez's expression told Saddiq that the man agreed with him, no matter how much Galvez didn't want to. Which meant there had to be a traitor somewhere in the cartel.

After a long moment, Galvez said, "Francisco will stop at nothing to find out who is responsible for this, *señor*. He will question everyone who can be questioned, he will turn over every rock—"

"Until he finds the scorpion he has taken to his bosom," Saddiq finished. "That is all well and good, Galvez, but it means nothing if I fail to reach my destination safely and cannot put my plan into operation."

"We will not fail," Galvez said again, but he sounded slightly less convinced now.

Saddiq fumed a moment longer, then asked, "How soon will we reach this town you spoke of earlier?"

"Hachita?" Galvez frowned. "Another two, three minutes. We are almost there."

"It seems logical that will be the next place the Americans attempt to stop us," Saddiq said as he peered through the windshield with narrowed eyes. "So we will know one way or the other whether they will succeed very soon now, eh?"

CHAPTER 20

Jake kept one eye on the convoy in the rearview mirror, half a mile behind him, and the other on the gauges in the pickup's dashboard.

The pickup had labored valiantly, but the temperature gauge's needle had finally started to creep over toward the red. He knew he risked damaging the engine if he kept up this pace much longer. If the pickup ground to a halt, he and Barry would be sitting ducks for their enemies.

Luckily, he wouldn't have to keep going this fast for much longer. He could see the scattered, run-down buildings of Hachita up ahead. As they came closer, he was able to pick out the red sheen of Barry's truck parked next to Chet Taylor's mobile home a couple hundred yards off the highway.

At the last second, he braked as he reached the dirt road leading to Taylor's place. The tires left deep skid marks as they swerved to a stop.

Jake wrestled the vehicle back into line and raced down the narrow dirt road with clouds of dust boiling into the air behind the pickup.

Barry was out the door before Jake brought the pickup to a complete stop.

"Come on!" he called over his shoulder. "And bring that Tommy gun!"

The Thompson was lying in the floorboard on the passenger side, where Barry had put it earlier. Jake grabbed the machine gun and the semi-auto rifles and bailed out the other side, running to the passenger door on the big Kenworth.

Barry had unlocked it with his remote as soon as they were in range of the signal, so Jake was able to haul himself up, yank the door open, and dive in as the big truck's engine rumbled to life.

Barry threw the Kenworth into gear. The passenger door was still open, but the sudden start slammed it. Jake hit the button to roll down the window.

"That's bulletproof glass, you know," Barry reminded him.

"Yeah, I know. Which means we won't be able to shoot through it, either."

Barry grinned. "Yeah, there's that to consider."

He hauled the wheel around as he backed up the truck. Neither of them had really considered the possibility that they might need to pull out of there in a hurry.

That was an unacceptable lack of foresight for a pair of professionals, Jake told himself—but nobody could think of everything all the time.

That was why nobody lived forever in this game. Statistically, Barry had been living on borrowed time for a couple of decades now. The odds should have caught up to him a long time ago. The fact that they hadn't spoke volumes about his skills.

The truck powered away from the mobile home with a throaty roar from its massive engine. Jake looked past

Barry and saw the three SUVs rocketing along the highway toward Hachita. It was going to be close . . .

The convoy was still a hundred yards away when Barry pulled smoothly onto the asphalt. The truck stretched nearly from one side of the highway to the other.

Barry had rolled his window down, too. "Hand me that Tommy gun!" he called.

Jake had watched plenty of World War II movies when he was growing up. He had been hoping he'd get to shoot the Thompson, like the GIs he'd seen in those movies, but he was on the wrong side of the cab.

Without hesitation, he thrust the machine gun into his uncle's hands. As the driver of the lead SUV stood on his brakes to avoid T-boning the truck, Barry racked the Thompson's slide back and opened fire.

The sustained belch of automatic fire chewed into the front of the SUV and sprayed glass everywhere as the windshield shattered into a million pieces. A red mist seemed to fill the inside of the vehicle as the slugs shredded the driver and the man beside him on the front seat.

The SUV slewed sideways, completely out of control. Tires gave, axles snapped, and the vehicle rolled over and flew into the air—heading straight for the truck parked across the road.

CHAPTER 21

Jake ducked instinctively and lifted an arm in front of his face even though he knew that wasn't going to do any good. It was just a human reaction.

He expected the SUV to smash into the side of the truck. At the speed it was going, the impact might be enough to knock the massive Kenworth over on its side.

Nothing happened in the next couple of heartbeats, though. The seconds seemed to stretch out much longer than they really were. Jake couldn't see the SUV anymore.

Then a huge crash from his side of the truck made him jerk his head in that direction.

To his amazement, he saw that the SUV had narrowly missed the truck and flown completely *over* it to land on the pavement beyond and explode into a ball of flame. The heat from the blast beat against Jake's face.

The Thompson in Barry's hands started its crazed chattering again. Over the racket, he called, "They weaved around and switched places again! The vehicle with the package is in the back now!"

Jake wasn't sure how his uncle knew that; the black SUVs all looked identical to him. He wasn't surprised that Barry had noted some minor difference between the vehicles, though. Barry was that observant.

Jake peered past Barry and saw the lead SUV skidding and swinging around sideways as the driver braked, skillfully bringing it parallel to the truck parked across the road. Movement at the rear passenger window caught Jake's eye, a familiar shape protruding from it.

"Barry, down!" Jake yelled. Barry trusted his nephew enough that he reacted instantly and bent forward so that Jake had a clear line of fire through the window on his side.

Jake had seen the grenade launcher with an RPG loaded in it sticking out the window and knew one of the cartel soldiers was trying to draw a bead on them with it. Using both hands on the 9mm, he took swift but careful aim and squeezed off three rounds.

At least one of the bullets hit the pressure trigger on the grenade. It exploded before the man in the SUV could fire it. Flames engulfed the vehicle, roasting anyone left inside it and turning it into a shattered hulk that continued skidding along the pavement toward the truck.

There was no way to avoid this collision. Barry didn't have time to pull forward or back up. But he was able to get the window beside him part of the way up and duck down behind it before the blazing wreck slammed into them. The bulletproof glass would stop burning chunks of debris, too.

The crash rocked the Kenworth but didn't tip it over. The SUV's gas tank hadn't gone up yet, but it was bound to in a matter of moments.

Barry dropped the Thompson, threw the truck in

gear, and slammed his foot down on the gas. The powerful, finely tuned engine responded immediately as he hauled the wheel to the right, grunting with the effort.

The truck leaped ahead as Barry turned, the cab going across the shoulder and onto the softer ground to the left of the highway. The eighteen huge wheels dug big ruts in the dirt but continued turning.

Barry circled the still-burning SUV that had flown over them before crashing. The truck's front end lurched back onto the pavement and lunged northward just as the second SUV's gas tank ignited and an even larger ball of hellish flame swallowed up the vehicle.

The third SUV darted around the explosion and whipped past on the right-hand shoulder. Jake pounded a hand on the dashboard in frustration.

"They're ahead of us!"

"For now," Barry said as he straightened the truck and increased its speed.

"Can they outrun us?"

"We're gonna find out."

By now, the SUV and the pursuing truck were barreling through what amounted to "downtown" Hachita, past convenience stores, gas stations, a couple of cafés, and a bar. The explosions just south of town had drawn people out of the buildings. They stood, using their hands to shade their eyes from the noonday sun as they indulged their curiosity and tried to see what was going on.

Then, as the remaining SUV raced past, some of the citizens began stumbling backward and clapping their hands to their chests. As Jake saw them collapse, he shouted in fury, "They're shooting those people!"

Flame flickered from the barrels of weapons protruding from the SUV's windows. As the citizens of Hachita became aware of the slaughter being carried out on them, they tried to scramble back to safety inside the buildings. Some of them made it, but others went down with crimson flowers blooming on their backs.

Grimacing, Jake leaned out the window with his pistol, intending to take a few shots at their quarry, even though he knew that if the "package" was a person, they needed to take him or her alive.

Before he could do that, however, the SUV reached the northern end of the little town and the shooting from it stopped. The vehicle continued heading in that direction at high speed.

The Kenworth roared after it.

"Should we go back there and try to help those people?" Jake asked.

"Don't think it didn't occur to me," Barry answered tightly, "but our job is to find out what's going on here. It has to be something pretty important for the Zaragosa cartel to go to this much trouble."

"Yeah, I know." Jake muttered a couple of curses under his breath, then said, "I can't believe they just mowed people down like that!"

"You've been in this business long enough to know that animals like the Zaragosas don't worry about hurting people. Anybody who gets in their way isn't even human . . . just something to be brushed aside or stepped on, like a bug."

"I know," Jake agreed, "but that doesn't mean I have to like it."

"No, it sure doesn't. I don't like it, either." Barry's gaze was fixed intently on the SUV in front of them. "That's why we're going to make them pay for what they did."

CHAPTER 22

Bandar al-Saddiq lifted his hand and looked at it.

Not a single tremor.

That was what believing in the rightness of his cause did for a man. It brought him peace and strength.

And righteous anger, as well. Saddiq closed his hand into a fist, and in his mind, he visualized crushing the life out of the infidels who pursued him. He could see their blood oozing between his fingers . . .

Beside him, Enrique Valdez twisted around on the seat and peered through the SUV's rear window. He banged his fist against the seat as a burst of Spanish profanity erupted from him.

"Still back there!" he said. "What does it take to get rid of these *gringos*?"

"I thought perhaps shooting those people in the town would make them stop," Saddiq said. "Obviously, they care nothing for innocent lives. But then, we already knew that. Consider how many millions of innocents the Americans have slaughtered in my homeland and in other countries on the other side of the world."

"You attacked them in their home," Galvez said. "Did you think they have no pride?"

Saddiq sneered. "I think most Americans are gutless

sheep, soft and easy to kill. Has your experience been any different, Galvez?"

The Mexican shrugged and said, "Many Americans are sheep to the slaughter, I agree." He glanced behind them again. "But some are wolves."

"This vehicle will go faster than that truck, will it not?"

"As you said earlier, *señor* . . . we will find out. In twenty minutes, if we live that long, we will reach the interstate, and another vehicle will be waiting there to pick you up. I promise you, the *gringos* will not be able to catch that one."

Barry and Jake knew from the drive down here into New Mexico's Bootheel that there wasn't much of anything between Interstate 10 and Hachita. As the road signs often warned out here in this part of the country, No Services for However-Many Miles.

So there was nothing to slow down the SUV as it fled north. Just open road, bordered on one side by telephone and power poles.

"If I remember the map right, this stretch runs almost straight as a string except for a couple of easy bends," Barry said.

Jake was already at work on the computer, calling up a map. As it appeared on the screen, he saw that Barry was right and said as much.

"Maybe we should call in the New Mexico highway patrol, get them to set up a roadblock at the interstate," he suggested.

"Neither of us have any official standing in this

case," Barry pointed out. "I don't carry any credentials, and you're taking time off from the FBI, remember?"

"Yeah, but I can get in touch with the bureau and request assistance anyway. And I know good and well you can make calls to people high up and get just about anything you want."

Barry laughed. "Things like that take time, though, and we don't have that luxury right now. Stopping whoever or whatever that is in front of us, that's up to us. The Zaragosas wouldn't be shooting RPGs all over the place and slaughtering civilians if it wasn't important."

That reminder of what had happened back in Hachita put grim looks on the faces of both men. Jake stared through the windshield at the black SUV, visible half a mile ahead of them.

"How fast can this truck go, anyway?"

"With the special modifications to the engine, top speed is 125 mph. We can't maintain that for more than an hour or so, but if we can catch them before they get to I-10, we won't have to."

"If that SUV belongs to the Zaragosa cartel, it's probably been souped up, too," Jake said. "The question is how much."

He leaned over slightly, enough to see that the needle on the speedometer was hovering just above 120. Barry had said he could coax a few more miles per hour out of the Kenworth if he needed to, and it was starting to look as if that was going to be necessary.

"Maybe it's just wishful thinking," Barry said after a few moments of taut silence, "but I believe we're getting closer to them."

"Maybe," Jake replied. "I mean, maybe closing in on them, not about it being wishful thinking."

The miles flashed by and the minutes crept along, and little by little, the truck drew closer to the SUV.

Then Jake said, "Isn't that the highway up there?"

Out here in this pancake-flat country, any elevation was easy to see from a good distance. That was why the humpbacked mountain ranges scattered around the vicinity looked almost close enough to reach out and touch when they were still miles away.

What Jake saw in the distance was the overpass where Interstate 10 went over New Mexico State Road 146, the highway they were on at the moment. There were no businesses at that intersection, Jake recalled, nor did the state road continue north of the interstate. It ended right there.

"They'll have to go either right or left," he said.

"Yeah." Barry's eyes narrowed. "What're they doing up there?"

The SUV swung out from the northbound lane into the southbound, revealing a motor home that the SUV's driver intended to pass.

A horrible thought occurred to Jake. He said, "You don't think they would—"

That was all he got out before a couple of the men inside the SUV opened fire on the motor home, hammering bullets all along its left-hand side and shattering the driver's window.

CHAPTER 23

Jake yelled in incoherent rage as the motor home began weaving back and forth across the road. The SUV had already spurted ahead of it, so the people in it didn't have to worry about the motor home blocking them.

Barry did have to worry about that, however, which was exactly why the murderous scum inside the SUV had opened fire. Barry had to brake as the motor home slowed but continued lurching unpredictably from side to side.

Jake was sure the driver was riddled with bullets and no longer in control of the vehicle. He had no way of knowing who else was in the motor home or how badly injured they were.

Then the motor home veered too far to the right and went off the pavement. There wasn't much of a drop-off, but enough of one that the top-heavy vehicle began to lean, then went over and began to roll. It made two revolutions before coming to a stop on its side.

Barry kept slowing down. "Can you see if anybody was thrown clear?"

Jake peered at the wreck, which they were rapidly approaching. He said, "I don't see anybody—"

That was as far as he got before the motor home exploded. The blast swallowed it completely. There was no chance that anyone still inside had survived, and since it didn't appear that any of the passengers—if there were any—had been thrown clear, he said, "We can't do anything here. Keep going!"

Grimly, Barry nodded. As he pressed down on the gas again and the truck surged forward, he said in a bleak voice, "Yeah, that's what I was thinking."

The SUV had picked up more ground. As Jake leaned forward to peer after it, the vehicle suddenly veered to the right, taking an exit on a paved road that curved back to the east.

"That's the access road!" Jake exclaimed. He glanced at the map display on the computer screen to confirm his memory. "They can't get onto the highway from there without going through a rest area a couple of miles east of the intersection. That might slow them down."

"Or give them a bunch more innocent people to kill to slow *us* down," Barry said.

He had the gas pedal all the way to the floor, but he had to let up on it as he approached the turnoff. He didn't want to slow down, but he couldn't make the exit onto the access road at this speed.

Even braking, the turn wasn't easy to accomplish. If the angle had been sharper, the truck probably would have gone off the road or jackknifed.

Barry kept it under control, though, and started speeding up again. The black SUV was visible up ahead, as were the buildings and covered picnic tables of the rest area Jake had mentioned.

The frontage road ran close to the actual lanes of the interstate in places. It looked like the SUV could have made it across that narrow median onto the highway without much trouble if the driver had wanted to, even though it would mean busting through a flimsy-looking wire fence.

Jake thought about that and said, "They're heading for some kind of meet at that rest area. Otherwise, they'd be on the highway by now."

"Yeah, I think you're right. Wonder if they're passing the package off to somebody else. That might give us a chance to grab it."

"Right now, I'll take any chance we can get." At the thought of all the wanton killing their quarry had carried out, deep trenches marred Jake's cheeks.

The frontage road was a narrow blacktop with no shoulder and a dotted white line down the middle. A dirt lane leading to a trailer house several hundred yards off the highway flashed past.

Jake wasn't sure why anybody would want to live in a place like that, out here in the middle of nowhere. The solitude would drive most people crazy.

On the other hand, if you didn't like people, southern New Mexico was the place for you.

The SUV's brake lights flared as it reached the rest area. Jake and Barry were close enough now that Jake could see the low, brick building that likely housed restrooms and vending machines. A parking lot for cars was in front of it, and a lane where trucks could park was farther out, closer to the interstate. Picnic tables were scattered around the outer edge of a large open area behind the building. A few scrubby trees grew back there, but it wasn't exactly parklike in its vegetation.

A couple of big rigs were parked in the truck lane. Half a dozen cars had pulled up to the curb on the other side of the parking lot. One of them, a low-slung, dark blue sports car, backed out quickly as the SUV entered the lot, still going pretty fast.

Barry didn't veer to the left toward the truck lane. He kept going straight ahead, aimed at the parking area for passenger vehicles. As the SUV skidded to a stop, Jake leaned forward and said, "A couple of guys just jumped out of the SUV. They're going for that sports car!"

"I see 'em," Barry said. "One of them must be the package."

That would be the sleek, dark-haired man in an expensive-looking, light-colored suit and an incongruous straw cowboy hat he held one-handed on his head, Jake thought. The man hustling him along was a burly Mexican, probably one of the Zaragosa lieutenants charged with delivering the other man to the next stop on his journey.

Three more men piled out of the SUV and opened fire on the Kenworth with machine pistols as Barry sent the truck barreling toward them. The slugs rebounded off the heavily armored front end and didn't even star the windshield.

A few people had been wandering around the rest area. When the shooting started, they scrambled for the cover of the brick building.

Jake worried that the cartel soldiers might open fire on those innocents as a distraction, as they had done twice previously, but this time it looked like a stand-up, face-to-face fight. The smugglers were done running.

Barry slowed down, but not by much. When the gunners realized that he was still coming at them and their bullets weren't doing any good, they tried to dive out of the way.

Two of them weren't fast enough. Jake caught a glimpse of them throwing their arms up in front of them, as if that would somehow protect them from the rushing steel behemoth. Their mouths were open in screams, inaudible over the roar of the Kenworth's engine. He barely felt the thud as they went down under the front bumper and the tires turned them into gory pulp.

The third man managed to dart out of the way. He tried to circle the front end of the SUV, which was parked crossways in the lot to take up as much room as possible.

Barry angled a little to the left so the right front of the truck struck the front end of the SUV, crumpling its fender and spinning it out of the way. The vehicle clipped the fleeing man and knocked him off his feet. A split second later, the Z1000 thundered over him as well.

Up ahead, the man they were after was climbing into the passenger seat of the sports car. He paused just long enough to gaze over the vehicle's roof at the truck coming toward him.

Then he finished leaping inside and slammed the door. The sports car took off, its tires smoking as they left rubber on the pavement.

The last of the cartel soldiers, the one who'd probably been in charge of this leg of the operation, turned to face Barry and Jake. He pulled a small revolver from his pocket, leveled it, and fired at them. He had to know those puny bullets weren't going to stop them, but he was defiant to the last.

The truck steamrollered over him.

Barry pushed the gas pedal to the floor again as he

gave chase to the sports car, which by now had pulled out onto the interstate itself. Traffic wasn't very heavy, so Jake had a good view of the fleeing vehicle as it weaved around the few cars on the road.

"Holy cow! He's taking off like a jet."

"I know," Barry said tersely. "And I can tell just by looking at how fast he's going that we can't catch him. We can't even keep up with him. That little jackrabbit can probably do a hundred and fifty, at least."

"You mean he's going to get away?"

"I mean we can't catch him," Barry said again.

"After they killed Mr. Taylor and shot up all those people in Hachita . . . after they wrecked the motor home and killed everybody in it . . . they delivered the guy they were supposed to deliver and he's going to get away."

Jake's voice was as flat as the bleak, lunar landscape around them.

"For now," Barry said as he began slowing the truck. "He's going to get away for now. That doesn't mean we won't catch up to him later."

"How do you figure that?" Jake asked in obvious disbelief.

"Because I got a good look at his face," Barry said, "and I know who he is. That's the first step in figuring out why he's here and where to look for him next."

CHAPTER 24

"Bandar al-Saddiq," Barry said as he nodded toward the screen of the open laptop on the desk.

Jake studied the lean, handsome, fashionably beard-stubbled face and said, "Are you sure it was him?"

"I got a good look at him at that rest area," Barry said with a nod. "The 'package' the Zaragosa cartel was delivering was Saddiq, all right."

They were in a motel room on the outskirts of Las Cruces, New Mexico, having driven through most of the afternoon to get there after leaving the rest area. The motel wasn't the best in the world—but it was the sort where nobody asked too many questions, either.

The big Kenworth was parked out back, where it wouldn't be as noticeable. After everything that had happened today, it was entirely possible that BOLOs had been issued for it.

Jake had made an anonymous call—Barry always had several burners available—to the New Mexico state police to alert them to a dark blue sports car (make, model, and license number unknown) that was traveling east at a high rate of speed on Interstate 10.

Jake had informed the cops that the car had been involved in several fatal shootings and crashes, and that whoever was in it should be considered heavily armed and highly dangerous.

Of course, the same thing could be said of him and his uncle. He was sure that law enforcement had gotten numerous reports today about a pair of maniacs in a big truck rampaging through that isolated corner of New Mexico. The people who had seen them wouldn't have any way of knowing they were the good guys.

Neither of them really expected Jake's call to the law to do much good as far as locating the man they were after. The driver of the sports car might have even slowed down to a normal speed once he judged he was so far ahead the truck wouldn't be able to catch him.

Chances were that the car had gone on through Deming and at least as far as Las Cruces. It was entirely possible the "package" could be in El Paso by now, or even farther along toward his ultimate destination—wherever that might be.

"So tell me about him," Jake said with a nod toward the face on the screen. "Have the two of you tangled before now?"

"No, I've just seen his name and picture before, that's all."

Barry had a near-photographic memory. If he actually studied something, he knew it forever. Jake had something of the same skill, but not as highly developed.

"He's from Afghanistan and has operated a lot there, also in Pakistan. He's a member of Lashkar-e-Taiba, the Pakistani terrorist organization that's been behind a number of attacks on the Indian military." Barry frowned in thought. "Haven't heard much from them lately."

"Wait a minute," Jake said. "Lashkar-e-Taiba . . . that sounds familiar, somehow."

"It means Army of the Righteous."

"No, I was thinking I'd heard something about it recently . . ." Abruptly, Jake shook his head. "Oh, it wasn't Lashkar-e-Taiba. It was Lashkar-e-Islami."

"The Army of Islam," Barry said. "The group that claimed responsibility for that train derailment in Nevada the other day." He nodded. "That's where we heard it, all right. Over the past forty years, there have been several Islamic terrorist organizations calling themselves the Army of Something or Other. Makes me wonder if a bunch of offshoots from them have gotten together and dubbed themselves the Army of Islam."

"Maybe they thought they weren't getting enough press," Jake suggested. "So they formed their own group of murderers and terrorists."

Barry chuckled. "Actually, you could be on to something. Saddiq was rumored to be involved in several of those attacks Lashkar-e-Taiba pulled off, but he was never the top dog in any of them. He could have figured he'd never get to be the boss if he stayed where he was."

"You make it sound kind of . . . corporate."

"Well, what's more cutthroat than corporate politics?"

Jake didn't have a good answer for that question. Instead, he asked, "What's our next move?"

"I'm going to get in touch with some of the people I've worked with in the past. Word needs to get out to the intelligence community and law enforcement that Saddiq is in this country and may be connected to the incident with the train in Nevada. That way the authorities will know to be on the lookout for him. And I should be able to get any effort to haul *us* in quashed, too."

"You've never talked that much about the people you work for," Jake ventured.

"Work *with*," Barry corrected. "Not for. And I don't talk about them because they don't like to talk about me. I guess we all just figure it's better to act like the others don't exist." He smiled. "Plausible deniability and all that."

"The secretary will disavow any knowledge of you or your mission, as they used to say on that TV show."

"Yeah, that's it exactly." Barry closed the laptop. "I'll make those calls, and then we can go get something to eat."

"After everything we saw today, I'm not sure I have much of an appetite," Jake said with a sigh.

"Maybe not . . . but Saddiq's out there somewhere, and he's plotting something bad. When we figure out what it is, we'll probably have to move fast to stop him. The truck can't go without being fueled up, and neither can we."

"When you put it like that . . . maybe a nice thick steak's not a bad idea."

CHAPTER 25

The dark blue sports car pulled up to the entrance of an exclusive gated community in El Paso. It was late enough in the evening that the guard on duty in the little brick gatehouse during the day had left.

The driver of the sports car knew the code to punch into the keypad that controlled the gate, though. It swung open, and he drove through at a careful, deliberate pace.

Beside him, Bandar al-Saddiq looked back at the gate closing behind them and said, "Typical of the West's decadence. The Americans are weak, so they fear and have to hide behind walls and gates."

"I seem to remember seein' plenty of footage of the compounds where your leaders live behind walls and gates," the driver drawled. "So I don't reckon you've got a lot of room to talk, *amigo*."

He was a lantern-jawed man in a cowboy hat, which, unlike Saddiq's, looked right at home on him.

"Usually drone footage, right before bombs blow the places to smithereens," he continued. He paused, then repeated, dragging it out, "Smithereeeens. What a great word. It's a shame folks don't use it much anymore."

"You should not make light of my people's sacrifice," Saddiq snapped.

"Sorry, hoss. I'm just sayin' that folks all over the world are kind of alike. Your country or mine, if they've got something to be scared of, and they have the money to do it, they're gonna build themselves a big ol' fort." The driver waved a hand at the huge, cookie-cutter houses they were passing as they drove serenely through the neighborhood. "Or the twenty-first century equivalent of one, anyway."

He brought the car to a smooth stop in front of a house with a real estate company's sign in the yard. Saddiq looked at it and said, "This house is for sale?"

"A good way to make sure it's empty in the middle of the night, wouldn't you say?"

Saddiq made a vague, revolving gesture with his hand that took in all their surroundings. "Aren't there security cameras everywhere in a place like this? I thought Americans had no privacy anymore and were always under surveillance. For their own good, of course."

"Sure, but by the time anybody looks at the footage from those cameras, you'll be long gone—and I will be, too. This car will be in pieces, bein' scattered all over the country. Nobody'll ever be able to trace it."

"But certainly, a car like this is very expensive, isn't it?" Saddiq protested. "You can afford to destroy it just to cover your trail?"

"I'm not affording anything. I'm just a hired hand, old son. Come on."

The driver got out and led Saddiq up a flagstone walk to the house's fancy entranceway. He had a key ready and unlocked the door.

Inside, a few dim lights burned, as they might in an empty house that was for sale. Saddiq and the driver waited in the gloomy, marble-floored foyer. In front of them, a staircase curved down from the second floor. As they watched, a pair of female legs, indecently bare atop garish high heels, descended those stairs, followed by the young woman they belonged to.

She was a blonde in a little black dress who looked more like she was heading for some high-society cocktail party than meeting a notorious terrorist in an empty house.

She barely gave the driver a look, her gaze flicking over him without real interest for identification purposes only, and then moved on to Saddiq, where her eyes lingered as she took him in from head to toe. Something that might have been approval showed on her face, but only for a second.

"Bandar al-Saddiq," she said.

"His own self," the driver replied with a grin. The blonde ignored him.

Saddiq took a step toward her. A frown of disapproval creased his forehead. He was a man, and certainly not blind, so he was aware of her beauty. But she was a decadent American slut, not worthy of his time or attention.

"Where is your master?" he asked harshly.

Her chin lifted and jutted out defiantly.

"There's a man I work for, but he's hardly my master," she said. "And if you're thinking of auditioning for the position, you can just forget it."

"I have no interest in a shameless woman," he said with a shake of his head. He looked at the driver. "Take me away from here. I will not deal with this female."

The driver held up his hands, palms out, and started backing away.

"My part of the job's done, hoss. I got you here. That's all I was supposed to do."

Saddiq reached for something under his coat at the small of his back. "You will—"

He stopped short both his movement and the angry words as he found himself caught between two guns, a revolver in the driver's hand and a flat little automatic pointed at him by the blonde. He hadn't known the driver was armed, and it was definitely a mystery where the blonde had produced her gun from, since it didn't look like there was room to hide anything in that little black dress other than the firm female flesh that was already packed into it.

"Mr. al-Saddiq," the blonde said, "I realize there are substantial cultural differences in play here. But that doesn't mean we don't have the same goal. If you'll just cooperate with me, I'll see to it that you're reunited with your allies before the night is over."

Saddiq jerked his head toward the driver. "Why can't he take me to them?"

"For the same reason you've been handed over to someone else several times during your journey. We don't want you leaving a trail."

"A trail that could lead to you and your . . . the man you work for."

"We just don't want anything to disrupt your plan. It's vital that every step be carried out."

Saddiq stared at her for a long moment, then nodded.

"All right," he said. "I suppose it makes sense. No one who knows anything about me would ever think to look for me"—his lip curled—"traveling with an American whore."

"If you think being called names bothers me, you're wrong. I'm devoted to my cause, just as you are. Now . . . shall we put away these guns and get you started on the next leg of your journey?"

Saddiq nodded. He would do what the whore said . . . for now.

But when this was over, he vowed, she would be punished for her shamelessness. And who better to carry out that punishment than him?

Chapter 26

The blonde didn't tell Saddiq her name during the drive to their next location, which was perfectly all right with him. He had no desire to be friends with *any* female, and certainly not this arrogant infidel woman.

The same was true of the mouthy American cowboy who had driven him to El Paso. Clearly, the man was selling out his country for money. Saddiq could have no respect for a man such as that.

The two Americans in the big truck—*those* men he could respect, even while he hated them and wanted to see them dead for trying to interfere with his plans. Fortunately, they had failed to stop him.

Perhaps when this was all over and the Great Satan had been vanquished and a different order was in charge, not only in America but worldwide . . . perhaps then, he could have them hunted down and dealt with. That was something to look forward to.

In the meantime, there was much work to be done, and Saddiq was ready to take the next step.

When they reached their destination, a small apartment, Saddiq saw a familiar face. He embraced Omar Habib and pounded the hulking man on the back.

"Omar, my great and good friend! How wonderful it is to see you again."

"You, too, Bandar."

Omar had been born and raised in America—Houston, Texas, to be precise—so instead of the faintly British accent in Saddiq's voice, Omar had an unfortunate twang. Not much of one, but enough for Saddiq to be annoyed by it.

He always put those feelings aside, however, because Omar was a good man, big and dependable and reasonably smart.

"I heard you had some trouble getting here," Omar went on.

Saddiq waved away that concern. "Nothing that the Mexicans could not deal with, although it was a bit irritating at times."

"Well, you're here now. Is the plan still on track?" Omar smiled. "So to speak."

"Nothing has changed." Saddiq's tone was a little sharp. Their holy mission was nothing to joke about. "You and your group performed well in Nevada. You left nothing that would lead back to you?"

"Nothing," Omar said.

Saddiq believed him and nodded in satisfaction.

Briefly, when the blonde had first brought Saddiq here and told him that Omar was waiting inside, Saddiq had suspected a trap. He had looked over at the blonde in the faint glow from the instruments of the luxury sedan she was driving. Her short dress had ridden up even more, leaving her long, sleek legs indecently bared for almost their entire length.

She had smiled an infuriatingly smug smile when she saw him looking at her.

"It drives you crazy to have to work with somebody like me, doesn't it?"

"Someone who would betray her country for money, you mean?" Saddiq's casual gesture dismissed that. "I expect that sort of dishonorable behavior from an American slut."

That had gotten under her skin. She snapped, "It's not the money. I'm loyal to my boss. I happen to believe what he's doing is right."

"It is ordained by Allah."

"If that's what you need to tell yourself, you go right ahead. It's enough for me to know that I'm doing the right thing."

Unable to stomach any more of her, Saddiq had gone into the apartment to be reunited with Omar. He felt cleaner now that he no longer had to look at the blonde.

However, the comfortable, middle-class apartment with its flat-screen TV and other symbols of Western decadence also made him a bit uncomfortable. He and Omar sat in armchairs, and Saddiq asked, "Tell me about the plan's progress."

"It's going really well, my friend," Omar assured him. "The explosives are all lined up. We're going to take delivery on them tomorrow night."

"From Francisco Zaragosa's people?"

"That's right. You met Zaragosa himself, didn't you?"

"And his wastrel brother." A curt shake of Saddiq's head. "Such creatures will have no place in our new world."

"The cartel has been useful, though," Omar pointed out.

Saddiq shrugged. "The time will come when their usefulness is at an end."

"Yeah, I suppose . . . Anyway, once we have the explosives, we'll split them up among the men who'll plant them on the tracks. Everyone knows his assignment. We've been over and over the plan. When that eastbound freight rolls into El Paso a couple of mornings from now, the explosions will derail it right there next to downtown." Omar chuckled. "The city won't know what hit it."

Saddiq studied the other man for a moment, then said, "An accident like that in an area with a high concentration of people should cause considerable loss of life. Your fellow Texans, Omar. Does that bother you?"

"My duty is to Allah and to my brothers in Islam," Omar answered without hesitation. "An accident of birthplace does nothing to change that. I realized that a long time ago, Bandar. It's why I first traveled to Afghanistan several years ago, to help my Islamic brothers."

"The Americans would consider you a traitor if they knew that you'd turned your back on them."

Omar blew out a disgusted breath.

"Do you think that I care for one second what the infidels think? What I do for the glories of Allah is all that matters."

Saddiq nodded slowly and smiled. "It is good to hear you say such a thing, my friend. That way, I will not worry when the blood of the Americans is spilled."

Omar shook his head. "No need to worry at all," he assured Saddiq. "Bring on the blood of the infidels. Rivers of it."

CHAPTER 27

A notification chimed on Barry's phone just a minute or so after he and Jake returned to the motel room after eating supper at a restaurant across the street. It was no fancier than the motel, but the steaks were good.

Barry looked at the phone, then went to the computer on the desk and opened it. He tapped a couple of keys, and a video call screen opened up with an angry-looking man's face on it.

"The first thing I want to know," the man said, "is if you're all right."

"I'm fine," Barry said.

"Physically, you mean. Because I know you've lost your mind."

Jake laughed and nodded toward the screen.

"Whoever he is, he's obviously well acquainted with you," he said.

"Wait a minute," the man said. He appeared to be in his forties, but his hair was already a premature iron gray. "That's your nephew, isn't it? You've dragged him on this . . . whatever it is?"

"Jake's giving me a hand."

"You've compromised the FBI?"

"He's not here officially. He's off duty." Barry's voice

sharpened. "Anyway, I seem to recall that the bureau did a pretty good job of compromising itself for a few years, or at least the leadership did, what with trying to undermine a legally elected president and all."

The man on the computer screen waved that away.

"Ancient history."

"Not so ancient. And a lot of people still remember it." Barry shook his head. "But as far as I know, that doesn't have anything to do with what's going on here. And don't worry about Jake. Like I said, he's here on his own time."

The man on the screen sighed wearily.

"All right," he said. "I'll just worry about you being charged with a couple dozen murders. How about that?"

"I didn't kill anybody who didn't need killing," Barry said. "It was the fellas we were after who were shooting civilizans."

"Actually, I figured that was the case, but that's not what the official reports are going to say. There are several dozen versions of the story going around—"

"Because there were several dozen eyewitnesses," Barry broke in.

"That's right. Officially, you haven't been identified yet, and there aren't any charges pending. But whoever was in that big rig of yours is definitely regarded as a person of interest in a whole slew of serious crimes."

"I can tell you what actually happened," Barry offered. "I assume this is a secure connection."

The man on the screen answered by rolling his eyes, then said, "I'm assuming this has something to do with you reaching out a few days ago about anything unusual happening along the border."

"That's right." Barry launched into a quick summation

of recent events, starting with the meeting with his old friend working undercover for the DEA.

He concluded by saying, "The man we were after turned out to be Bandar al-Saddiq. I imagine you recognize the name."

The man on the screen frowned and said, "Minor-league Afghan terrorist?"

"Maybe not so minor-league anymore. A new group, Lashkar-e-Islami, claims responsibility for that train derailment in Nevada the other day, and then Saddiq shows up, being smuggled into the country by a Mexican cartel. I can't believe that's just a coincidence."

"It does seem like quite a stretch to think so," the man on the screen said slowly. "Let me look into this, Barry, and see if I'm hearing whispers of anything."

"I was going to get in touch with you and ask you to do that exact thing."

The man snorted. "I'm always quicker on the uptake than you are. I'll be back in touch."

"Thanks," Barry said. He closed the laptop.

"Okay," Jake said, "are you going to tell me who that was?"

"One of those people I work with that we were talking about earlier."

"Yeah, but I recognized that guy. I've seen him before, maybe on TV at, like, presidential news conferences . . ."

"You might have," Barry admitted.

"He's one of the guys who stands in the background—"

"A lot of good work gets accomplished in the background."

"Yeah, I know." Jake frowned. "Is he going to tell my boss that I'm mixed up in this?"

"He has a habit of not telling anybody anything

unless he believes they have a need to know." Barry chuckled, but the sound didn't have much genuine humor in it. "That tendency has bitten me on the butt more than once. I think there's a good chance he'll give us both free rein and do what he can to help us . . . for now. As long as we don't embarrass too many of the wrong people."

"Like starting World War III in southern New Mexico."

"Yeah, something like that."

They didn't really expect to hear anything else that night, but as they were about ready to turn in, Barry's phone chimed again. He checked it and opened the computer. The same young-old face looked out from the screen, a bit wearier now, it seemed.

Without preamble, the man said, "According to one of my sources in the DOD, a significant amount of C-4 went missing from Fort Bliss a couple of days ago."

"Was the army going to tell anybody about this?" Barry asked.

"What do you think? Not if they didn't have to. They're conducting their own investigation, of course, hoping to recover it before anybody else knows it's missing. All they've found so far is that an enlisted man, a clerk who might have been able to get his hands on the stuff, has gone missing. And he has family connections with the Zaragosa cartel."

Jake leaned forward over Barry's shoulder and said, "Nobody knew about that when this guy joined the army?"

"You think they've got the time and the manpower to do extensive background checks on everybody who enlists?" the man asked sharply.

"If they did, maybe so many bad actors wouldn't

have gotten through and caused trouble later on," Jake said.

Barry said, "We're not going to solve that problem tonight. Just give us the guy's name and a way we might be able to get a line on him."

"His name is Carlos Molina. His cousin Paco Reyes is a low-level cartel soldier. Reyes could have put pressure on Molina to steal those explosives. Molina's parents are both still alive, and he has two little sisters. Reyes could have threatened them if Molina didn't cooperate, too."

"A guy would do that to his own family?" Jake said.

"Somebody who'd work for the Zaragosas would do just about anything," Barry said. "Send me the address of Molina's family."

"Already done. You'll be heading for El Paso tomorrow?"

"No," Barry said. "Tonight."

He closed the computer, looked at Jake, and added, "Aren't you glad we got something to eat? Now we can keep going all night if we need to."

CHAPTER 28

Despite it being the middle of the night, Barry made a call ahead, so somebody was waiting when he pulled up to a huge, cinder-block building in one of El Paso's industrial areas.

The place had an oversized door. It rolled up as a motor hummed, and Barry drove into a vast garage.

Even before Jake opened his door, he detected the sharp tang of paint fumes. They started a dull ache behind his eyes. He hoped they wouldn't have to be here for long.

"Big Mike!" Barry greeted the tall, burly man in coveralls who met them. "Good to see you again."

They shook hands. Mike ran an admiring gaze over the truck and let out a low whistle.

"What model is that?" he asked. "I don't think I've seen one just like it before."

"You haven't," Barry told him. "It's a prototype. The Z1000."

"Sweet. And what a beautiful paint job."

"Yeah, that's the problem. It's too sweet, too eye-catching. I need you to rough it up for me."

Mike pressed a ham-like hand against his chest and said, "Rough it up? That'd be a sin, Barry!"

"Maybe so, but that's what I need."

Mike gave him a searching frown. "You hot, Barry?"

"Warm," Barry qualified. "I have friends working to take some of the heat off, but in the meantime, the last thing I need is for some eager-beaver state trooper to pull me over."

Mike nodded, sighed, and said, "You got it. I can give you a completely different color if you've got a few days."

"We don't. Do what you can to make it not stand out, and in the meantime, we need another vehicle."

If they had been able to double back to Hachita, they could have gotten his pickup, Jake thought. Plus, the pickup was registered under a false name. Some of his uncle's natural caution—some people might call it paranoia—must have rubbed off on him. The pickup wouldn't put the cops on his trail. But the place would have been swarming with law enforcement officers by then, and they hadn't wanted to risk it.

Mike frowned and said, "I got an old panel truck you can use, if you want."

"That's perfect," Barry said. "Nobody pays any attention to those."

Mike pointed to the brown truck on the far side of the garage, then dug the keys out of his pocket and handed them to Barry.

"Thanks. We'll take good care of it."

"Shoot, you couldn't hurt that old thing!"

Jake said, "Don't tell him that. He'll take it as a challenge."

"Come on, Junior," Barry said as he started toward the truck. He tossed the keys to Jake. "You drive."

They had left their semi-automatic rifles in the big

rig, but each man was armed with a pair of 9mm pistols, as well as backpacks with other gear they might need. According to Barry, this was more of a surveillance mission than anything else—but there was no way of knowing what they might run into.

Once they'd left Big Mike's garage in the nondescript old truck, Jake said, "Is that guy on the up-and-up?"

"It didn't look like a chop shop to you, did it?"

"No, but I guess I'm just naturally suspicious of anybody who knows you."

"That would include you, you know."

"I'm suspicious of myself half the time," Jake said. "What about Big Mike?"

"He's clean," Barry said. "He handles jobs for me and other operators. A buddy of his is a world-class mechanic. They're sort of a tag team when it comes to automotive matters for guys in our line of work."

"So you trust him?"

"Absolutely."

Jake listened to the truck's engine and said, "I'll give him credit. He, or his buddy, have this old beater running like a top."

"Mike wouldn't have anything else."

Barry got out his phone and studied the information his nameless friend had sent him. He read an address to Jake and went on, "That's where Carlos Molina's family lives. We'll keep an eye on the place for a while to see if he shows up there."

"Your friend said the army was conducting its own investigation. Don't you think we're liable to trip over some of those on their own stakeout?"

"Please," Barry said. "If they're there, we'll see them,

but they'll never see us. We'll just stay out of their way and hope they don't get in ours."

The GPS in Barry's phone directed Jake to a lower middle-class residential neighborhood. It was still a couple of hours before dawn. He slid the truck up to the curb, which was crumbling in a few places, and killed the engine and lights. Quite a few cars and pickups were parked along both sides of the street, but there were a number of open spaces, too.

"The house is three up on the other side of the street," Barry said.

"Got it."

Nobody was parked in front of the Molina house. An older pickup was in the driveway. Jake estimated that most of the houses in this neighborhood had been built in the sixties or seventies. From what he could tell, they were well kept up, the sort of neighborhood where people had pride in their homes, even if they didn't make much money.

Jake got a pair of night vision binoculars from his pack and studied each of the vehicles parked along the street for as far as he could see in both directions.

"Doesn't seem to be anybody in any of them," he reported as he stashed the binoculars. "My guess is they all belong to the people who live along here."

"More than likely," Barry agreed. He was using regular binoculars to scan the houses, looking for lighted windows. He saw a few, but the lights inside the houses were dim, as if someone were sitting up reading or watching TV or surfing the Internet. Overall, the neighborhood was quiet and peaceful.

"I thought El Paso was supposed to be full of crime," Jake commented quietly.

"Parts of it are. But parts of it are just like places anywhere else.

Jake didn't say anything else. He concentrated on the house where Carlos Molina's family lived instead. Time passed. They got thermoses of coffee from the backpacks and sipped them.

Then, when the sky in the east was starting to turn gray, a car with a lowered chassis came along the street with its headlights out. It drifted to a stop at the curb in front of the Molina house.

"Is that a lowrider?" Jake asked in a half-whisper. "I didn't know they had such things anymore!"

"Some *hombres* follow the traditions of their forefathers," Barry said.

He had his own night vision glasses out now and used them to study the two men who got out of the car and started across the neatly kept lawn toward the house.

"That's Molina," he reported after a second. "And the fella with him is his cousin, Paco Reyes. We got lucky, Jake. Maybe we'll stay lucky and those boys can tell us what happened to all that C-4 that went missing."

CHAPTER 29

Molina knocked on the door. Jake could tell by the way he did it that he was trying to be quiet about it. After a moment, a dim yellow light came on in what was likely the house's living room. The glow illuminated the two young men standing on the small concrete porch.

From where they were, Jake and Barry couldn't tell who opened the door, but when Molina and Reyes went into the house, the man who had answered their summons lingered. Short, thick-bodied, he was probably Carlos Molina's father. He closed the door.

"What do you think they're doing here?" Jake asked.

"I don't know, but I think it's a good idea if we try to find out."

Barry had already popped the bulb out of the dome light, so the interior of the truck remained dark as they opened their doors and slipped out. They pressed the doors closed with faint clicks rather than slamming them, then cat-footed across lawns toward the Molina dwelling.

The houses were fairly close together on this street, with hedges separating very narrow side yards. Jake and Barry moved through deep shadows in the side yard of the Molina house toward a lighted window at the back.

All the windows had bars on them. Tranquil though it looked, the neighborhood probably had its share of crime—maybe more than its share. But at the lighted window, the pane inside the bars was raised a couple of inches to let fresh air in. The curtain was pulled, so Jake and Barry couldn't see in, but they could hear what was being said.

The voices spoke in Spanish. A woman asked what was going on. A man rumbled in reply, "It's Carlos and that no-good Paco."

"Carlos!" the woman exclaimed. "Is he all right?"

"He looks fine."

"What does he want?"

"I don't know. To talk to us, he said. About something important."

"I'll get dressed. Tell them to wait. Don't let them leave!"

"I can't stop them if they want to go," the man said. "Paco has a gun." He added some uncomplimentary things about Paco's parentage and the fact that he was in a gang, then said worriedly, "Carlos has a gun, too. It's all that Paco's fault!"

Jake and Barry heard *Señor* Molina hurry back out. Barry motioned for them to head back to the front of the house. They stepped up carefully onto the porch and knelt in front of the big living room window. With a light on inside and none out here, their shadows wouldn't be visible against the glass.

The curtains were pulled over this window, too, but there were a couple of gaps. Jake leaned close to peer through one of them. He saw Carlos Molina pacing around nervously while the other young man, Paco Reyes, sprawled in an armchair as if he didn't have a care in the world.

Molina was stocky and muscular with close-cropped dark hair. An army haircut, for sure.

Reyes was skinny, with a bowl haircut, a thin mustache, and a little wisp of beard on his chin. He reminded Jake of a praying mantis.

Barry took a small piece of equipment out of his backpack, ran a wire with a suction cup at the end of it to the glass, and pressed it into place. He handed Jake a small, wireless earpiece and slipped one just like it into his own ear. When Jake inserted the comm device into his ear, he heard a reedy voice say in English, "—easy, man. We got nothin' to worry about."

"You don't know how stubborn he is, Paco."

"It'll be all right. Just think about how much money we're gettin' paid."

"I can't put a price on how much my old man means to me!"

"No, no, dawg, that ain't what I mean." Reyes leaned forward in his chair. "Just tell him you'll pay him however much he'll lose in wages by stayin' home today. You can afford it, right?"

Molina paused in the pacing that was carrying him back and forth, in and out of Jake's line of sight. He scratched at his chin and said, "Yeah, I guess so. Maybe."

He turned as his parents came into the room followed by two girls, one an older teen, the other probably twelve or so.

"Hey, I didn't mean to wake up you two," Molina

said to the girls, who had to be the sisters Jake and Barry had heard about.

"Carlos, we've been so worried about you," the older girl said. She came over to him, put her arms around his neck, and hugged him. "Are you all right?"

"Yeah, I'm fine," he said as he returned the hug.

The girl turned to look at Reyes with a disapproving frown. She asked, "What's *he* doing here?"

"Hey, girl, is that any way to act when your cousin comes to visit you?" Reyes said. "We used to be friends, remember?"

"That was before you turned into such a sleaze," the girl snapped.

Señor Molina said, "Anita, you and Elisa go back to your room. I just wanted you to know your brother is safe." He cast a disapproving glance at Reyes, too. "At least for now. Who knows what *that one* has gotten him mixed up in."

Reyes stood up and said, "I didn't mean to cause trouble by comin' here. Maybe it'd be best if I just left."

"That would be a good idea," Anita said.

Reyes jerked his head toward the door. "Come on, Carlos."

"Not yet," Molina said. "I haven't done what I came here for. Papi, I have to talk to you . . . alone."

Señor Molina drew himself up straighter.

"Anything you have to say to me, you can say in front of your mother," he told his son stiffly.

"No," Molina insisted. "This is just for you to hear."

Señora Molina spoke to her husband in Spanish, telling him it was all right. She came over to her son, hugged him, and told both girls to hug him again as well. They did so, and then the woman ushered them out, all of them leaving with some reluctance.

When Molina, his father, and his cousin were alone in the living room, the fugitive soldier said, "Papi, you can't go to work today."

The older man stared at him in utter confusion.

"Not go to work?" he repeated. "I always go to work. You want me to lose my job?"

"No, but you got to call in sick today. Just today. That's all. You can go back to work tomorrow."

Señor Molina shook his head and said, "That's crazy. Why would I do that?"

Reyes spoke up, saying, "Because we're tryin' to do you a favor, *viejo*."

"Watch it," Molina snapped at him. "Don't talk to my father like that."

"Look, man, we shouldn't even be here," Reyes said. "You know what those guys would do to us if they found out what we're doin'. You know how they are about anything that throws a wrench in their plans."

He drew a finger across his throat in a curt, meaningful gesture.

"I don't care," Molina said. "They can't go ahead without my help. And I'm not going to let my father get hurt." He turned back to the other man. "Look, something's going to happen tomorrow. Today, I mean. Later today. And you can't go to work at the yard."

On the porch, Jake and Barry exchanged a glance. "Yard" could mean rail yard. And that brought things right back around to the railroad connection.

Señor Molina looked intently at his son for a moment, then said, "Carlos, what have you done?" He jerked a hand toward Reyes. "What have you let this jackal talk you into?"

"Papi, please—"

"Get out of my house," the older man said. "If you're mixed up in some trouble with this animal, I won't have it touching the rest of my family. Get out, and count yourself lucky that I don't turn you in."

"Papi—"

Reyes broke in, "You're not gonna change his mind, homes. I told you it was a bad idea to come here." He sighed and shook his head. "Now we gotta make sure he don't talk to nobody."

Jake stiffened. Reyes's words set off alarm bells in his mind. But it was too late for either of the men on the porch to do anything. Paco Reyes reached under his shirt, pulled out a pistol with a silencer screwed onto the barrel, and shot *Señor* Molina in the head.

CHAPTER 30

The murder of his father was such a shocking, un-expected act that all Carlos Molina could do was stand there and stare in horrified disbelief at the red-rimmed bullet hole in *Señor* Molina's forehead. After a second, the older man's knees buckled and he crumpled to the floor.

Reyes swung around, thrust the gun toward his cousin, and fired twice more, putting both rounds into Molina's chest. Molina staggered back, tripped over a coffee table, and went down hard to the floor.

The silenced rounds might not have been loud enough to warn *Señora* Molina and her daughters that something was wrong, but the crash certainly was. Reyes pivoted toward the opening between the living room and the hall that led to the rest of the house, obviously ready to gun down the females as they rushed to see what was wrong.

By that time, though, Jake was already at the front door, ramming it open with his shoulder and lunging into the house. Reyes twisted toward him, eyes so wide with alarm—and possibly drugs—that they seemed on the verge of popping out of their sockets.

Jake slapped the silenced pistol aside with his left

hand. His right shot out and closed around Reyes's throat. Jake was a lot bigger than the scrawny cartel soldier, so he had no trouble lifting Reyes off his feet by the neck and slamming him against the wall. Reyes's head thudded so hard that the Sheetrock cracked from the impact. He went limp.

Jake let go of Reyes, and he slid down the wall to the floor. At the same time, *Señora* Molina and her pajama-clad daughters ran into the living room, saw the two bodies sprawled on the floor, and started screaming.

Barry was in the doorway, gun in hand. The older Molina daughter threw herself at him, throwing wild punches as she cried, "You killed them! You killed them!"

Jake turned from the unconscious Reyes and said, "No! We didn't do this. Paco did. He's the one who shot them."

Señora Molina had fallen to her knees beside her husband's body. She lifted his bloody head and cradled it in her lap as she rocked back and forth, wailing.

The younger daughter went to her brother and bent over to touch him tentatively, saying, "Carlos? Carlos? Please don't be dead . . ."

Still under attack by the older girl, Barry stuffed his gun back in its holster and caught hold of her wrists as she tried to claw his face. He said, "Listen to me, *señorita*, we just want to help. We didn't shoot your father and brother. You need to calm down—"

On the floor beside the overturned coffee table, Carlos Molina moaned and moved his head back and forth.

"Barry!" Jake said. "He's still alive."

"You hear that?" Barry said to the girl he was holding

off as gently as possible. "Carlos needs help. Call 911! Now!"

He took the chance of releasing her. She dropped her arms and stumbled back a couple of steps. Then she turned and ran to join her sister on the floor beside her brother.

"Carlos!"

The young man's eyes fluttered open in response to her voice. Jake knelt on the other side of him. He leaned closer and said in an urgent voice, trying to get through the pain Molina must be feeling, "Carlos, listen to me. Why are the Zaragosas selling the explosives you stole to terrorists? What are Saddiq and his men going to do with them?"

Some of what he said was speculation, of course, but he was convinced the assumptions were solid. He and Barry had connected up the items of information they knew in the only way that really made sense.

Molina's eyes were unfocused. He coughed and blood came out of his mouth. He said in a raspy voice, "Anita?"

The older girl said, "I'm here, Carlos! I'm here!"

"Make sure Papi . . . doesn't go to work . . . today . . ."

Molina sighed and his eyes started to glaze over. Jake knew he was gone.

So did both girls, who collapsed onto his bloody chest and sobbed.

Jake scowled. He was saddened and angered by *Señor* Molina's murder and frustrated by Carlos Molina's death. The young man had died taking the answers they needed with him. He started to rise to his feet and was halfway there when a scuffling noise behind him made him turn sharply in that direction.

Paco Reyes had regained consciousness and was lunging at him with a knife extended in one hand. The blade scraped along Jake's side, ripping his shirt but not slicing the flesh underneath. Instinctively, Jake brought his right elbow up in a sharp blow that caught Reyes under the chin. Reyes's head jolted back—

The crack of bone was loud in the room. Reyes dropped the knife. His eyes rolled up in their sockets. He fell to the floor again, and the limpness with which he collapsed this time made it plain he wouldn't be getting back up. Jake had just broken his neck.

Jake grimaced. Another possible source of information gone.

Maybe not all was lost, though. Barry knelt next to the older woman and said, "*Señora* Molina, please listen to me. My friend and I are trying to stop whatever it is that Reyes got your son mixed up in. Reyes killed your husband and Carlos because he was afraid they would tell the authorities about something very bad that's going to happen. You can help us keep that from happening. Tell me . . . where does your husband work?"

Tears covered the woman's face. Barry had to ask the question again before she looked up from her husband's dead face and said, "*Qué? Qué?*"

"Where your husband works, that's where the bad thing is going to happen. That's why Carlos didn't want him going to work today. Where is that, *Señora* Molina?"

"He . . . he works at . . . the rail yard."

Anita, the older girl, had been listening to the conversation. She used the back of her hand to wipe away some of her tears and said, "The Santa Fe Freight House, next to the yard where all the BNSF trains come through."

"Where's that?" Jake asked. He knew that BNSF referred to the Burlington Northern and Santa Fe Railway.

"On Santa Fe Street," the girl replied impatiently, as if that were the dumbest question ever.

Jake and Barry looked at each other. Explosives and a train yard were a bad combination. Lashkar-e-Islami might be planning another derailment, and in crowded conditions like that, the damage and loss of life probably would be considerably worse than what had happened in Nevada.

Barry said, "I'm sorry this happened, *Señora* Molina. We'll stop them. We'll make sure your husband and son didn't die for nothing."

She just started sobbing again as she stroked her husband's cheek.

Jake started toward the door, but Anita got in his way. Her eyes still shone with tears, but they burned with an angry fire, too.

"Who are you guys?" she demanded. "Are you cops? How do we know you didn't kill Carlos and Papi?"

"You know what kind of guy Reyes was, what he was mixed up in, so you probably have a pretty good idea what he was capable of," Jake said. "And you know he was in here talking to them. We didn't come in until after they were shot."

Anita still glared at him, but there was a note of uncertainty in her voice as she said, "He was part of the Zaragosa cartel . . ."

"That's right, and we're trying to stop them. We're not cops, though," Jake added. "But we *are* good guys."

He could tell she wanted to believe him. He went on,

"Before Carlos went AWOL, did he say or do anything that might tell us what the Zaragosas are mixed up in?"

Anita started to shake her head, then stopped abruptly and stepped over to a desk in the corner of the living room. She pawed through some papers on it, then turned to thrust one of them toward Jake.

"My father worked in the scheduling office at the freight house. Every time Carlos came by lately, he asked him about what trains were coming in. Last time he was here, Papi was showing him on the schedule." She stopped and had to swallow hard. "Before that, Carlos never showed much interest in what Papi did. I . . . I think it made Papi happy."

That was a bittersweet thing to hear, and Jake knew it must have been painful for the girl to say. He nodded, took the printout she handed him, and said, "*Gracias*." He could see pencil marks next to several items. "This may be a lot of help."

"We'd better get going," Barry said quietly. The silenced shots wouldn't have drawn any attention, but the screams might have. On the other hand, folks around here probably minded their own business. But there was no point in taking a chance.

"Thank you again," Jake said as he started after his uncle. "And we're very sorry for what happened here."

"You . . . you'll really stop the bad guys?" Anita said.

"We'll stop them," Jake promised.

CHAPTER 31

Jake listened for sirens as he and Barry hurried back to the panel truck parked down the street from the Molina house. He didn't hear any, but that didn't mean nobody had reported the screams coming from the house. Their best course was to get out of here.

"You've got that railroad timetable the girl gave you?" Barry asked as he slid behind the wheel.

"Yeah, right here," Jake said, touching his shirt pocket where he had stuck the folded paper. "You think they're going to try another derailment at the yard where *Señor* Molina worked?"

"The BNSF handles more freight than any other line in the country," Barry said by way of reply as he drove along the street at a moderate pace, making sure to be a model driver and stopping at the stop sign at the end of the block. "They have more routes, more locomotives than anybody else. El Paso isn't as important a hub as some of the other terminals they have around the country, but a derailment right there in the yard would disrupt a lot of shipments all over the southern half of the country." Barry paused. "There'd probably be quite a few casualties, too. And no telling how much environmental damage, depending on which trains they're targeting."

Jake pondered on that as they left the residential neighborhood behind them and started back in the direction of the garage where they had left Barry's truck.

After a few minutes, he said, "Something seems off about this, Barry. Terrorists usually go after targets that offer them the potential for the greatest number of innocent casualties. That's why they call it terrorism, after all. They're trying to scare us. Something like this . . . yeah, it'll kill some people if they pull it off and hurt the economy some, more than likely, but it doesn't seem . . . well, dramatic enough."

Barry nodded slowly and said, "Think about how they started, though, with one lone train in the middle of nowhere."

"That was a test run, clearly."

"Yeah, but it got people talking about railroads and terrorism. Like we talked about before, most people don't naturally link those two things in their minds."

"But it drew more attention to the railroads, and that heightened awareness has got to make it harder for them to strike again." Jake gestured at himself, then included Barry in the motion. "I mean, just look at us. If not for that incident in Nevada putting us on the trail, we might not have any idea what they're up to."

"It's a fine line," Barry admitted with a shrug. "And you can't ask for too much logic from fanatics. But going by everything we've found out, they're planning *something* at that rail yard today. That's why Molina didn't want his dad to go to work." Barry paused, shook his head, and added grimly, "So in trying to save him, he just put a target on him, and on himself as well."

"He didn't think his own cousin would turn on him like that."

"A scorpion is always a scorpion."

A few minutes later, they reached the garage. Big Mike opened the door for them, their arrival having been announced by a pressure plate outside, a buzzer inside, and a closed-circuit TV camera to tell Mike who they were. The big man rolled the door down after them.

As they got out of the old panel truck, Mike held his hands up and said, "I'm sorry, Barry."

"What're you apologizing for?" Barry asked. He looked at the Kenworth. "You did just what I asked you to."

"Yeah, but it was like defacing a work of art!"

The Z1000 didn't look new anymore. There already had been dents and dings on the layer of steel over the armor plating due to the bullets that had struck the rig during the chase over by the Big Hatchets. Mike had added some scrapes on the paint job and daubed primer on them. The chrome looked tarnished in places. A patina of mud coated the whole truck, as if it been caught in a rain shower and then driven through a choking dust storm. Jake wasn't sure how Big Mike had managed all the effects, but now the Kenworth looked like . . . just another truck.

There hadn't been anything he could do about the extra-large sleeper, of course; that was built in. And all the special additions inside were still there, too, but at least the rig wouldn't instantly draw attention anywhere they went.

"You did a fine job, Mike," Barry told him. "Just what I wanted."

"Yeah, I guess. But it's still a shame."

Barry clapped a hand on the big man's shoulder.

"Maybe when this is all over, you can put everything back the way it was before."

That brought a smile to Big Mike's face. He nodded and said, "No, I'll make it even better. You wait and see."

"That's a deal. Now, Jake and I need to have a little council of war, if you've got a place we can use."

"Right over there in my office." Mike pointed to a door at the side of the garage. "There's coffee on, too. I'm gonna step out for a while. Whatever you guys need to talk about, it's probably better if I don't know anything about it."

Jake didn't blame him for feeling that way.

A few minutes later, they had poured foam cups of coffee for themselves and spread the printed-out timetable on Mike's desk in the cluttered office. The coffee was mediocre, but mediocre caffeine was better than none.

After studying the pencil marks on the paper—some of them so faint that it looked like somebody had merely rested the pencil point on it—for several minutes, Barry said, "It looks like Molina was interested in three trains." He touched the listings with a fingertip. "These two are being made up in the yard this morning, and this one"—he moved his finger—"will be coming in from the north a little after eight o'clock."

"Yeah, and this tells us which tracks they'll all be on, but we don't have a map of the yard. We don't know where exactly each of them will be."

"No, but you ought to be able to find out when you get there."

Jake frowned and said, "You mean when we get there?"

"No, we're going to have to split up on this one,"

Barry replied with a shake of his head. "You'll go out to the yard and have a look around, see if you can figure out their plan from what we know, and stop them if you can. You'll have to borrow Mike's panel truck for that."

"What are you going to do?"

"I'm heading for Las Cruces in the rig to see if I can intercept that train coming in from there and stop it. That has to be the one they're planning to derail, and if it doesn't roll in on schedule, their attack won't come off, either."

Jake nodded as he took in the plan. He asked, "Should I alert the people at the yard? I can use my FBI credentials, and they'll pay attention to me, I guarantee that."

"Scout around some first. But make it official if you have to."

"Once I do that, though," Jake said, "that'll be the end of us investigating this discreetly."

"Yeah. Better that, though, than some sort of catastrophe downtown."

Jake agreed. He put the timetable back in his pocket since Barry had committed to memory the identification numbers of the train he was looking to stop before it reached El Paso. They left the office to find Big Mike standing beside the Kenworth, still shaking his head regretfully.

"We need to borrow that panel truck of yours again, Mike," Barry told him. "Will that strand you here?"

"Naw, I'll just call a buddy to pick me up if I need to leave. Anyway, I got enough work to do that it ought to keep me busy all day."

"We don't know for sure when we'll be back," Jake told him.

"That's all right. I don't know what it is you guys are doing, but if Barry's mixed up in it, it's bound to be something important. And with Barry, well, I know I'm on the side of the good guys."

"Appreciate that, Mike," Barry said. He shook hands with the big man, then with Jake, and added, "Good luck."

"You, too," Jake said.

Big Mike looked back and forth between them, frowned, and said, "You guys sound like you're goin' off to war."

"Let's hope it doesn't come down to that," Barry said.

CHAPTER 32

The GPS on Jake's phone took him to Santa Fe Street without any problem. The sun was up, painting the peaks of the Franklin Mountains just north of town with slanting red rays. Later, the day would be hot, but for now the air held a hint of coolness, enough so that Jake enjoyed having the window down in Big Mike's truck as he drove toward the BNSF freight yard.

He cruised by the place first to get an idea of what he was dealing with, trying to be unobtrusive about it. The main building was beige stucco over cinder block to make it look like adobe. Long and narrow, it angled slightly as it stretched back from the street. Two pairs of railroad tracks running across Santa Fe Street and parallel to the building, acres and acres of the freight yard on both sides.

A sign reading SANTA FE FREIGHT HOUSE was above the door, flanked on both sides by the old Santa Fe Railroad logo. A few cars and pickups were parked in the lot on the opposite side of the building from the tracks. Jake figured the place was open around the clock since trains came through at all hours of the day and night.

He drove on past, turned at the next cross street, and

made a block. This time as he went by, he looked out into the yard itself. The tracks split into numerous sidings, several of which had strings of freight cars and empty flatcars on them.

Two such strings ran farther than Jake could see from his angle. They flanked one of the sets of main tracks. As he circled again and headed back toward the yard, he considered the situation.

The sets of rails were all fairly close together. If a train heading down the main track between those two sidings where the strings were being assembled happened to derail, there was a good chance the jackknifing freight cars would take out the cars on both sidings as well.

Such a catastrophe would cut a wide swath of destruction right through the heart of the yard. The loss of life might not be staggering, but Jake had seen quite a few people working out there—loading goods into parked freight cars with forklifts, coupling and uncoupling cars, making repairs, tooling around in golf carts and checking on things. No telling how many of them would be in harm's way in the event of a major derailment.

Jake drove on past. The tall buildings of downtown El Paso were visible directly in front of him, a few blocks away. All sorts of toxic fumes might be unleashed by an accident of the magnitude he was imagining, and if the wind was right, those fumes would sweep right over the city center. He couldn't risk that happening.

There was no parking on the right side of the street, but cars were at the curb on the left side. Jake hung a U-turn, hoping no city cops were sitting around unnoticed to see him do that. He didn't need any distractions or delays if he got pulled over.

Nothing of the sort happened as he eased the old panel truck to the curb beside what appeared to be a one-story office building. From where he sat, he could see the freight yard office building and the long warehouse extending from the back of it, as well as part of the yard itself.

According to the timetable, the freight from the north that Carlos Molina had been interested in was due at 8:17. It was a little after seven now. A little more than an hour away . . . enough time to plant the explosives Molina had stolen from Fort Bliss if the terrorists hurried.

Jake's eyes narrowed. The terrorists might still have *time*, yeah, but how could they plant the C-4 in broad daylight? When he and Barry had tried to figure out the plan, they hadn't known the layout of the freight yard or the conditions under which the terrorists would have to make their strike.

Another thought occurred to him. They had no way of knowing when the Zaragosa cartel had turned over the explosives to the terrorist cell. That exchange could have been done earlier in the night. In fact, that was more likely. So the odds were that Bandar al-Saddiq and the other fanatics from Lashkar-e-Islami already had the C-4.

Had, in fact, in all likelihood planted the bombs before now, so they were just waiting for the targeted train to get here.

Jake opened the truck door and stepped out. He needed to get a look at those tracks. If BNSF security caught him snooping around, he could always play the ace up his sleeve—his standing as an FBI agent.

Of course, he *wasn't* here officially, and when his

superiors found out what he'd been up to—especially if he roped the bureau in on it—he was liable to be in a lot of trouble. But if he and Barry stopped a terrorist attack, it would be worth it.

He left his backpack and the gear it contained in the truck, but he had both pistols, one in a belly holster, one at the small of his back, both hidden by the tails of his shirt. He ambled to the corner and paused, taking out his phone and pretending to look at something on it while actually he was studying the layout in front of him.

The entrance to the yard had four broad lanes, two going in, two coming out, where trucks could drive. A small, shedlike office for the yard attendants sat between the entrance and exit lanes, surrounded by low concrete barriers painted bright yellow. Just beyond the shed was a large sign with the yard's rules and procedures printed on it. The gates on both sides were wide open.

A man wearing a hard hat and carrying a clipboard came out of the shed. Jake thought the guy might intend to come over and ask him why he was hanging around, but instead the man barely glanced in his direction, then walked briskly toward the main office building. Jake waited until the man had gone inside, then slipped his phone back in his pocket.

There might be another attendant in the shed, and there were windows in the main building that looked in this direction, as well. For all Jake knew, there were eyes on him right this minute. But he had to get in there and take a look around, so he started walking briskly toward the nearest gate, which happened to be the exit side.

Act like you're supposed to be there, like you know

what you're doing, like you're just doing your job . . .
That attitude worked a lot of the time. Not as much as it
used to, according to conversations he'd had with Barry
about the old days. People were just too paranoid in the
twenty-first century for it to be effective all the time.
But it was still the best bet.

Jake strode purposefully into the railroad yard, and
nobody tried to stop him.

He might not know the official designations of the
tracks and sidings, but he had his eye on what he believed would be the terrorists' target and headed in that
direction.

A man driving a forklift passed him and gave him a
curious glance. Jake paused, took out the timetable he
had gotten from Anita Molina, and unfolded it to look
at it. That was for show, more than anything else, and it
seemed to work because the guy on the forklift went on
and didn't look back.

Jake made a mental note of the numbers that had interested Carlos Molina, though. Maybe he would see
some signs that matched up with them, and that would
confirm his guesses.

Other men were around, but none of them paid any
attention to him until he came even with the end of the
string being put together four sidings deep into the yard.
Without pausing, Jake started across the empty sidings
toward it.

"Hey, buddy, what are you doing?"

The voice made him pause and look around. A guy in
a hard hat was walking quickly toward him. Jake lifted
the piece of paper in his left hand, thumped it with his
right middle finger, and said, "Just got to check on
something real quick."

"Not without a hat. You know the rules."

Jake made a face. "Yeah, when I came out here I wasn't planning to go on into the yard. I just happened to remember—"

"All right, all right, it's your butt, not mine." The man pointed an admonishing finger at Jake. "But if anybody asks you, I told you—you got that?"

"Sure," Jake agreed with a grin. "I'll make it fast. No problem."

The man shrugged and turned away. Jake watched him walk off for a second, then headed for the freight cars again. The line of them already stretched for a long way down the yard.

He moved around the one on the end and looked along the empty tracks between this siding and the next one over, where the other string was being assembled. He heard faint clanking noises from the far end of the string.

More cars being coupled on? He supposed that was possible. He didn't know anything about trains. Barry seemed pretty knowledgeable on the subject . . . but then, Barry knew a lot about everything.

Between the two lines of freight cars like this, Jake suddenly felt a little cut off from the rest of the world. Not claustrophobic, exactly. He didn't suffer from that, and the cars weren't *that* close together. But he couldn't be seen up in here, except through the narrow gaps between the cars.

He moved along the rails, his eyes darting back and forth studying each one, searching for anything that looked odd or out of place. C-4 could be molded against the rails, but it still had to have a detonating mechanism attached to it, so *something* ought to be visible if the explosives had already been planted. Jake still felt that it was more likely the terrorists had gotten in here and done their evil work under cover of darkness.

He had gone about thirty yards along the narrow canyon between the looming freight cars when he spotted a small, oblong shape against the outside of the right-hand rail. He went to a knee to examine it more closely and wished there was more light. The sun wasn't high enough for its rays to penetrate directly into the space between the lines of cars.

He didn't know what sort of equipment might legitimately be attached to the rails, but he figured he would know a bomb when he saw one. And as he bent closer, his heart began to slug harder in his chest. It didn't take an expert to know that what he was looking at wasn't right. Wasn't right at all.

"Don't move! Put your hands up and then get down on your belly!"

The sharp command possessed the unmistakable tone of having a gun to back it up. Jake recognized that, too.

What surprised him was the fact that a female voice had just issued that unexpected order.

CHAPTER 33

Jake didn't get down on the ground, but he *did* raise his hands so they were in plain sight. The woman didn't shoot him, so he supposed obeying half of the order was better than none.

"Hold your fire," he said in a calm voice. If she actually was pointing a gun at him, he didn't want her getting jumpy. "How about if I stand up and turn around, and we'll talk about this?"

"I said get on your belly, and I meant it!"

"Okay, okay. Take it easy. A filthy railroad yard isn't a very good place to be lying down, though. My clothes are gonna get pretty dirty."

"I don't care. Do what I told you."

Jake lowered himself to a knee, then stretched out on his stomach next to the rails. He didn't care for being that close to the explosives. He didn't like the way the cinders poked against his skin through his clothes, either.

He heard her feet crunching on the gravel as she approached. She didn't get too close but stopped far enough back that he couldn't take her legs out from under her with a quick sweep of his leg. Evidently, she wasn't a total amateur, anyway.

"You have a gun at the small of your back," she said. "Reach around with your left hand, slowly, and take it out, then toss it out of reach."

"Sure," Jake said. He didn't mind all that much giving up one gun, as long as he had another. He reached back with his left hand, eased the 9mm out of its holster, and tossed it gently to the side.

"Roll over now, away from the gun," she told him. "And keep both hands where I can see them while you're doing it."

"This is really uncomfortable—"

"Not as uncomfortable as a bullet."

"Nice hard-boiled line. You delivered it well, too."

"Shut up and roll over."

"And now you're trying to sweet-talk me," Jake said.

She didn't shoot him for that crack, so he supposed he ought to count himself lucky. He turned over onto his back. Some of the gravel and cinders clung to his clothes.

"Now the other gun," the woman said. "I figure you had one in a belly holster, too."

Jake was considerably more reluctant to follow that order. He had thought at first that the woman might be one of the terrorists. Most of the time, Islamic terror groups used females as couriers or suicide bombers, but occasionally they toted guns just like the men.

This one didn't *look* like an Islamic terrorist, though. In boots, jeans, and a black T-shirt that showed off an excellent figure without being overly tight, and with blond curls falling to her shoulders and part of the way down her back, she looked more like a Texas cowgirl. All she was missing was the hat.

She held the Glock in her hands like a Texas girl, too, one who knew how to use it.

He was stereotyping, he told himself, and racially profiling, too, but both of those things had some basis in fact to them, no matter how much the progressive, politically correct crowd liked to deny it. Technically, he was even assuming her gender, but the way she was built, it was difficult not to.

Still, quite a few all-American-looking kids had gone to the Middle East over the years to join up with ISIS or al-Qaeda or whatever the terrorist group of the month was. Assuming too much about this woman might get him killed, Jake warned himself.

"Where did you come from?" he asked. "I didn't see anybody around."

"Maybe I'm just that good," she said with a faint smile, then turned serious again. "And you're still being slow to do what you're told. I don't like that."

"What gives you the right to give orders, anyway? Are you a cop?"

"I'm the person pointing a gun at you, that's who I am." Her shoulders rose and fell maybe an inch. "But I guess I should identify myself. My name is Gretchen Rogers. I work for the Department of Homeland Security."

Jake couldn't help but frown a little in surprise at that revelation—assuming she was telling the truth, of course. At the moment, she didn't look like she'd be too receptive to a request for identification.

She was sharp enough to take note of his reaction. She said, "That's right, you're in trouble, mister, so don't make it any worse on yourself. You'll be better off if you cooperate and do as you're told."

"All right, all right," he muttered. "But here's the thing . . . I'm not giving up my other gun."

She looked angry and jabbed the Glock at him. "You'd better—"

"What I'm going to do," Jake overrode her, "is stand up, and then you and I are gonna talk about this. Time's too short and the stakes are too high for you to be showing off how tough you are."

This time it was her eyes that widened in surprise.

"Why, you—"

Jake sat up. He kept his hands in sight and well away from the gun at his waist. Just because he wasn't going to let her ride roughshod over him didn't mean he had to give her a good excuse for shooting him.

He put his left hand on the ground to brace himself and climbed to his feet. Gretchen Rogers kept the gun pointed at him and said, "Stop! Stop what you're doing. Throw your gun away and get back down on the ground! Do it now or I'll shoot!

"Stop it," Jake said. "My name is Jake Rivers. I'm FBI."

Her head jerked back slightly as if he'd just slapped her.

"You expect me to believe that?" she demanded. "Why would an FBI agent plant a bomb on a railroad track?"

"I didn't. It was already there. But I'm glad you realize it's a bomb, because we need to get this rail yard shut down and a demolitions team in here to check for explosives all over the place."

Making it official like this would shut down the independent investigation he and Barry had been carrying out. Barry was convinced they were more effective as lone wolves, and most of the time Jake thought he was right. Bringing in other agencies might make it harder for them to find Bandar al-Saddiq and discover what else he was planning, but they couldn't let this bombing succeed, either.

Gretchen Rogers shook her head, though, and said, "I'm going to have to see some ID, Rivers . . . or whatever your name really is." Then she frowned. "Wait a minute. Rivers . . . Seems like I've heard that name before."

Jake wasn't going to mention Barry. Only a very few select people within the government knew that Barry Rivers—the legendary "Dog"—was still alive.

But he had his own degree of notoriety, so he said, "Kelton College a few years ago. I was involved in an incident there—"

"When terrorists took over the campus. I remember that. *You* were the one who stopped them?"

"A lot of people stopped them," Jake said, remembering some of the unlikely heroes who had stepped up to do the right thing that bloody, fateful day. "I helped."

Gretchen squinted at him and said, "Seems I remember hearing something about the fellow who was there going into federal law enforcement."

"Walt Graham at the FBI will vouch for me."

"I know the name," Gretchen said. "One of the bureau's top anti-terrorist people, isn't he?"

"That's right. He was there at Kelton that day. He helped me get into Quantico." Jake had been keeping his hands partially raised. He went on, "Is it all right if I lower these now? Are you going to take a chance on believing me until you can check out my bona fides?"

"Maybe . . ."

"If you are, I wouldn't mind moving a little farther

away. Being this close to a chunk of C-4 like that is a little nerve-wracking."

"You're right about that," she agreed. She lowered the gun, but not completely. She could still raise and fire it in less than the blink of an eye if she needed to. "Is this the only IED?"

"The only one I've found so far . . . but I suspect there are more."

"We'd better have a look, then. Do you know who's responsible for planting them?"

"I suspect it's a group calling themselves Lashkar-e-Islami."

"The Army of Islam," Gretchen translated. "The ones who claimed responsibility for the train derailment in Nevada."

"That's right." They started walking along the tracks on opposite sides of the steel rails.

"So the bureau is working on that case? I hadn't heard. But then, maybe I wouldn't have. The bosses over there still like to keep things to themselves, like information . . . and glory."

No matter what, Jake thought, interagency rivalries would never die out completely. He said, "And Homeland Security never plays anything too close to the vest in order to make themselves look better. Got it." He paused. "How come *you* showed up here today?"

"And caught you skulking around, you mean? I got a tip. One of my sources got wind of something big that might be about to happen. She didn't know what, but she thought it might involve this freight yard."

That ambiguous answer made Jake a little suspicious, but he had to admit, what Gretchen described was a very similar situation to the way he and Barry had gotten mixed up in this. Law enforcement on all levels couldn't function without shadowy sources and vague tips.

They walked another hundred yards along the tracks, passing some flatcars on Jake's side that were loaded with lashed-down crates. Gretchen stopped short and said in a slightly hushed tone, "Look."

Jake saw the same thing she had spotted: another lump of C-4 molded to one of the rails with a small detonator attached. The knowledge that all it would take to set off the explosives was a radio signal put his teeth on edge.

"We don't need to keep looking," he said. "I think we've found enough."

"More than enough," a harsh voice said behind them.

CHAPTER 34

Jake and Gretchen whirled toward the voice at the same time. A man stood there with a gun pointed at them. Jake could tell that the stranger had climbed over the load on one of those flatcars because two more armed men were scrambling over the crates, as well.

In a flash, his keen eyes and brain took in several more items of information. The pistols the men carried had suppressors on them, like the one Paco Reyes had used to kill Carlos Molina and his father.

These men weren't Zaragosa cartel soldiers, though. At a quick glance, they might have been mistaken for Hispanic, but Jake could tell they were Middle Eastern.

Unless he missed his guess, he was looking at three members of the Army of Islam.

And those soldiers wanted to slaughter him and Gretchen Rogers.

The man who had spoken opened fire. Since Gretchen's gun was in her hand already, he must have figured her for the bigger threat. The suppressed pistol barked a couple of times, the reports no louder than polite, restrained hand claps.

Gretchen reacted swiftly to the threat, though, and was moving already. Unfortunately, in this narrow canyon between railroad cars, there wasn't much of anywhere to go. All she could do was dive headlong to the ground and hope the man's shots would go over her.

The bullets sizzled through the air where she had been an instant earlier. The Glock in her hand went off twice, the blasts a lot louder than those from the suppressed weapon had been.

Her aim was better, too. Both slugs punched into the gunman's chest and rocked him back. He took a couple of stumbling steps, tripped over the rail, and fell between the tracks in a loose-limbed sprawl that testified he was either dead already or mighty close to it.

The other two terrorists had guns in their hands, as well, and they were getting ready to leap down from the flatcar. Jake drew his gun with smooth, practiced speed and brought it up to squeeze off two rounds.

One of his bullets smacked into a crate on the flatcar, but the other thudded into the second man's body as he jumped down. The impact twisted him in midair. He cried out and landed in a tangled heap of arms and legs.

Jake couldn't tell how badly the man was hurt, but he seemed to be out of the fight, at least for the moment. Jake swung his gun toward the third terrorist.

Obviously facing more dangerous opposition than he had expected, this man caught himself before leaping off the flatcar. He flung himself backward and rolled over the pile of lashed-down crates. Jake caught a glimpse of his face before he dropped out of sight, though, and recognized the worker in the hard hat who had stopped him a short time earlier.

That meant the terrorists had infiltrated the workforce at the freight yard. Jake wasn't surprised. Saddiq and his associates would want men on hand to keep an eye on things and make sure the attack went off as planned.

Jake heard gravel crunch under the third man's feet as the guy jumped off the flatcar on the other side. A long step brought him to Gretchen's side. With his gun in his right hand, he reached down with his left and caught hold of her arm.

"Are you hit?" he asked.

"No, I'm all right."

When he heard that, he lifted her to her feet almost effortlessly. She was a solidly built young woman, not model-skinny and waifish like many of the female cops and special agents on TV and in the movies who threw around men twice their size with apparent ease.

"Don't manhandle me—" she started to say angrily, but before she could finish, Jake gave her a hard shove that sent her sprawling to the ground again.

In a continuation of the same move, he darted in the opposite direction and raised his gun. A bullet went past his left ear, through the space where Gretchen had been a heartbeat earlier, and whined off one of the freight cars behind them. Jake had caught a glimpse through the gap between cars of a man drawing a bead on them and had reacted instantly.

Jake returned fire, aiming through the same gap the terrorist had used to fire at him and Gretchen. He heard a yelp and thought he saw blood spray in the air, but wasn't sure.

Somewhere not far away, rapid footsteps slapped against the ground. Several people were rushing in this direction, but were they cops or freight yard workers checking out the shooting—or more members of Lashkar-e-Islami hurrying to protect their plan?

The sound of angry voices exclaiming in a foreign language that wasn't Spanish answered that question for Jake. He *thought* the men were speaking Pashto, although he wasn't an expert on Middle Eastern languages.

If it was Pashto, that meant the men were from Pakistan or Afghanistan, which had that language in common. Also, that would tie in with the earlier organization, Lashkar-e-Taiba, which was where they believed the Army of Islam had its origins.

Those thoughts flashed through Jake's mind in a heartbeat. At the same time, he muttered, "Sorry for the push," to Gretchen, who scrambled back to her feet.

"No need to apologize for saving my life," she said as she lifted her gun. "Sounds like more trouble coming."

"Yeah." The gaps between the freight cars were too small for a human being to slide through, so climbing over those three flatcars was the easiest way into this artificial canyon.

The other terrorists must have seen the man Jake had shot through one of those gaps because they didn't rush blindly over the load on any of the flatcars. Instead, a man stuck his head up, saw Jake and Gretchen, and yelled in alarm. He ducked down, thrust a gun over the crate behind which he crouched, and opened fire.

"Move!" Jake said as he grabbed Gretchen's arm again. He broke into a run along the tracks as more of the terrorists started shooting.

As long as the men stayed behind the cover of the crates, though, they had a limited field of fire, and that narrow angle didn't include Jake and Gretchen hurrying along between the rails.

Gretchen jerked her arm free from his grip and said, still running, "You're awfully free with your hands!"

"You mean while I'm saving your life? Don't be so blasted sensitive about it!"

"I'm not—" She stopped in mid-argument as she glanced over her shoulder. "Here they come!"

She wheeled around and started shooting at the men who were now climbing over the crates and leaping to the ground. Muzzle flame stabbed from their guns, splitting the gloom in the narrow corridor between freight cars.

Jake would have joined in with Gretchen, but at that instant, he caught a glimpse of movement in the corner of his eye and turned his head to look along the rails and up to the top of a freight car several yards farther along the string to the left.

A man crouched there, trying to draw a bead on them. Jake didn't want to find out whether he or Gretchen was the target. He whipped up his own gun and stroked the trigger. The ambusher's head jerked as the bullet blew a fist-sized chunk out of his skull. He fell backward, out of sight.

"They're climbing on the cars!" he called to Gretchen.

Her fire was too accurate for the terrorists to stand against. When one of them pitched to the ground, drilled cleanly, the others clambered back up on the flatcar and used the corner of the freight car directly ahead of it as cover while continuing to snipe at her and Jake.

Meanwhile, Jake twisted swiftly from side to side, snapping shots at the tops of the cars wherever a terrorist poked his head up. He advanced at a deliberate pace while Gretchen backed away from the threat in the other direction.

They weren't quite battling back-to-back—but almost.

Then a shot roared to Jake's right. He felt the hot breath of a slug as it passed close beside his cheek.

Jerking around in that direction, he realized that one of their enemies had fired through another gap between freight cars. Jake sent a bullet sizzling through that same narrow space, then an instant later heard the wind-rip of a bullet passing his ear from the left.

The terrorists were on the other side of the string being assembled on the siding to the left of the rails— and hidden by the cars to the right. *And* they were still coming up from behind, with Gretchen trying to hold them back.

All of which, Jake thought bleakly, meant that they were surrounded . . .

CHAPTER 35

Barry's Kenworth was far from the only truck heading north on Interstate 10 this early morning. After the beating it had taken during the running fight over in New Mexico's Bootheel the day before and the camouflage job Big Mike had done on it, the Z1000 didn't stand out that much.

The highway made the northward jog from El Paso to Las Cruces before turning almost due west and continuing in that direction all the way to Los Angeles. It was a vital conduit for traffic along the southern border, so there were plenty of trucks for Barry's to blend in with. He made good time and reached Las Cruces before the sun was very high in the eastern sky.

Trains didn't stop here on a regular basis anymore, freight or passenger, but the tracks that passed next to the old depot were still in use, with a number of BNSF freights rumbling through every day.

The depot itself had been converted into a railroad museum by the city, Barry had discovered by doing some research on the computer during the drive up here. The voice-controlled software made it almost like working with a human assistant.

He hadn't been in touch with Jake since they'd split

up, and he wondered how his nephew was doing with his part of the job. Barry had every confidence in Jake. The boy was a natural at this kind of work, although now and then he tended to *think* too much instead of trusting his instincts. But if anybody could stop those terrorists from blowing up the tracks in the El Paso freight yard, it was Jake.

Barry found the old depot. The museum was closed this early in the morning, not long after seven o'clock. With its tan walls and red-tiled roof, it was a charming example of Spanish-style architecture, but Barry wasn't really interested in that right now. He pulled into the parking lot next to the museum and looked through the fence that ran along the back of the lot.

On the other side of that black metal fence were the two sets of railroad tracks that carried trains back and forth through the city.

The fence wouldn't be hard to climb. It was only about five feet tall with black metal pickets, each of which came to a point on top, but not a sharp one. There was no barbed wire. No security system sensors that Barry could see. It was designed mainly to keep kids and animals from wandering out onto the tracks, and it would do that job just fine.

It wouldn't keep Barry out, though.

He put on a blue jean jacket to help conceal the fact that he was carrying a 1911 .45 and the Browning Hi-Power. In the early morning, the air had enough crispness in it that the jacket didn't look out of place. And he was an old guy. Old guys got cold easily, he thought with a wry smile.

He got out of the truck, locked it, and leaned on the fence to study the situation before climbing over. He looked around for some way he could stop the freight train coming through shortly, some excuse to explain why it had to be held up here instead of continuing on to El Paso.

There were several electronic signal boards along the tracks, but he would have to get into the BNSF computer system to activate them.

He glanced toward the old station building, then looked again. The old flag signal was still there at the edge of the small platform where passenger trains had stopped in times past. That wasn't surprising, since the building was now being used as a railroad museum. Barry went along the sidewalk behind the building. It turned into the old platform. The signal pole stood at the edge of it, next to the tracks.

The "flag" was actually a wooden bar painted red that could be raised or lowered depending on whether a train passing through was requested to stop. Under past conditions it had been operated by an electric motor so all the stationmaster had to do to control it was push a button.

There was a manual control mechanism still in place, though, consisting of a metal pole in a roller bracket that ran up the side of the signal post. That pole worked a lever at the top of the post. Would it still function? Barry took hold of the pole and pulled down on it. The lever at the top moved and raised the flag until it stuck straight out horizontally in the STOP position.

Would the engineer see the signal? If he did, would he be curious enough to stop? He might radio the control center in El Paso and ask them what was going on.

Of course, it was possible Jake might have dealt with the threat there already and it was all right for the train to proceed. But until he knew that for sure, Barry was going to do his best to stop it here.

If he could do that, he carried several different sets of identification, in several different names, and one of them ought to be enough to convince the engineer to cooperate.

For the most part, his real name carried no weight, he reflected wryly, because to the world at large, Barry Rivers was dead and had been for more than three decades. And "Barry Rivera" was just a shadow man, a rumor, someone that no one could say existed for sure.

He didn't want to draw any more attention to himself than he might have done already, so he stood next to the old depot's rear wall and waited to see what was going to happen. He wasn't sure when, exactly, the freight train was supposed to pass through Las Cruces, but if it was going to arrive on schedule in El Paso, it had to be soon.

Sure enough, Barry had been standing there less than five minutes when he heard a rumble in the distance. He knew that if he went out there on the tracks and pressed his ear to the rail, like someone in an old Western movie, he would be able to "hear" the train approaching.

His muscles tensed as he spotted the train coming toward him. Would the engineer even notice the old flag stop, or would he just barrel on through? If the train didn't stop, Barry would have to run back to the truck and try to get ahead of it somehow. He might find a crossing somewhere down the line and block it with the truck . . .

The train began slowing. Barry didn't relax yet, though. The engineer could still change his mind.

The train gradually came to a halt with the engine

next to the old station, the freight cars seeming to stretch out endlessly behind it. There was a gate in the black metal fence, but it had a padlock on it. Barry climbed over without much trouble and went to the steps leading up to a small metal platform attached to the front of the engine.

The engineer opened the door leading into the cab and said, "Mister, what are you doing here? You can't be here."

"Problem down the line in El Paso," Barry said. He moved forward confidently, and just as he expected, the engineer gave ground and let him step into the cab.

The cab had two well-upholstered seats in it, the one on the right for the engineer while the conductor sat on the left. Each seat had a large instrument panel in front of it below the big double windows. The engineer's console had a lot more gauges and dials on it, enough that Barry thought it resembled the cockpit of an airliner. In fact, the whole cab reminded him of that. A good engineer, like a pilot, had to be able to watch a dozen read-outs at once.

The conductor had swiveled his chair toward the doorway where Barry stood. He frowned and said, "We haven't heard anything from BNSF. Mister, you'd better identify yourself."

His hand moved toward a pocket on the side of the seat. He might have a gun in there, or some other sort of weapon like a Taser.

"Take it easy," Barry said. He lifted both hands, palms out. "I'll get my ID."

The engineer had both hands clenched into fists, ready to swing a punch if he needed to. Moving deliberately, Barry reached inside his jacket and slipped a leather folder from a pocket. He flipped it open to reveal a badge and an identification card with his photo on it.

"I'm an inspector for the FRA," he said as he held out the bona fides. The ID was actually from the Department of Transportation, rather than the Federal Railroad Administration, but since the FRA was part of the DOT, that was plausible enough.

The conductor frowned dubiously, though, and shook his head.

"I didn't know the FRA had inspectors," he said. "Not ones who hang around old abandoned stations, anyway."

"And use old-fashioned flag signals," the engineer added. "Something fishy's going on here. Jamal, get on the radio to El Paso."

The conductor reached for a microphone hanging on the console in front of him.

Barry said, "Listen, we have credible evidence of a terrorist threat to the freight yard in El Paso. According to information we've uncovered, a group known as Lashkar-e-Islami plans to derail this train when it reaches that freight yard. You'll be between two other trains being assembled on sidings, and if you go off the rails, it'll cause all sorts of havoc."

The engineer grunted and said, "If you ask me, *you're* the one who's off the rails, buddy." He turned his head. "Jamal, you got El Paso yet—"

The engineer obstructed Barry's view of the conductor. Otherwise, the conductor never would have gotten the gun out of the pocket on the side of his chair without Barry seeing what he was doing. Barry heard the suppressed snort of the shot, though, and saw the engineer's eyes widen in shock and pain as the bullet struck him in the back of the head.

Letting his instincts guide his actions, Barry ducked down and to the right so the engineer's body, still on its feet but bound to collapse any second, shielded him from the conductor's gun. He rammed his shoulder into the dead man's belly and drove him back against the conductor.

He wasn't in time, though, to stop the conductor's left arm from lashing out, grabbing a lever on the engineer's console, and shoving it forward.

The locomotive lurched forward and started rolling down the tracks toward El Paso.

CHAPTER 36

The jolt of the train starting up again wasn't enough to throw Barry off balance. He kept pushing against the luckless engineer's body, pinning the treacherous conductor in his seat. Barry reached past the engineer, sliding his hand under the dead man's arm, and tried to get hold of the conductor's wrist.

The man's murderous actions hadn't taken Barry completely by surprise. It only made sense when he was actively battling terrorists from the Middle East that he'd notice the conductor's dark hair and skin when he stepped into the cab. Although Barry had taken the man for Hispanic at first glance, the engineer calling him "Jamal" had set off further alarm bells in Barry's brain.

Even so, he hadn't been able to save the engineer's life, and the train was picking up speed.

He clamped his fingers around the killer's wrist and shoved the gun aside as the man fired again. Barry heard the slug *spang!* around the cab but wasn't sure where it hit. It hadn't drilled him, and that was all he cared about at the moment.

Holding the gun away from him, he elbowed the corpse aside and grabbed the killer's throat with his other hand. The man's left arm was pinned momentarily, but he worked it free and hammered a punch to the side of Barry's head. The blow packed enough force that Barry was knocked to the side for a second. The conductor shoved the dead man off him. As the engineer's body slumped downward, his legs tangled with Barry's. Barry's feet went out from under him, but he hung on to the killer's throat and hauled him down, too.

All three men sprawled on the cab's metal floor in a tangle of arms and legs.

Barry hung on for dear life with both hands. The conductor triggered the pistol twice more, and again the slugs bounced around the cab. There was no telling what damage they were doing to the locomotive's control board, but it wasn't enough to stop the train. With its low, throaty rumble, the locomotive continued pulling the lengthy line of freight cars along the tracks.

Barry writhed out from under the corpse and saw an opening to headbutt the conductor. Blood spurted from the man's nose under the impact, and he stopped his feverish struggles long enough for Barry to bang his gun hand twice against the floor. The man's fingers opened involuntarily. The pistol with its attached suppressor skittered across the cab.

The terrorist recovered quickly, lifting his knee toward Barry's groin. Barry twisted aside to take the blow on his thigh. He pulled the man up by the throat and bounced his head off the metal floor. The man was starting to look pretty groggy. Barry let go of him and hit him twice on the jaw, short, sharp blows that made his eyes roll up in their sockets. He went limp.

Barry pushed to his feet and picked up the man's

pistol. He had been certain already that there was nothing he could do for the engineer, but a glance at the back of the man's head where the bullet had gone in confirmed it. There was no exit wound, which meant the slug had bounced around inside the skull, turning the man's brain to mush. He'd been too dead to feel it, though.

Barry's lips pulled back from his teeth in anger. A part of him wanted to plant a bullet in the middle of the terrorist's forehead. The guy had it coming. But he might have valuable information, so killing him out of hand could turn out to be the wrong move.

It was still frustrating and annoying to let a criminal like that continue drawing breath, though.

He turned to the control board and started trying to make some sense of it. Barry could fly a plane and he had cut his teeth on the big rigs, but he'd never operated a massive locomotive like this before. Still, he asked himself, how hard could it be?

A lot harder than it should have been. At that moment—just before he could press the right button to stop the train—the door into the cab swung open and a gunshot blasted. No suppressor this time, so the report slammed painfully against Barry's ears in the cab's close confines.

The bullet went over his right shoulder, narrowly missing his right ear. It struck the windshield and punched through, leaving a hole and a star shape around it. The glass didn't shatter.

Barry still had the conductor's gun in his hand. He returned fire without thinking about it, triggering two shots from the semi-automatic pistol. The bullets punched into the chest of the man who had just tried to kill him and drove the guy backward against the short railing around the platform. He flipped over it, his legs going high in the air for a second before he vanished.

In the split second Barry had gotten a good look at this second would-be killer, he had recognized another Middle Eastern face. Obviously, Jamal had friends on board. Most freight trains operated with only two-man crews. Barry wondered if the unfortunate engineer had been aware that his conductor had smuggled a passenger on board the train. Probably not.

Passengers, Barry corrected himself. The second man wasn't alone. A third terrorist leaned forward far enough to snap a shot through the open door, then ducked back. This one missed Barry and hit the windshield, too.

Barry fired but knew he had missed. In a burst of anger, he threw the suppressed pistol out the door. It sailed away from the train. It was just a cheap piece of crap for his warm-up.

He reached under his jacket and drew the 1911 and the Browning, confident that he had just improved his firepower immensely.

But they weren't going to help him against what came next. A small canister flew into the cab from the train's outside walkway that ran to the rear of the locomotive. As it started spewing noxious fumes, Barry cursed under his breath. Tear gas? What were his enemies doing with tear gas?

He supposed one of them believed in being prepared for any eventuality. What mattered was that the stuff was here, filling up the cab, and in an instant, he began to choke and his eyes watered. He had to get out of there.

The terrorist—or terrorists, he didn't know how many more were out there—would be watching the door, though, ready to open fire at the first sign of movement.

He might pass out if he stayed in there, and he couldn't afford to do that. Holding his handkerchief over his mouth and nose, for what little good *that* did, he sat down on the console in front of the controls, drew his legs up, turned around, and lashed out at the windshield with both feet.

Weakened by the bullets hitting it, the glass gave way, shattering and spraying outward onto the platform attached to the locomotive's nose. That newly created opening caused enough wind to blow through the cab that the fumes from the tear gas canister were whipped away. Barry's eyes, nose, and throat still smarted miserably, but at least he could breathe again without choking and kind of see.

He didn't know if any of the terrorists were lurking on the platform at the locomotive's nose. He lifted both guns, ready to blaze away through the opening if anybody opened fire on him.

Nothing happened, though, leading him to believe that the enemy was still on the walkway, farther back on the locomotive. He used the 1911 to rake shards of glass out of the windshield frame, then stuck his legs out.

Jake was too big to have made it out this way; his shoulders probably would have gotten caught. Barry was built leanly enough that he was able to wriggle through the opening and drop to the platform.

The train had left Las Cruces behind and was rolling south through semi-desert covered with scrub brush. Interstate 10 was visible several hundred yards away, running parallel with the railroad.

The racket from the engine was too loud for Barry to hear anything else, so he risked a glance around the corner of the cab, along the walkway. As he suspected, he saw three men at the far end of the narrow path, all of them armed. More of Jamal's friends. Judging by their angry expressions and gestures, they were arguing about who was going to ease along the walkway and take a look to see if the hated infidel was dead.

Quickly, Barry pulled back out of sight before they spotted him. He drew in a couple of deep breaths, then wheeled around the corner of the cab with both guns thrust out in front of him, the 1911 in his right hand, the Browning in his left.

The gun-thunder that rolled from both weapons added to the cacophony filling the air. Barry emptied both guns. The storm of .45 and 9mm slugs ripped through the terrorists and slammed them off the walkway. Their bullet-riddled bodies sailed through the air and crashed to the ground alongside the tracks, rolling and flopping limply.

The dead men soon faded out of sight as the train continued rolling.

Barry had spare magazines for both guns in his pockets. He swapped them out quickly, then moved toward the still-open door into the cab. He had left

Jamal in there unconscious, but the man might be coming to.

On the other hand, breathing all that tear gas could have caused some serious damage to Jamal's lungs. It was possible he wouldn't wake up again after being exposed to such a high concentration of the gas.

Barry was ready for either of those possibilities.

He wasn't prepared for Jamal to attack him like a red-faced berserker, screeching like a howler monkey. But that was what happened, and the unexpected impact drove Barry back against the railing. He had to drop the Browning to grab the rail and keep himself from going over. The gun fell at their feet and began to slide around as the two men kicked it while they struggled.

Barry chopped at Jamal's head with the 1911. Hate, rage, and desperation gave the terrorist strength and speed he might not have possessed otherwise. He avoided the blow and rammed his shoulder against Barry's chest, trying to knock him off the train.

Barry hung on and struck Jamal a glancing blow with the .45's barrel. Jamal sagged. That put him in position, though, to clamp both arms around Barry's knees. With an incoherent cry, Barry lost his grip on the railing and went up and over, pinwheeling through the air.

The ground came up and crashed into him, knocking all the air out of his lungs and stunning him. The world spun crazily around him. He had fallen beside the tracks, rather than landing under the train's wheels, but that was the only bit of luck he'd had.

He was able to lift his head for a second and peer after the locomotive. His vision was blurred, but he was able to make out Jamal staggering back into the cab. The train was still headed for El Paso, but now a terrorist was at the controls.

And Barry was losing consciousness. It slipped away from him, despite how desperately he tried to cling to it.

CHAPTER 37

There was nowhere for them to go except up, Jake realized as he fired again through one of the gaps between freight cars. Metal ladder rungs were attached to the side of the car next to him. He called to Gretchen, "Climb! I'll cover you!"

She immediately grasped what he meant and shoved her gun into its holster at the small of her back. She grabbed one of the rungs, got a foot on the lowest one, and started hauling herself up. Jake sent a couple of rounds along the tracks to make the guys who'd tried to climb over the freight car keep their heads down, then swiveled and shot a man off the car opposite just as he was trying to draw a bead on the climbing Gretchen.

When she reached the top of the car's ladder, she rolled onto the roof and jerked her gun out again.

"Come on!" she shouted to Jake as she fired across the tracks toward some of the other cars.

He holstered his gun and started climbing, going up the ladder with a lithe agility unusual in a man of his size. Gretchen continued twisting, rolling, and shooting.

If he had seen her in other circumstances and she'd claimed to work for Homeland Security, he would have figured she was a pencil-pusher or at best some sort of cyber-warrior. Clearly, that wasn't the case. She was a good shot and apparently had nerves like ice.

Right now, that was helping to keep them alive.

Jake heaved himself onto the top of the freight car beside her. Her deadly accurate fire had driven the terrorists off the other cars, but they were still surrounded.

"How many guys do they have working in this yard?" Gretchen asked in frantic exasperation as she paused to reload.

"Too many," Jake said. "Listen."

Sirens wailed somewhere not far away. The sound of a small war breaking out in the freight yard had drawn the attention of the cops, just as Jake had known it would.

The terrorists who had infiltrated the workforce at the yard must be hearing those sirens, too, and they knew what it meant. They were running out of time to wreak the havoc they had intended.

"They'll go ahead and blow those bombs instead of waiting for the train," Jake said, "unless we keep them too busy."

"You mean we take the fight to them?"

"Yeah. You ready?"

Gretchen looked a little pale and scared now, but her nod was decisive enough as she said, "Let's do it."

"We'll clean out this side first. Ready . . . go!"

Jake sprang to his feet, leaned out, and opened fire on the three gunmen he spotted running along the siding to a new position. They weren't expecting the counterattack. Jake drilled all three of them cleanly and sent them spinning off their feet.

Gretchen turned the other way and fired as a man sprang onto the roof of the car across the tracks. The

he searched for more explosives. He heard Gretchen mutter something. Then, when he glanced up, he saw that she was running along the tops of the cars, keeping pace with him.

"Get out of here!" he yelled at her.

"Then you come, too!"

Instead of answering, he ran faster as he spotted something else attached to the outside of the right-hand rail. It was another of the C-4 charges, he confirmed as he came closer. He waved his arm at Gretchen again and told her, "I'll just get this one and then leave. Go on, I'll catch up to you!"

He could tell that she was torn about what to do, but sheer stubbornness won out.

"Just go ahead and disarm it! I'll wait."

It was Jake's turn to mutter now. He knelt next to the rail, studied the deadly little package to make sure it was set up the same way the others had been, and took hold of the pair of wires and ripped them loose.

A noise made him look up. A wiry figure stood beside the tracks about fifty yards away, where he had just jumped down from one of the freight cars. He jerked a gun up and threw a shot at Jake, who dived forward so the bullet went above him, through the space where he had just been. Not all the terrorists had fled, he thought as he tilted his gun up and pulled the trigger.

The slug punched into the man's midsection and doubled him over. He dropped the gun as he collapsed. Jake sprang to his feet and raced forward. If he could force this guy to talk, he might find out how many of the C-4 charges had been planted.

The man was extending a shaky hand toward his fallen gun when Jake got there and kicked the weapon out of his reach. Jake hooked his toe under the terrorist's shoulder and rolled him onto his back. The man's shirt was soaked with blood from the belly wound.

"Listen to me," Jake said as he bent over the man. "You're hurt bad, but you'll be all right. We'll get you to a doctor. You just need to tell me how many of these bombs you guys planted."

The man's eyes were unfocused. Sweat coated his face. He rasped something in a foreign language—Jake was almost certain it was Pashto—but his voice was so choked that Jake couldn't understand the words.

Then he picked up the man repeating the word "Allah" several times and realized the guy was praying. Under these circumstances, most likely he was praying for a swift passage to paradise, where all those unlikely virgins would be waiting for him.

The man had one hand pressed to his bleeding belly. The other came out from under him clutching something—a cylinder with a button on the end. Jake would have tried to slap it out of his hand, but the man's fanaticism gave him a final burst of speed. He rammed the detonator button down.

Jake was already turning and running, yelling, "Fire in the hole!," hoping Gretchen Rogers would have the sense to jump off the other side of the freight car so it would shield her from the blast.

Then the world came apart behind him in flame and noise, and the explosion's force picked Jake up and flung him forward through the air.

CHAPTER 38

Barry didn't know how long it had been since he passed out, but as his senses came back to him and he heard the train still clattering and rumbling past him at full speed, he knew it couldn't have been any more than a few moments. A minute or so, maybe.

The length of time didn't matter. The length of the train did.

Barry lifted his head, looked back along the tracks, and saw that a couple of dozen cars remained before the end of the train. He pushed himself to his hands and knees, shook his head for a second to clear some of the cobwebs from it, and then shoved to his feet. He broke into an unsteady run alongside the tracks, angling closer as the cars rolled past him.

Nearly all the cars had ladder rungs welded onto the side at one end or the other. Barry edged nearer and nearer until he could reach out and close his left hand around one of them. Calling on all his reserves of strength, he lunged forward. He flung his right hand up and grabbed the next-highest rung. With a grunt of effort, he heaved himself up so his feet wouldn't drag as the freight car carried him along.

Knowing that freight trains, like any others, had

emergency braking systems, as soon as he was stable on the ladder he studied the maze of couplings, cables, and hoses between the cars. Spotting a hanging chain with a metal label above it that read EMERGENCY, Barry leaned in, grasped it, and pulled as hard as he could. If that worked as it should, it ought to vent the pressure from the air brakes and stop the train.

Nothing. Barry grimaced, knowing that the terrorists must have sabotaged the emergency system somehow.

He wasn't going to get any results here.

He climbed hand over hand, his arms and shoulders aching from the strain of supporting his weight. It got a lot easier when he was able to get a foot on the bottom rung. From there, he went on up to the top and rolled onto the car's roof.

Lying spread-eagled on his belly, Barry stayed still for a long moment, catching his breath and letting the trembling in his muscles subside. Even though he was amazingly strong and vital for a man his age—or even one a lot younger—he had put in quite a few years on this earth, and no one could completely escape the ravages of time.

When he trusted himself to move again, he lifted his head and peered along the train toward the locomotive. There were quite a few cars between him and the engine. It would take some time, but nothing would stop him from getting there.

Jamal would believe that he was gone, Barry thought as he made his way forward. He'd think Barry was thrown off the train either to his death or at least left unconscious and far behind. He wouldn't be expecting any more trouble between here and El Paso.

Barry crawled to the center of the car and rose to his

feet. Jamal was in for a surprise, he thought as he trotted toward the locomotive.

The gaps between cars were narrow enough that Barry had no trouble jumping over them. He closed in steadily on his objective. By the time he finally reached the one directly behind the locomotive, he had shaken off most of the effects of being thrown from the train. His right knee still twinged a little. He must have twisted it when he landed, he thought.

He had been concentrating on what he was doing, so he hadn't really looked ahead much. He paused now and glanced around to see that there were streets and houses and businesses on both sides of the tracks. The streets weren't crowded, but they definitely weren't out in the semi-desert anymore.

Barry lifted his gaze and felt a little shock go through him as he spotted a cluster of tall buildings in the distance with some mountains off to the left. That was downtown El Paso, he thought. The train had made good time from Las Cruces—and maybe he'd been unconscious a little longer than he had thought at first.

What it amounted to was that his opportunity for stopping the train before it reached the rail yard was dwindling with every second that sped past. He moved into action again.

The ladder was at the front end of the car, so he was able to descend part of the way and reach over to grasp the railing beside the walkway leading to the front of the locomotive. It was a long step from the freight car to that walkway, but he made it. He edged along the narrow metal walk.

Instead of an old-fashioned cowcatcher, modern loco-motives had a small platform on the front with steps leading down on at least one side and sometimes both. That was where the door into the cab was located, too. Barry eased up to it and grasped the handle.

If Jamal had locked the door, Barry would have to try to get in through the broken windshield. Jamal would have plenty of time to shoot him if he did that, but he didn't see any other option.

Barry blew out a relieved breath when the door handle moved slightly under his careful touch. Jamal believed he was home free. As far as he knew, he was the only person still on the train.

The door latch disengaged, and Barry eased it open. He didn't think the door had made enough noise for Jamal to hear it over the steady thrum of the engine. Through the narrow gap, he saw the terrorist sitting in the engineer's seat, watching the control board.

Jamal might not have *heard* Barry open the door, but with the windshield being broken out like it was, the door being open changed the wind patterns in the cab. Jamal noticed that. His head jerked around, and he twisted his body up out of the seat as Barry threw the door wide open and charged into the cab.

He slashed at Jamal's neck, hoping to end the fight quickly, but Jamal raised his shoulder and took the blow there.

At the same time, Jamal's right fist shot out and drove into Barry's solar plexus. Barry grimaced and bent forward, but he managed to hook a left that caught Jamal on the jaw and knocked him back against the engineer's seat.

Smooth as a cobra, Jamal brought his right leg up and snapped a kick into Barry's chest. The terrorist seemed to be recovered from their earlier clash. The savage kick made Barry fly back toward the open door.

He wasn't getting thrown off this train again. He flung his arms out at his sides and caught hold of the opening as he reached it. The muscles in his arms, shoulders, and back bunched as he used that grip to launch himself toward Jamal again. The two of them grappled, staggering back and forth in the close confines of the locomotive's cab.

Jamal got one hand on Barry's throat and the other on his face. His fingers hooked into claws and dug for Barry's eyes. Barry got his right fist inside the circle of Jamal's arms and brought it up in a short, sharp punch that landed under the terrorist's chin and rocked his head back.

Jamal let out a strangled cry of pain as blood gushed over his lips. He had been panting for breath as he struggled, and Barry's punch had caused him to bite all the way through his tongue.

The pain and shock galvanized Jamal. He twisted and slammed Barry against the control board. The edge of the console cut into Barry's side just below his ribs. He brought up his arm and hit Jamal under the chin again, this time with his elbow. More blood flew, not from a fresh wound but from the crimson lake that had filled Jamal's mouth.

With a little gap between them now, Barry had room to hook a left into Jamal's ribs. He followed that with a right to the chest that knocked Jamal back a step. Jamal caught his balance and swung wildly at Barry, who ducked or blocked all the blows except one, which clipped him on the side of the head just above his left ear. That one packed enough power to make Barry's head spin for a second.

Jamal tried to seize the advantage and crowd in, throwing a flurry of wild punches as he did so. Barry hunkered down, absorbed the punishment, and let Jamal get close enough to land a right in the terrorist's belly. Barry's fist sunk almost all the way to the wrist.

Jamal's breath gusted foully in Barry's face as he bent over from the blow. Barry chopped down on the back of his neck and knocked him to his knees. Jamal tried to ram his head into Barry's groin, but Barry pivoted out of the way. There wasn't room in the cab to swing a full-fledged spinning side kick, so he settled for just pulling his leg back and then kicking Jamal in the back of the head.

Jamal went down on his face and skidded halfway through the open door.

Barry turned to the controls. He glanced through the windshield and saw that the train was rolling past downtown El Paso now. The freight yard was only a mile or so away. He needed to start slowing down if he was going to stop the train in time.

Not one hundred percent sure that he was doing the right thing, he grasped a handle and pulled back on it. The sound of the engine changed slightly. He thought it had throttled down, but he couldn't tell right away if the train actually slowed any. He eased the handle back more.

That was doing it, he told himself. He felt a slight but perceptible change in the train's speed, but it wasn't enough. He wasn't sure what would happen if he hauled back hard on the handle. That might cause problems he couldn't deal with. So he wouldn't risk that unless he had to, he decided.

Jamal kicked him in the side of the knee. Barry yelled as his leg buckled. The wiry little terrorist was nothing if not resilient. Barry had thought he was out cold this time.

Instead, Jamal scrambled up, leaped past Barry, and shoved the handle forward again before Barry could tackle him and knock him away from the controls. They rolled over on the cab's floor but couldn't go far before they ran out of room. Jamal pinned Barry against the wall and peppered his body with punches.

Barry grabbed him by the throat. Blood still welled from Jamal's mouth and splattered down on Barry's wrists. Barry surged up and banged Jamal's head against the metal plates of the floor. Jamal didn't even seem to notice. He was completely in the grip of his frenzied hatred now. He wouldn't stop fighting until he was unconscious—or dead.

Barry got his feet under him and surged upright. He hauled Jamal up with him, grimacing from the effort. Jamal kept flailing at him, but the blows were feeble and ineffectual now. Barry staggered out onto the platform, forcing Jamal ahead of him, and rammed the man's back against the railing. He felt as much as heard the crack as Jamal's spine broke under the impact.

Jamal turned into deadweight. He crumpled into a senseless heap on the platform. Confident that his enemy was finally out of action, Barry turned back toward the cab, intending to try again to slow down the train, when he heard a sudden blast and looked ahead to see a ball of fire, maybe half a mile away, in the middle of what he recognized as a train yard.

Jake hadn't been able to keep the terrorists in El Paso from setting off at least that one explosion, Barry realized, and from the size of it, that was enough to have damaged the tracks. And he knew he couldn't stop the train in the distance he had left.

But he could slow it down as much as possible and maybe minimize the damage. He leaped into the cab, grabbed the handle he had been using earlier, and hauled back on it as hard as he could. Something screeched and the train lurched heavily—but kept going.

Up ahead, a chain-link fence stretched on both sides of the gate into the freight yard. The gate was open— not that it would have stopped the train anyway. Barry stood on the platform until the locomotive cleared the gate, then jumped.

CHAPTER 39

Jake had gotten chewed out many times while he was in the army, but few if any of those dressings-down had been as vehement as the butt-blistering he was getting from Walt Graham right now.

"And the worst of it is, I put my own career on the line for you more than once," Graham concluded, evidently having run out of profanity. He had been stalking back and forth in the office of the Special Agent in Charge of the El Paso branch of the FBI, but now he stopped, pushed back his coattails so he could rest his hands at his waist, and glared at Jake and Barry as they sat in uncomfortable chairs in front of the desk. "Clearly, being an irresponsible cowboy runs in the family."

"Some of us might consider that a compliment, Walt," Barry drawled.

Graham looked like he was about to explode again. He was a large, burly black man with graying hair and one of the deepest voices Jake had ever heard. He controlled his anger with a visible effort, propped a hip on the corner of the desk in the borrowed office, and said, "You're both lucky you're not in jail right now."

said, "Hello, Mitchell. You got here pretty quickly from Washington."

"I'd already been hearing rumors you had a rogue agent stirring up trouble."

Graham bristled at that. "Special Agent Rivers has hardly gone rogue," he snapped.

"Oh? What would call running around over two states while blowing things up and killing people? Do you know how many civilian casualties he's been involved with over the past two days? I believe the death toll right now stands at thirty-seven."

"I'm right here," Jake said, not bothering to conceal his irritation. "And that death toll might have been a lot higher if I hadn't tried to stop those terrorists."

"Alleged terrorists," the white-haired man said. "Why don't you ask the citizens of Hachita what they think of your involvement, Rivers? Or Vincent Gilpin, who was killed along with his family when their motor home crashed and burned?"

Barry spoke up, drawling, "That's not fair, Cavanaugh. The men we were trying to stop committed those crimes, not us."

"But would they have killed those people if you and your nephew hadn't gotten involved?" the white-haired man shot back at him.

Jake had heard the name Mitchell Cavanaugh before. He was some sort of high-ranking official in the Department of Justice. Probably reported directly to the Attorney General. That meant he *wasn't* Gretchen's boss, since DOJ was separate from Homeland Security, but Cavanaugh still had a lot of clout.

Graham said, "You can't blame these two men for the actions of others. We've been questioning people all morning, and it's obvious that if they hadn't stepped in, we would have had a major terrorist attack here in El Paso this morning."

"They stepped in with no authorization or supervision."

"That's true," Graham admitted with a shrug. "But there were special circumstances—"

"No circumstances warrant such dangerous, irresponsible behavior." Cavanaugh looked at Barry and sneered. "It's a cliché to call someone a loose cannon, but I can't think of a better term to describe you. And you've *been* a loose cannon for far too many years. You believe you're above the law and can just take whatever actions you deem necessary—"

"That's how the people we've both worked for wanted it," Barry broke in.

"—no matter how dangerous and crazy they are," Cavanaugh finished. "Well, that's over. You're officially suspended, pending further investigation." He looked at Jake. "And so are you, Special Agent Rivers."

That was like a punch in the gut to Jake. He frowned and looked at Barry, who didn't seem all that perturbed.

"I don't think you *can* suspend me, Cavanaugh. I believe that's above your pay grade."

Cavanaugh's beefy face got even redder.

"Don't worry, I'll be speaking to the White House later today," he said. "Then we'll see just how high and mighty you are."

"Yeah, I guess we will," Barry said.

Cavanaugh turned to include Gretchen in his ire for the first time since entering the room.

"I haven't forgotten about you, Ms. Rogers. I'll be speaking to the Secretary shortly, as well, and I'm going to recommend in the strongest possible terms that you be suspended. When you found out what Agent Rivers was doing, you should have arrested him rather than joining in his lawless behavior. Have you never even *heard* of due process? Those men you shot at the freight yard were either American citizens or else were here in this country legally."

Barry said, "So were the men who hijacked those planes on 9/11."

Cavanaugh ignored that and went on, "It's entirely possible that all three of you will be arrested on murder charges before the day is over."

"Are we to consider ourselves in custody, then?" Jake asked tightly.

Cavanaugh looked like he wanted to say yes, but after a second, he shook his head.

"Not at this point. If any of you leave this jurisdiction, however, you'll be considered fugitives." Cavanaugh looked around the room, snapped, "That's all," and walked out, his back stiff with obvious anger.

An ominous quiet hung over the room for a long moment before Walt Graham sighed.

"Cavanaugh was right," he said. "You're lucky, all three of you. I'm not sure why he *didn't* just have you arrested." Graham looked at Barry. "Could be he's a little leery of the pull you've got. He knows you have some friends in high places."

"Maybe," Barry said with a shrug. "After all this, maybe not."

In a hollow voice, Jake said, "The worst part about it is that, in a way, he's right. Some of those innocent people wouldn't have died if we hadn't been trying to stop the Zaragosa cartel from getting Saddiq into the country."

"Don't do that," Barry said sharply. "Don't take their evil on your shoulders. They're the ones who pulled the trigger. Nobody forced them to."

Graham said, "Barry's right. Don't try to rationalize what they've done. There's no excuse for any of it. None."

Jake knew they were right. He said, "What are we going to do now, Mr. Graham?"

A grunt of humorless laughter came from Graham.

"You heard Cavanaugh. You're suspended, Rivers. You won't be doing anything."

"But this wasn't the end of Saddiq's plan. As bad as it would have been if we hadn't interfered with their plans, derailing that train in the freight yard wasn't nearly dramatic enough. They wouldn't have gone to so much trouble to get Saddiq into the country just for that."

The creases on Graham's forehead deepened as he said, "That sounds suspiciously like you're planning to continue poking your nose into this."

Barry said, "Do you have any confidence that a bunch of Deep State bureaucrats like Cavanaugh will actually investigate what's going on? Or will they concentrate on damage control and covering up anything and everything that might make them and their agencies look bad?"

Gretchen spoke up, saying, "Homeland Security's not like that. We'll get to the bottom of this, you can count on it."

"If you really believe that, sweetheart," Barry said, "I've got some of that proverbial oceanfront property in Arizona to sell you."

"Don't call me sweetheart," she snapped. "Or honey, or dear, or anything else like that."

Barry held up his hands, palms out. "Sorry. You've got to remember I'm a dinosaur, a relic of the patriarchy."

"Well, you don't have to revel in being out of touch with the times."

Barry shrugged and grinned at her, then turned back to Graham, "I want to get my truck. I left it up on Las Cruces."

"I can send someone to get it," Graham said.

"No, you can't. There are fail-safes. It can only be started in certain ways."

"You didn't *booby-trap* it, did you? Is somebody else going to get hurt?"

"No, of course not." Barry paused. "Probably not. But I still think you need to let me pick it up. I'll bring it back down here."

"Blasted right you will. I'm sending a couple of men with you to make sure of it."

"That's fine," Barry said. "And I want Jake to come along, too."

"Why?" Graham's eyes narrowed. "What are you up to, Barry?"

"Me? Nothing."

Barry's tone of mock innocence didn't fool anyone in the room.

"Well, I haven't been suspended yet," Gretchen said. "Not officially. So I'm going along, too."

"Fine. I don't trust any of you, so having you all in the same place with my agents keeping an eye on you is probably a good idea." Graham looked from one to the other of the three of them. "But I'm warning you right now . . . if you try anything else crazy, there won't be a thing in the world I can do to help you."

"You don't need to worry about us," Barry said. "It's Bandar al-Saddiq—and whatever he's got planned for this country—that ought to be on your mind. Because I've got a hunch it's not going to be anything good."

CHAPTER 40

The Pacific Northwest

The driveway to reach the estate was actually an asphalt road that climbed more than a mile to the top of a hill with a spectacular view of waves crashing against the rocks at the bottom of a steep cliff. The ocean stretched as far as the eye could see to the west.

The house was a massive fortress of stone, concrete, steel, and glass arranged in a stunning vision of cubist architecture. Few, if any, would call the place pretty, but no one who laid eyes on it would ever forget it.

A vast parklike area surrounded the mansion. Walking and biking paths serpentined their way through groves of trees and colorful flower beds. Nearer the house were tennis courts, an Olympic swimming pool, and a helipad. Clearly, whoever lived here was as rich as Midas, with such a staggering amount of wealth that it was almost meaningless.

When one could buy *anything*, what was the point of life? Bandar al-Saddiq asked himself that question as the luxury car in which he rode rounded the last turn in the long driveway and he got his first good look at the bizarre castle on top of the hill.

The driver was a jovial, round-faced man, who, after

several futile attempts at making friendly conversation, had given up the effort. The man sitting next to Saddiq was a much more somber sort, with close-cropped dark hair and the bulge of a weapon under his suit coat. He was a professional security man, either privately employed by the man who owned this estate or a member of an executive protection firm. Saddiq had seen plenty of them over the years. He had said almost nothing during the drive from the private airport where Saddiq had been picked up after the flight from Texas in his host's jet.

"Why wasn't I brought out here on a helicopter, instead of making this long drive?" Saddiq asked when he noticed the helipad.

"The chopper's got mechanical problems right now," the driver replied with a glance over his shoulder.

"Your employer doesn't have more than one?" Saddiq asked dryly. "Judging by the looks of this place, I would think he'd have an entire fleet of them."

"Well, actually, he does own several more of 'em. But they're all in use at other locations right now. Far-flung business empire and all, you know."

"Of course."

Saddiq looked over at the expressionless bodyguard. The man might as well have not even heard the conversation, for all the reaction he showed.

The road turned into a circular driveway. The man at the wheel followed it around the house—which actually looked a little like something out of a nightmare to Saddiq—past the swimming pool and tennis courts, past a large garage with room for at least a dozen vehicles, past a barn and stables with an attached corral in which four magnificent horses grazed, and through the park to a small, graveled circle with a gazebo in it.

To the left of the gazebo was a golf driving range, to the right a gun range with a long open shed where several people could stand to shoot. There was also a machine to throw clay pigeons for skeet shooting.

No one was at the gun range, but a lone man stood at one of the tees with a golf club in his hands. He drew it back, poised for a second, and hit his drive. It flew straight and true, at least two hundred yards. Saddiq didn't know much about golf, but he was impressed anyway.

The man turned away from the tee and put his club back in a golf bag that was sitting nearby. He wore khaki trousers and a polo shirt. He was in his sixties, or perhaps his seventies. His eyes had the deepest bags under them that Saddiq had ever seen on a human being. The man reminded him a little of a basset hound, only instead of drooping, his ears stuck out straight from his head like wings. The large skull between them was naked and shiny. A small tuft of silver hair adorned his chin.

"Welcome to my home," the man greeted Saddiq in a gravelly voice. He put out his hand. "I'm Alexander Sherman."

"Mr. Sherman," Saddiq said as he shook hands with the American billionaire, overcoming the natural revulsion he felt at such familiarity with an infidel. "It's good to meet you at last."

"I feel the same way," Sherman assured him. "I heard that you had a little . . . trouble on your way here."

"On my way into the country, yes. But not since then."

"My apologies for the inconvenience. I was told that

Francisco Zaragosa would be the best man to handle the job."

Saddiq shrugged and said, "There was nothing wrong with his plan, really. It was just that two extremely stubborn individuals took it upon themselves to stick their noses into something that was none of their business."

"Yes, I know the men of whom you speak. I assure you, they will be dealt with."

"They ruined our operation in El Paso, too," Saddiq said. He tried to control the fury that burned within him, but it threatened to boil to the top and explode.

Sherman waved a thick-fingered hand and said, "Not at all, not at all. The end results matter less than the fact that there was another terrorist attack directed at a railroad. That's the second one in less than a week."

"Yes," Saddiq agreed. "But it draws attention to what we're doing without the sort of damage we wanted and anticipated."

"No matter." Sherman laughed. "It's still plenty to scare people, and that's what we're after!" He gestured toward a golf cart parked nearby. "Come on, let's go to the house. My chef is preparing dinner. Everything will be halal, I assure you."

For some reason, that assurance annoyed Saddiq, but he put a smile on his face and got into the golf cart. Sherman put his golf bag in the storage area behind the seat and then climbed in next to Saddiq. The bodyguard stepped up onto the back of the cart and hung onto its frame, obviously intending to ride back to the house with them.

"Harry, just put the car out front. You'll be taking Mr. Saddiq back to the city later," Sherman told the driver. He started the golf cart and followed the asphalt drive back toward the monstrosity that was his home.

As they approached the place, Sherman chuckled and said, "Ugly son of a gun, isn't it?"

"The house, you mean? No, it's quite striking."

"You don't have to lie," Sherman said. "It looks like something a toddler would build out of blocks. I know that. But it serves my purpose. Only a filthy rich eccentric would live in an eyesore like this, right?"

"You . . . want to be considered eccentric?" Saddiq asked with a frown.

"Eccentric and colorful. When you act like that, people laugh at you behind your back. When they laugh at you, they don't take you seriously." Sherman looked over at Saddiq, who realized suddenly that the older man's gray eyes were as cold as chips of ice. "And when they don't take you seriously, they don't pay any attention to what you're *really* doing."

For the first time, Saddiq thought that perhaps Allah had brought him together with a suitable partner in the war against the Great Satan.

Sherman had reached out through intermediaries in Paris and let it be known that he wanted to get in touch with an ambitious young leader in the network of Islamist terror groups. Saddiq had investigated the man as thoroughly as he could from long distance and had not been impressed. Sherman struck him as a buffoon. But a very rich buffoon, and there was a chance he might prove to be a useful idiot.

America was full of those.

Now, however, Saddiq saw that Sherman might bring something to their partnership other than limitless funds.

Whatever the man was really after, he believed in it. Saddiq had seen that in his eyes.

For the moment, Sherman resumed his charming patter as he drove the golf cart to the garage and left it there for someone else to deal with. The casual, uncaring nonchalance of the very rich.

Another bodyguard was waiting at what Saddiq assumed was the house's rear door. Both black-suited men fell in behind Sherman and Saddiq as the American led the way into the house.

It was as luxurious inside as it was odd-looking outside. Spanish tile, gleaming marble, gold and silver and chrome, thick carpet, paintings and sculptures that should have been in a museum somewhere, every sort of electronic gadget imaginable . . . Everywhere Saddiq looked was something else that loudly proclaimed Alexander Sherman's wealth.

A woman in a burqa met them in a large, comfortably furnished room with one wall that was almost entirely glass. The view was of the pine-topped cliff rising on the other side of a little cove.

"Bring us juice," Sherman told the woman, who bowed slightly and withdrew. He turned to Saddiq and went on, "I've told my servants to dress so that their appearance won't be offensive to you."

"That was not necessary, but it is appreciated," Saddiq said with a smile. "Even in the short time I've been here in America, I have seen many women dressed shamelessly. This will be different someday."

"If good fortune smiles on us, it will be."

Saddiq decided to be blunt. He said, "Mr. Sherman, you are not Muslim."

"Nope, not even close. I was raised a Catholic, but I

left the Church—or the Church left me, however you want to put it—and these days religion has no real part in my life. I'm more interested in something that will actually help people."

"You do not believe that religion serves a purpose?"

Sherman shrugged and said, "It helps some people get through the misery of their lives, I suppose. Pie in the sky by and by, by and by. I'd rather change things right here on Earth, in *this* life." He seemed to be warming to his subject as he went on. "This country is deeply, severely flawed at its core. It's badly in need of real, fundamental change."

Saddiq cocked his head to the side and said, "I believe you supported someone who claimed he would bring fundamental change to this country. For his trouble, his defenders were soundly rebuked and almost everything he accomplished was demolished by the one who came after him. That trend has continued, has it not?"

"Unfortunately, yes. I really thought he would make a difference; that was why I helped get him elected. But then he turned out to be just a slick bag of hot air, and the country turned their backs on us." Sherman's voice had started to tremble with anger. He drew in a deep breath and controlled himself. "That's water under the bridge. Mistakes were made. But I learned from those mistakes. I learned that you have to break something apart before you can remake it in the image of what it should be."

Again, the coldness in Sherman's eyes made a tiny shiver go down Saddiq's own spine. But they were getting down to the basics of what had brought him here, so he pressed on.

"These attacks on the railroads we have planned, their intended result is economic damage?"

"People have forgotten about the railroads," Sherman said. "There was a time when everybody *knew* they were the lifeblood of the country. But now, with trucks and airplanes, some people probably spend most of their lives without ever thinking about railroads. They still carry more freight than any other means of transportation. Without them, goods don't move in this country."

Saddiq thought that his host was overstating the situation. If all the railroads were to collapse overnight and stop rolling, the situation would be bad, certainly. But other methods of transportation would take up the slack, and business would go on.

"And in a lot of places," Sherman continued, "it's not just goods. *People* don't move without the railroads, either."

Saddiq nodded. "The subways, the commuter trains . . . the famous El in . . . Chicago, is it?"

"That's right. Every large city in this country has an extensive rapid transit system. What happens if people can't get to work? Businesses don't open. The whole thing snowballs. The stock market starts to drop, panic sets in . . . This country operates on a very delicate balance, my friend. It doesn't take much to upset that balance."

Saddiq didn't consider this infidel his friend, but he didn't correct the man. Instead, he said, "We have struck twice now at the railroads that carry freight—"

Sherman chuckled and said, "Yeah, I lost some business myself with that derailment in Nevada. One of my companies owns that hazardous waste containment facility, you know."

"Yes, I am aware. But now that we have warned the Americans that their rail lines are at risk—"

"We wake them up even more," Sherman interrupted again. He smiled. "We're going to derail a commuter train on the Babylon Branch of the Long Island Rail Road."

"Babylon . . ." Saddiq breathed. "A name from my part of the world."

"That line is one of the busiest commuter rail lines in the country, if not *the* busiest. We take one of those trains off its tracks as it's coming into a station, thousands of people will die." Sherman lifted a finger. "It won't be as symbolic as taking down the Towers, of course . . . but the death toll is what we want. We want people afraid to ride the trains. We want people afraid to go to work. That's what will start the economy spiraling down, and once that happens, it'll be impossible to stop."

"If no one interferes with our plans."

Sherman gave an impatient shake of his head.

"Are you talking about those two troublemakers down in New Mexico and Texas? I tell you, you don't have to worry about them. By now, steps have been taken to make them back off, and if they don't . . . well, they can be gotten rid of . . . permanently."

Saddiq smiled as the woman in the burqa came back into the room carrying a tray with glasses of fruit juice on it. He nodded and told Sherman, "I like the sound of that."

Chapter 41

Sherman and Saddiq discussed the plan on through dinner, which, as Sherman had promised, was halal, and Saddiq was able to enjoy it without reservation.

Sherman knew that some Muslims, even among the die-hard terrorist groups, were not as stringent about following Islam's dietary laws, but his research had told him that Saddiq was particularly fanatical about his faith's tenets, so there was no point in offending him.

Hence the burqas on his female servants, to hide their shapely forms from Saddiq's eyes. Sherman preferred that all the women around him be attractive and as young as legally feasible—and in some cases, younger—but he had no objection to denying himself that pleasure for a while, if it was in a good cause.

His cause was the best of all, and Saddiq was a useful tool in achieving his ends.

As the terrorist took his leave that evening, to be driven back to the expensive hotel in Portland where he was staying, Sherman smiled, lifted a hand in farewell, and wondered if Saddiq was planning to have him killed at some point in their future partnership.

Sherman would have been shocked if Saddiq *didn't*

intend such a double cross. Sherman certainly planned to have Saddiq put down like the rabid animal he was—as soon as he had outlived his usefulness.

He turned away and closed the door, starting back toward the glass-walled room that was his favorite sanctum in this hodgepodge of a house.

Terry Morse emerged from a door along the way and asked, "Shall I bring you a drink, Mr. Sherman?"

"Yes, please," Sherman replied.

Terry had discarded the burqa, revealing the blue bikini she wore underneath it. It wasn't an extremely small bikini, but she was so abundantly blessed that it almost appeared so. Her long red hair was loose now, spilling down her back. It had been a real shame to cover up such sensuous beauty, and Sherman was glad that it was back on full display.

"And bring the others to me as soon as they arrive," he added.

"Of course, sir."

Sherman watched her walk away, admiring the view, and then went on into the study. He took a cigar from an antique humidor on the desk, lit it with an engraved, gold-plated lighter, and strolled over to peer out into the night.

With the light behind him like that, he would have made a good target for any sniper on the opposite cliff, had the glass not been thick and bulletproof. Not only that, it also possessed a special refractive quality that made him appear from outside to be five feet to the side of where he actually was. It was a precaution, one of many he had taken to ensure that he was safe here.

No man could have as much money as he did without also possessing a proportional number of enemies.

Terry returned with a Scotch, handed it to Sherman, and said, "The helicopter will be here in five minutes, sir."

"Excellent." Sherman sipped the Scotch. "The news and the drink."

He stayed where he was, staring out at the darkness and musing over his plans. It was closer to ten minutes before Terry came back onto the room and announced, "Your guests are here, Mr. Sherman."

He tossed back the rest of the drink and turned from the glass.

"Thank you." He nodded a greeting to the five men and one woman who came into the big, comfortable room, then said, "Gentlemen. Madame Speaker."

The woman, a sharp-faced blonde in her forties, said without smiling, "It's a bit high-handed, isn't it, Alexander, summoning us here this way? A command performance, is that it?"

"Not at all," Sherman said with an easy smile. "I meant no offense, Doris. I just knew that I'd be meeting with a key ally of ours this evening, and I wanted to fill all of you in on how our plan is progressing. Also, I suspect that some of *you* have information for me. Isn't that right, Mitchell?"

A white-haired, ruddy-faced, well-built man stepped forward and said, "I've dealt with the problem that's cropped up over the past few days, if that's what you mean."

Mitchell Cavanaugh's jaw jutted out defiantly. He always looked like he was ready for a fight. That was just his nature. A good man to have on your side, but a bad enemy.

He wasn't the only government bureaucrat in this group. An undersecretary of state was there, too, and the bald-headed black man who was high up in the Department of Defense. The other two men were United States Senators, one from California, the other from New York.

Including Representative Doris Farrington, the Speaker of the House since the Democrats had retaken it in the most recent midterm election, it was a high-powered group indeed, split between three elected positions and three appointed.

All of them actually worked for him, Alexander Sherman mused, although to help themselves sleep at night, they probably thought of it as working *with* him for the greater good. Whatever it took. The results were all that mattered.

"I'm glad to hear that, Mitchell," Sherman responded to Cavanaugh's statement. "I've promised our associate from the Middle East that Barry and Jake Rivers won't cause any more trouble, and that if they try to poke their noses in again, they'll be eliminated."

The senator from California said nervously, "I'm not sure we need to discuss that, Alex."

Sherman's weathered features hardened. He said, "Oh, but we do, Bradley. We need to be very clear about what's going on here and what we're going to do. If Barry and Jake Rivers cause trouble for us again, they're going to be killed. Mitchell has men sympathetic to our cause who will be happy to eliminate them for us. Isn't that right, Mitchell?"

Cavanaugh looked like he would just as soon not be discussing this, either, but he said, "There are a number of agents, men and women both, in DOJ, the FBI, Homeland Security, DOD, and elsewhere in the government who understand how vital it is that we take back control of our country from the . . . the rabble who keep foisting these unsuitable leaders on us!"

The Speaker of the House said, "If you give the voters an actual choice, inevitably they make the wrong one. We've seen that time and again." Her lips tightened into a thin line and barely moved as she added, "We're not going to allow that to happen again."

"Indeed, we are not," Sherman said. "We've taken the first steps on that path already." He turned toward the glass wall again and clasped his hands behind his back. "People know what they want, but they don't know what's good for them. They're grasping and greedy and, in the end, think only of themselves." A harsh laugh came from him. Without turning to face the others again, he went on, "I know what you're thinking. How ridiculous it is for a man of my wealth to be ranting about people's selfishness and all the inequality and discrimination that breeds. But I'd give away all my money tomorrow if that would actually make a difference. It wouldn't," he said flatly. "No amount of money in the world will change human nature. So the changes that we need will have to be *forced* on the American public, and to do that, we need the power of the government. We need the best people running things, the people who *know* what needs to be done and how to go about doing it. That's how my money can make a difference, by helping to make sure that the right people are elected and appointed and put in a position to enact those changes. *That* is how we'll make this a different country, my friends. A better country."

"Are you making a speech or giving a sermon, Alex?" the senator from New York asked. "Why don't *you* run for office?"

Sherman said, "Bah!" and made a curt, chopping gesture. "And waste my efforts by setting my sights so low? I can do a lot more good by working behind the scenes like this."

"By working with a known terrorist who wants to supplant the rule of law in this country with his religious law," the man from the Department of Defense said. "I'm not sure that's the best way to proceed—"

That made Sherman swing around from the window. He said, "You can leave right now, Clark. You know that. You don't have to be part of this."

The man's eyes widened a little in visible fear. He said hurriedly, "Don't get me wrong. I know we're just doing what has to be done in order to preserve a system that those who came before us built over the past hundred years. I mean, all the way back to FDR—"

"Wilson, you mean. Before FDR." That came from the Speaker of the House, who before entering politics had been a professor of history at one of the Ivy League universities.

"Yeah, whatever," the man from DOD said. "All I'm saying is that we're following traditions that go way back, and I know we don't have any choice in the matter. Since we don't have full control over the media and mass communication—"

"We have people working on that at all the social networks," the senator from California said.

"I know, I know." It was cool inside the house, but the man from DOD had a few beads of sweat on his forehead. Sherman saw that and knew they were there because the man understood how close he had come to making a fatal mistake. "I'm just saying I don't like working with terrorists. But it's necessary, I'll give you that. And I assume, Alex, that when we don't need them anymore . . ."

"They'll be squashed like bugs," Sherman said. "All of them."

The man from the Department of Defense swallowed and nodded, obviously relieved to have dodged the bullet of seeming to have wavered in his devotion to the cause.

Sherman would remember what had happened, though. And when the time came, Bandar al-Saddiq might not be the only one who had outlived his usefulness.

"Once we've created enough economic chaos to justify removing the President and Vice President from office, you'll be in charge, Doris," Sherman went on, feeling his fervor growing stronger once more. "You can start setting things right again. Congress will go along with whatever executive orders you issue, and for those who don't want to cooperate, we'll have facilities where we can show them the errors of their ways." He smiled. "I have a lot of property in Nevada and Utah, after all, that's not being used. Plenty of room there for dissidents who need to be reeducated."

"You mean . . . camps," one of the bureaucrats said.

Sherman shrugged and said, "It's a word that's taken on unpleasant connotations, but really, what better way to bring people around to the proper way of thinking than to remove all the distractions of modern life? Harsh conditions breed hardy organisms. We see that in nature all the time. And those who can't, or won't, adapt . . ."

Sherman's voice trailed off, but his meaning was clear.

Once the members of the Washington elite were running things again, the common people would toe the line.

Or they would die.

Sherman looked around the room, saw that knowledge on their faces . . . and didn't care one whit whether they liked it or not.

CHAPTER 42

Jake swung his legs off the hotel room bed when somebody knocked on the door. He stood up and went to see who was there, feeling a little uncomfortable as he did so because he was unarmed. When he and Barry had been taken into custody, all the weapons on them had been confiscated.

Jake didn't know what would happen to all the guns in Barry's truck. More than likely, the authorities would grab them, too—if Barry let them. Jake worried about what the outcome of such an attempt might be.

Right now, however, there was nothing he could do about it, so he just bent over a little to look through the peephole in the hotel room door.

He grunted in surprise. He hadn't expected to see Gretchen Rogers standing out there in the hall.

She had changed clothes, now wearing dark green trousers and a matching jacket over a white top. Her curly blond hair was still loose around her shoulders.

Jake couldn't help but notice how attractive she was. Under the circumstances, such thoughts probably weren't appropriate; they had a lot more important things to worry about. But there was no denying it, either.

As far as Jake could tell, Gretchen was alone. He opened the door and said, "Hello."

"Where's your uncle?" she asked, which he thought was a little abrupt.

"He hasn't gotten back from Las Cruces yet. He went up there to pick up his truck, remember?"

"You mean he was escorted up there."

"Well, yeah." Jake shrugged. "I kind of thought he might be back by now, but I haven't seen him."

It was early evening. He'd been stuck here in this hotel room since the middle of the afternoon, when Walt Graham and several other high-up FBI agents had stopped interrogating him.

"Can I come in?" Gretchen asked. "I'd hoped to talk to both of you, but since your uncle's not here . . ."

"Oh. Yeah." Jake stepped back. "Didn't mean to be impolite. Come on in. Please."

Gretchen walked into the room. Jake closed the door behind her. It didn't occur to him to ask if she wanted it left open. They were both adults. She could speak up if she didn't like something he did.

Besides, he had seen her in action. He knew she couldn't kick his butt—she wasn't big enough to do that—but there was a good chance she could hurt him if she wanted to. Not that he intended to give her any reason to want to.

Irritated with himself, he shoved those thoughts out of his head.

"I don't know what's in the minibar," he told her. "I haven't broken into it. But if you'd like a drink . . ."

"No, thanks." She turned to face him and put the small purse she carried on the desk under the flat-screen

TV. "I want to talk about what we're going to do about this."

"About . . .?"

"This." She gestured impatiently, as if she couldn't understand why he didn't read her mind. "This whole business of being stuck in here like prisoners."

"Mighty fancy jail," he said. His broad shoulders rose and fell. "But yeah, if we're not prisoners, we're the next thing to it."

"And while we're stuck here, there's no telling what those terrorists are going to do next."

"I guess somebody else will have to figure that out," Jake said.

"Do you really think they will? This whole thing has made your bosses, and my bosses, look bad."

"Walt Graham is a good man and a good agent. There's no way he'll just brush something under the rug."

"I hope you're right, but I'm worried that you might not be." Gretchen shook her head. "I don't trust that man Cavanaugh."

Jake grunted and said, "That makes two of us. He had Deep State written all over him."

"You believe in the Deep State?" Gretchen asked, cocking her head a little to one side.

"How can you not?" Jake asked, surprised by the question. "Anybody who's been paying attention during the past ten years has seen plenty of evidence of it, over and over again. Any time the President did anything to buck the elites, everybody in both parties freaked out! They believed they had a firm grip on everything that went on in Washington, and they didn't like it when that hold started to slip. Mostly the left, but some on the right, too. And they all have one thing in common."

"Oh?" Gretchen said. "And what's that? Please, continue pontificating."

"I don't mean for it to sound like that. But the answer to your question is a simple one. Power. That's what they all want. They believed they had it and nobody could take it away from them. And they'll fight to the death to keep it."

"And yet you work for people you evidently believe are awful."

Jake shook his head and said, "No, not most of them. The vast majority of folks who work for the government are all right. Most of the FBI agents I know, for example . . . we're just cops. We're out there trying to bust the bad guys and keep them from hurting innocent people. It's only when you get into the upper ranks, not just in the FBI but across the board with all the Alphabet Boys, that thinking starts to get twisted and corrupted. Must be something in the air up there. You see it over and over again. They start thinking they're above the law."

"Didn't you and your uncle do pretty much the same thing, going after that Mexican cartel and those terrorists on your own?"

Jake looked at her for a long moment and then said, "Aren't you arguing both sides of the case here? When you came in, you seemed to be worried that this whole thing would get covered up, and now you're acting like nobody in the government would do that to save their own butts . . . or their grip on power."

Gretchen blew out an exasperated breath, shook her head, and said, "I don't know what I'm arguing! I don't know what to *do*. I want to trust the people I work for, but at the same time, I don't like being shunted aside like this."

"You want to be in on the action," Jake told her.

She looked at him and said, "Yeah. Yeah, I guess I do."

"Welcome to the club." Jake smiled and shook his head in frustration. "I've been going nuts ever since they put me here. But there are guards by the elevators and stairs, and I don't want to give a guy grief just for doing his job. They don't have anybody watching you?"

"Not so far. I haven't received any notice that I'm officially suspended, either. *And* I still have my badge and gun."

Jake couldn't tell she was carrying, but that came as no surprise. These days, even amateurs could carry without it being obvious.

"So what are you gonna do? Bust me out of here?"

"I could, you know."

Jake could tell she was serious. He shook his head and said, "No, I don't want you getting in more trouble than you already are. Just keep your head down, and maybe everything will blow over without doing too much damage to your career."

"I don't care as much about my career as I do stopping whatever Saddiq and his friends are planning to do next."

"You don't think they're through?"

"Not at all," Gretchen replied with a shake of her head. "Do you?"

"No," Jake admitted. "I don't. And I have a bad feeling that whatever they're going to try to pull off next, it'll be worse than what they've already done. A lot worse."

A feeling of gloom settled over the room. After a

moment, Gretchen said, "Well, we can stand around here moping, or we can go down to the restaurant and get some supper." She summoned up a smile. "You're buying."

"You really think they'll let us do that? I was told if I wanted anything to call room service."

"Your guards can follow us, can't they? Besides, you'll have your own personal guard in the form of a Homeland Security agent."

"Who's also in all kinds of trouble," Jake pointed out.

"The guy at the elevator may not know that. We can give it a try, anyway."

The idea of having dinner with Gretchen held a lot of appeal, Jake realized. They had fought side by side, which created a near-unbreakable bond . . . and she really was very attractive, as well as smart and tough.

"All right," he said. He gestured at his jeans and T-shirt. "I'm not dressed for anything fancy, though, and nobody's brought me the rest of my stuff yet."

"Trust me, the hotel restaurant isn't that fancy." Gretchen picked up her purse. "Let's go."

The elevators were only a couple of doors away, and just as Jake expected, as soon as the FBI agent posted there saw them coming, he stepped forward and said, "Hold it, Rivers. You're not going anywhere."

"We're just going downstairs to get some dinner," Gretchen said. "Agent Rivers is in my custody."

She reached for her ID, but the guard said, "Yeah, you showed me your badge and papers earlier. I know you work for Homeland, Ms. Rogers, but I also know you were mixed up in the same incident that got Rivers here in trouble. I'm gonna need the word of somebody a lot higher up than you before I'm letting him off this floor."

"You can follow us down there," Jake said. "I give you my word, man, I'm not trying to get away—"

His efforts at persuasion were probably doomed to failure, but he didn't get to finish because at that moment, the elevator dinged and the door of one of the cars slid open.

Barry stepped out in his casual, loose-limbed way, by himself, no FBI agents in sight. Jake, Gretchen, and the guard turned to look at him, and the guard exclaimed, "Hey, aren't you—"

"I sure am, son," Barry said, and in the next split second his right fist rocketed out to crash against the man's jaw and knock him back against the wall. The agent's hand had barely twitched toward the gun under his coat.

As he bounced off the wall, Barry slipped behind him, got an arm around his neck, and clamped down on the hold until the man passed out. Barry lowered him gently to the floor, glanced along the corridor, which was empty, and then straightened to grin at Jake and Gretchen.

"Are you two ready to get out of here and get back on the case?" he asked.

CHAPTER 43

"I promise you, I didn't hurt either of those agents who went up to Las Cruces with me," Barry told Jake and Gretchen as the Kenworth Z1000 rolled east out of El Paso on Interstate 10. "They just went to sleep for a little while, like the guard up there at the elevator."

Barry was behind the wheel, Gretchen in the passenger seat. Jake sat on the sofa in the sleeper, leaning forward so he could take part in the conversation.

"I know that," he said in response to his uncle's promise. "I still feel a little bad about it. They were fellow agents, after all."

Without taking his eyes off the road unrolling in front of them, Barry asked, "Would you rather be stuck on the sidelines while the rest of this plays out?"

"You know better than that."

Gretchen said, "So you don't think this is over yet, Mr. Rivers?"

"Call me Barry. And I figure Saddiq is just getting started. The two attacks they've carried out prove they can do it, even though we kept the one this morning from being as bad as they wanted. Next time they'll try for something even more spectacular."

"We were talking about that earlier," Jake said. "It

seems to me that after hitting a couple of freight trains, they'll go after a bigger target."

"A passenger train," Gretchen said, nodding. "The same thought had occurred to me."

"There are hundreds of them, from commuter lines to the Amtrak trains that run all across the country. How are we going to figure out which one they're targeting?"

"I have informants all over the country," Barry said. "I'll put the word out again. That led us to the Zaragosas smuggling Saddiq into the country. Maybe we'll get lucky again."

Gretchen said, "I have some sources I can reach out to as well."

Barry glanced over at her with slightly narrowed eyes and said, "No offense, Ms. Rogers, but you don't hardly look old enough to have developed any sources."

"I was recruited into Homeland Security while I was getting my master's in Criminal Justice." She looked back at Jake. "The FBI wanted me, too. And so did the CIA. That was five years ago, and I've done a lot since then."

Jake held up his hands and said, "Hey, it was him who doubted it, not me."

Barry said, "Do you think any of those sources are going to help you? The word's going to get around pretty quickly about you being in trouble with your bosses."

"I'll do what I can," Gretchen said with a shrug. "Anyway, I've gone rogue now, haven't I, just like the two of you? That's liable to make some of my contacts *more* likely to help me."

"Speaking of going rogue," Jake said, "maybe we ought to ditch the truck, Barry, and find a more inconspicuous means of transportation."

"The license plates and all the identifying numbers have already been changed," Barry said. "And after everything that's happened, it's not as noticeable as it was. I think we still blend in all right."

"I get it. You just don't want to give it up."

"I will if I have to. But I think we're okay for now."

The big rig rolled on into the night.

Francisco Zaragosa stalked back and forth across the terrace next to the swimming pool at his estate outside Ciudad Juárez. The night was warm and fragrant with the smell from the gardens next to the terrace. Lights glowed warmly in the trees. The scene was tranquil, even serene.

But rage burned in the heart of Francisco Zaragosa, and all he wanted to do was kill.

Daniel Colón was dead. One of his most trusted lieutenants. Maybe his *most* trusted. And more than thirty other members of the cartel had been killed in the past two days, as well, including that *idiota* Paco Reyes.

All of them wiped out by the same two men.

Those two had disrupted the operation at the freight yard in El Paso, too, and no doubt displeased Bandar al-Saddiq. Zaragosa didn't really care about that, but he had taken money from the man to assist with the operation, and he didn't like being interfered with. He'd been brooding about that all day.

Such defiance could not be allowed to go unpunished.

Laughter made Zaragosa stop pacing and turn toward the house. Angel and two of his girls were headed toward the pool, obviously bent on a nighttime swim.

All three were nude. The girls were fifteen years old—maybe.

"Angel." Zaragosa spoke sharply, although his voice was not loud. "I am expecting a phone call, and until I get it, I must think."

Angel stopped and looked embarrassed, not by his nudity but because he had annoyed his brother. The girls stood there giggling quietly, completely unashamed. Zaragosa could tell by looking at their eyes that all three of them were high as could be.

"I'm sorry, Francisco," Angel said. "We just wanted to swim. It's a warm night."

Zaragosa controlled his temper. He nodded and said, "I know you meant no harm. But take your friends and go back inside, please."

Angel bobbed his head eagerly.

"Come on, girls," he said. They didn't argue with him as he turned them back toward the house and started them on their way by patting their rear ends. They all must have enjoyed that, because he continued patting and they kept giggling.

Zaragosa rolled his eyes and sighed as one of the servants stepped out of the house carrying a specially shielded and scrambled satellite phone.

"The call you were expecting, *señor*."

That was sooner than Zaragosa had anticipated, but at the same time, he was eager to talk to Bandar al-Saddiq.

"*Señor* al-Saddiq," he said into the phone. "I hope you are well."

"I have no time for pleasantries," Saddiq replied coldly. "I would rather talk about those two men who have been such an annoyance to us."

"Jake Rivers," Zaragosa said. "I am unsure of the other man's name. His identity seems to be quite an enigma. But Rivers, I know, is an agent of the American FBI. The other man is probably some sort of federal law enforcement officer, as well."

"His name is Barry Rivers," Saddiq said. "He is the younger man's uncle and is sometimes known as Dog. From what I've been told, he is a somewhat legendary figure in the American intelligence community. Some even doubt that he is real. But he is very real—we've seen plenty of proof of that."

Zaragosa raised his eyebrows even though Saddiq wasn't there to see the reaction and said, "You have better sources of information than I do, it seems."

"I visited with one of my other associates earlier today, and then he contacted me later to give me the names. He assures me that the two men have been dealt with and will no longer interfere with us."

"Dealt with how?" Zaragosa asked harshly.

"Jake Rivers has been suspended from the FBI and placed in protective custody along with his uncle," Saddiq said. "In a hotel, no less. House arrest, I believe they call it. The woman who was at the freight yard with Rivers works for the American Department of Homeland Security and will be prevented from interfering in the future by her superiors."

Zaragosa sat there for a couple of long seconds, then said, "That is all? A slap on the wrist?" His voice rose in anger. "They killed more than thirty of my men! They killed my friend Daniel!"

"And nearly a dozen of my men died at the freight

yard this morning," Saddiq said. "Such an affront to Allah cannot be allowed to stand."

Zaragosa leaned forward and pressed the phone more tightly to his ear.

"What did you have in mind?"

"If you can find out where the two men and the woman are, I believe they should be killed. Not only will it prevent them from possibly interfering with our plans in the future, they deserve death for what they have done already."

Zaragosa didn't actually care whether Saddiq's plans succeeded or failed, but he agreed completely with the man's final statement.

"If they are still in El Paso, I can find them," he declared. "And once found, we can take steps to ensure they will never bother us again."

"I'm glad we see this matter the same way, my friend."

"Allow me to make some other phone calls," Zaragosa said. "I have contacts at all the hotels in El Paso, as well as among the authorities. I can locate them. If you'd care to wait, I'll use another phone . . ."

"I'll hold," Saddiq agreed.

Zaragosa took his regular cell phone from his shirt pocket and made several calls, speaking in quiet but intense Spanish to the people on the other end of the connections.

When he picked up the satellite phone, he reported, "The wheels are in motion. My people will be reporting back soon."

"Very good. We can sit and talk while we wait."

That prospect didn't really appeal to Zaragosa, but he

didn't see a gracious way to refuse. These Islamists were just another bunch of religious fanatics, as far as he was concerned. But their money spent as well as any other.

Saddiq went on, "You are very devoted to your brother, are you not?"

"I promised our mother that I would take care of him," Zaragosa replied. "And he has a good heart. Just not a very good brain. Not everyone is blessed to have both."

"True. And who is to say which one is the best to have, eh?"

Zaragosa didn't want to talk about Angel. He said, "Is there anything I can do to assist you in the future, *Señor* Saddiq? Other than to dispose of those troublesome *Yanquis*, that is?"

"You have done more than enough, my friend. Our operation will be moving on to a different part of the country."

"I have connections from one end of the country to the other," Zaragosa said. He added proudly, "There is nowhere the Zaragosa cartel cannot reach."

Saddiq said, "I will bear that in mind."

Zaragosa's cell phone buzzed in his pocket. He took it out and said to Saddiq, "You will excuse me." He thumbed the phone and said, "*Qué?*"

He stiffened in anger as he listened to what was said. Then he responded in a burst of furious Spanish and broke the connection. His face was dark with rage as he picked up the satellite phone.

"What is wrong?" Saddiq asked. He must have heard Zaragosa's angry response to the news.

"Jake and Barry Rivers and the Rogers *señorita* are gone. They eluded the agents guarding them and disappeared. They are wanted fugitives now."

"But if the law finds them, they will just be arrested again."

"I know," Zaragosa said as he got his anger back under control. "That's why I've given orders that my men must find them first." He shrugged. "Now it may even be easier. We won't have to kill any police or FBI agents. And in the end . . . those three will still die."

Chapter 44

"I think you *wanted* them to get away," Mitchell Cavanaugh said as he stared coldly across the desk at Walt Graham.

It was the next morning, and the two men were in the federal building office Graham had borrowed from the SAC in El Paso. Cavanaugh had stormed in here a few minutes earlier, having just found out that Jake and Barry Rivers were no longer in custody.

"You should have detailed more agents to guard them," Cavanaugh went on. "Better yet, you should have locked them up! You know that Barry Rivers is too much of a . . . a madman . . . to ever cooperate if he doesn't want to!"

"That's right," Graham said, making an effort to keep his own temper under control. "But I had no reason to suspect that Barry wouldn't respect my authority."

"Since when has Rivers respected *anybody's* authority? The man's been a loose cannon for decades!"

What Cavanaugh was saying was true, of course, and Walt Graham knew it. Younger agents might believe that "Dog" was just some intelligence community urban legend, but Graham had been around long enough to know that he existed—and to be aware of all the good he had done over the years. Only a few people in the government knew how much justice Barry had dealt out—and how many evil men he had sent to the hell they so richly deserved.

"Look, I'm sorry they got away," Graham said. "Maybe I should have done more to prevent it." He spread his hands. "What can I tell you? It was a judgment call."

Tight-lipped, Cavanaugh said, "Maybe a man with such questionable judgment shouldn't have such an important position in the FBI."

Graham stood up, leaned forward, and rested his fists on the desk.

"If you want to get me fired, Cavanaugh, you just go right ahead," he said, not even making any pretense of civility anymore. "I'll stack my record as an agent up against anybody's, and I have some friends in high places, too, just like you do."

"I *am* the friend in high places for a lot of people," Cavanaugh sneered.

"Well, if I have to walk away from this job, so be it. Anyway, you don't know how many times I've been tempted to do just that over the years . . . every time I have to deal with some *politician* like you."

The contempt dripped from his voice as he said it.

Cavanaugh went pale. He lifted his hand, pointed a shaking finger at Graham, and said, "You'd better deal with this, and deal with it quickly, or you're going to regret it."

With that, he turned on his heel and stalked out of the office.

Graham straightened, glad to see the pompous Cavanaugh go. After the door had slammed behind the man, Graham lifted a hand and scrubbed it wearily over his face.

He shouldn't be this tired so early in the morning. Maybe it *was* time for him to get out of the game, he told himself. Maybe for more reason than one.

Because honestly, he couldn't swear that he *hadn't* hoped Barry and Jake would slip away. It hadn't been a conscious thought on his part . . . but it could have been in the back of his mind.

That was no way for a man sworn to uphold the law to be thinking.

He hadn't expected the Rogers girl to disappear with them, however. But on thinking about it, he wasn't really all that surprised. He had spent only a short time around her, but that had been enough to tell him that she had the same sort of stubborn, wild streak that ran through Jake and Barry. They were devoted to fighting the bad guys, but they were going to do it their own way.

Well, in the end, if that got the job done . . . and if he was being honest, they might stand a better chance of it, not being bound by rules and regulations . . .

"Wherever the three of you are," Walt Graham whispered, "good luck, and Godspeed to you."

Van Horn, Texas

It was just a little roadside motel, not part of a nationwide chain, but it was affordable, easy off and on from the interstate, and Barry's Kenworth wasn't the only big rig in the lot. It didn't stand out from the other four trucks parked there, either.

Jake and Barry had shared a room. They would have gotten Gretchen the one next door, but there weren't two adjacent units available when they pulled in late the previous night. In fact, they had gotten the last two vacancies.

Jake trusted Gretchen to be able to take care of herself. He had seen ample evidence that she was capable of that. And as far as he was aware, the night had passed quietly and peacefully.

Even so, he was going to be glad to see her again and *know* that she was all right. He lifted his hand and rapped his knuckles on the door of her room.

She opened it a moment later and said, "I'm just about ready to go." She was tucking her shirt into her trousers as she spoke.

"You, uh, look good this morning," Jake said.

She stopped what she was doing and looked at him. "Really? You feel like you have to pay me a compliment?"

"No, I'm just, uh . . . Well, it's the truth."

"No, it's not," she said. "These are the same clothes I had on yesterday, and I don't even have a brush for my hair."

"Doesn't matter. You still look great."

She rolled her eyes and shook her head. "Next time we go on the run together," she said, "remind me to pack a few things first, okay?"

"We can stop and get you whatever you need," Jake said. "You don't have to worry about anybody tracking your credit card, either. Barry's got plenty of cash."

"I'll bet he does. Operators like him, they pick up whatever they come across while they're working, right?"

"Well . . ."

Gretchen held up a hand and said, "Never mind.

None of my business. Let me get my purse, and we can get out of here."

"There's a fast-food place just down the highway. We figured we'd stop there and get some breakfast since the motel doesn't have a coffee shop."

"That's fine," Gretchen said as she came through the door carrying her purse. Her jacket was draped over her arm. "Is this what it's going to be like from now on? Cheap motels and fast food?"

"Life on the run," Jake ventured with a smile.

Gretchen shook her head again and walked toward the truck.

Barry met them there. He nodded to Gretchen and said, "Ms. Rogers. You look—"

"Don't you start," she said.

"Just trying to be polite," he said with a shrug. "But I guess there are more important things. Nobody bothered you during the night?"

"I killed a cockroach in the bathroom. Other than that . . ."

"That's better than some of the vermin we may have to deal with pretty soon."

"What do you mean by that?" Jake asked.

Barry didn't answer until they had all climbed into the truck. Then he said, "I don't think Saddiq will just sit back and wait for us to interfere in his plans again. Once he hears that we're not in government custody anymore, he'll figure that we intend to come after him, so he'll think it's best to eliminate us first."

"Wait a minute," Gretchen said. "How is a terrorist going to find out we're not in custody anymore?"

"He's working with the Zaragosas," Barry explained. "Francisco Zaragosa has eyes and ears all over the

Southwest. If he's paying any attention at all, he knows by now that we're on the loose and ready to cause trouble."

Jake said, "I thought Saddiq just paid the cartel to smuggle him into the country."

"Maybe . . . but teaming up with Zaragosa gives him a lot of soldiers to draw on for help, the way Paco Reyes recruited Carlos Molina to steal that C-4 from Fort Bliss. That makes me think there's a good chance they're still working together."

"Great," Gretchen said. "So now there are probably drug cartel death squads looking for us."

"Could be," Barry said with a grin.

"Well, I suppose that means things can't get any worse, anyway."

"Never say that," Jake told her.

It was two hours earlier in the Pacific Northwest, but Alexander Sherman sounded wide awake as his voice came over the secure, scrambled phone.

"What is it, Mitchell? I assume my pilot got you back to El Paso last night?"

"Yes, yes, no problem with that . . . but I found out this morning that Jake and Barry Rivers have disappeared."

Several seconds of silence from Sherman, then an edge of annoyance had crept into his voice as he said, "I thought the FBI had them in custody."

"They did. They gave their guards the slip. And I'm convinced that Walt Graham, the agent who's taken over the case, intended for that exact thing to happen. Graham has known Jake Rivers for five years and helped him get into the FBI. I have no idea how well or how long he's known Barry Rivers."

"This is unacceptable, Mitchell. Based on everything that's happened so far, those two will crop up again and cause trouble for us."

"I know. That's why I intend to get rid of them." Cavanaugh bit back the curse that tried to escape from his lips. "We've taken the discreet approach for long enough."

Sherman grunted and said, "Too long, maybe. You have men you trust to handle this job?"

"Yes. There are any number of men in the bureau, at Langley, and in other agencies who agree with our objectives. It won't be any trouble to find volunteers to deal with those two, and the woman with them."

"Woman?"

"Gretchen Rogers, the Homeland Security agent who was with Jake Rivers at the freight yard."

"I see," Sherman said. "She's disappeared, too?"

"That's right. I have absolutely no doubt that she's with them."

"Then she'll share the same fate that they do. We can't afford to be sentimental about this, Mitchell."

"That never even entered my mind," Cavanaugh said honestly.

"Very good." Sherman's tone was brisk and business-like again. "Let me know when it's done." He paused. "Those rogues are about to discover that they're on the wrong side of history."

CHAPTER 45

Jake, Barry, and Gretchen holed up at a motel in one of the suburbs of Fort Worth for a few days while all three of them worked their contacts through burner phones and the dark web.

Jake and Gretchen took the law enforcement angle through friends in the FBI and Homeland Security who, while they couldn't exactly be *trusted* completely, were at least unlikely to try to track them down. And with Barry's vast experience at staying off the grid, by following his advice they were going to be almost impossible to find by conventional methods, anyway.

Barry himself navigated a much more shadowy path, since he could reach out not only to people in the intelligence community but also to criminals. Living as Barry had in the past three decades sometimes required more of an amoral, pragmatic approach. As he had phrased it to Jake, sometimes you couldn't clean up the bigger messes without wading into the edge of them.

On a practical level, the motel was a good place to lie low. The parking lot extended around to the back of the property in an L shape, and there was plenty of room back there to leave the truck where it was mostly out of sight.

Across the highway, less than a quarter of a mile away, was a Walmart where the three of them were able to buy clothes and personal needs. Also, there were seven or eight fast-food joints within walking distance, so they didn't have to take the truck out in order to get meals. Gretchen complained some, but Jake and Barry had figured out by now that this was just her nature.

All three of them were looking for increased traffic among suspected terrorist cells or unusual activity involving weapons dealers, especially those who sold explosives. The first two attacks had centered on blowing up railroad tracks, and as Barry put it, "Once terrorists try something that works, they tend to stick with it. That's why you saw a lot of activity directed at air traffic after 9/11. Actually, that goes all the way back to the rash of plane hijackings starting in the seventies. They've targeted trains a few times over the years, and that seems to be what Saddiq's bunch likes."

"Then we should also be on the lookout for any unusual activity involving railroad employees," Jake pointed out. "They had gotten a number of men into that freight yard in El Paso as workers just recently. Any spate of new hires might be worth taking a look at."

"That sounds like something your contacts at the FBI might be able to find out," Gretchen said.

"Like Homeland Security doesn't do domestic surveillance all the time?"

"Well, that's sort of our job by definition, isn't it?"

Barry said, "We'll all look into it, and I'll work the munitions angle extra heavy. Somebody out there knows something that'll start us in the right direction.

We need to just keep on trying to shine some light into the dark corners."

As time went by with no real results, however, their frustration grew. Jake was restless, wanting to be on the move again, and he could tell that Gretchen felt the same way.

Unfortunately, until they had a lead, there was no point in going anywhere else. At least here in North Texas, they were in a good central location and could head for any part of the country if they turned up something to indicate another attack was brewing.

By the time five days had passed, Jake's nerves were stretched almost painfully tight. The gap between the attacks in Nevada and El Paso had been only a couple of days. Whatever Saddiq and Lashkar-e-Islami tried next probably would be a more complicated operation that would take more time to set up, but it could be happening soon.

He was on his way back to the motel from the Mexican food place down the road, walking alongside the four-lane farm-to-market road with a plastic bag holding an order of super nachos each for him and Barry and a plain bean burrito with no onions and no sauce for Gretchen. The road was busy with midday traffic, and so was the state highway down the hill. Out of habit, Jake watched the passing cars for signs of trouble.

Everything appeared normal as he approached the motel. The office was in the front of the complex, which stretched away from the road in an L shape that matched the parking lot. The room Jake and Barry were sharing was at the far end of the L's longer leg, and Gretchen's room was right around the corner.

A car turned into the parking lot as Jake started along the sidewalk that would take him past the office entrance and to the room doors. The driver went all the way to the back corner of the building before pulling into one of the empty parking spaces. Some instinct made Jake stop and turn toward the office window as if he were looking at something there. He lowered his head and hunched his shoulders a little to make his height less conspicuous.

And then he watched from the corner of his eye as five men got out of the newly arrived car, two from the front seat, three from the back. All five looked Hispanic, and despite the warmth of the day, each wore a fairly long coat.

Jake breathed a curse and set the bag of Mexican fast food on an iron bench just outside the office door.

It looked like lunch was going to be delayed today.

He had the Browning Hi-Power under his shirt at the small of his back. Moving his hand to wrap it around the grip, he angled across the parking lot as if going to one of the cars parked on the far side. With his left hand, he took the burner phone he was currently using from his shirt pocket and thumbed a quick text message to Barry, warning him that trouble was about to erupt.

By now, three of the guys from the car had pulled handguns, and the other two were holding sawed-off pump shotguns. One of the guys with a pistol lifted his foot and poised it, ready to kick the room door open.

Barry opened the door before the would-be assassin could kick it open. He said something—Jake couldn't make out the words—and then the 1911 in his hand boomed as he slammed a round into the man's chest.

The .45 slug knocked the man back off his feet. His arms and legs flew out to the side as he skidded across the asphalt.

The men with the shotguns were on either side of the door. By now, Jake had the Browning out and shouted, "Right!" as he aimed at the man on Barry's right. Barry pivoted to take the man on his left.

The Browning and the Colt went off at the same instant, as perfectly timed as if Jake and Barry had practiced it that way. Jake's man went down with his shotgun unfired as the 9mm round drilled through his head and dropped him instantly, like the proverbial puppet with its strings cut.

Barry's man jerked the trigger of his shotgun, but he was already going backward as the weapon boomed and sent a load of buckshot harmlessly into the air. Blood geysered from the man's throat where the bullet from Barry's gun had torn through the big artery there. He would bleed out in less than a minute and was already too weak to pump the shotgun again.

Three members of the death squad were down in as many seconds, but the other two were diving for cover and wouldn't be as easy to kill. As they leaped behind cars, Jake angled sharply toward the motel building, gun up and ready to fire. Barry went the other way along the sidewalk instead of ducking back into the room. The motel's thin walls wouldn't stop high-caliber bullets.

They might have been able to reach cover and trap the assassins in a crossfire, but at that moment Gretchen ran around the corner, holding her gun in front of her. Her momentum took her right past one of the men, who surged up from behind the car that had been protecting him. He grabbed her from behind with his left arm and reached around with his right to chop down with his pistol on her wrists. She cried out in pain and dropped her gun.

The man swung around toward Jake and hauled Gretchen with him, using her as a shield. Jake crouched at the back end of a parked car and grimaced. The gun in the man's hand spouted fire at him.

Jake dived to the asphalt as the slug spanged off the trunk. From his belly-down position, he had a good view of the gunman's feet, as well as Gretchen's. She was struggling in the man's grip, which meant they stumbled back and forth. Jake cursed again as he tried to aim at the moving feet.

Then he squeezed the trigger. The bullet sizzled underneath the car and struck the assassin's left ankle, shattering the bones into millions of pieces. He screamed as that leg went out from under him.

Gretchen must have helped him fall, maybe with a well-placed fist or elbow, because he landed hard and seemed stunned as he writhed from the agony of his wounded ankle.

Jake put him out of his misery with a head shot.

Bouncing to his feet, Jake saw Gretchen scoop up her fallen gun and then fire twice, aiming down into the space between cars where the man had fallen. Jake knew the guy was already dead, but he didn't try to stop Gretchen from letting out her anger. If she wanted to blast his head so that it looked like a broken gourd, then so be it.

A few yards away, the last member of the death squad

let out an incoherent yell of fury as he charged around a car to blast shots at Barry as fast as he could pull the trigger. Barry had to dive and roll as the slugs chewed up asphalt around him.

He came up on a knee as the slide on the guy's gun locked back. The weapon was empty. But he was still barreling down on Barry.

Barry fired. Pure bad luck made the man juke slightly to one side just as Barry squeezed the trigger. The bullet ripped the top of the man's left ear off instead of going right between his eyes as Barry had intended.

Momentum kept him going. He crashed into Barry, bowling him over. The impact sent the 1911 flying out of Barry's hand. Both men rolled across the parking lot.

They came up at the same time. The assassin had dropped his empty gun, but he tore his coat off and reached behind his back to pull a machete from a sheath strapped there.

"Oh, you've got to be kidding me," Barry said in disgust.

With blood gushing down the side of his head from the mutilated ear, the man waved the machete and rushed forward. Barry ducked as the blade swept over his head. He thrust out a leg to try to trip the man, but he leaped over it with surprising nimbleness and slashed back at Barry, who barely avoided the machete this time and had to go to ground and roll in order to do so.

The guy was good with the big blade and must have had quite a bit of experience fighting with it, Barry realized. He sprang up and had time for a glance toward the motel, where Jake and Gretchen appeared to have finished off the other members of the death squad. The two of them hurried toward him, guns in hand.

As the killer came toward Barry, slowly weaving the blade back and forth through the air, Barry said, "You'd better drop that machete and get on the ground, *amigo*. That's the only way you're gonna live through this."

The man spat curses in Spanish at him, then said, "Are you afraid to fight me, *mano a mano*?"

"Nope," Barry said, "but I'm also practical."

He nodded to Jake and Gretchen.

Too late, the machete wielder realized his mistake. He tried to spin around, but two shots rang out, and the bullets ripped through him, driving him off his feet. The machete clattered away. The man gasped a couple of times, then lay still.

The whole town seemed to have gone silent, except for sirens wailing not too far away.

"Grab your stuff, or as much of it as you can in thirty seconds," Barry told Jake and Gretchen. "Time for us to move."

Jake glanced toward the office, where the bag of food was still sitting on the iron bench.

Well, they could always pick up something somewhere else, he thought as he sprinted toward the room.

They made it out of the parking lot and onto the farm-to-market road heading north just in time. Barry looked in the truck's mirrors and saw the flashing lights as the local cops reached the motel. He drove at a deliberate pace, staying right at the speed limit and stopping at the red light beside the town's high school.

Five minutes later, there were fields on both sides of the road. Probably not many big rigs used this route, but Barry was sure that some did. They shouldn't draw too much attention.

Jake was in the passenger seat, monitoring the mirror on that side. He said, "I don't see anybody who might've followed us from the motel. I was worried somebody would feel like he had to do his civic duty and trail us while he called the cops."

"Could have happened, easily enough," Barry agreed.

From the sleeper, Gretchen asked, "What *was* that back there? Who were those guys?"

"Zaragosa cartel death squad," Barry said.

"That's what I thought as soon as I saw them get out of their car," Jake said. "Maybe they came after us because they're still working with the terrorists, or maybe they just want revenge for all their guys we killed over in New Mexico."

"And to let other people know it's not a good idea to interfere in their plans," Barry added. "Like any other cartel, they rule by fear."

Gretchen said, "How did they find us? Law enforcement's been looking for us for several days now—"

"The cartel's got eyes and ears just about everywhere in the Southwest," Barry said. "More and better sources than the Feds, that's for sure, because most of them lead law-abiding lives 99.9 percent of the time. But they have friends or relatives in the cartel, or family back in Mexico, and they want to keep everybody safe. So Francisco Zaragosa puts the word out to watch for a truck like this and three people matching our descriptions, and that word goes far and wide."

Jake said, "It's probably not that bad farther north and east, but Zaragosa will have a network of some sort that stretches all the way across the country."

"That's right. That means we'll still have to be careful once we get to Long Island."

"Long Island?" Jake and Gretchen asked in unison.

"That's where we're headed," Barry said. "While you were gone to get lunch, Jake, I heard back from one of my sources with a tip . . . and I have a hunch it's a good one."

Chapter 46

"One of the things I had my sources look for was un-expected and unexplained turnover among railroad employees," Barry explained a short time later as he drove the big Kenworth through rural North Texas.

In a few miles, they would reach an intersection with a state highway and turn east, Barry had said. Once they were on that road, the truck would blend in even more with all the traffic headed toward Dallas.

"So the tip you got points toward Long Island?" Jake asked.

"The Long Island Rail Road, to be precise," Barry replied. "We know from the way the terrorists got their men jobs at the freight yard in El Paso how they like to operate. Getting away with sabotage like that requires inside men, some to do the actual work and others to protect them. The Long Island Rail Road has had more employee turnover in the past six weeks than any other commuter line in the country."

From where she sat on the bed in the sleeper, Gretchen said, "That seems pretty thin to me. There could be other reasons for the turnover. Maybe a real jackass got promoted and is running people off."

Barry chuckled and said, "That *does* happen from time to time. But this didn't happen all at once. Employees left and new ones came on at a higher rate than normal, but at a fairly steady pace, not suddenly. Just in a shorter period of time than usual. So it's hard to point to a management change and blame it on that. Also, a lot of the new employees work at the same place: the Babylon station on Long Island, one of the busiest stations in the country. Nearly all the passengers who go in and out of that station every day work in Manhattan . . . most of them in the financial district."

"So it would be a big hit to Wall Street if a bunch of them were wiped out," Jake mused.

A grim expression came over Barry's face as he nodded. "It could damage some of the banks and brokerage houses to the point that they wouldn't be able to operate for a while. They might be crippled permanently."

"Well, we can't take a chance on that happening," Jake declared.

"That's why I figured we'd better head in that direction."

From the sleeper, Gretchen asked, "Do I get a vote in this?"

Barry glanced at her in the rearview mirror and said, "Don't start acting like this is a democracy or anything . . . but sure, what do you think about it?"

"If you're right about the next attack happening in New York, shouldn't we try to get there faster than driving?"

"In a perfect world, yeah," Barry said with a shrug. "But all the airports are going to be watched closely. The FBI won't like us giving them the slip the way we did."

"You don't know somebody with a private jet and their own airstrip?" Jake asked.

"Of course I do. I don't want to get anybody else in trouble, though."

"Just Jake and me," Gretchen put in.

Barry grinned and said, "You knew the job was dangerous when you took it."

She frowned.

"Is that a quote from something? It sounds kind of familiar."

"Never mind," Barry told her. "It's before your time. Jake and I will trade off driving. We'll only stop for food and fuel. Doing that, we can be in New York by tomorrow night."

"I could maybe take a turn driving," Gretchen offered.

Jake turned his head to look at her.

"How many big rigs have you driven?" he asked.

"Well . . . none. But how hard can it be?"

"We'll handle it," Barry said. His flat tone of voice ended the discussion.

Jake looked over his shoulder as Gretchen. She glared, then stuck her tongue out at him. Jake just laughed, shook his head, and faced forward again.

They headed east, getting back on the interstate and taking it to Texarkana, then on into Arkansas and Tennessee. Every couple of stops, Barry changed the license plates and the identification numbers. There was no logo painted on the doors, so they didn't have to worry about being identified from that.

They angled northeast at Knoxville and traveled on into Virginia through the night, cutting across a corner of West Virginia as the sun came up. A bit of Maryland, and then through Pennsylvania as the day began to get warmer.

Gretchen had gotten a decent night's rest in the sleeper, and Jake and Barry had switched back and forth between the captain's chairs in the cab, one driving and the other dozing. That wasn't the same as actually stretching out and resting, but Jake didn't feel too weary as he took his latest stretch at the wheel and piloted the truck through rolling, wooded hills toward New York City.

"Before we get there, I'll call my contact and find out where he wants to meet us," Barry said. He had slept for a bit but was awake now. "And I'll take the wheel again before we're in the city."

"You think I can't handle New York?" Jake asked as he glanced over.

"I imagine you can, but I've got a lot more experience steering a big rig through city traffic. Decades more, in fact."

Jake couldn't argue with that. He shrugged and said, "All right. Let me know when you want to make the switch."

"You're still all right out here on the highway."

"Thanks," Jake said dryly.

They continued rolling along for a few more minutes, then a frown creased Jake's forehead. His eyes began to dart from the road ahead to the side mirror.

Barry, as observant as ever, noticed and asked, "Something wrong?"

"Two cars have been taking turns being in front of and behind us for the past fifty miles or so," Jake said. "One tails us for a while, then goes around us, while the other one—the one that was in front—drops back behind."

"You're sure it's the same cars?"

"Yeah, once I got an inkling of what's going on, I watched them pretty closely. The dark blue Ford is behind us now, three cars back. That silver Toyota four cars ahead is the other one."

"How many men in each?"

"I can't tell. The windows are tinted fairly dark in both vehicles."

From the sleeper, Gretchen asked, "What's going on up there? You guys sound very serious all of a sudden."

"There may be another hit squad getting ready to make a move on us," Jake said.

"From the cartel?" Gretchen's response was swift and tense.

"Don't know who they are, but my gut tells me they're looking for trouble."

Barry popped open the console between the seats, reached into it, and brought out the 1911. He turned his head and said to Gretchen, "I showed you how to get into the gun stash. Open it up and break out an AR-15. I suppose you know how to use one?"

"I've fired one," she said. "I wouldn't say I'm an expert."

"If there's trouble, stick to that handgun you're used to. But have the rifle handy in case you need it, or one of us does."

While Gretchen was doing that, Jake studied their surroundings. Along this stretch of road, the divided highway had a wide median between the eastbound and westbound lanes, with enough trees growing in the parklike area that the view from one set of lanes to the other was somewhat obscured. The road made gentle curves between thickly wooded hills, too, and in some of those places, the hills themselves completely cut off Jake's sight of the westbound lanes. It was beautifully picturesque—but it was also a good place for an ambush.

Traffic had been heavy in some of the towns they'd passed through, but that wasn't really the case out here on the open road. At the moment, there was only one car between the Kenworth and the Toyota, which had slowed down and prompted the others to pass while Jake and Barry were talking, and none between the big rig and the Ford. They were almost boxed in, Jake realized.

He wondered how far it was to the next exit.

He didn't get to find out. At that moment, the Toyota in front braked again, and the crossover behind it swung out into the left lane and accelerated past. Jake pressed down on the gas and picked up speed, too, but as he started to move over, thinking maybe he was wrong and the Toyota and the Ford actually *didn't* contain any enemies, the Toyota confirmed his hunch by swinging over and going down the middle of the road, partially blocking both lanes.

"That's it," Barry said as Jake hit the brakes to keep from plowing into the sedan. "They're not our friends, that's for sure."

"I can knock them out of the way," Jake said.

From behind him, Gretchen protested, "You can't do that. They might just be jerks, not killers."

Jake glanced in the side mirror.

"The Ford's closing in on us," he reported. "And

you'd have to be a pretty big jerk to stick a gun out your car window like the passenger in the front seat is doing."

The gun looked like a machine pistol of some sort, and even more so when flickering flames suddenly spurted from its muzzle. Jake didn't think the bullets would penetrate the armor plating that covered almost the entire truck—except for the bulletproof glass in the windows—but being shot at bothered him. It always had, going all the way back to his army days.

"Gun up here, too," Barry said. "We don't have to worry about them being civilians. Go ahead and bump him off the road."

Jake gave the Kenworth gas and sent it surging ahead. The Toyota's driver saw that and accelerated, too. Their car was faster than the truck and gained enough ground to avoid being rammed.

The Ford was hanging tight behind, with the passenger still firing ineffective bursts at the truck.

All three vehicles were racing along at around 80 mph now. Over the rising roar of the engine, Jake said, "We'll start catching up to slower-moving traffic soon. You know these guys won't be careful not to hurt any innocents!"

"I think they've shown enough to prove that," Barry replied. "And here comes more proof."

A guy hanging out the rear driver's-side window on the Toyota opened fire. Bullets sprayed and whapped across the truck's windshield but didn't have any effect other than to mar it slightly.

"Damn it!" Jake reached down into a pocket on the door beside him and pulled out the Browning Hi-Power. He rolled down the window, and then, steering with his right hand, he stuck the left out and opened fire with the pistol.

Jake's shots came close enough to make the man in the Toyota duck back into the vehicle. He directed a couple of bullets at the back window, but it failed to shatter.

"Looks like we're not the only ones with bulletproof glass," Barry said.

Gretchen said, "What if the ones behind us shoot out our tires?"

"Not gonna happen," Barry told her. "They're run-flats, but not ordinary run-flats. You'd have to hit one of them with a bazooka to do much damage."

"I wouldn't put it past them to *have* a bazooka," Jake said grimly. "Or some RPGs, more likely. Remember, we've run into those before in this mess."

"I'm not likely to forget," Barry said. "What are they—"

He didn't finish the question because it was obvious what the men in the Toyota were doing. The silver car leaped ahead, going well over 100 mph now, and quickly opened a large gap between it and the truck.

"I don't like the looks of that," Jake said.

"Neither do I," Barry said.

That concern proved to be justified. The driver of the Toyota suddenly slammed on the brakes. The car's rear end slewed to the side. It came to a stop across the two lanes of the highway about a quarter of a mile in front of the Kenworth.

"They can't stop us like that," Jake said as the men from the car scrambled out. "We'll just knock it out of the way."

One of the men was at the trunk. The lid popped up, and he reached inside to take something out—something big and bulky enough that he needed another man to help him.

"RPG?" Jake asked tensely.

"No, I don't think—Good Lord!" Barry exclaimed. "That's a blasted Stinger missile!"

CHAPTER 47

The Stinger was a surface-to-air missile, designed for ground forces to be able to shoot down low-flying airplanes and helicopters. The launcher was bigger and bulkier than that of a rocket-propelled grenade, and usually two-man crews were assigned to handle it.

But one man could lift the launcher to his shoulder and steady, aim, and fire it if he needed to. The two men who'd just gotten the SAM out of the trunk of the Toyota had no trouble sending the missile sizzling down the highway toward the Kenworth with Jake at the wheel.

The big rig's armor would stop bullets, but even that was no match for a Stinger. In the split second Jake had, he wrenched the wheel to the left as hard as he could and sent the truck bouncing and bounding into the grassy median.

He knew that a Stinger's guidance system homed in on the heat from its target's engine, but he hoped there wouldn't be time for the missile to make a course correction.

There wasn't. The Stinger screamed past the Kenworth's cab and missed its rear end by no more than a foot.

The driver of the Ford roaring up from behind didn't

have a chance to react like Jake had—and probably didn't have Jake's lightning-fast reflexes to begin with. The missile slammed into the car's grille and detonated.

A ball of fire completely engulfed the Ford. Jake and Barry both saw the explosion as Jake wrestled the big rig into a turn that took it back toward the highway. The force of the blast flipped the blazing hulk of the car into the air. It turned over a couple of times before crashing down on its top.

From the sleeper, where she was hanging on for dear life, Gretchen cried, "What was that?!"

"We just almost got blown up," Barry told her. "Missed it by a whisker."

"And the bad guys behind us weren't so lucky," Jake added. "Now to deal with the rest of that bunch."

He sent the Kenworth barreling toward the Toyota stopped across the highway. The men who had gotten out of the car either didn't have another Stinger or didn't think they would have time to use it. Instead, they used the vehicle for cover and blasted away at the onrushing truck with handguns and semi-automatic rifles.

The bullets were like gnats trying to stop a charging bull.

Jake aimed the Kenworth straight at the car. He was still fifty yards away when the would-be killers' nerve broke. Still shooting on the run, they dashed out from behind the Toyota.

That gave Jake his first good look at them. He'd expected the assassins to be more soldiers from the Zaragosa cartel, but if they were, they dressed oddly for drug dealers and killers. All four men who'd gotten out of the car wore dark suits and ties and looked more like government bureaucrats.

That made him think twice about bulldozing right over them with the truck. Might be a good idea to try to take at least one of them alive, he decided, so that the prisoner could be questioned. Instead of veering toward them as he'd planned, he turned the wheel and circled around them as they ran along the highway's shoulder.

Another turn and a hard push on the brakes brought the truck to a stop across both lanes of the highway, two hundred yards past where the Toyota had stopped. The four men were halfway between the vehicles. They stopped and hesitated like they couldn't decide which way to run next.

One of them dashed into the median. Jake didn't know where he was going, other than away from here. The other three started back toward the Toyota.

Jake glanced past the silver sedan and saw that several cars had stopped on the shoulder in the distance. It appeared that their drivers had spotted what was left of the burning Ford off to the side of the road, as well as the Toyota and the big rig parked crosswise in the highway.

That was more than enough to tell them that something was wrong, prompting them to pull over and try to figure out what was going on. A couple of them had their emergency flashers going to alert the traffic coming up behind them. One man got out of his car and waved his arms in the air, signaling for other drivers to stop.

Jake was glad to see that. He didn't want a bunch of civilians cluttering things up.

"I'll get the one who split off from the others," he said as he threw the door open.

"We'll try to round up the other three," Barry said.

He had noticed the same unexpected attire Jake had and added, "They don't look like gangbangers."

Jake didn't take the time to explain that the same thought had crossed his mind. He just jumped down from the truck with the Browning in his fist and took off after the man who had fled into the median.

The man was still in sight, heading toward a rugged, rocky, brush-covered hill that blocked the view of the highway's westbound lanes. If he reached the little crag, he might find some pretty good cover, and he had a big enough lead that Jake didn't know if he could stop him in time.

Of course, Jake could stop and try to wing the guy, maybe shoot a leg out from under him, but at this range that would be difficult, even for an excellent shot like Jake. And you never could tell where a bullet would go. It might sever an artery and quickly prove fatal.

So Jake kept running, hoping to cut down the lead with his long legs.

The man started climbing the slope, ducking behind an upthrust of rock. Jake was expecting what happened next. His quarry stuck a gun out from behind the rock and took a shot at him.

Jake veered sharply to the left, then back to the right. He didn't know where the bullet went, but it wasn't close enough for him to hear it.

He fired the Browning on the run and saw a shiny streak appear on the rock, not far from the head of the man he was after. The bullet coming that close made the guy jerk back, as Jake hoped it would.

A couple of long strides sent him up the hill and kept the rock between him and his quarry. The man had thought to use it as cover, but it actually protected Jake now. He charged up the hill, keeping the stony upthrust on his right.

He reached the top of it, leaped out onto the rock itself, and saw the man trying to scramble away. Jake launched himself in a diving tackle.

His shoulder caught the man in the small of the back as his arms wrapped around the guy's legs. The impact brought the man down, hard. He cried out in pain.

But that didn't stop him from twisting around and lashing out with a kick aimed at Jake's head. Jake got his right shoulder up and took the kick there. It landed with enough force to make that arm go numb all the way down.

The guy tried snapping another kick at Jake's face. This time, Jake caught his ankle with his left hand and stopped the kick before it could land. He twisted hard, and the guy had to roll over onto his belly to keep his knee from snapping.

Jake pushed himself up, landing with both knees in the small of the man's back. The man screamed and arched the top half of his body off the ground. Jake looped his left arm around the man's neck and tightened his grip as he pulled up.

The man pawed feebly at the forearm pressed across his throat like an iron bar. After a moment, his hands fell away from Jake's arm, and he went limp.

Jake maintained the choke hold for a little longer, just to make sure the man actually was unconscious, but not long enough to risk killing him. When he let go, he stood up and shook his right arm, trying to get the feeling back into it more quickly. It was already starting to tingle as the momentarily deadened nerves came back to life.

He was about to turn and see how Barry and Gretchen were doing in their pursuit of the other would-be assassins when a flurry of gunshots sounded from the direction of the highway.

Chapter 48

"Hand me that AR-15 I had you get out," Barry said to Gretchen as they got ready to go after the other fleeing members of the hit squad. "And that extra magazine."

She handed them over. "Are you going to shoot them?"

"Those guys?" Barry shrugged. "I'll give them a chance to surrender."

He stepped down from the truck, brought the rifle to his shoulder, didn't seem to aim at all, and squeezed off three shots in the space of an indrawn breath.

One of the bullets knocked the side mirror off the Toyota's passenger side. The other two starred the front passenger window.

The three men stopped in their tracks, turned, and returned the fire with their handguns. They were still within range for the pistols to be effective, but they must have been pretty shaken by everything that had happened. Their shots fell well short, chewing up the pavement.

Barry took a little more time before triggering his fourth shot. One of the men spun off his feet, dropping his gun and grabbing his thigh where Barry had just drilled him.

The other two started running again. Barry shot a leg out from another one, who tumbled to the ground in an awkward roll. The remaining man made it to the Toyota, circled it, and jerked open the rear door on that side.

What he brought out and set on the car's roof made a huge racket—like a hundred hammers striking a hundred nails almost but not quite in unison—and it kept going. Barry grabbed Gretchen's arm and ran for the safety of the truck as bullets tore up the highway almost at their feet.

The hail of lead from the full-auto weapon wasn't able to follow them as they darted around the Kenworth's front end. Its armored cab blocked that death storm.

"That's a machine gun!" Gretchen exclaimed. "Like, a big machine gun!"

"Yeah," Barry agreed.

"How are we going to stop him? If we set foot out of the cover of this truck, he'll shoot us to pieces!"

"Let me get into the sleeper. I've got something that'll deal with him."

With slugs still hammering into the armor plates, Barry climbed into the cab. He stayed low. He believed the bulletproof glass would withstand the continued pounding of the full-auto fire, but nothing would hold up forever, no matter how strong.

When he emerged a couple of minutes later, dropping to the ground beside Gretchen, he held a long-barreled revolver that prompted her to ask, "What in the world is *that*? It looks like an Old West revolver, only the giant-sized version."

"That's pretty much what it is," Barry told her, raising his voice to be heard over the racket. "It's based on the Colt Single Action Army, only it fires a .600 Nitro Express round instead of a .45. An Austrian company made a few of them. With as big and heavy and awkward as it is, it's not really good for much except a few very special circumstances." He looped his right thumb over the hammer and drew it back to full cock. "Like this one."

With that, he waited a couple of seconds until the assassin's weapon fell silent. Had to be changing magazines. Barry stepped out from behind the big rig's front end, leveled the revolver in a two-handed grip, and fired.

The Toyota rocked on its shock absorbers as the huge slug struck the passenger-side window, blowing it inward, smashing through the driver's-side window, and plowing a fist-sized hole through the body of the machine gunner.

Through the now blasted-out windows, Barry saw him flop on the ground behind the car. The way he went down told Barry that he wouldn't be getting back up again.

Barry lowered the massive gun and said, "That guy won't tell us anything. Let's go check on the other two."

He set the revolver on the floorboard inside the truck and picked up the AR-15. Taking the lead, he moved toward the two men whose legs he had shot out from under them. Gretchen was close behind and slightly to one side with the Glock held ready.

"Here comes Jake," she said.

Barry glanced toward the median and saw his nephew trotting toward them with a motionless figure draped over his left shoulder. Given Jake's size and strength, an unconscious man didn't seem like too much of a burden.

One of the men Barry had shot was out cold, too. From the looks of the bloody welt on his head, he had hit it and knocked himself out when he fell.

The other man was still clutching his thigh and moaning as he writhed around on the ground. A pistol lay a few feet away from him. He glanced at it as Barry and Gretchen came up to him.

"I know what you're thinking, *amigo*, and I wouldn't try it," Barry advised him. "Anyway, I'd say there's a good chance if you let off the pressure on that leg wound, you'll bleed out pretty quick."

The man spewed rage-filled obscenities at them, but he didn't reach for the gun.

He was in his late thirties, probably, with curly brown hair and a cleft chin. The all-American sort, although the way he was cursing them, he didn't sound that way.

Gretchen lowered the Glock slightly, stared at the man on the ground, and exclaimed in obvious disbelief, "Jason Harwell!"

Barry's eyes narrowed in surprise as he looked over at her and asked, "You know this guy?"

"I ought to," Gretchen said. Her voice shook a little. "I've worked with him before. He's an agent for the Department of Homeland Security."

CHAPTER 49

Jake came up, carrying the man he had captured, in time to hear what Gretchen said. Her statement shook him, but he didn't let it show.

Instead, he lowered the unconscious man to the ground and said, "How about this guy? Do you know him, too?"

Gretchen swallowed hard.

"I do," she said. "His name is Alex Durant. He works for the TSA. We were on the same task force for a little while."

The Transportation Security Administration was part of the Department of Homeland Security, Jake knew, a different branch from the investigative arm Gretchen worked for—or *had* worked for, since she probably didn't have a job anymore after throwing in with him and Barry.

The thought had crossed Jake's mind earlier, when he first got a look at the hit squad, that they looked like government bureaucrats.

He hadn't expected to discover that his wild idea was actually right.

"Take a look at the other guy who's knocked out," Barry told Gretchen with a bleak note in his voice.

The wounded man she had called Jason Harwell snarled and said, "I'll save you the trouble. He's Dave Clemons. You remember him, Rogers?"

"Yes, I do." Jake could tell Gretchen was fighting to keep her voice from shaking even more. "Who . . . who else was with you?"

"Steve Frazier."

Gretchen closed her eyes and sighed. Her face was drained of color now.

"You know him?" Jake asked gently.

"He brought me coffee once, during a meeting."

"And you killed him!" Harwell burst out. "This . . . this traitor here shot him with that cannon!"

"I'm not a traitor, son," Barry said flatly. "Whoever told you that has sold you a bill of goods."

"Maybe not a traitor," Harwell responded through clenched teeth, "but you've been running around murdering people all over the country. You've gone rogue, mister, and you need to be put down like any other mad dog!"

"Does that go for me, too, Jason?" Gretchen asked.

"You were a good agent, Rogers. But these men are a danger to the country! They don't follow orders—"

Jake said, "When it comes down to following orders or saving lives, I'm going to do the right thing."

"Following orders *is* the right thing," Harwell spat. "The people running the government know what they're doing. You can't just . . . just let normal people decide things. They're too stupid! I mean . . . look who they've been voting for."

"Yeah," Barry said, "the people got in the way of your Deep State train and derailed it a few elections ago, didn't they? You've been trying to get it back on the tracks ever since, but with only limited success." Barry shook his head. "Too bad for you that you don't control *all* the news anymore."

Gretchen said, "Wait a minute. That whole Deep State business people have been talking about for years is just an urban legend. There's not some sort of secret . . . cabal . . . inside the government bent on running everything."

"The hell there's not," Barry snapped. "It's cropped up in agency after agency. Those Alphabet Boys just love to take orders like good little Nazis."

"Hey!" Jake said. "I work for the FBI, remember? At least, I did. I'm one of those Alphabet Boys."

Barry shook his head and said, "Not really. That's why you're on the run now, and statist bottom-feeders like this slug are trying to kill you."

Gretchen stood there shaking her head slowly, struggling to accept what was obvious. It went against everything she had believed. But the bloody evidence was right in front of her.

She took a deep breath, moved a step closer to Harwell, and lifted her Glock to aim it at his face in a two-handed grip. His eyes rounded with surprise and more than a little fear.

"Who sent you after us, Jason?" she said. "I want a name."

He spewed another torrent of profanities, interspersed with a few uses of "slut" and "whore" that made Jake's jaw tighten. He stepped forward and said, "Mister, I'm about to plant my boot in the middle of your face."

"Back off, Jake," Gretchen said. "This is between me and Jason. And he's going to tell me what I want to know . . . or maybe I'll shoot him in the other knee."

"You don't have the—"

Sneering, Harwell was about to name the requisite part of the male anatomy when Gretchen shifted the Glock, squeezed the trigger, and put a round into the dirt no more than two inches from his left knee. He jerked, which made him scream from the pain in his already wounded right leg.

"Now, Jason," Gretchen said as the echo of the shot faded.

"C-Cavanaugh."

"Mitchell Cavanaugh?" Barry asked sharply. "He's DOJ."

"Doesn't matter. He . . . he's coordinating things . . . it's like a task force, although they're not calling it that. He's brought in people . . . from several different agencies. Their job is . . . to run you to ground."

"And kill us," Jake said.

"Those weren't . . . explicit orders for everybody. Just . . . some of us."

"The deepest of the Deep State," Barry said. "The ones Cavanaugh can trust to commit murder."

"Our own people," Gretchen murmured.

Barry looked at her and said, "It's been going on for a long time. Since the 1990s, anyway. Remember what happened to anybody who was . . . inconvenient . . . or posed a threat to those in power? Plane crashes, 'muggings' gone wrong, three shots to the back of the head getting an official verdict of suicide.

"The more things change, the more they stay the same. The monsters doing that crap get a free pass from the news and half the country. That inner circle's grip on things has been shaken in the past ten years, but it hasn't come loose yet. Not completely. And they're going to hang on until they've drawn their last breath—"

Barry stopped abruptly, shaking his head.

"Rant's over. What's important is that you know the truth now, Gretchen. Cavanaugh's unleashed the full power of the government on us, and that means local law enforcement won't know any better and will be after us. And the Zaragosas still want our heads, too."

Jake said, "So all we have to do is dodge all that while we find out what those terrorists are planning and stop them from killing a bunch more innocent people."

"Yeah," Barry said, "that's—"

He didn't finish the sentence because at that instant, a shot cracked. Gretchen made a little noise, dropped her gun, staggered to the side. She looked down in shocked horror at the crimson flower of blood blooming on the front of her shirt.

CHAPTER 50

Barry reacted instantly, turning, bringing the AR-15 to his shoulder, and squeezing the trigger all in one smooth, swift move. The rifle cracked.

The man Harwell had identified as Dave Clemons jerked as the bullet bored through his brain and snapped his head back.

Clemons had regained consciousness, listened to the interrogation of Harwell long enough to know what was going on, and found the strength to raise his gun and fire the shot at Gretchen. He would never do anything else, though.

Jake leaped to catch Gretchen as her knees buckled and she started to fall. As his arm went around her, another shot sounded close by. Harwell had let go of his wounded leg and lunged toward his gun, snatching it up and triggering as he angled the barrel toward Jake.

The wind-rip of the bullet was loud in Jake's left ear as it passed close by. An instant later, the AR-15 in Barry's hands barked again. The close-range shot turned Harwell's all-American face into a bloody, ugly mess.

Gretchen sagged in Jake's grip and moaned.

"You're all right," he told her, because that was what

you said to people who'd just been shot. "You're gonna be all right."

She looked up at him, her eyes wide with pain and shock, and tried to say something. But although her lips moved, no words came out. Her eyes rolled up.

For a second, Jake thought she was gone. He could still feel her breathing, though, as he cradled her limp form against him.

"We have to get her to a doctor!" he told Barry.

"I know. Let me give you a hand. We'll put her on the bed in the sleeper." Barry shifted the rifle he held. "Let me take care of that other one."

He pointed the AR-15 at the man Jake had captured. Alex Durant, that was what Gretchen had called him. Jake knew Barry was about to shoot him.

"Wait."

"We can't take a chance on the guy waking up and trying to kill us like the others did."

"But they *were* trying to kill us. He's unconscious. This would be an execution."

Barry looked like he wanted to ask what was wrong with that, but then he jerked his head in a curt nod.

"I'll secure him."

He took zip ties from his pocket, went to Durant, and fastened them around the man's ankles and wrists after pulling Durant's arms behind his back.

Then he hurried over to Jake and took Gretchen from him. She was unconscious now. Jake stepped up into the cab, reached down, and took her from Barry to carry her into the sleeper.

Barry lifted Durant and dumped him into the truck, as well, handling him like a sack of feed and not being too gentle about it, either. He went into the sleeper, where Jake was kneeling beside the bed and working to stop the bleeding from Gretchen's wound.

"It looks worse than it is," Barry said over Jake's shoulder, "*if* the bullet missed the lungs. You can tell it didn't hit her heart or the spine."

"There's no exit wound," Jake reported. "So the slug's still in there somewhere, and there's no telling where it bounced around."

"We can't go digging for it . . . but I know somebody who can."

Jake glanced up at him.

"A doctor?"

"Yeah, a really good one." Barry frowned in thought. "Lives about an hour away from here, or at least he did the last time I was in touch with him."

Jake looked at Gretchen and said, "I don't know if she has an hour."

"She's tough. She'll make it. And we need to be gone from here."

"You're right," Jake said with a sigh. "I'll do what I can for her. You get us out of here."

"My thoughts exactly," Barry said.

The next hour seemed longer—a *lot* longer—to Jake than it really was. Using the first aid supplies in Barry's truck, he stopped the bleeding from Gretchen's wound, taped a rough dressing in place, and gave her shots of painkillers and antibiotics.

But he had no way of knowing whether she had internal bleeding, and if so, how bad it was. Judging by how pale and drawn her face was, he didn't think the situation was good.

After leaving the scene of the shoot-out, Barry had taken the first exit off the interstate and stuck to back roads and smaller highways as he drove through this mostly rural area of Pennsylvania. There were bound to be APBs out on the truck by now. Even with the armor plating, the big rig had taken enough damage that it really looked beaten up, which made it distinctive.

After a while, Jake called up to the cab, "Are we getting anywhere close yet to this doctor you know?"

"Not much longer," Barry replied.

"I assume he won't feel duty bound to report a gunshot wound?"

"I think that's safe to say."

A few minutes later, Barry turned off the county road he had been following onto a paved driveway that ran between a pair of hedges. The driveway was a long one, at least a quarter of a mile. It ended in a parking lot with room for a dozen vehicles. Barry pulled the truck to one side of the lot.

A concrete walk led from the parking lot across a well-kept lawn to an old farmhouse, with a newer brick building set to the right of it.

"We're here," Barry told Jake, who already had his arms under Gretchen's shoulders and knees as he prepared to lift her from the bed.

With Barry's help, Jake got her out of the cab and turned toward the building with her in his arms. He paused when he saw the sign on the wall that read McIntire Animal Clinic and Hospital.

"Wait a minute," Jake said. "You brought us to a *veterinarian*?"

"Still a doctor," Barry said. "And don't be so quick

to jump to conclusions. I texted Doc that we were on our way."

Indeed, there were no other vehicles in the parking lot, and in the middle of a weekday like this, at least a few clients should have been there with their sick pets. Unless whoever ran the place had canceled all the existing appointments.

A man came out of the farmhouse. Jake could tell that he'd been watching for them. The stranger was a tall, middle-aged, muscular black man with a closely trimmed beard. He moved like a soldier, so Jake wasn't surprised when Barry said, "Hello, Captain."

The man made a slight gesture as if swiping that away.

"That was a long time ago," he said. He went on, addressing Jake, "I'm Caleb McIntire. You'd be Jake. I'd shake hands, but you've got yours full right now. Bring the young lady inside."

Jake carried Gretchen up the steps to the porch. As he did, a couple of dogs pushed out through the screen door, a good-sized golden retriever and a shaggy little miniature schnauzer with just about the happiest expression Jake had ever seen on a dog's face.

"Max, Clifford, get back," McIntire said in a firm but kind voice. The two dogs responded instantly, moving over to the side of the porch to give Jake plenty of room. Their tails wagged with great enthusiasm.

McIntire held the door open and told Jake, "Down that hall there, first door on the right."

Jake nodded. He assumed this was the veterinarian's residence, with the brick building next door housing his office and practice.

There was a hospital bed in the room Jake entered,

along with several pieces of medical equipment such as IV stands, a blood pressure monitor, and a pulse oximeter. From the looks of the setup, Gretchen wasn't the first human patient McIntire had treated.

Carefully, Jake placed Gretchen on the bed. She stirred a little, making a small sound of pain, but she didn't regain consciousness.

Jake stepped back, looked over at McIntire, and said, "Iraq? Afghanistan?"

"Yes," McIntire said.

From the doorway, Barry said, "If there's been a hot-spot anywhere in the world in the past thirty years, odds are that Doc has been there. Isn't that right, Doc?"

"Both of you get out and let me get to work," McIntire said.

That seemed to Jake like good advice to follow.

CHAPTER 51

"So . . . is he a real doctor, or a vet?"

"He's both," Barry answered Jake's question as they sat in the parlor of McIntire's house. "Doc Caleb finished top of his class in med school, was a surgical resident at one of the best hospitals in the country . . . and then enlisted. He didn't just stay at a hospital on one of our bases, though. He wanted to be out in the field." Barry shrugged. "I suppose he saw more than he expected out there. He came back, said he didn't want anything more to do with humans, and got his veterinary degree and license. But I guess he couldn't stand the peace and quiet. I met him in Central America, where he was working as the medical officer for a private contracting company."

"Mercenaries, you mean," Jake said.

"Call it whatever you want. Point is, there's not much he hasn't seen or can't handle when it comes to the damage human beings can do to each other. Gretchen's in good hands, I promise you."

They were quiet for a few moments. Then, to distract himself from worrying about Gretchen and to satisfy his curiosity, Jake asked, "How did he wind up back here taking care of animals again?"

"Finally burned out on that other life for good, I suppose. We've never really talked about it. I don't normally pry into another man's life. All I know for sure is how good he is at what he does."

"He's patched you up before?"

"Once or twice," Barry replied with a smile.

Jake nodded, then frowned in thought.

"Wait a minute. You said the two of you met in Central America. I thought you operated in *this* country."

"For the most part, that's what I've done. But now and then somebody would come to me with a job outside the country, and I'd take it on . . . if I believed it was the right thing to do."

"Do you even remember all the places you've been and all the things you've done?"

"I don't even *try* to remember all that," Barry said. "The past is over and done with and never coming back. And all it's good for is meeting some people you might need to connect with again later . . . like the doc in there."

They fell silent again. Time stretched out. Jake thought about how many trees and how much brush there was on McIntire's property. That made the buildings and the parking lot difficult to see from the road. It wasn't likely anybody would spot the truck.

That kept him from thinking about Gretchen for a while, but really, it didn't take long for her to fill up his thoughts again. He had known her for only a few days, and he had a hunch that they were in fundamental disagreement about some things, yet despite that, she took up a sizable amount of room in his mind.

Jake didn't want to think too much about what that might mean. Not while she was lying in there, maybe on the verge of death, maybe gone already . . .

McIntire came back into the room. Jake and Barry both stood up hurriedly.

"Take it easy," McIntire advised them in his deep, solemn voice. "I believe there's a good chance the young lady will be all right."

Relief flooded through Jake, but wariness tempered it only a few seconds later.

"A good chance, you said. What are the percentages?"

"Percentage is a mathematical term," McIntire said, "and mathematics is an exact science. Medicine isn't. But I'm guardedly optimistic about her survival. That's the best I can do." His formal attitude unbent a little as he went on, "I was able to extract the slug without much trouble. It missed all the vital organs, but there was enough internal bleeding for it to be a problem. I cleaned that up, tied off the bleeders, and closed the wound. The blood loss is what I'm worried about, but I've given her a transfusion, have IVs hooked up for plasma, antibiotics, and anti-inflammatories, and her condition is stable. Now she'll get some rest, and we'll see what happens. Barry, I don't believe you told me her name."

"It's Gretchen," Barry said. "Gretchen Rogers."

"Is she in the same line of work as you, or is she an innocent bystander?"

"Does that make a difference?"

McIntire shook his head and said, "Only in satisfying my curiosity."

Jake said, "She was an agent for the Department of Homeland Security."

"Was?" McIntire repeated with an arched eyebrow.

"After everything that's happened, she probably doesn't have a job there anymore."

"She started keeping unsavory company," Barry added dryly. "Us."

McIntire snorted and said, "I knew who you meant. Do I need to know the details?"

"Not really. I can tell you, though, that no matter what you might hear, Jake and I are the good guys."

"I never doubted that. The way Clifford and Max seemed glad to meet you was enough for me to go by. If there's one thing I've learned, it's to trust dogs."

Jake asked, "When will Gretchen be able to travel again?"

McIntire frowned at him and said, "She shouldn't move much for a couple of days. And she won't be able to run around and keep up with you two for a month."

"We don't have that long to wait," Barry said. "We'll have to leave her here, Doc."

Jake was about to object, but he knew his uncle was right. With another terrorist attack looming, one that might be carried out at any minute, they had to get on the move again and check out the lead Barry had turned up on Long Island.

"I thought maybe that was going to be the case," McIntire said, nodding. "It won't be a problem."

"Taking care of her won't interfere with your practice too much?"

"I have a partner who can handle most of the regular patients, and she can help me out with Ms. Rogers, too, if need be."

"You can trust this woman?" Jake asked, maybe a little more sharply than he meant to.

McIntire smiled and said, "I hope so. We're engaged to be married."

"Oh. Well, in that case, I'm sorry."

McIntire made that waving-off gesture again and said, "Don't worry about it. And even if it meant closing down the vet clinic for a while, I'd do that. Your uncle saved my life more than once, you know."

"I didn't know," Jake said, "but I'm not surprised."

Barry said, "We're going to have to ask another favor of you, Doc. Is there a place where we can leave my truck, and maybe a vehicle we can borrow?"

McIntire looked surprised. He said, "You're going to leave that big rig of yours, Barry? I thought you were too attached to it for that."

"I don't like to," Barry said with a sigh, "but enough people are looking for us now that even with all the things I can do to make it harder to recognize, the odds of somebody spotting us in it are just too high. We need to move fast, and we can't afford to be looking over our shoulders all the time."

McIntire thought about it for a moment, then nodded.

"Follow the little dirt road to the left of the house," he said. "It goes back to a barn that dates from the days when this was a working farm. There's room in there for the truck, and nobody would have any reason to go poking around. It'll be safe and out of sight. As for another vehicle, you can use my old pickup. I've hauled a few hogs and goats in it, but these days I pretty much confine my practice to small animals."

"We don't want to cause any extra trouble for you—" Jake began.

"It's no trouble, son. If it was, I'd say so."

Barry stood up. "That's settled, then." He extended his hand. "We can't thank you enough, Doc."

McIntire shook hands with both of them and gave Barry the keys to the pickup. Jake said, "Can we see Gretchen for a minute before we go?"

"That should be all right. She's sleeping, though, so don't expect her to talk to you."

Jake nodded and followed McIntire into the room where Gretchen was lying in the hospital bed. The sheet was pulled up over her breasts, but her shoulders and arms were bare after McIntire had had to cut her clothes off her to get to the wound. She had two IVs going, one in each arm.

Barry and McIntire stood back while Jake went to the side of the hospital bed. Gretchen was still pale, but Jake thought her face had a little more color in it now than the last time he'd seen her.

"You rest easy," he told her quietly. McIntire had said she couldn't talk, but maybe, somewhere deep inside her, she could hear him. "We'll take care of this."

He reached out tentatively with his left hand, closing it around Gretchen's right hand.

Jake couldn't see it, but over by the door, McIntire

looked at Barry and cocked an eyebrow. Barry nodded. It was clear to both of them that Jake had fallen for Gretchen, whether Jake had come around to understanding that himself or not.

After a moment, Jake let her fingers slip out of his and turned to the other two men.

"Let's go," he said to Barry. "The sooner we take care of this mess, the sooner we can get back here."

CHAPTER 52

Dr. Caleb McIntire's pickup was ten years old and as nondescript as could be, so it was exactly what Jake and Barry needed as they drove across a couple of towering bridges, through New York City, and onto Long Island.

Barry looked at the city in the rearview mirror and said, "I don't think I could ever get used to being around that many people all the time."

"You don't like people," Jake said.

"That's not entirely true. There are a few I like. It's just that most of the ones I run into in my line of work are pretty sorry specimens of the human race."

Jake couldn't argue with that. He had encountered the same thing as an FBI agent. Like the rest of the law enforcement community, it wasn't a profession designed to make anybody optimistic about the future.

Jake was driving while Barry did the navigating. His contact was a transit cop who worked for the Long Island Rail Road, he explained between telling Jake which turns to make, and worked mostly out of a station called Babylon, about forty miles out on the island.

"Lots of passenger traffic through there, according to

Hank," Barry said. "It's supposed to be one of the busiest train stations in the whole country. And nearly all of them are commuters who work in the city."

"Sounds like a perfect target for that sorry bunch of terrorists," Jake said. "With the tension those earlier attacks have caused, if Saddiq pulls this off, the nerves of everybody who rides a train will be so tight they're liable to snap." He paused. "Of course, we don't know for sure that this is the next target. It's only a possibility, based on the information you've turned up. Like Gretchen said—"

He stopped short. A scowl appeared on his face. Barry saw that and said, "I know you're worried about her. I am, too. But she'll be all right. She's in good hands."

"Medically, maybe. But what if one of those blasted death squads, either from the government or the cartel, tracks her there?"

"Then the doc will deal with them," Barry said confidently. "You don't think anybody could just waltz in there, do you? If I hadn't let him know we were coming, we might have had an unexpected and unpleasant welcome."

"How's that possible?" Jake asked. "He has to deal with the public to run that vet clinic. He can't have booby traps all over the place."

"You'd be surprised. Just figure that if anything comes up, Doc McIntire will find a way to deal with it, and Gretchen will be all right." He pointed at an intersection ahead of them. "You're going to want to turn right when you get to that red light."

Jake did so, and the road he followed took them

through what seemed at first glance to be a picturesque fishing village. Long Island Sound was visible in several places, and they passed nice housing developments arranged along the banks of canals.

Just looking at the place, it was hard to believe that the population was well over two hundred thousand. The people must be really packed in, but somehow, the village didn't give the appearance of it.

"We're going to your friend's house, right?" Jake said.

"Yeah. We've been messaging back and forth, and he said to meet him there instead of at the station. That'll give him the chance to give us the lay of the land first."

That sounded like a good idea to Jake. He made a couple more turns, following Barry's directions, and then pulled up in front of a small but neatly kept frame house with a postage-stamp front yard in a neighborhood of similar houses. He could see the waters of the sound several blocks away.

The street was empty at the moment. At this time of day, most of the people who lived around here were at work.

A short driveway led to a closed one-car garage. Jake and Barry walked past a mailbox with the name GLENNON on it and started up the drive toward a concrete walk, which jogged over to the tiny front porch.

"Hold on a minute," Barry said.

"Something wrong?"

"I want to send Hank another message."

Jake gestured toward the house and said, "You can just tell him whatever it is."

"Nah. Besides, I want a picture of the place."

Barry lifted the phone in his hand and snapped a picture of the pleasant little cottage.

This was definitely strange behavior on his part, and as Jake realized that, he felt the skin on the back of his neck prickle. His uncle never did anything unless there was a good reason for it.

Barry's thumbs moved with the speed and efficiency of a millennial who'd been to Starbucks one too many times that day. As he typed in the message he was going to send, he spoke the words out loud. Maybe it was for Jake's benefit, although Jake didn't understand why.

"Hey, buddy, nice place you have here. A far cry from that dump in Lisbon where we met."

Barry pressed the icon to send the message.

Less than ten seconds later, the phone dinged, and Barry read the reply.

"Thanks, come on in." Barry's thumbs flashed again with his response. "Just a second, I forgot something in the truck." He inclined his head toward the pickup and said, "Give me a hand, Jake."

Still puzzled but sure now that something was wrong, Jake turned away from the house and followed Barry toward the pickup parked at the curb.

The middle of his back crawled as if a target were painted on it—which might not be far from the truth.

"Let me guess," Jake said quietly. "You didn't meet this guy in Lisbon."

"Not hardly," Barry replied. "The first time we ran into each other was in Hawaii. I doubt if he's ever been to Lisbon, or anywhere else in Europe."

"Somebody's got a trap set for us in there. They realized that your friend was poking around in things he shouldn't have been, and they're guessing that he's connected with you."

"That's the way I sized it up when I realized those

text messages I was getting were coming from his phone, but not necessarily from *him*," Barry agreed.

"What tipped you off?"

Barry shook his head and said, "Nothing in particular. Just being careful. I should have checked before we ever got here. Maybe I'm getting too old for this life, Jake."

"I don't believe that for a second," Jake declared. "Think how much worse things would have been in El Paso if you hadn't figured out what Saddiq was planning. And I'll bet you're right about what's going to happen here, too."

"And soon," Barry said grimly. "It could be they're getting ready to strike any time now, and that's why they want us out of the way."

"What are we going to do?" They had reached the pickup. Barry opened the driver's door as Jake spoke. "Should we dive in and get out of here, maybe head straight to the train station?"

"Hank may be in there, in the house," Barry replied, "and there's no telling what they might have done to him. I'm not going to just abandon him to animals like Saddiq's men, or those cartel butchers, or those weasels from Washington, whoever it is that's trying to ambush us."

Jake grunted and said, "That's what I was hoping you'd say. How do we play it?"

"Take your phone out, act like you got a call, and stroll on down the sidewalk while you're pretending to talk. Wave your free hand around a little like you're arguing with somebody. I'll go on up to the front door, so they'll be watching me. You can go around the house next door and cut through to the back, then come in that way."

"Why not do it the other way around? If you go up to

the front door, you're just asking for them to open fire on you through it."

"I don't think so. I think they'll try to get me inside before killing me so as not to attract any attention. But that's the way we're going to do it, anyway."

Jake looked at Barry for a second, saw the determination in his uncle's eyes, and sighed and nodded.

"All right," he said. "I think I'm getting a call right now."

He took his phone out of his shirt pocket, pretended to thumb the screen, and held it to his ear.

"Yeah, this is Jake," he said. "Oh, hey, man, how are you? Were you able to find out that stuff I asked you about?"

He strolled along the sidewalk away from the pickup as if distracted by the imaginary conversation.

"See you inside," Barry called after him, reinforcing the idea that neither of them was suspicious about the situation. Without turning around, Jake waved a hand in acknowledgment and continued walking away.

Barry closed the pickup door and turned to the driveway, going up it again to follow the walk to the front porch. As he approached the door, every instinct in his body told him that he was being watched. He didn't show it, though. Anyone observing him would believe that he was relaxed, not expecting trouble.

Barry hooked his right thumb in the front pocket of his jeans so he could easily sweep his hand around to his back and pluck a Smith & Wesson 9mm from his waistband, where he had tucked it before getting out of the pickup. He raised his left hand and knocked on the door.

A muffled voice called from inside, "Hey, come on in. It's unlocked."

Barry reached down and turned the knob. He swung the door back and stepped across the threshold. He had never been here before, but his keen eyes instantly took in every available detail. He was in a foyer that turned into a hall running toward the back of the house. There was a small living room to his right; to his left was a wall with a few framed photos on it, and up ahead a door that opened into a dining room.

Barry took another step into the foyer, and as he did, he rammed his shoulder against the door and drove it back against the wall, pinning the man who had been waiting behind it to ambush him. Barry had smelled the man's rank scent as soon as he moved across the threshold.

As he pinned the man with the door, he also reached behind him and snatched out the 9mm. Just in time, because another man appeared in the hallway ahead of him, swinging up a full-auto machine pistol.

Barry triggered two swift shots before the would-be killer could bring the weapon to bear. The slugs punched into his chest and knocked him back a step but didn't put him down. He was still a threat as long as the machine pistol was in his hands. Barry shifted his aim and drilled him between the eyes.

That dropped the man to the hallway floor. The gun clattered down beside him.

Barry kept his shoulder pressed hard against the door while he was taking care of the man in the hall, so the lurker behind it was still pinned against the wall. As soon as the man in the hall was down, Barry stuck the 9mm's barrel around the edge of the door at head height and fired twice more.

Then he stepped quickly away from the door. The man who'd been behind it collapsed, his head a bloody ruin, and his fall pushed the door toward Barry, who hooked it with his toe and kicked it shut.

No need to risk any passersby glancing in here and seeing what was going on.

He had three rounds left in the pistol, but a couple of extra loaded magazines were in his pocket. He advanced slowly toward the back of the house, tracking the gun from side to side as he did so.

A man whirled out of the dining room and slashed a curved scimitar at his head.

With his mouth wide open in a shout of rage and the scimitar clutched in a two-handed grip, he looked like something out of the Arabian Nights. Barry had just enough time for that thought before he put a bullet into the wide-open mouth and blew the back of the guy's skull out.

A gun thundered somewhere close behind Barry.

He felt the heat of the bullet on the left side of his neck. It came close enough to leave a little burn, but that wouldn't stop his momentum. Barry twisted around, saw another ambusher pointing a big revolver at him, and dropped to one knee as he fired twice. The bullets punched into the man's gut and doubled him over.

The man was trying to lift the revolver again, though, stubbornly doing his best to carry out his mission and kill this infidel. The slide on Barry's gun was locked back, empty. He could have dropped the magazine and slapped another one in, but instead he used his right hand to scoop up the scimitar the last guy had dropped.

As he came to his feet, Barry swung the curved blade over his head and brought it flashing down.

The scimitar split the man's skull, cleaving it in two almost down to its base. He collapsed in a loose-limbed welter of arms, legs, blood, and brains. Barry wrenched the blade free.

The back door crashed open and Jake rushed in, the Browning held ready in his hands. He stopped short, staring at Barry, who stood there in the hall with an empty gun in one hand and blood dripping from the scimitar he held in his other hand. Jake exclaimed, "Good Lord!"

"This may not be all of them," Barry said. "We need to clear the rest of the house." He added grimly, "And then we need to find Hank."

CHAPTER 53

The rest of the house was clear of enemies, and Hank Glennon was in the garage.

Perhaps surprisingly, he was still alive—but not for long.

Glennon, a burly, mostly bald man with a fringe of reddish-gray hair around his ears, was tied onto a kitchen chair sitting in the middle of a large pool of blood.

He had been worked over with a blade, obviously tortured for information. But some of the cuts had gone too deep, and he was on the verge of bleeding out.

Somehow, he found the strength to lift his head and smile at Barry, though.

"Knew you'd . . . be here," Glennon rasped. "You get . . . those lousy . . ."

"We got 'em," Barry assured him.

"I di'n't . . . di'n't tell 'em . . . a thing."

"I know that, Hank. You always were a stubborn cuss." Barry leaned closer, locking his gaze in on his old friend's eyes and not seeing, for the moment, the damage that had been done to Glennon's face. "They're going to derail a train at the station, aren't they?"

"Dunno . . . what the plan is . . . lotsa new guys . . .

working there . . . M-Middle Eastern . . . guys." Glennon managed a hollow laugh. "It's only that . . . so many new . . . at once? Made me . . . suspicious."

"What's the busiest time at the station?" Jake asked.

"That's your . . . nephew . . . you told me about?"

"Yeah," Barry said. "He's got the right idea. They'll hit when they can inflict the most casualties."

"Six . . . six-twelve . . . train from . . . the city . . . always packed . . ."

"Barry, it's 6:03 now," Jake said tensely.

"I know. Hank, we'll call 911—"

"Don't waste . . . even that much time . . . Just go . . ."

Glennon's head fell forward. The breath that eased out of him had a rattle of finality to it.

"I'm sorry, Barry," Jake said.

"Time to be sorry later. We've already been here too long."

Barry was right about that. No matter how deserted the neighborhood appeared, there were bound to be people around, and they would have reported the gunshots inside Glennon's house. The cops had to be on their way already.

Jake didn't hear any sirens when he and Barry left the house, but that didn't mean anything. The responding officers could be running silent. They got in the pickup, Jake taking the wheel again. He drove off without seeming to be in a hurry because that would draw attention, too.

But with every second that passed, his nerves grew tauter. The time for that crowded commuter train to roll in to the Babylon station was drawing steadily closer.

Barry gave him directions to the station in a voice that showed the same strain Jake was feeling.

"How far away are we?" Jake asked after several blocks and a couple of turns.

"A mile, maybe two."

"And the traffic will be worse around the station. Barry, we're running out of time."

"We'll make it, we'll make it—"

The sudden roar of an explosion in the distance interrupted what Barry was saying.

Barry grimaced and pounded the pickup's dashboard with a fist.

"It's not time!" he said. "We still had a few minutes." His face settled into bleak lines. "They jumped the gun for some reason. Maybe those guys who were waiting at Hank's house were supposed to report back in, and the rest of the bunch panicked when they didn't."

Jake's foot came down harder on the gas pedal, and the pickup leaped forward.

"Maybe we can still help," he said.

"Yeah, we don't know how bad it is yet."

A ball of black smoke had begun to rise in the distance, though, so it didn't look good. Jake didn't need directions anymore. He just headed toward the scene of the obvious disaster.

A fire truck came screeching around a corner ahead of them and straightened up to race in the same direction. Jake saw the flashing lights of other emergency vehicles. He and Barry were about to be surrounded by cops, a situation which normally they would have tried to avoid.

Under the circumstances, though, it seemed unlikely

that any of the law enforcement officers responding to what had to be an outpouring of desperate calls from the train station would pay any attention to them.

They were fairly close—it looked like within three or four blocks of the smoke, which was even thicker and blacker now—when Barry suddenly leaned forward and said, "Turn around."

"What?"

"Turn around!"

Jake had no idea what was going on, but Barry usually knew what he was doing. Jake hit the brakes and hauled the pickup into a skidding U-turn after waiting a second for traffic going the other direction to clear.

"What's this about?" he asked his uncle as he started to accelerate again.

"See that blue van up there, three cars ahead of us?"

"Yeah."

"Follow it!"

Jake sped up even more and said, "Sure, but why are we chasing it?"

"When it met us going the other way, I noticed that it's packed full of guys who look like they'd be friends with Bandar al-Saddiq. They seemed pretty excited about something, too. Giddy, almost."

Jake's eyes narrowed as he glanced over at his uncle.

"Most people would call that racial profiling," he said.

"Yeah, well, most people are full of crap these days, instead of the common sense that they used to have. If you've got a wolf snarling at you all the time, it doesn't take much deep thought to realize that it means you harm. And if you've got a van full of men laughing when hundreds of people are dying, there's something wrong."

Jake said nothing, which Barry seemed to take as disagreeing.

"Just call it my gut," Barry snapped. "My instincts haven't led us wrong so far, have they?"

Jake had to admit that they hadn't. Barry had a remarkable track record for finding the bad guys. He'd always had that ability, going back for decades now.

Jake worked his way through the traffic, gradually getting closer to the blue van. They were leaving the smoke behind now, and while it galled him not to be helping out at the scene of . . . whatever had happened back there . . . he had to admit that it might be more important at this point to catch the murderers responsible for it.

The fact that they might be up there not far ahead of him, joyously celebrating their destruction and wanton slaughter of innocents, just made him want to catch up to them even more.

If Barry was right and that van was full of terrorists, they were probably flush with the success of their attack and not that observant about what was going on around them. They might not notice that Jake was tailing them. He kept moving up until he was directly behind them.

The road was two lanes each way, and up ahead at the next intersection was a traffic light that had just turned red.

"Pull up beside them," Barry said.

Jake nodded. He steered the pickup into the left-hand lane, slowed down a little to make sure the light would catch him, and braked to a stop next to the van.

The pickup was tall enough that Barry had no trouble looking into the van. He glanced over at the driver in apparent nonchalance. He could see the man in the passenger seat as well, and also a couple of men who leaned forward into the gap between the front seats to talk excitedly. They were young Middle Eastern men in their twenties, and all of them seemed extremely animated and happy. They were even exchanging high fives.

Then the driver must have felt Barry's gaze on him, because he looked over and an angry scowl replaced his grin. He said something quickly to the others, and they turned hostile stares toward Barry and Jake as well.

Barry lifted his hand in a mocking wave as the light turned green. The van spurted ahead as the driver tromped the gas.

"That's them, all right," Barry said.

"We don't have any proof of that," Jake pointed out.

"Fall back some and keep following them. Maybe we will."

Jake did as Barry said. Trailing the van brought them to an area along the sound, outside of Babylon, where there weren't many houses. Sand dunes topped with coarse grass ran down to the water. A few old farmhouses and fishing cottages were visible here and there.

The van turned off the highway onto a dirt road that led toward the water and one of those ramshackle old buildings. Jake and Barry cruised on past.

"The next road you come to that leads toward the water, take it," Barry said.

"We're going to sneak up and see what those guys are up to?"

"That's the idea."

Jake nodded. Half a mile farther on, another dirt road turned to the left, in the direction of Long Island Sound. From the lack of tire tracks, no one had driven along it for quite a while. Jake pointed the pickup along the road, and in less than a minute, they spotted an old fishing shack at the end of it.

Jake didn't think anybody was likely to spot them out here, but he parked where the shack partially obscured the pickup anyway. As he and Barry got out and checked their weapons, he looked along the sound toward Babylon. The column of smoke was still visible, as were flickering red and blue lights, a veritable sea of them. Things were bad there, very bad.

And there was a very good chance the men they were closing in on were responsible for that tragedy.

"We'll stay low going through the dunes," Barry said. "They're not likely to spot us."

"They'll have guards posted, if they're the ones we're after," Jake pointed out.

"Yeah, but how watchful are they going to be right now? They're flush with success. They've just struck a blow against the Great Satan, and they believe they've gotten away with it. They probably figure that nobody knows what they did. They'll celebrate a little, then move on to the next act in their cowardly little drama."

"You seem to know this type pretty well."

"I've been killing them for a long time," Barry said.

CHAPTER 54

The sun was far down in the western sky, making Jake and Barry's shadows long as they stole through the grassy sand dunes toward the shack where the van had gone. When they were close enough, they dropped to hands and knees and crawled up the last dune so they could peer over its top toward the shack.

Fires were still burning in Babylon, they saw, and a pall of smoke covered the sky in that direction. Jake felt his guts tighten at the sight of it. He tried not to think about how much death and destruction the men in that ramshackle building in front of him had caused today.

The shack had a porch built onto it that faced the water. Several men came out of the house onto the porch, talking excitedly and laughing. Jake couldn't hear them well enough to understand the words, but he thought it was probably Pashto.

"You catching any of that?" he whispered to Barry.

"A little here and there. Enough to tell that they're talking about that commuter train derailing when it reached the station and how many infidels they killed today. They're talking about some friends of theirs, too, who must have been killed in the attack. They're actually jealous because they figure those fellas are in paradise right now, each of them enjoying the favors of seventy-two virgins."

Jake's hands clenched into fists. He had never been able to comprehend what sort of sick, twisted mind could genuinely believe that murdering innocent people was the best way to get into heaven.

If it hadn't been for the heat, he wouldn't have minded being in hell when those killers got there, just so he could see the looks on their faces when they realized where they actually had ended up.

"You see any guards?" Jake asked.

"No, but there's probably somebody inside watching the road. A man might be able to approach the place from the side, though, if he stayed down and moved slow and easy so the grass didn't wave around too much. You want to give that a try?"

"Sounds good to me. What are you going to be doing?"

"Oh, I thought I'd take a stroll along the beach," Barry said.

Jake glanced over at him and frowned.

"What are you talking about?"

"There's nothing unusual about somebody walking along the water in the evening. They'll figure I'm a tourist, or somebody staying up at that place where we pulled in."

"Unless they're just paranoid enough they go ahead and shoot you."

Barry shook his head and said, "They've pulled off their big plan. It would be stupid to call attention to themselves now."

"Do you think this is the end of it? Derailing that

commuter train was what they were after all along, and the other attacks were just practice?"

"I don't know," Barry mused. "We don't have any idea how bad the casualties are, but it could be the worst attack since 9/11. I just have a hunch they're not finished, though." His voice hardened. "That's why we should try to take one of them alive, so we can question him. And after what the rest of the bunch did to Hank, I won't be worried about how far we have to go in order to get the info we need."

Jake couldn't help but agree with that.

"Maybe we can find out," Barry went on, "but first we have to get our hands on one of them. They'll be watching me, so they won't be likely to see you sneaking up on the shack. When you get there, go in from the front and take care of any resistance you find. Then we'll have them in a crossfire."

Jake nodded in understanding. He said, "I'd tell you to be careful, but that would be just a waste of time, wouldn't it?"

Barry chuckled and said, "More than likely."

He slipped off to the right through the sand dunes toward the water. Jake lost sight of him after a moment.

A couple of minutes went by. The celebration on the shack's porch was getting louder and more raucous. The terrorists were probably debating how many women and children had died at the train station, Jake thought bitterly.

Then Barry came into sight, strolling along the edge of the water about fifty yards from the shack. He was carrying his shoes in his left hand and had the legs of his trousers rolled up a couple of turns. He looked about as harmless as a man could look.

Jake wasn't sure, but he could have sworn he faintly heard Barry whistling the theme song from *The Andy Griffith Show*.

The talk on the porch trailed off as the men caught sight of Barry. Knowing that their attention was on his uncle now, Jake slid over the top of the dune, bellied down in the coarse grass, and began crawling toward the shack.

When he heard Barry call, "Howdy, fellas!," Jake lifted his head enough to look in that direction. Barry was waving as he walked toward the house with a big friendly grin on his face. "Fixing to have yourselves a clambake?"

One of the men said something as Jake resumed crawling toward the shack. Again, Jake couldn't make it out.

Barry responded, "Oh, I'm renting a place just along the water here. Thought I'd do some fishing. You boys look like fishermen."

The man on the porch spoke again. This time the words had a definite unfriendly tone to them.

"Sorry, boys," Barry said. "Didn't mean to interrupt whatever it is you're celebrating. You just carry on and pretend I'm not here. Say, though, seems like something mighty big happened in town. I saw a lot of smoke and heard a bunch of sirens earlier. You fellas happen to know anything about that?"

Jake was close enough now to hear one of the men on the porch say angrily, "Go away, old man! Do not bother us."

Jake had reached the shack. He crawled to the front corner, stood up, and pressed his back against the wall.

He slid a hand behind him and pulled out the Browning from where he had tucked it at the small of his back.

After a minute of careful listening, during which he didn't hear anyone breathing or moving around in the front part of the shack, he slipped around the corner. A long step brought him to the front door. He grasped the knob with his left hand. It turned, and he eased the door open.

The shack had only two rooms, not counting a tiny bathroom in one corner. The room Jake had just entered had four bunks in it, as well as several bare mattresses lying on the floor. The members of this terrorist cell had really been crammed in here. Just beyond, through an open door, was a combination kitchen and living room.

Barry had been wrong about a sentry being posted. The men were so high on their bloodlust, so confident they were immortal and invincible, that they had let down their guard completely. All of them were outside on the porch except for one burly, bearded man rummaging around inside an open ice chest sitting on the table in the kitchen. He had his back to Jake, who approached him soundlessly.

However, some instinct must have warned him, because he suddenly jerked his head around to look over his shoulder. His eyes widened in surprise as he caught sight of the big American.

Jake twirled the Browning in his hand so he could strike with the butt as he lunged at the terrorist and lashed out. The man moved with surprising speed for his size, darting his head to the side so that the blow Jake intended to knock him unconscious scraped along above his ear instead.

Even so, the gun butt struck the man with enough

force to make him grunt in pain and stagger against the table. That impact knocked the ice chest to the floor with a loud crash.

The man kept his feet by slapping his right hand on the table and bracing himself. He swung his left arm in a sweeping, backhanded blow at Jake, who had to duck to avoid it.

The racket from the falling ice chest attracted the attention of the men on the porch. They yelled angrily as they looked into the kitchen and realized that one of the hated infidels had invaded their temporary sanctum.

They had to turn their backs on Barry to look into the shack, and that was a mistake. He dropped the shoes he'd been carrying, pulled up his shirt, and yanked the 1911 out of his waistband, triggering three fast shots. The heavy .45 caliber slugs smashed into two of the terrorists from behind and knocked them off their feet.

After the things Barry had heard them saying, the way they had laughed about all the innocent people they had killed, he didn't hesitate for even a second before shooting those monsters in the back.

The other two yelled in alarm and jerked their heads back and forth, unsure what to do. They tried to claw out pistols they had stuck in their pants. A couple of old wooden deck chairs sat on the porch, and the men frantically dropped behind them, hoping the chairs would provide some cover for them.

Inside the kitchen, Jake grappled with the big terrorist and tried again to wallop him with the Browning's butt to knock him out. He had a feeling that Barry was likely to kill the others, so if they wanted to have a prisoner to question, it was up to Jake to get him.

The man shrugged off the effect of the blow to the

head pretty quickly, though, and while he wasn't as tall as Jake, he probably weighed a few pounds more. The T-shirt he wore revealed thick slabs of muscle on his chest, arms, and shoulders.

He landed a punch to Jake's jaw that rocked him back a step. That gave the man room to grab the wrist of the hand that held the Browning, ram his shoulder into Jake's chest, and drive Jake back against the wall.

The shack was pretty flimsily built. The wall quivered under the impact. If they ran into it like that again, they might both crash through it.

Jake got his left arm between him and the terrorist and brought it up so that the heel of his hand lodged under the man's chin. He shoved upward, hard, levering the man's head back and forcing him to give ground. He tried to twist his other hand free so he could slash the gun across the guy's face, but the terrorist was hanging on for dear life.

Outside, Barry fired twice at one of the chairs where the men had taken cover. The flimsy wood was no match for the .45 slugs. They ripped right through it and the man's body, one in his chest, one in the throat. He dropped his gun and started flopping like a fish on the porch as blood sprayed from the wound in his throat. It spattered across the planks like crimson paint shaken from a paintbrush.

The fourth man was able to get a couple of shots off in Barry's direction. One missed wildly, but the other came close enough that Barry heard the flat *whap!* as it passed through the air mere inches from his ear. He dove forward onto the sandy ground to make himself a smaller target.

Another bullet struck the ground in front of him and

kicked grit in his face, stinging his eyes and making them water. He grimaced and blinked in an attempt to clear his eyes faster. Instinct made him roll to the side. More slugs marched through the space where he had been a second earlier.

Coming to rest on his belly again, he found that his vision was good enough to aim and fire at the last man on the porch. The bullet struck the chair back, drove on through, and blasted a chunk out of the terrorist's skull. The man toppled out from behind the chair and sprawled on the planks, not moving again.

So much for taking any of these terrorists alive, Barry thought. He hoped Jake was having better luck inside the shack.

While the big man he was battling was still a little off balance, Jake lowered his head and butted him in the face. The man howled in pain and stumbled back even more as blood welled from his broken nose. Jake bull-rushed him and forced him back until the man ran into the table again. The table slid, coming up against the counter where the kitchen sink was, and when it couldn't move anymore, Jake's momentum drove the terrorist down on top of it, on his back.

That finally knocked loose the man's grip on Jake's wrist. With his gun hand free again, Jake whipped the Browning's butt across the man's jaw, raking a long gash in the bearded flesh.

While the man was stunned, Jake grabbed the front of his shirt and heaved him up, then shoved him forward so that his head dangled in the sink. Jake twisted the faucet handle and sent water gushing down into the terrorist's face.

That made the man start to thrash, but Jake clamped

his left hand around the guy's throat and bore down on it with most of his weight, keeping him pinned there under the steady stream from the faucet. The water went up the man's nose and filled his mouth and throat. Desperation made the man fight, but Jake had him in a bad position. He couldn't get any leverage to throw off Jake's weight.

Jake kept it up until the man stopped struggling and slumped, apparently senseless. Lifting him again, Jake let him slide to the floor, where he landed in a sodden heap, gasping and retching. Air wheezed through the misshapen nostrils of his broken nose.

From the doorway, Barry said, "Looks kind of like a waterlogged rat, doesn't he?"

Jake glanced toward his uncle and asked, "What about the others?"

"All dead," Barry replied.

That wasn't surprising. Jake had been vaguely aware of gunshots outside and had figured Barry was dealing with the other men in his usual lethal fashion.

"I'm glad you got one of them alive," Barry went on. "Let's see what he's got to say for himself."

He used a foot to roll the man onto his back, then hunkered on his heels next to him. Barry slapped him lightly on both cheeks.

"Time to wake up, my friend. Wake up and talk."

The man coughed and sputtered, turned his head to the side and spewed water from his mouth. Once he'd stopped doing that, he spewed what Jake assumed were curses instead, although he didn't know enough of the language to recognize any of the words.

"He's cussing you out, isn't he?"

"Oh, yeah," Barry said. "It's safe to say he's not a happy little mass murderer anymore."

Barry took out the 1911 and rested the muzzle between the man's eyes. From that angle, the barrel must have looked as big around as a cannon.

"I said it's time to talk. What's the next part of Saddiq's plan?"

Jake saw a tiny flicker of surprise in the man's eyes. Maybe these terrorists hadn't known that they were aware of Saddiq's presence in the United States and had figured out that he was the mastermind behind what was going on.

Barry put more pressure on the gun and said, "Considering what you fellas did today, I don't have a whole lot of patience. Now, I know you understand English, so tell us what we need to know." He paused. "If you don't talk, I don't have a single reason in the world not to blow your evil, twisted brains out."

"You Americans," the man rasped. "Sick, disgusting, immoral . . . so arrogant . . . so proud of your eagle . . . you will learn . . . and then you will die!"

Jake frowned and said, "Eagle? What's he talking about? The rest of it's just the usual blustering—"

Jake stopped short as Barry raised the gun away from the prisoner's head and made a curt gesture with it.

"Somebody's coming," he said.

Chapter 55

"Check the door," Barry went on as he pressed the 1911's muzzle to the terrorist's forehead again.

Jake straightened and hurried into the other room. A glance out the door told him that two cars were approaching along the dirt lane from the highway. He could see them in the dusk even though they didn't have their headlights on.

"We have company," he told Barry as he turned his head. "Two vehicles."

"Cops?"

"I don't think so. I don't see any light bars on them. Of course, they could be unmarked."

"Most of the cops around here, if not all of them, will still be in town at the scene of that attack, probably all night. Somebody might've heard gunshots out here and reported them, but it's not that likely."

"So whoever's coming, they're friends of these guys?"

"Maybe," Barry said. "Could be different unfriendlies, though."

He lifted the gun again before, without warning, chopping down with it. The weapon thudded against the prisoner's skull.

Barry got to his feet and went on, "Cut some strips

from this guy's shirt and tie his hands and feet. We don't want him running out on us when he wakes up."

Jake tucked the Browning away, pulled out his pocket knife, and did as Barry said. Once he had the unconscious terrorist's wrists and ankles tied securely, he cut two more strips of cloth from the man's T-shirt. He wadded up one of them and forced the man's jaws apart so he could cram it in the guy's mouth. He tied the gag in place with the other strip and left the man lying there.

Barry was in the other room by now. He had closed the door most of the way and was looking out through the narrow gap he'd left. With his jeans and dark shirt, he was hard to see in the gathering gloom inside the shack. The fading gray light from outside didn't penetrate much in here.

"Both cars stopped about fifty yards away," he reported. "Guys got out of both of them. I couldn't tell for sure how many, but they seemed pretty full."

"So eight or ten, total," Jake said.

"Yeah. And once they were out of the cars, they split up and spread out."

"Definitely not cops, then. They could be members of the same terrorist cell as these guys, but more than likely they're either more of Cavanaugh's Deep State killers or else they're from the Zaragosa cartel."

"That's the way I see it, too," Barry agreed. "No matter who they are, they have us outnumbered at least four to one, and with the water behind us, there's really nowhere for us to go."

"They figure to surround the shack, close in, and finish us off." Jake paused, then added, "I wonder where they picked up our trail again."

"There's no telling. The cartel and the government,

they've both got eyes and ears all over the place. We live in a surveillance state, and have for a long time."

Jake sighed and shook his head.

"Do you think this country will ever get back to being what it once was?"

"I don't know," Barry said, "but I plan to keep fighting for that ideal, however long I still have any fight in me."

That seemed like a pretty worthwhile goal to Jake, too.

He looked around the room and, in the last of the light, spotted a trunk of some sort shoved underneath one of the bunks. He got hold of the handle on one end and dragged it out.

"What's that?" Barry asked.

"Let's find out."

Jake unfastened the catches and lifted the lid. He couldn't help but laugh at the sight that met his eyes.

The trunk was full of guns, most of them full-auto machine guns, by the look of them.

Barry let out a low whistle and said, "I hope those ammo boxes down at the end are full. Our odds just got better."

"Yeah, I'd say so, too," Jake replied as he reached into the trunk and lifted out one of the weapons. It already had a full magazine inserted in it. "We still have the problem of this shack being almost as flimsy as balsa wood, though."

"And that's why we can't just hunker down here. We're going to have to take the fight to them. The light's getting bad out there, which is an advantage for us. As long as we stay together, we know that anybody else we run into is an enemy."

Jake handed the machine gun to Barry and picked up

another one for himself. He opened one of the boxes stacked at the end of the trunk and found extra loaded magazines for the weapons. He and Barry shoved as many of them in their pockets as they could.

"We'll go out the back," Barry said. "You take the left corner, I'll take the right."

Jake nodded. "Got it."

They slipped out the back door after checking to make sure none of the men were already sneaking up on them from that direction. Jake went to his corner and propped his shoulder against the wall as he waited for the action to start.

He didn't have long to wait. A man popped out from behind one of the dunes on his side of the house and started to dash toward another little hillock of sand. He was carrying a shotgun.

Jake worried for a second that the man was a legitimate law enforcement officer. But then, as the man he was watching dived behind that dune, somebody else called softly in Spanish, "Kill them all!"

An honest cop wouldn't be giving an order like that. That plus the Spanish indicated they were dealing with cartel killers. When the shotgunner sprang up again and tried to charge toward the shack, Jake was ready for him.

He pressed the machine gun's trigger and sent a stream of lead hammering into the twilight.

The bullets caught the shotgunner in mid-stride and flung him backward. The stuttering muzzle flash from Jake's weapon gave the other men a target, and they opened fire instantly, forcing him to duck back around the corner. Slugs chewed into the shack's wall and sent thousands of splinters spraying in the air.

At the other corner, Barry's gun was pounding out a deadly rhythm, too. After a moment, it fell silent and he called, "Moving! On me!"

Jake poked his gun around the corner long enough to let out a burst, then wheeled away from the wall and dashed after Barry, who was firing on the move as he headed for the dunes.

The cartel soldiers hadn't been quick enough to set up a perimeter. They couldn't stop Barry and Jake from reaching the rolling, grassy terrain along the edge of the sound. Bullets whined nearby, and flashes of orange muzzle fire split the gray dusk.

"Alternate fire!" Barry called. He stopped first, whirling around and dropping to one knee to spray slugs back at their pursuers.

Jake raced on, his long legs carrying him for twenty yards or so before he turned. He made sure Barry wasn't in his line of fire and opened up again with the machine gun.

"Covering!" he shouted just before he pressed the trigger.

"Moving!" Barry replied.

The running battle continued like that as they made their way through the dunes, drawing the death squad away from the shack where they had left the prisoner. Neither Jake nor Barry had abandoned the idea of further interrogating the terrorist.

They were heading toward the place where they had left the borrowed pickup. The sun was down and the shadows were closing in quickly when they reached it.

Barry said, "I want you to get in the pickup and drive off."

"You mean I should leave you here? No way!"

Barry pushed a fresh magazine into the weapon as he responded, "No, just start to drive off. That ought to draw them out, and I'll be waiting for them. Then you circle back and give me a hand finishing them off."

"Got you."

Jake ran to the truck and got in while Barry retreated behind the other shack. The pickup started instantly— Doc McIntire kept it in top-notch running order—and Jake tromped the gas hard enough to make the engine roar as he started toward the highway.

Yelling angrily, seven men emerged from the dunes and fired after the vehicle, thinking both of the men they were after were getting away.

Barry stepped out of concealment as they did that. Clearly, they weren't expecting him to open up on them like he did. Three men went down almost immediately, kicking out their lives.

The pickup's brake lights flared as Jake slammed his foot down on the pedal. He hauled the wheel around and sent the pickup sliding into a turn that threw sand in the air around the tires.

Then the pickup surged back toward the surviving members of the death squad as Jake steered with one hand and held the stuttering machine gun out the window with the other.

Even under these grim, dangerous circumstances, he couldn't resist the urge to let out a loud whoop. He was caught up in the exuberance of battle.

Once again, Jake and Barry had trapped their enemies in a crossfire, and with Jake charging toward them in the pickup and Barry coming up behind them, it took only a minute or so to wipe out the rest of the gang of killers. Jake brought the pickup to a halt while Barry checked the bodies.

"Any survivors?" Jake asked as he stepped down from the pickup.

Barry shook his head.

"Not the way we were cutting them up with these guns," he said. "We'd better make tracks. Shots from handguns are one thing, but playing these typewriters the way we were is bound to attract some attention, even with all the chaos going on in town."

"Typewriters?" Jake repeated with a bleak grin. "Just how old *are* you?"

"Never mind that. Come on, let's go grab our friend in the shack."

Driving, it took only a minute to get there. When they pulled up after circling around the parked cars left by the cartel death squad, they saw that the flimsy building had a lot of bullet holes in it.

"Uh-oh," Jake said. "Looks like they shot it up pretty good. Maybe we should have taken the guy with us."

"He would have slowed us down enough that we never would have gotten away," Barry pointed out. "Come on, let's hope for the best."

What they found hardly qualified as "the best." The terrorist was still tied up on the kitchen floor, but he was lying in a pool of blood now. At least one stray bullet had found him.

He wasn't dead yet, though, so there was that to be thankful for. Barry knelt beside him, being careful to avoid the spilled blood, and took the gag out. He said, "Listen to me. You're hurt bad, but you're going to be all right. We'll get you to a doctor as soon as you tell us what else Bandar al-Saddiq is planning."

Jake wasn't sure the man even heard what Barry said, but after a few seconds, his eyelids fluttered and he stared up, his eyes unfocused.

"I will never . . . betray my brothers," he rasped as he struggled to draw another breath into his badly wounded body. "Soon I . . . will be in paradise . . . A joyous reward . . . awaits me . . ."

"No, it doesn't," Barry said. "You don't get any reward, because you failed."

"No! The infidels . . . died . . ."

"Some did. But the eagle still flies."

"The eagle . . . will crash . . . and die . . . and with it . . . America . . ."

The man's head lolled to the side. He wasn't going to say anything else, now or ever.

"Blast it!" Jake said. "If we'd just had a chance to question him more." He frowned. "What was that you brought up about an eagle? I know he mentioned it before . . ."

"Just something I thought might spook him into spilling something," Barry replied with a shake of his head as he straightened to his feet. "He made it sound like there was something important about an eagle. But maybe it didn't mean anything. The eagle's one of the symbols of America, after all."

"I wouldn't think a guy would try to be symbolic with his dying breath." Jake shrugged. "But I've never died, so what do I know?"

"What I know is that it's time for us to get out of here." Barry's voice was icy as he went on, "We were too late this time. We weren't able to do a thing to stop them, and a lot of people died. I don't intend to let that happen again."

"Neither do I," Jake said, "but right now, we don't even know where to pick up the trail of the rest of them. *And* we've still got guys after us who are determined to kill us. We need to regroup and figure out our next move . . . and I want to make sure that Gretchen's okay."

Barry nodded and said, "All right. We'll head back to the doc's place."

CHAPTER 56

Gretchen Rogers stirred, felt a little twinge of pain at the movement, and winced. Her eyes opened slowly. She looked around, trying to figure out where she was and what had happened.

Then the details of the battle she and Jake and Barry Rivers had waged against the Deep State assassins—men she had considered, if not friends, at least coworkers—came flooding back into her brain. She didn't know who had shot her—she had assumed the fight was over—and she didn't even know for sure that she'd been shot, but that seemed like the most probable explanation.

She also wasn't sure how badly she'd been hurt, but at least she'd had some medical attention. She knew that by the dressings on her wound and the IVs that were set up on both sides of the bed, a tube running to the back of each hand.

And she was alive, so that was something.

She could tell she wasn't in a hospital, although she was lying in what was clearly a hospital bed and there were glass-fronted cabinets of medical supplies arranged along one wall. This looked more like a bedroom in somebody's house, judging by the rugs on the floor and the curtains on the window.

At least there wasn't a guard at the door. She wasn't in some prison hospital, under arrest for aiding and abetting federal fugitives.

Worry gnawed at her and hurt worse than the pain from her wound. That was slight enough that Gretchen knew she'd been pumped full of painkillers. There were pills to get rid of worry, too, but she must not have been given any of them because she wanted desperately to know if Jake and Barry were all right.

Jake . . .

She frowned a little as a memory . . . a half-memory, more like . . . drifted into her mind. Even though it wasn't possible, she seemed to recall him standing beside her, so big and formidable, and yet so gentle as he slipped his hand around hers . . .

The door opened. A tall black man with a closely trimmed beard stepped into the room. Gretchen had never seen him before. Her eyes darted around, searching for something, anything, she could use as a weapon if he tried to hurt her.

Instead, he stopped just inside the door, as if he didn't want to make her nervous, and said in a deep voice, "I'm glad to see that you're awake, Ms. Rogers. I know you must be curious. My name is Caleb McIntire. I'm a doctor, and this is my house you're in. Barry Rivers is an old friend of mine. He and his nephew Jake brought you here earlier today and asked me to take care of you. I've attended to your wound, and you've been sleeping. Does that bring you up to speed?"

Gretchen had to make two attempts to speak, because her mouth was dry as cotton. She asked, "W-Where are Jake . . . and Barry?"

"I'm not sure, exactly. They had something else they needed to go and take care of, but they promised to come back here when they were done."

Gretchen's eyelids were incredibly heavy. She believed she could risk closing them for a moment. McIntire was on the other side of the room, and if he made a move toward her, she would hear it.

She wasn't sure what she would do if he did, but at least she would know it.

Even though it felt wonderful just to lie there with her eyes closed, the urgency of the mission they had set out on prodded her into opening them again. When she did, she asked, "Barry . . . trusts you?"

"I hope so," McIntire said. "We've saved each other's life more than once, so he ought to."

"You're in . . . the same line of work?"

"Not exactly, but close enough that our paths have crossed from time to time. All that's in the past, though. These days, I'm just a simple country vet."

"V-Vet? As in . . ."

"Veterinarian." McIntire smiled. "I prefer animal patients to human. But don't worry. I started out treating people. I just think that, by and large, animals are more deserving of my services. I'm not that fond of people in general anymore."

Gretchen sighed, nodded, and said, "Most days I tend to agree with you, especially recently." Her voice was stronger now. "Thank you for . . . making an exception."

"I was glad to do it. Any friend of Barry's is worth the effort."

"How badly am I hurt?"

McIntire came a little closer to the bed as he said, "You lost a considerable amount of blood. The bullet did some tissue damage, of course, but it missed the vital organs. You'll be laid up for a while, but as long as there's no infection, you should make a full recovery." He smiled again. "And the scar won't even be that bad."

"I don't care about that," Gretchen said with a sigh. "I just wish I knew . . ."

"Whether those two are all right? So do I."

"How . . . how long has it been? Since they left here?"

"About eight hours. It's night now. They didn't say when they would be back. I don't think they knew."

"No, I don't imagine they did." She remembered where they had been headed, and after a moment's thought, she decided she trusted McIntire enough to ask him more questions. "Has anything happened today? Anything . . . bad?"

McIntire's expression became solemn again. No, more than solemn, Gretchen thought. Grieving.

"You mean like . . . a terrorist attack?"

"Ohhhh," Gretchen moaned. "What happened?"

"There were several explosions at a train station in New York, on Long Island," McIntire said flatly. "And the commuter train that was arriving at the time derailed. The wreck destroyed what was left of the station after the explosions. It's too early for anything except rough estimates of the death toll, but it's believed to be somewhere between a thousand and fifteen hundred."

Gretchen tried not to sob, but she couldn't help it. All those people, those poor, innocent people.

"Was that what Barry and Jake were going to try to stop?"

All Gretchen could do was nod.

"So . . . since they didn't succeed, there's a chance that they . . ."

McIntire didn't finish the sentence, but he didn't need to. Gretchen knew exactly what he meant.

Jake and Barry might have failed to stop the attack *because they were dead.*

After a moment, McIntire drew in a deep breath and said, "I know what you're thinking, Ms. Rogers, but we don't have any way of knowing what happened. But I *do* know that Barry Rivers is a very difficult man to kill, and although I just met that young man of yours, his nephew, today, I have a feeling that Jake is pretty resilient, too."

Gretchen was about to automatically correct him and say that Jake wasn't *her* young man when a buzzer sounded somewhere else in the house.

She knew from the way McIntire stiffened that that wasn't necessarily a good thing.

"We have company," he said. "I need to go see about that."

"You have alarms set up?"

"Given my past, it seemed like the prudent thing to do."

Which meant that he had enemies, too, who might show up to settle a score with him. As he quickly left the room, Gretchen wondered what he might have done in the past and just what his connection with Barry Rivers was.

None of that mattered at the moment, however. She looked around to see if she could find her pistol. It wasn't in sight, and she wished somebody had thought to leave it within her reach.

Flat on her back in the hospital bed, attached to the two IV stands, all she could do was lie there and wait.

Nobody could turn off the highway onto the road leading to the clinic without tripping a motion detector. McIntire went into his big study and library, which had several video monitors mounted on one wall. The closed-circuit infrared camera that covered the parking lot revealed a car coming to a stop.

It was too late for any patients to be showing up. The clinic offered after-hours emergency services, but clients had to call first, and McIntire had set his voice-mail message to say that he had been called away.

The man who got out of the car didn't have a sick dog or cat with him. Instead, he was alone as he walked toward the house, a well-built, middle-aged man in a dark suit.

McIntire was sure this nocturnal visit had something to do with Barry and Jake and the blonde in the other room. He already had a small Smith & Wesson revolver in a belly holster under his shirt. He opened a drawer, took out a 1911, and stuck it behind his belt at the small of his back. He didn't have to check to make sure it was loaded. He knew it was.

He opened the door as the man stepped up on the porch. He didn't have either gun in his hand, but he could draw them fast enough if he needed to.

"That's far enough, friend," McIntire said. "What can I do for you?" He added, "The clinic is closed."

"Yes, I'm aware of that," the man said.

"Kind of late in the evening to come calling if there's no emergency."

The man smiled.

"Who said there was no emergency? I believe that the reason I'm here qualifies."

"Why don't you explain what that is?" McIntire suggested.

"I've come for Gretchen Rogers."

The man must have seen McIntire's hand move instinctively toward the belly gun. He held up his own hand in a conciliatory gesture.

"There's no need for that," he went on. "Listen, Dr. McIntire—"

"You know who I am."

"I know a great many things. That's my job. My name is Mitchell Cavanaugh. I'm with the Justice Department."

"So what you're saying is . . . 'I'm from the government, and I'm here to help'?" McIntire shook his head. "That doesn't resonate with nearly as many people as it used to, Mr. Cavanaugh. At least half the country stopped believing that a long time ago."

"Well, I can't be held responsible for what people think, but I know the truth." Cavanaugh nodded toward the house. "Gretchen Rogers is in there, and I need to speak with her."

"You believe she's here because—"

With a testy note of impatience in his voice now, Cavanaugh said, "Because I saw Barry and Jake Rivers bring her here earlier today."

McIntire cocked his head a little to the side.

"Satellite surveillance? Or drones? You *do* use drones in American airspace now, don't you?"

Cavanaugh waved the question away and said, "That

doesn't matter now. Look, Doctor, I realize that you and Barry Rivers go way back—"

"That's putting it mildly."

As if he hadn't even heard McIntire's interruption, Cavanaugh continued, "But that doesn't really matter. I'm here on official government business, and I need to speak with Ms. Rogers. You know that she works for the Department of Homeland Security?"

"I know that she did."

"She still does, as far as I'm concerned. I don't know what lies those two traitors told you, but Ms. Rogers isn't in trouble. I just want to help her, but to do that, I have to talk to her. Technically speaking, I *am* her boss, you know."

McIntire wished Barry or Jake were here. He didn't know what to do. Was this man Cavanaugh one of the group that wanted them dead, or did he really have Gretchen's best interests at heart?

"Wait here," he said. "I'll go see if she's willing to talk to you."

Under the circumstances, he didn't see any reason not to admit that Gretchen was here. Obviously, Cavanaugh and his people had been tracking Barry and Jake and knew what they had done.

Cavanaugh nodded and said, "All right. But just so you know, I'm not accustomed to being left standing on somebody's front porch in the middle of the night."

"And this isn't just anybody's front porch," McIntire snapped. He closed the door in Cavanaugh's face and got a little satisfaction out of that.

He went back to the room where he had left Gretchen and opened the door. As he stepped in, he caught sight of something from the corner of his eye and suddenly crouched as he reached for the gun at his waist.

He stopped short, and so did Gretchen, with one of the IV stands poised to drive its feet into his face. She was pale, washed-out looking, and none too steady on her feet, but fierce determination burned in her eyes.

"Good grief, what are you doing out of bed?" McIntire exclaimed. "You shouldn't have taken that IV loose."

"Wasn't sure . . . who was gonna come through the door," she said. She swayed, and he reached out to take hold of her arm so she wouldn't fall.

"There's a man out there who wants to talk to you," McIntire said. "He claims he's one of your bosses. A man named Cavanaugh."

Gretchen's eyes widened with shock, and McIntire knew he'd been right not to trust Cavanaugh.

"No," Gretchen began. "You can't—"

That was when something crashed through the window, followed by a blinding flash and an earsplitting explosion of sound.

CHAPTER 57

Pain shot through Gretchen as McIntire lost his grip on her arm and she fell to her knees. Her head rang like she was trapped inside a giant bell, and she couldn't see a thing. A part of her brain still worked well enough that she was aware a flash-bang grenade had just gone off, but mostly she was just in agony and wanted to collapse cringing onto the floor.

She wouldn't allow herself to do that. Outrage stiffened her spine and galvanized her muscles. She made it back halfway to her feet, but then someone grabbed her from behind and jerked her the rest of the way up. Her arms were pinned to her sides. She tried to struggle, but the strength she had summoned rapidly deserted her. She sagged in her captor's grip.

As stunned as she was, it was difficult to say how much time passed before she began being able to see and hear a little. As her vision gradually cleared, the first thing she saw was Dr. Caleb McIntire lying face-down on the floor and not moving.

Even though she had just met him, horror went through her at the thought that he was dead. She knew his medical attention probably had saved her life.

Then her eyesight sharpened a little more, and she

could tell that he was breathing. That was a relief, anyway, although how long either of them would survive was very much in doubt.

Men in tactical gear had crowded into the room. Gretchen didn't know how they had gotten there, but it didn't matter. One of them held her while a couple of others stood by with their guns trained on McIntire in case he regained consciousness and tried anything.

She took that in instantly since being observant had become second nature to her, but most of her attention was centered on the man who stood in front of her with an annoying smirk on his ruddy face—Mitchell Cavanaugh.

"Can you hear me, Gretchen?" he asked.

"I can hear you," she said. Her voice sounded strange to her inside her head. "I just don't like you. Or trust you."

"Well, that's where you're making a mistake. Because, you see, I'm the only way out of this mess you've gotten yourself into."

"My way out? Ha! You sent men to kill me!"

Cavanaugh shrugged and said, "That's regrettable. However, Barry and Jake Rivers were the primary targets. I'll admit, you might have been collateral damage—"

She tried to surge forward as her lips pulled back from her teeth in a savage grimace, but the grip on her was too strong.

"But now the situation has changed," Cavanaugh went on. "Since you're not with those two traitors anymore, there's no reason you have to come to any harm. In fact, I believe we might even be able to salvage your career in government service."

"The only traitor here is you!"

"I'm sorry you feel that way. It's a shame you believe all the lies those two have fed you. I want only what's best for this country . . . and I know who's best qualified to decide what that is."

"And that's not the common people, right?"

Cavanaugh cocked his head to the side and said, "You have to admit, they don't have the best track record over the past two hundred and fifty years, do they?"

Even wracked with pain, Gretchen saw that it was useless trying to argue with Cavanaugh's smug elitism. She glared at him and asked, "What is it you want from me, anyway?"

"Tell me where Barry and Jake are."

Gretchen shook her head slowly.

"I don't know. And that's the truth."

"Then you know where they were going."

"No, I don't," she declared. "I don't have any way of knowing. I was unconscious when they brought me here. If you were spying on them with some sort of eye in the sky, you ought to know that. I'd been shot by one of those flunkeys you sent after us."

"You mean those dedicated federal agents Jake and Barry Rivers murdered?"

"We were just defending ourselves!"

"Careful," Cavanaugh said. "You don't want to say too much and incriminate yourself."

A look of sly, evil anticipation appeared in his eyes for a fraction of a second as he said that. In that moment, Gretchen knew that any promises Cavanaugh made regarding getting her out of trouble and saving her job were just lies. He was only trying to get her to tell him what he wanted to know, and once she did, he would kill her.

She wasn't going to give Mitchell Cavanaugh what he wanted. She might be almost completely powerless right now, but she could still deny him that much.

"Go to hell, Cavanaugh," she rasped. "I'm not going to cooperate with you, no matter what you do."

"Is that so?" He reached under his suit coat and took out a small, flat, semi-automatic pistol. As he pointed the gun at the back of McIntire's head, he went on, "Even if it means saving the life of the good doctor here?"

Gretchen's head was starting to spin. As McIntire had said, she'd lost a lot of blood, and it was going to be a while before she recovered from that—if she ever did. The way things were going, that looked doubtful.

"I don't think . . . the doctor would want me . . . to betray his friend . . ."

Cavanaugh sighed, shook his head, and started to take up the slack on the trigger.

"Wait!" Gretchen said. McIntire had told her about the terrorist attack on Long Island. Jake and Barry might not have survived it. If they hadn't, then Cavanaugh couldn't hurt them anymore.

If they *had* survived, they would be on the move already, trying to figure out what to do next. That meant they probably weren't on Long Island anymore.

She had to swallow a couple of times before she could speak again. She was still having trouble because her mouth was so dry. But she managed to say, "They were going to New York. One of Barry's contacts told him . . . that something funny was going on . . . at a railroad station on Long Island. He and Jake . . . were going to check it out. That's all I know . . . I swear."

"A railroad station on Long Island? What station?"

Gretchen made herself look like she was trying to

think. After a moment she said, "Baghdad . . . No. Babylon. That was it. Babylon."

"You haven't heard anything about Babylon station this evening?"

"I just woke up a little while ago!" she said. "I've been shot, remember? I . . . I don't know what's going on here." She moaned and let herself sag even more, trying to sell the idea that she was telling the truth. "It's all so crazy . . . I just can't understand anymore . . ."

Cavanaugh looked intently at her for a few seconds, then jerked his head toward the hospital bed.

"Help her lie down," he told the man holding her.

"Thank you," Gretchen said with a big sigh of relief. "I was about to pass out again."

With the help of Cavanaugh's goon, she climbed back onto the bed.

"I probably ought to reattach that IV I took loose," she said.

"Oh, I don't know that that's necessary," Cavanaugh said with the smirk reappearing on his face. He swung the gun up, away from McIntire, so that it pointed in Gretchen's general direction. "I've decided that I believe you, Agent Rogers. You've told me everything you know."

A ball of ice started to form in Gretchen's belly. She said, "Does that mean you don't need me around anymore?"

"That's right. You . . . or the good doctor. It makes more sense to dispose of both of you and then arrange things so that it looks as if, say, a gas explosion destroyed this house and the adjoining clinic." Cavanaugh made an eloquent gesture. "Regrettable, to be sure, but for the best overall."

"You're a monster," Gretchen said through clenched

teeth. She looked at the three men in tactical gear, who stood in the room with their faces carefully expressionless. She demanded of them, "Are you going to let him just get away with murder like this?"

"It's for the country's good, ma'am," one of them said. "Mr. Cavanaugh wouldn't say so if it weren't true."

Gretchen stared at him in disbelief. Cavanaugh put his gun away and stepped toward the bed.

"This won't take long," he said, smiling. "And if you'll just cooperate, it won't even be that unpleasant. I'll just take that pillow and hold it over your face—"

"You can't blow up the clinic," Gretchen said. "There are bound to be animals over there, sick animals—"

Cavanaugh stopped and frowned at her, as if she had just started pleading with him in a foreign language.

"Animals?" he repeated. "I don't care what happens to a bunch of stupid dogs and cats!"

He lunged at her, the suave mask gone now.

Gretchen grabbed the IV stand on that side of the bed, shoving it into his path. He stumbled over it, cursed, tried to bat it out of the way.

The other three men started to leap forward to help him, but gunshots suddenly blasted out somewhere nearby.

"Go help the others!" Cavanaugh told his men. "I'll take care of this bi—"

Gretchen pushed herself halfway up from the bed, swung a leg off, and kicked him in the belly before he could finish what he was saying. He bent over, cursed, and slammed the IV stand out of the way with his forearm. Lunging forward, he wrapped both hands around her neck and shoved her down on the bed. She tried to gasp for air, but nothing could get through her windpipe with Cavanaugh throttling her like that.

"Just for that, you can die painfully," he rasped as he bore down on her.

Smothering her with a pillow would have left her without any telltale marks, but since they were going to blow the place up anyway, she supposed that didn't really matter. She fought back as he choked her, but she was so weak from her wound that the blows she struck with both fists were pretty feeble. Cavanaugh just ignored them.

But those gunshots meant one thing to Gretchen: Jake and Barry were back. The three men in tactical gear had rushed out of the room to help the rest of Cavanaugh's henchmen, but that wouldn't be enough. Jake and Barry would take care of them, Gretchen was sure of that.

And then they would take care of Mitchell Cavanaugh, she told herself as her consciousness started to fade. She could cling to that hope on her way out of this life. No matter what happened, Cavanaugh wouldn't get away with it . . .

CHAPTER 58

Jake felt weariness gripping him as he slowed down to turn from the highway onto the lane leading to McIntire's house and clinic. It had been an incredibly long, violent day, and even though he still had strength and stamina to spare if he needed them, he was starting to wear down.

Sometimes he didn't have any idea how Barry still did it at his age. But Barry, in most respects, seemed ageless . . .

"No, don't turn in," Barry said suddenly in an urgent voice. "Keep going."

Without thinking too much about it, Jake took his foot off the brake and put it on the gas again. He hadn't slowed down much, hardly enough to be noticeable.

"Drive on past and find a place to stop where the pickup will be out of sight," Barry said.

They continued along the dark road for another quarter of a mile until Jake spotted a clump of trees with a big enough gap in it for the pickup. He turned and drove through the opening. He had to force the vehicle through some underbrush and was sorry that

McIntire's pickup was probably getting quite a few scratches on it.

When he had penetrated about fifty yards into the trees, Barry said, "That ought to be far enough."

Jake eased the pickup to a stop, killed the lights and the engine, and looked over at his uncle.

"What's wrong?" he asked. "Something tip you off?"

"Yeah. The doc." Barry held up his phone, which had a text message displayed on the screen. It was nothing but a long line of exclamation points. "An alarm signal we've used before."

"So we need to go in discreetly."

"That's right. But we have to get in there so we can find out what's going on."

Gretchen, Jake thought. She could be in danger. Barry was right that they needed to be careful, but at the same time, a part of him wanted to go charging in with all guns blazing.

Just in case that turned out to be necessary, Jake checked both of his pistols, making sure the magazines were loaded and that he had loaded extras ready. Barry did the same.

Then they started through the trees toward McIntire's place, moving carefully and quietly—but not too slowly. They had no idea how much danger McIntire and Gretchen might be in.

Neither of them wanted to get there too late.

Although the vegetation was thick in the area, a wide space around the house and clinic had been cleared. That was because the life McIntire had led had gotten him into the habit of caution, Jake thought. It would be more difficult for anyone to sneak up on the place that way.

After a few minutes, Jake and Barry reached a spot where they could crouch down, part the brush, and peer through the narrow gap they'd created.

A sedan and a couple of SUVs were in the parking lot. Jake didn't recognize any of them, but every instinct in his body told him that they were a bad sign.

"You see anybody?" he whispered to Barry.

"No, but they're around. Not any doubt of that."

"Cartel? Terrorists?" Jake paused. "Or federal agents?"

"Doesn't really matter, does it?"

"It does," Jake said tautly. "I still don't like killing anybody who's supposed to be working for the same government I am."

"They're not. You work for the government that was elected legally, by the people. Cavanaugh and his ilk, they're part of a *different* government, a shadow government of bureaucrats who've been appointed . . . in some cases, *self*-appointed . . . and they believe the rules don't apply to them. They're above the law, in their eyes, and when the average citizens stand up and say, hey, we don't like what you're doing, the elites try to shout them down at first, and if that doesn't work, they don't have a problem putting down any dissent with force. The ones who accidentally tell the truth admitted a long time ago that they don't see anything wrong with locking up their political enemies . . . or killing them, if that's what it takes."

"I know, I know, blast it. You're preaching to the choir, Barry." Jake sighed. "I just hate that things ever got to that point in this country."

"You and me both, son. You and me both. Blame the people who bought into blatant lies for decades." Barry peered intently though the gap in the branches and went on, "There, in that shadowy area between the house and the clinic. Two of them."

Jake looked where Barry indicated, and after a moment his keen eyes made out the shapes there. They were nothing more than man-sized patches of deeper darkness, but Jake knew his uncle was right.

"If we take them, we can get around to the back."

"Yeah. We'll have to try. But crossing that open ground, we're liable to be spotted if there are more of them." Barry shrugged. "Chance we'll have to take. But let's circle around to the other side of the clinic. Better angle of approach that way."

They moved off to the left, staying well back in the brush so there was less likelihood of them being spotted. As they made their way into position, Jake listened intently for any noises coming from inside McIntire's house. He knew that if he heard screams or gunshots, he wouldn't be able to hold himself back but would have to charge in there and do whatever he could to help Gretchen.

He was surprised by the depth of feeling he had developed for her in just a few short days, but he realized there was no point in questioning or analyzing it. He felt what he felt, and that was all there was to it.

He didn't hear anything that signified trouble as he and Barry crossed the open ground, but as they pressed their backs against the brick wall at the far end of the clinic from the house, however, he was able to hear barking inside the building. One of the dogs staying there overnight because of some ailment was announcing his presence to the world.

Jake took a little comfort from that. A dog barking was a normal sound . . . a sign that the whole world hadn't gone crazy.

They eased along the wall to the back corner, then around it and closer to the gap between clinic and house. They could have made a run for the back door from there, but the watchers in the shadows were almost certain to see them if they attempted that. Better, instead, to go ahead and deal with that threat first.

Barry had brought along a piece of a broken branch, about a foot long, that he had picked up in the woods. When he and Jake reached the other corner and stopped there, Barry took the piece of wood from behind his belt and threw it toward the brush. It made a little racket when it landed—not much, but enough to attract the attention of the guards.

"What's that?" one of the men quietly asked the other.

"Don't know, but we'd better check it out."

Barry whispered to Jake, "You take the first one who sticks his head out."

Jake nodded, even though it was probably too dark back there for Barry to see him. He was the nearest to the corner, so he set his feet and waited for the guy to get close. He heard stealthy footsteps approaching. The guard was being careful—but not careful enough.

As soon as the man took one step past the corner, Jake struck with blinding speed. His hands shot out and grabbed the guard's shoulders, jerking him closer. Jake's right arm went around the man's neck and clamped down like an iron bar. He hung on until the guard slumped into unconsciousness—or death.

Right now, Jake didn't particularly care which one it was.

While that was going on, the other man realized something was wrong and exclaimed, "Hey!" as he lunged forward. Barry swung around Jake and was ready to meet that charge. With a lithe agility much belying his age, he bent sideways at the waist and snapped a kick into the second guard's midsection. Breath gusted out of the man's lungs as he doubled over.

Barry chopped a sidehand blow down onto the back of his neck. The guard collapsed on his face, out cold.

Barry stepped back from the fallen sentry and said quietly, "Now let's see if we can get in through the back door."

They moved toward it, but before they could get there, the door swung open and a man stepped out with an automatic rifle in his hands. There was nowhere for Jake and Barry to hide. This guard, who wore tactical gear like the others, saw them immediately, let out a yell of alarm, and jerked his rifle up.

Barry was too fast for him, bringing up the 1911 he carried in a two-handed grip and firing a pair of swift shots to the man's chest. The guard's vest stopped the slugs, but at that range the .45 caliber rounds packed enough punch that they knocked him back off his feet and made him drop the rifle. Barry rushed forward and kicked him in the jaw to finish knocking him out.

Another man had been following the first one along

the hallway toward the back door. When he saw what was happening, he fell back, also shouting an alarm.

He tried to bring his rifle into play, too, but Jake had already stepped up with the Browning outthrust. There was no time now to be less than lethal. Flame spat from the pistol's muzzle. The guard went down hard with a third eye in his forehead.

Someone shouted, and more heavily armed men charged into the hallway from the room where Gretchen was supposed to be recuperating from her injury. Clearly, Jake and Barry would have to go through them to reach her.

Well, if that was the way it had to be . . .

Jake dropped to one knee and resumed firing. Barry crouched behind him, shooting over his head.

Outnumbered and outgunned as they were, they had to get their shots in first and make them count. That meant more head shots because of the body armor the enemies wore. The rogue enemy agents had visors on their helmets, but that protection wasn't lowered in place. They hadn't been expecting trouble, and they hadn't reacted as well as they should have.

That carelessness cost two of them their lives right away. They tumbled off their feet, drilled through the head. The remaining man was able to get his rifle working. Its ferocious hammering filled the corridor. Jake flung himself one way, Barry the other, as the slugs stitched the air between them.

They ended up on opposite sides of the hall, both of them triggering their pistols as they lay on their bellies. Firing from this angle meant that when one of their slugs—they never did know which one of them fired it—caught the man under the chin, it angled on up through his brain and rattled around inside his skull, turning the man's brain to mush.

He hit the floor hard and fast.

Jake scrambled to his feet first and pounded toward the door of the room where they'd left Gretchen.

The first thing he saw as he loomed in the doorway was the back of a man bending over the hospital bed, apparently struggling with someone. A fraction of a second later, Jake realized the man had his hands wrapped around Gretchen's throat and was trying to choke her. Barry was about to go after the guy when another figure rose up from the floor.

Dr. Caleb McIntire had a loose IV stand in his hands. He swung it like a baseball bat and slammed the metal pole against the back of the man's head.

That jolted loose the man's grip on Gretchen's neck but didn't knock him out. With an angry roar, the man swung around toward McIntire. Jake recognized Mitchell Cavanaugh, who was high up in the conspiracy—whatever it was—that threatened the United States.

Jake wanted to put a slug in the middle of Cavanaugh's face, but he realized in time that the man might have valuable information. So he blasted Cavanaugh's right kneecap into a million pieces instead. Cavanaugh screamed as that leg buckled underneath him and dropped him toward the floor.

McIntire hit him again with the IV stand on the way down. Cavanaugh was out cold when he hit the floor.

McIntire was reeling. A line of dried blood ran down

one side of his face from the wound on his head where somebody had clouted him, probably with a rifle butt.

Barry came into the room behind Jake. He grasped McIntire's arm to steady him and said, "Sit down over here, Doc. Jake, I'll keep Cavanaugh covered. You check on Gretchen."

That was exactly what Jake was doing already. Gretchen lay there, pale, gasping, and coughing as she gulped down air through her tortured windpipe. Jake stuck his gun behind his belt and took hold of her shoulders.

"Gretchen, are you okay?" he asked, knowing it was kind of a dumb question even as the words came out of his mouth.

"Yeah . . . other than . . . being shot and then choked half to death!"

There was fresh blood on the hospital gown McIntire had put on her, which meant the gunshot wound had probably broken open again, but the crimson stain wasn't very big and didn't appear to be spreading fast. Jake figured that the bleeding likely wasn't bad.

"Where did Cavanaugh come from?" he asked.

"They've been spying on you . . . with satellites."

Barry said, "They must've lost sight of us part of the time. If they'd known where we were for any length of time, I wouldn't put it past Cavanaugh to call in a drone strike on us!"

"An . . . American citizen? On . . . U.S. soil?"

"You're still clinging to the idea that all those Deep Staters aren't the bad guys," Barry told her. "After what happened here tonight, though, I'll bet you're starting to think differently about that."

"Jake . . ."

He leaned closer over her and asked, "What is it? Do you need something?"

"Yeah . . . Give Cavanaugh . . . a good swift kick for me!"

"We can do better than that," Barry said. "We're gonna make him tell us at last what this is all about."

CHAPTER 59

The first order of business was to check on the men Cavanaugh had brought with him and make sure the ones who were still alive were secured properly so they couldn't cause any more trouble or send for help.

Jake went to do that—reluctantly, since he didn't want to leave Gretchen's side—while Barry talked to McIntire in the hallway just outside the room where Gretchen was resting again with her IVs hooked back up.

"I'm sorry to get you mixed up in this trouble, Doc," he said. "It may cost you your practice. Once the bureaucrats in the state capital find out that you gave Jake and me a hand, they'll probably pull your license to practice veterinary medicine."

"Maybe, maybe not," McIntire said as he taped a bandage over the gash on his head. He had already cleaned it with disinfectant. "Could be the government will be giving you boys medals before this is all over."

Barry let out a cynical laugh.

"Not hardly. Even if we find out what's going on and put a stop to it, they'll never acknowledge what happened. The powers that be will move heaven and earth to cover it up." Barry shrugged. "That's what governments do."

"Well, however it plays out, I'll never regret giving you a hand. Not after all the things you've done for me."

"I appreciate the heads-up you gave me about trouble waiting for us here. Otherwise, Jake and I might have waltzed right into it with our eyes wide open."

McIntire let out a snort and said, "I doubt it. That instinct of yours would have warned you, Barry. I've never known it to fail yet. But when I came to on the floor, I figured it wouldn't hurt to send you a message in case you were nearby. I was able to get my hand into my pocket and reach my phone without Cavanaugh or his men noticing. They were too busy paying attention to Cavanaugh questioning Ms. Rogers. I'd programmed the number of that burner phone of yours into mine before you left, and I can send a text message just working by feel."

"I guess that makes you as talented as a millennial," Barry commented wryly.

McIntire just snorted again, then looked down at the still-unconscious Cavanaugh.

"I suppose I'd better tend to that piece of scum before he bleeds to death."

Barry had been standing where he could keep an eye on Cavanaugh. The man hadn't regained consciousness. Gretchen had dozed off, so Barry went into the room, got hold of Cavanaugh's collar, and dragged him out, leaving a trail of blood smeared on the floor. Luckily, the tile was the sort that would clean up easily.

"You may be doing more damage to his knee by hauling him around like that," McIntire said with a slight frown.

"You swore an oath to do no harm," Barry replied, "but I never did."

"We've both done plenty of harm in our lives . . . most of it justified."

McIntire and Barry lifted Cavanaugh onto the metal table in McIntire's bare-bones operating room for human patients. McIntire cut away the man's trouser leg, revealing the bloody mess that Jake's bullet had made of Cavanaugh's knee. White bone fragments were visible through the gore.

"Shooting a man like this strikes me as a little cruel," McIntire commented to Barry. "I don't know Jake well, of course, but it seems a little out of character for him." He smiled bleakly and added, "More like something you would do."

"Are you saying I'm cruel?"

"No . . . but you *are* practical."

"And Jake saw Cavanaugh trying to strangle Gretchen."

"That *does* help to explain it. Well, I'm no orthopedic surgeon, so there's not much I can do here except clean up the blood and stabilize the knee."

"Oh, I think there's something else you can do," Barry said. "You still have any of that special serum of yours?"

McIntire frowned and said, "I've told you, Barry, there's no such thing as truth serum."

"No such thing as a foolproof one, you mean. But we both know there are drugs that can help get information out of somebody who doesn't want to part with it." Barry nodded toward Cavanaugh. "He certainly falls into that category."

McIntire thought about it for a moment, then said, "Let me see what I can do for his knee first. Or do you plan on using that injury to help extract what you want to know? Am I just wasting my time because you'll damage it even more?"

"I'll do whatever's necessary," Barry said. "But I can't question him if he bleeds to death, so go ahead and work on his knee."

He stood in the doorway, leaning a shoulder against the jamb, while McIntire cleaned the blood away from Cavanaugh's bullet-shattered knee and bound it up. Cavanaugh started to stir and moan a little while McIntire was working. The doctor went over to a cabinet, opened it, and took out three bottles and an equal number of hypodermic syringes.

"Two of these are drugs to help with the pain and ward off infection," he said as he filled those syringes. "The other one . . ." He drew the third syringe full of liquid from the last bottle. "It's what you asked for."

"Thanks, Doc. I have to admit, I'm a little curious why you have it on hand."

"The old days are just old," McIntire said. "That doesn't mean they're completely gone. I have other friends who need favors now and then, you know."

"I'm not surprised to hear it. I figured you'd keep a hand in if you could. If this wasn't so important—"

"Save any apology you were about to make," McIntire said. "After what this man tried to do, I'm not exactly overcome with sympathy for him."

Jake came back into the house while McIntire was giving Cavanaugh the injections. He saw Barry in the hallway and joined him.

"The two who are still alive are secured and gagged. I dragged them out to the barn. They won't give us any more trouble." Jake nodded toward the metal table where Cavanaugh was stretched out. "What's going on there?"

"Doc's patching up Cavanaugh's leg where you shot him."

"I figured he had it coming," Jake said.

"Nobody around here is going to argue with you." Barry paused, then added, "The doc's going to help us find out what we need to know, too."

McIntire stepped back and said, "He's starting to come around now, but with everything I've given him, he won't be awake for long. So you'd be well-advised to ask your questions fairly quickly. As for me . . . I'm going to go check on Ms. Rogers."

Barry nodded. He knew exactly what his old friend meant. McIntire didn't want to be in here while the questioning was going on. It wasn't that he had gone squeamish over the years since Barry had last seen him. Caleb McIntire had always operated by a strict moral code of his own.

Barry understood that. He was the same way. And *his* code meant saving lives was more important than handling evil men such as Mitchell Cavanaugh with kid gloves.

When McIntire had left the room, Barry stepped up next to the table and lightly slapped Cavanaugh's cheeks until the man's eyes opened. He stared up at Barry uncomprehendingly for a moment.

Then pain and memory hit Cavanaugh at the same time, and he snarled in rage.

"You . . . you'll never get away with this, you . . ."

He sputtered out curses and obscenities for several seconds before Barry rested his hand on the man's right knee and put just a little pressure on it. That was enough to make Cavanaugh choke off his tirade and gasp in agony instead. Tears began to well from his eyes.

"I don't like you, Cavanaugh," Barry said. "Not even a little. You've got an arrogant little Washington bureaucrat's mind, and you think you and your friends are better than everybody else. You believe that everybody who doesn't live in the Beltway, New York, Los Angeles, or *maybe* San Francisco and Chicago are just redneck rubes who shouldn't have any say in how their country is run. Because you know better than them, don't you? The best and the brightest, that's what you boys used to call yourselves. But you were never the best at anything except hoarding power, lining your own pockets, and turning yourselves into petty tyrants."

Barry paused and drew in a breath. After a second, he went on. "But I'm wasting time telling you things we both already know. What *you* need to tell *me* is what the endgame is. What have you and Bandar al-Saddiq cooked up that'll ruin this country?"

Cavanaugh's eyes were starting to turn a little hazy now as the cocktail of drugs McIntire had given him began to affect his brain.

"Saddiq is . . . a fool," he said in a slightly slurred voice. "A useful idiot. As if we'd ever let them . . . actually run anything. They think they're gonna come in here . . . with their sharia law . . . and turn this country . . . into a caliphate . . . That'll never . . . happen."

"Well, what do you know?" Barry said. "We actually agree on something, Mitch. But if Saddiq and his people aren't going to be running things when you're finished with whatever this is, then who is?"

"The people who . . . deserve to. Not a bunch of . . .

self-aggrandizing buffoons . . . Time's come . . . to take
the government back . . ."

Jake said quietly, "He's talking about a coup."

Barry nodded and said to Cavanaugh, "You can't get
away with removing the President. And if you did, you'd
still have the Vice President—"

"No! Speaker of the House! The Speaker of the
House . . . is third in line . . ."

"Good Lord!" Jake said. "They mean to assassinate
the President *and* Vice President."

"I'm not so sure," Barry said with a shake of his
head. "Too many people wouldn't stand for that. It'd be
the boogaloo to end all boogaloos. And since this group
has never succeeded in disarming the American people
the way they want to, I don't think they'd even attempt
such a thing. No, they'd have to come up with a way to
get more than half the country to go along with—"

"Only way . . . to keep the Chinese out . . ." Cavanaugh
said. "Once the econ . . . economy . . . is just . . . smoking
ruins . . ."

Jake said, "Attacking the railroads has hurt the economy, sure, but not enough to make it tank to that extent.
Barry, this isn't making sense."

"I know." Barry frowned for a long moment, then
leaned closer to Cavanaugh and said, "We know about
the eagle project, Cavanaugh." The glance he threw
toward Jake indicated that he knew he had tried this
tactic before, but maybe this time it would work. "It's
too late. We're going to stop it."

Cavanaugh moaned. His consciousness was fading,
that was obvious. But he found the strength to shake
his head and said, "You can't . . . stop the eagle . . . The
eagle . . . goes through . . . Silver . . . silver eagle . . ."

His eyes closed, and he seemed to have slipped into a deep sleep.

Barry leaned on the wounded knee again. Cavanaugh screamed as his eyes flew open.

"The silver eagle," Barry said sharply. "What's the silver eagle?"

"Can't stop it!" Cavanaugh cried. "They'll all be there!"

His head fell back. He was out cold this time, and he wasn't going to wake up no matter how much pain Barry dished out. Barry knew that, and despite what some might think, he wasn't a cruel man.

He stepped back from the table.

"What in blazes is the silver eagle?" Jake asked.

"That's what we have to find out," Barry said.

CHAPTER 60

By the next morning, Gretchen was feeling a lot stronger and her color was better. Jake knew she must have a lot of resilience to be bouncing back that quickly from everything she had gone through.

Even so, she was going to need a lot of rest and medical care before she was completely recovered. Which meant she couldn't continue trying to help Jake and Barry stop whatever the conspiracy was. She wasn't physically capable of it right now.

When Jake told her that, she was predictably irritated.

"What am I supposed to do?" she demanded. "Just lie here and wait?"

"Actually, Dr. McIntire is making arrangements with some other friends of his to have you moved to a safe house. Cavanaugh and the other prisoners will be moved, too, and cleaners will be here later today to make sure nobody will ever be able to tell that anything happened here."

Gretchen stared at him with a puzzled frown on her face.

"You make the doctor sound like some sort of, I don't know, superspy," she said.

Jake shook his head and said, "No, just a guy who's made a lot of friends in, well, circles that might be considered a little shady . . ."

"Friends like Barry," Gretchen said.

"Yeah, that about sums it up."

She shook her head and said, "I never knew there was so much going on behind the scenes. It's like there's a whole dark world out there that normal people aren't even aware of."

"If people ever learned the whole truth about what goes on behind the scenes . . . well, most people wouldn't want to know about it, I imagine," Jake said.

Gretchen started to say something but hesitated, then said instead, "While you're trying to track down that silver eagle business with Barry . . . you're going to be careful, aren't you, Jake?"

"I always am," Jake replied. Then, realizing how ludicrous that probably sounded, he shrugged and added, "Well . . . as much as I can be, anyway."

She reached out with a hand that had an IV needle inserted into a vein and taped down on the back. Despite that, she was able to slip her fingers into his hand and squeeze.

"Thank you for everything you've done," she said softly.

"I haven't done anything except get you right in the middle of bad trouble—"

"That's not true at all, and you know it," she interrupted him. "I got myself into this trouble, and I could have gotten myself out of it any time I wanted to. It just so happens that I think it's important to stop whatever it is that Cavanaugh and Saddiq and whoever else is mixed up in it plan to do."

Jake nodded and said, "Yeah, it's a bad combination—"

Barry came into the room behind him and said, "Hate to bother you two, but I may have a lead."

Gretchen took her hand away and used it to push the button that raised the head of the hospital bed a little more. Just like that, she was all business again.

But Jake wasn't going to forget the look he had seen in her eyes a moment earlier.

"What is it?" she asked Barry. Jake turned toward his uncle, eager to hear the answer as well.

"I did some research and found out that there's a train called the Silver Eagle," Barry said. "One of those luxury excursion trains that people take vacations on. It runs from Denver through the Rocky Mountains and on west to San Francisco."

Jake frowned and said, "Attacking a train like that might have some *symbolic* value . . . you know, striking against the wealthy, since I guess you'd have to be rich to afford it . . . and they've certainly made it clear that they like going after trains. But I can't see that it would do much practical damage to the country, so what would their motive be?"

"That's what we have to figure out, and that means going to Denver."

"When are you leaving?" Gretchen asked.

"Right away. The sooner we get there, the better. And we're taking the truck," Barry added. "Driving straight through, we can be in Denver by the morning of the day after tomorrow."

Jake said, "With everybody we have gunning for us,

is it a good idea to travel in something as recognizable as that truck?"

"If we have to make it through a gauntlet of killers, I can't think of anything better to be in."

Jake nodded in acceptance of that. He knew from experience how tough that big Kenworth Z1000 was.

"The doc's going off the grid and taking you with him," Barry went on to Gretchen. "Nobody will be able to find you . . . but when this is all over, I'll get in touch with him, and Jake and I will come for you."

"I told Jake earlier, and I'll tell you, too," Gretchen said. "Be careful, Barry."

"Oh, I intend to be," he replied with a reckless grin. "But you know what they say about good intentions."

"The road to hell is paved with them."

"Maybe this time that old saying will be wrong," Barry said.

Jake hoped so—but he couldn't quite bring himself to believe it.

With memories of his bittersweet farewell with Gretchen in his head, Jake had to force himself to concentrate on the mission. It was almost nightfall when he and Barry left McIntire's place and headed west.

By now, somebody was bound to have noticed that Mitchell Cavanaugh and the agents he had brought with him were missing. From the passenger seat, Jake asked, "You think we have eyes in the sky watching us?"

"I wouldn't doubt it."

"They may try to drone us."

Barry thought about it and shook his head.

"Cavanaugh has to be pretty high up in this conspiracy.

I'm not sure any of the others would make a move like that without his approval. And it's possible they believe he's with us. They wouldn't want to blow him up."

Jake snorted and said, "I'm not so sure about that. From what I've seen, these guys would kill anybody if it helped their agenda. Like you pointed out, there's a long trail of suspicious deaths and outright murder behind them, and they're used to having the media cover up for them."

"That's true. They were untouchable and could do pretty much whatever they wanted for close to a hundred years, until talk radio and then the Internet came along. Things have changed . . . some . . . but they're still pretty blatant about their power grabs. They've got another one going on now, so you might be right. They're working with Islamic terrorists and have already killed more than a thousand people to further their goals. They probably won't hesitate to blow us up to keep us from interfering, even if it means a lot of collateral damage."

"So what are we going to do? It's like we've got a target painted on top of the truck!"

Barry smiled and said, "We're going to be doing something about that."

"Well, don't be all enigmatic about it."

Barry's smile just turned into a grin.

It was dark when Barry piloted the truck off the highway and turned onto a smaller road. It was paved but narrow and old, probably a hundred years or older judging by its macadam surface. It led into some thick woods. The trees that crowded in both sides of the road were tall, and their arching branches stretched out and tangled with each other.

374 *William W. Johnstone*

"I get it," Jake said. "Darkness might not be enough to get away from their satellites, but they can't see through the trees." He thought of something. "What about thermal imaging? That big engine must put out a lot of heat."

Barry reached over and pushed some buttons on the dashboard underneath the computer screen.

"Electronic countermeasures," he said. "We can block thermal imaging, infrared, and just about any other kind of surveillance equipment you can think of. The trees take care of visuals."

"How did you know this road was here? No, wait, let me guess. You've used it for something like this before, haven't you?"

"Maybe," Barry said. "Honestly, I didn't know if it was still here. They could have bulldozed all the trees and built a bunch of McMansions, for all I knew. But luck was on our side."

"Luck and a bunch of electronic gizmos. Whatever it takes, I guess."

"That's right."

They drove on in silence for a moment, but Jake's frown deepened until he said, "Wait a minute. If you had all these countersurveillance measures available, why weren't you using them all along? Then they wouldn't have been able to track us to Dr. McIntire's place."

"True, there's a chance we could have lost them, I suppose."

"Blast it!" Jake burst out. He stared at his uncle. "Barry . . . you *wanted* them to find us!"

"I thought there was a chance that if somebody made a move against us, it might wind up giving us another lead." Barry shrugged. "And it has. We wouldn't know about the Silver Eagle if we hadn't gotten our hands on Cavanaugh."

"But that nearly got Gretchen killed! You were willing to risk her life . . . *all* of our lives . . . just to get a lead."

With a grim note in his voice now, Barry said, "What the people plotting against this country have in mind isn't just harassment, or even a body count. They're after something a lot bigger than that. We know they plan to cause enough trouble to make it feasible for the President and Vice President to be removed. Anything that big will cause more death and misery than the U.S. has seen in a long time."

"I suppose you're right—"

"You know I am." Barry stared straight ahead through the windshield. "We've both suffered losses in the past from battling these people, Jake. And there'll be more pain in the future, because they won't give up. They're so convinced of the rightness of their cause that they'll cause countless deaths to get what they want. And if they ever succeed in forcing their deranged beliefs on this country, they'll just keep on hurting people, over and over again—"

Barry shook his head and blew out a breath.

"Sorry I started preaching," he said. "I just know how dangerous they are. I've been battling against that encroaching evil for three decades now. Sometimes it's frustrating because some people can't see . . . refuse to see . . . what these people are trying to do. There's no 'live and let live' with them. You agree with their philosophy . . . or you die. Whether they put you up against a wall for a firing squad or you starve to death in some gulag, if you don't think like them, they want you dead. That desire might be buried deep enough in some of them that they won't admit it, even to themselves, but it's there. And it comes out whenever they get any power. That's why we have to keep fighting them. This country won't survive if we don't."

Jake sat there in silence. He knew, logically, that his uncle was right. He had observed certain politicians long enough, and keenly enough, to realize the truth of everything Barry said.

But he still wished that Gretchen hadn't been hurt, and he was looking forward to seeing her again when this was over.

Sometimes the small things were just as important as the big, epic ones.

They emerged from the long, tunnel-like road and turned onto a smaller highway that also led west and eventually brought them to the interstate again. In the middle of the night, they stopped for gas and food at an isolated convenience store, avoiding the big truck stops where they were more likely to be spotted.

Then they rolled on through the darkness, with Jake behind the wheel while Barry dozed in the passenger seat. Jake punched up some jazz on the sound system to keep him company through the long night.

They continued across the Midwest and the Great Plains, the strong beating heart of the country so despised by those who huddled together in the great coastal cities congratulating themselves on how much smarter and better educated and just plain *better* they were than those rubes and yokels who couldn't be trusted to vote the proper way.

Jake had never tried to force his beliefs on anyone, only defended himself and others who were under attack. Even after all this time, he struggled to grasp the fact that so many of his fellow citizens were filled with hate for anyone who didn't support their so-called progressive agenda. As far as Jake could see, it wasn't progressive at all. Instead, it was a throwback to an earlier era, a time of thugs banding together to take down those they disagreed with—"canceling" anyone they wanted by shaming them on social media. He knew from bitter experience that a few of the modern-day leftists would be happy to do far more than just that if they ever got the chance.

It was a fight worth fighting . . . but it got awfully wearying after a while.

A day and another night of driving, and they approached Denver with the sun rising behind them and turning some of the heavily glassed downtown high-rises into towers of flame. Barry was at the wheel while Jake studied the computer screen for anything that might relate to their mission. They were still on the vast flatland east of the city when Jake said, with a hollow note in his voice, "Barry, here's something."

Without taking his eyes off the road, Barry said, "Something wrong?"

"Well, there's a news story talking about how the owners and CEOs of more than a dozen of the biggest companies in the country are meeting to discuss ways to limit the economic damage from the recent terrorist attacks."

Barry had to turn his head for that. He glanced back at Jake in the sleeper and said, "You mean they'll all be together in one place? The people who run the corporations that drive the huge majority of the economy?"

"Yeah," Jake said, and now his voice sounded like it

was coming from a grave. "And to keep distractions at a minimum, they're getting away from everything else by having their summit meeting on a train." Jake swallowed hard. "The Silver Eagle. And it rolled out of the station fifteen minutes ago."

CHAPTER 61

Barry pulled over into a rest area so he could join Jake in the sleeper and look over his nephew's shoulder at the computer screen. Jake had found several news stories about the corporate summit meeting on the excursion train, which, according to the stories, had been chartered by the billionaire industrialist and financier Alexander Sherman.

Sherman was quoted as saying it was vital that the current economic crisis be stopped in its tracks before it got bad enough to do any lasting damage to the country.

"I know that name," Barry said. "Alexander Sherman has given millions, maybe more, to so-called philanthropic causes over the past twenty years. The thing of it is, every one of those causes wound up giving the government even more power than it already had and furthered Sherman's agenda. He's a statist and a globalist who, despite what he's saying right now, would like nothing better than to kill the free market."

"But he's a billionaire," Jake said in obvious confusion. "How can he hate the free market and capitalism that much when it made him into the richest guy since Scrooge McDuck?"

"He figures he'll still be the richest guy around once

his side takes over, but then he and his handpicked politicians can tell everybody else what to do and control every detail of their lives from the proverbial cradle to the grave. They won't have to deal with those uppity common folks believing they know what's best for their own lives when it's so obviously Sherman and his ilk who know best." Barry shook his head. "I know, Jake. Guys like you and me and a lot of other people can't even comprehend how anybody could feel that way, but trust me. That's exactly what Sherman and his allies believe."

"I know," Jake muttered. "But you're right . . . I'll never understand it." A frown creased his forehead as he leaned forward and started typing on the keyboard again. "There's something bugging me, something I seem to remember . . . Look!" He pointed to the news story that had come up on the screen. "The train that was derailed in Nevada, the first attack Lashkar-e-Islami claimed credit for, was headed for a hazardous waste containment facility owned by Sherman Global Enterprises." His fingers flew across the keyboard again. "And as if you couldn't tell from the name, that company is owned by—"

"Alexander Sherman," Barry finished as the results of Jake's search came up. Jake didn't even need to click on any of the hits for them to see what they needed to know.

Jake turned in his seat to look up at his uncle.

"Sherman's behind this, Barry," he said. "He's got to be."

With a bleak expression on his face, Barry nodded and said, "Yeah, there's no doubt in my mind. Orchestrate things so the economy's in danger of melting down and use that as an excuse to get all of those CEOs together. Then there'll be another terrorist attack that wipes them all out—except for Sherman himself, of course—and when the economy actually does crater because of that, they'll use it as an excuse to remove the President and Vice President and form a new government. They won't be able to do it overnight, but they'll start beating the drums right away, and the Chinese will start making threatening noises, and it'll make the Depression look like a picnic. I'll bet within a year the country will be desperate enough to turn to them to take over and do whatever they want. Remember how Woodrow Wilson centralized the federal government during World War I, and then FDR strengthened the presidency even more during the Depression? Those extra executive powers didn't go away after the crisis ended."

"A little before my time," Jake said dryly, "but I remember reading about it. You really think that Sherman and his allies would inflict so much terrible suffering on the country just to get their own way? Just because they don't like how a few elections have gone?"

"Like we talked about, he'll do anything to further their cause," Barry said. "And he doesn't care how many bodies it costs to get it done."

"Then we have to stop them."

"You said the train's already left Denver."

"Yeah, but maybe we can catch up to it somehow and be there to stop whatever they've got planned." Regret tinged Jake's voice as he went on, "I know we weren't able to stop them completely in El Paso, and we weren't able to do squat on Long Island, but . . ."

"But the stakes are higher now," Barry said. "The

highest." He turned toward the truck's cab. "Come on. We'll figure out our next move as we go along."

Bandar al-Saddiq had never seen such luxury. The thick carpet, the lushly upholstered furniture, the richly paneled walls, the gleaming brass and chrome . . . The money it must have cost just to furnish this one railroad car could have fed an entire village in Pakistan for a year!

Soon, the Americans would pay for their immoral greed and arrogance, thanks to Saddiq and the man who sat across from him in this private train car. Outside, visible through the large windows, were rugged, snow-capped peaks. The mountains' white crowns gleamed in the morning sun.

"A beautiful day, isn't it?" Alexander Sherman said.

"A momentous day," Saddiq said. "The day the Great Satan finally begins to taste defeat."

"Yes, of course," Sherman said, nodding. His basset-hound face showed satisfaction. "All our plans are about to come to fruition, my friend. By the time this day is done, America will have experienced a fundamental change. Of course, people won't realize at first just how fundamental a change, but this country's history of evil will be at the beginning of the end."

"To be replaced by the holy reign of Allah," Saddiq said. He couldn't contain the boundless enthusiasm he felt. He stood up from the comfortable chair and went over to the window to watch the rugged, starkly beautiful landscape through which the Silver Eagle was moving. "This . . . United States . . . will be made over, molded anew into part of the worldwide caliphate." He smiled over at Sherman, who joined him in looking out the window. "I mean no offense, my friend, but I hope you will embrace Islam. Sometimes Allah makes use of infidels, but I hope for your sake you have seen the truth and the light and know what you must do to take your rightful place among the leaders of this new world."

Sherman nodded and said, "Oh, I know exactly what to do to take my rightful place."

He slipped a small, flat pistol from his pocket, held the muzzle less than an inch from Saddiq's head, and pulled the trigger. The spiteful crack of the weapon mingled with Saddiq's shocked cry. Saddiq's knees buckled, and he fell to the thick carpet. Shame about the blood, Sherman thought, but it could be cleaned—or the carpet could be replaced, if need be.

With an expressionless face, he fired a bullet into each of Saddiq's open, staring eyes, just to make sure.

The car's top-of-the-line ventilation system was already starting to clear away the smell of burned powder.

Sherman put the pistol away and forgot about Bandar al-Saddiq except for a fleeting thought about useful idiots. The man and his ragtag organization had served their purpose of stirring up fear in the American populace, and so Saddiq could be safely dispensed with.

Fear was the most potent weapon in his arsenal, Sherman mused as he left his private car, which was soundproofed well enough that the shots couldn't have been heard from outside, even without the noise of the train's wheels on the rails. Fear of the unknown, fear of the "other," fear of poverty and hard times, fear of death . . . All of those made people easy to manipulate.

Sherman sighed as he walked through the vestibule into the next car, where his guests were meeting. Some people just wouldn't learn how to accept what was good for them. The ones who wouldn't had to be taught—and taught *hard*.

This car was set up like a boardroom, with a long table surrounded by his two dozen guests. *Victims* would have been a better word, but if they had known what was in store for them, they wouldn't have accepted his invitation, now would they?

Some of them had been reluctant to do that anyway, since they disagreed with his politics. But he had appealed to them to put those differences aside in the spirit of patriotism. He had talked stirringly about the need for fast action to ward off the worst financial collapse in almost a hundred years. And they had accepted, never dreaming that such a catastrophe was exactly what he intended to precipitate.

The car was full of talk when he came in, not all of it serious yet. They were still visiting among themselves, comfortable in these luxurious surroundings, at ease chatting with fellow members of their elite, super-rich fraternity. The trip was just getting started. They didn't expect to reach San Francisco until the next morning.

They had no idea that none of them would ever leave Colorado alive.

Sherman raised his voice and said, "My friends, welcome! I hope you've enjoyed my hospitality so far."

"This is all so wonderful, Alexander," a thin, silver-haired woman gushed as she smiled at him. She was the majority partner in one of the biggest hotel chains in the country. "You're a real patriot for doing this."

Some of the others didn't look convinced of that, but they were willing to give Sherman the benefit of the doubt for now.

"Thank you, Margaret," he said graciously. "We'll be getting down to work shortly, but for now, I think we can take the time for all of you to have a look at some of the most impressive scenery in the world." He went to a console and pushed a button, and sections of the wall rolled up to reveal large windows through which the mountains were visible on both sides of the train. The Silver Eagle was climbing into the Rockies, and clichéd though it might be, "majestic" really was the best word to describe them. The route went through high passes and alongside gorges that seemed a mile deep, where rivers foamed and raced along the bottoms.

One of those gorges would seem even deeper when the tracks running beside it blew up just as the train got there and the whole length of cars derailed and tumbled down the slope to fiery destruction. It was utterly unthinkable that anyone would survive such a crash.

Which was why Alexander Sherman intended to be gone from the Silver Eagle before it ever reached that point.

For now, though, he stood watching in satisfaction as the company presidents, managing partners, and CEOs stood up from the table and went to the windows to gaze out and *ooh* and *ah* at the magnificent mountain landscape. Actually, Sherman thought, one of the biggest challenges of the whole scheme had been to find enough companies still owned by American interests to make a sufficient dent in the economy when they failed. So much of the economy was dependent on China now . . .

But that was good, because when the economy cratered, the Chinese would feel threatened enough by a possible worldwide collapse that they would be willing to send troops, and Sherman could play that off as an imminent invasion, an existential peril that only one man could defeat. The country would have to turn to him for salvation, and even though the Speaker of the House would ascend to the presidency, that terrible hag would be only a puppet leader.

The real leader of the country would be Alexander Sherman. America would be his. His ascension had been inevitable for more than a hundred years.

So it was blasted well about time. Sherman smiled as he pictured all the greedy capitalists in this car screaming in terror as they plummeted to their deaths.

Soon, soon . . .

CHAPTER 62

Barry drove on toward Denver while Jake stayed at the computer. As Barry put it, Jake had been born to that technology, while he'd had to learn it.

As he tapped away at the keyboard, Jake hoped he would be able to justify his uncle's faith in him.

He found surprisingly little information about the Silver Eagle and the special trip it was making with a large number of vital financial figures aboard. Alexander Sherman—if he truly was tied in with Bandar al-Saddiq, Mitchell Cavanaugh, and the other plotters—must have tried to keep a low profile on this part of the plan. It would have been difficult to get that many movers and shakers in one place without *some* news leaking, though.

"The Silver Eagle is following the same route as Amtrak's California Zephyr," he reported to Barry after more Internet searching. "That Amtrak run has been suspended for a couple of days. Sherman must have a lot of clout."

"That's putting it mildly," Barry said from the cab. "Having billions of dollars tends to make other people sit up and pay attention."

"It's making the trip nonstop, according to what I've read." Jake frowned. "But that doesn't make any sense. If Sherman plans to crash the train or something like that to wipe out all those big shots, is he going to do it with him on there, too? Is the guy the type to be a martyr? Honestly, from what I've read of him, he doesn't seem to be."

Behind the wheel, Barry considered that for a moment, too, and then said, "I agree with you. I never dealt with him, but I've heard plenty about him, and it seems to me like he's just the opposite, the kind who wants to be in charge and make sure everybody does what *he* thinks they should. He likes to pull those strings from behind the scenes, mind you, but I can't see him killing himself for *any* cause, because then he doesn't wind up on top of the heap."

"But it sounds like he was on the train when it pulled out."

"Then he plans to get off somewhere before things go bad. You can count on that."

"Go around Denver and head west as quickly as you can," Jake said after studying a map of the Silver Eagle's route. "Then cut northwest on Highway 40. The California Zephyr has stops at Granby and Glenwood Springs, so the Silver Eagle is bound to go through those places, too. Maybe we can get to one of them before the train does." He paused. "Of course, even if we do, I don't know how we can stop it."

"We'll find a way to stop it," Barry said in flat-voiced determination.

"Maybe we ought to bring in the law . . ."

"As far as every lawman in the country knows, you're

a rogue FBI agent and I'm your unidentified companion, and we're both murderers—and probably considered domestic terrorists, to boot. Nobody's going to take our word for anything, let alone stop a train on our say-so. *Especially* a train being paid for by Alexander Sherman."

"But you have friends in the intelligence community," Jake argued. "High-up friends. Surely you can call in a favor . . ."

"I've already called in a bunch of them. I don't know anybody with enough pull to step in and stop that train, Jake. It's up to you and me."

"Even if we're successful, we're liable to be arrested," Jake pointed out.

"I'll run that risk if it means keeping Sherman from wrecking that train."

"We're convinced now that he's the brains behind this whole thing? He pulled in the Islamic terrorists and the Deep State?"

"It's the explanation that makes the most sense," Barry said. "He's the only one I can think of who could bankroll this operation . . . and he's egotistical enough to do anything as long as he ends up in charge."

Barry circled Denver on the I-470 beltway, which had finally been completed a year or so earlier after many years of controversy and delays. Where the beltway connected with Interstate 70, Barry swung the Kenworth west again, with the Front Range of the Rocky Mountains looming right in front of them.

Barry pushed the truck's speed considerably higher than the limit. He was an excellent driver with decades of experience and the reflexes of a twenty-two-year-old professional athlete. It was easier to maintain such standards when your life might easily depend on them.

In addition, the truck had state-of-the-art radar-detection equipment built into it. They didn't want to risk being stopped by the cops for something as simple as speeding, so now and then when the alarm went off, Barry slowed down until they passed the unit running radar.

Each of those delays gnawed at their guts. They had no idea how much time they had left to stop whatever it was Alexander Sherman and his cohorts intended to do.

Dupes might be a better word to describe those helping Sherman, Jake mused. So far, it had been Saddiq's men carrying out all the actual sabotage of the rail lines. Jake suspected they had no idea what Sherman's true intentions were. No way was Sherman going to turn control of the country over to a bunch of terrorists. They were just cannon fodder for him.

The Deep Staters like Cavanaugh likely would fare better in Sherman's New World Order. Any bureaucracy needed soulless, heartless bureaucrats to run it. Cavanaugh would fit right in.

Jake didn't want to think about a country in which Sherman and Cavanaugh were completely in charge. It would be a totalitarian nightmare, worse than the old Soviet Union, worse than China, worse than Venezuela or Cuba. Sherman's plan *had* to be stopped.

Jake moved back to the passenger seat in the truck's cab. He had done all the computer work he could. Now it was up to Barry to coax all possible speed out of the truck.

The Kenworth roared along the interstate until the

GPS told Barry where to turn to head for Granby. Their route led up U.S. 40 from Clear Creek Canyon to Berthoud Pass, the high mountain pass that marked the location of the Continental Divide. The steep, pine-covered slopes and deep valleys with creeks bubbling through them were beautiful, but the grade was steep enough that even the truck's powerful engine labored slightly, not to mention how tricky it was navigating the big vehicle through the frequent switchbacks. Some might have looked at the two-lane road snaking its way through the mountains and shaken their heads in refusal.

Not Barry Rivers. Not Dog. He kept them heading toward their goal, no matter the risks.

Jake was a little white-knuckled in places where the earth seemed to drop away forever on the right and sheer rock walls rose to the left. The road in front of them looked extremely narrow from the vantage point of the truck's cab. It seemed impossible that Barry would be able to make it around some of the turns without driving right off the side of the mountain. The Kenworth's tires hugged the road, however.

"Nervous?" Barry asked at one point.

"I'm not part mountain goat, if that's what you mean," Jake replied. "I'll be glad when we get over this pass."

"This is God's country," Barry said with a grin.

"Yeah, well, I just hope we don't meet Him personally before we get down from here." Jake sighed. "Funny. I didn't know I was afraid of heights . . ."

Finally, they reached the top of Berthoud Pass and the sign declaring that they were at the Continental Divide, elevation 11,307 feet.

"It's not quite as bad on the other side," Barry said. "Fewer switchbacks, and it's not as steep."

"Good. I'd just as soon not go through that again."

"Seen any signs of those railroad tracks yet?"

"No, but from the maps I looked at on the computer, we should be spotting them before too much longer. The line passes through a tunnel under the divide and comes out not far from Granby."

"Keep an eye out. The train we're looking for should be the only one on this line today."

Jake nodded. On the map, the railroad tracks were a short distance east of the highway. He watched in that direction, eager for his first sight of them.

After a while, he pointed and said, "There!" The steel rails, just one set of them, were visible intermittently through the trees. The railroad came close to the highway at times, curved away from it at others, following a route that probably had been laid out when the highway was just a trail, if it was even there at all.

"Any sign of the train?" Barry asked.

"No, I don't see it. And I don't know any way of finding out where it is along the line. All we can do is get to the station in Granby as fast as we can, hope it hasn't gone past yet, and figure out a way to stop it."

"There'll be an emergency signal to stop it. We can use that."

"We'll have to get the personnel at the station to cooperate," Jake said.

"They'll cooperate," Barry said. "With the fate of the whole country at stake, we'll make sure they cooperate." He rubbed his chin as he frowned in thought. "If I have to, I'll blow up the tracks myself to keep the train from starting again, once it's stopped and not in danger of derailing."

"We're both going to prison. You know that, don't you?"

"Be worth it to save the country."

"Then who's going to save it next time?" Jake asked.

Barry glanced over at him, and for once Jake felt like he had thought of something before his uncle did. Most of the time, Barry seemed to be two or even three steps ahead of everybody around him. That was one of the things about Barry that had always impressed Jake the most.

"Well, if we can, we'll slip away, but the most important thing is stopping that train."

"Agreed," Jake said.

The terrain was just as rugged and scenic on this side of the divide, but the highway's path wasn't quite as treacherous. And since they were going downhill, the truck was able to travel a little faster. Not too fast, though, because they couldn't risk it turning into a runaway. Luckily, the Kenworth had state-of-the-art brakes along with everything else.

Jake watched the railroad tracks more than he did the scenery. They weren't far from the town of Granby, where they would find the station, when he spotted what he had been looking for.

"Up there!" he said as he pointed. "You see it?"

"I sure do," Barry replied grimly. "That's got to be it."

The Silver Eagle lived up to its name. All the cars were painted silver, including the sleek, bullet-nosed locomotive. As the train came in and out of their view through the trees, Jake tried to get a count of the cars. The train was a short one, only half a dozen cars behind the engine. Compared to freight trains that sometimes stretched for several miles, the Silver Eagle was nothing.

And yet it carried the fate of the nation aboard it.

Barry's foot pressed down harder on the gas pedal. It was an instinctive response to the urgency of the situation. The truck surged ahead. The train was going pretty fast, but the Kenworth drew even with it and slowly pulled ahead.

Probably no one on board the train even noticed the big truck on the highway. If they did, they wouldn't think anything of it.

"All right, now we need to get to the station," Barry said. "Navigate for me."

Jake returned to the computer and typed for a moment, then said, "It's on Railroad Avenue. Big surprise there. The road turns to the left off the highway. I'll tell you where."

When they got there, with the town of Granby spreading out on both sides of the highway, Jake didn't have to say anything because Barry spotted the sign for Railroad Avenue and was already slowing the truck for the turn before Jake could speak up. Jake spotted two old-fashioned, cream-painted frame buildings with dark green roofs up ahead on the left.

The tracks, which Highway 40 had crossed on an overpass a short distance to the east, ran behind the buildings. Jake and Barry leaned forward to peer back along the steel rails. The Silver Eagle hadn't come into sight yet.

Barry brought the truck to a stop in the parking lot, not caring that it blocked numerous spaces. With no regular trains running today, the lot was almost empty. Only two cars were there.

They checked their pistols—two each, as usual—and climbed down quickly from the Kenworth's cab. They started toward the entrance of the station itself, which was the second building. The first building appeared to be used for storage and maintenance.

They were hurrying along the road beside that first building when two men stepped out through the main building's double entrance doors and opened fire on them with automatic machine pistols.

CHAPTER 63

Born and raised in Denver, Tarik Duffar had been pretty much indistinguishable from any other American kid, interested mostly in video games, graphic novels, marijuana, and girls, with occasional forays into sports. He'd gone to college intending to "do something with computers," like so many others of the past few generations, and had taken little, if any, interest in politics until a friend of his started getting into the whole "Islamic heritage" thing.

Now Tarik was standing in a train station in a little mountain town holding a gun on the fat, terrified, middle-aged black man who'd been the only one working here today, while his friend Beni harangued the guy and threatened to blow his brains out.

"Hey, man, take it easy," Tarik said. "This gentleman's gonna cooperate. Aren't you, sir?"

Tarik had learned the whole "good cop, bad cop" business from movies and TV. He and Beni hadn't worked that out in advance, but now it seemed to Tarik like a tactic that might work, so there was no reason not to try it.

"J-Just what is it you boys want?" the station man

asked. "There's no money here, if this is a robbery. I mean, I'll give you what I got, but it's not much—"

"We don't care about your money," Beni said, adding some obscenities. "We want you to stop that train!"

"But . . . but I got my orders," the man sputtered. "It's a special train, goin' through nonstop—"

"We know that," Tarik said. "But you have an emergency signal, don't you?"

"Yes, sure, but I don't even remember the last time anybody used it—"

Tarik interrupted the man again.

"But you know *how* to use it, don't you?"

"Of course. I just have to use the computer in the office."

Tarik aimed his machine pistol right between the man's eyes and said, "Then go do it, and nobody has to get hurt here."

That sounded like something they'd say on TV or in a movie, too.

The leaders of their cell in Denver had gone over and over the plan. Tarik knew that his and Beni's part in it was redundant. Some of their members had gotten jobs on the train as part of the support staff, and one of them was tasked with stopping the train here in Granby so someone important could get off. Tarik didn't know exactly who that VIP was, but he suspected it was Bandar al-Saddiq, who had come to this country to lead them in their holy mission.

The man whose job it was to stop the train would remain on it, running the engine, until the very end, as would the others. They would die as martyrs to their glorious cause. Tarik was jealous of them. But his day was coming, he was sure of that. Soon, he would be in paradise himself, surrounded by all those virgins eager to welcome him . . .

The station man's face was covered with beads of sweat from the fear that gripped him. He said, "You boys goin' to all this trouble just to stop a train? You figure on robbing it, like old-time outlaws? You gonna be in bad trouble if you try to do that. Lots of important folks on that train, I hear. They'll all have bodyguards with them. You're just gonna get yourself killed. If you just leave now, I promise I won't call the cops—"

"Turn on the emergency signal!" Beni screamed in the man's face. He lashed out with the gun, hitting the man on the head, driving him to his knees. Blood began to drip from the cut the blow opened up. "Do it!"

Sobbing in pain and fear, the station man struggled back to his feet and stumbled toward the office.

"Wait!" Tarik said as he glanced through the window at the end of the building and caught a glimpse of a big truck turning into the station's parking lot.

Like everyone else in the group, he had heard the stories about all the trouble that had been caused by two Americans in a big truck. He had seen the photos of them that had circulated among all the Lashkar-e-Islami cells in the country. Surely those men hadn't shown up here, just at the wrong time—but he and Beni couldn't afford to take that chance.

"What's wrong?" Beni demanded irritably.

The words tumbled out of Tarik's mouth as he explained about the truck and the two men. Beni's lips curled in a sneer.

"If it's them, we'll kill them, that's all," he said. "They won't stand in the way of Allah's glorious plan."

Tarik opened one of the doors just a little and peeked out. His voice trembled with a mixture of excitement and fear as he said, "Two men are getting out of the truck . . . They're coming this way . . . I . . . I think it's them—"

The station man turned and tried to run. Beni chopped down at the back of his head with the gun. It connected with a solid thud, and the station man sprawled on his face, moaning.

"Let's kill them!" Beni said.

"But I'm not sure they're the same ones—"

"I don't care! They're infidels!"

Beni slammed the doors all the way open and charged out. Suddenly, Tarik was scared. His belly felt like it was filled to bursting with ice water. But he followed his friend anyway, an involuntary yell coming from his mouth as he thrust the gun in his hands toward the Americans and pulled the trigger.

Jake and Barry reacted to the attack instantly and instinctively, leaping away from each other and drawing their guns with blinding speed. The two attackers, both of them young, didn't seem to be very familiar with their weapons. They sprayed lead around wildly, filling the air between Jake and Barry but not coming too close to either.

Jake crouched, firing the Browning with a two-handed grip. His shot drilled through the shoulder of one of the young men, shredding flesh and shattering bone. The man screamed in pain and dropped his gun. He twisted halfway around and clapped his other hand to the wounded shoulder.

The 1911 in Barry's hand boomed. The .45 Automatic Colt Pistol round slammed into the other gunner's chest and lifted him off his feet as it threw him backward. His arms flew out to the side, and his machine pistol sailed through the air as he lost his grip on it. It landed in the middle of Railroad Avenue. The young man who'd been firing it landed on his back on the sidewalk in front of the station and slid a few feet before coming to a stop. He didn't move again.

The other attacker had fallen to his knees and stayed there, clutching his bloody shoulder and sobbing. Jake approached him carefully, with the Browning ready to fire again.

"Get down on your belly!" Jake ordered him. "Now!"

"Please don't kill me, bro," the young man whimpered in a thoroughly American accent. "Please don't shoot me again."

"Then do what I tell you and get down."

The man tried to follow orders but stopped and groaned as the movement made him hurt even more. Barry circled behind him, put a foot between his shoulder blades, and shoved, not giving him any choice in the matter. The guy sprawled on the sidewalk, howling now.

He shut up as Jake knelt in front of him and said,

"We won't hurt you anymore if you cooperate. What's your name?"

Through the blubbering, the young man said, "T-Tarik."

"Tarik, you're not going to die from that wound, but you *will* die if you don't tell me the truth. You understand?"

Tarik lifted his tear-stained face to look at Jake and nodded.

"What were you supposed to do here?" Jake asked.

"B-Beni and me . . . we were supposed to . . . stop the train."

"You're Lashkar-e-Islami?"

"G-Glory to the Prophet! All glory to Allah!"

"I don't want slogans," Jake snapped. "How were you going to stop the train? Is there a bomb in the station?"

"N-No . . ."

A new voice said, "There's no bomb, mister."

Jake and Barry looked up to see a heavyset, middle-aged black man stumbling toward them, holding a hand to his head as if he'd been clouted there. He went on, "Those two came in and started wavin' those ugly guns around and ordered me to turn on the emergency signal so the train that's comin' would stop. They yelled and threatened me a lot, especially that one"—he nodded toward the man Barry had shot, who was staring sightlessly up at the Colorado sky—"but that's all they'd had time to do before they spotted you two fellas."

Jake looked back down at the wounded man and asked, "Why did you try to kill us? Why start shooting?"

"We . . . we saw pictures . . . they sent us pictures . . . said you were trying to interfere with . . . the plan . . ."

"Why were you supposed to stop the train?" Barry asked. "Is somebody supposed to get off here?"

"Y-Yeah. I . . . I don't know . . . who . . ."

Jake glanced at his uncle and said, "Sherman."

"Yeah, and maybe Saddiq. So what we need to do is let the train go ahead and stop. That's what we wanted to start with."

The station man said, "Who *are* you guys? Do you work for the government?"

"That's right, sir," Jake said as he straightened. "I'm with the FBI. I don't have my credentials on me right now, but I assure you, we're trying to stop another terrorist attack on the railroad."

The man groaned and said, "Heaven help us, I thought it might be something like that when these two showed up. What can I do to help?"

"How badly are you hurt?"

The man gestured toward his head with a hand that had blood smeared on it and said, "This knock on the head? This is nothin'. I've got a nice thick skull."

"Let's get these two inside, out of sight," Barry said. "From where he'll be in the locomotive's cab, the engineer probably wouldn't be able to see them, but we don't want to risk spooking him and making him go on without stopping."

"You want to stop the train, like they did?" the station man asked in confusion.

"Yes, but for completely different reasons," Jake said.

"Okay. Should I call the police?"

"Not yet," Barry said. "We have jurisdiction over this matter."

"All right. You need a hand?"

"No, we can get them," Barry replied as he bent down, grasped the dead man's collar, and started to drag the corpse into the station.

CHAPTER 64

Ahmed Noorzai felt greatly honored. Pride filled him as he checked the gun in the concealed holster at his waist, under the waiter's jacket. With his experience at one of the best restaurants in Denver, he'd had no trouble getting the job on the Silver Eagle, especially when one of the regular waitstaff from the dining car had come down with a sudden illness and had to be replaced.

That "illness" was a slit throat, but no one knew it yet. The body had been carefully disposed of. It might never be found.

Noorzai had performed his job well during the short journey so far, but his real task was yet to come. He was about to set out on it now, as he opened the door of the car's vestibule, hung on, and reached carefully around into the gap between cars until he was able to grasp one of the rungs of the narrow ladder leading to the top.

Noorzai pulled himself around and climbed the ladder. He didn't like leaving the door open behind him like that, but there was no way to close it from where he was. He wondered if he would be missed before the train reached its ultimate destination: the deep gorge running alongside the tracks where the Colorado River leaped and danced over its rocky bed.

The train was about halfway between the western end of the Moffat Tunnel and the station at Granby, where it would be stopping to let Noorzai's leader, Bandar al-Saddiq, get off, along with the infidel Sherman. The unscheduled stop would be passed off as necessary to take care of an unexpected mechanical problem, and then the train would roll on with a delay of only minutes.

Noorzai would be at the controls, driving the locomotive on to its date with destiny. He was eager to meet his own destiny, as well, to die and awaken in paradise.

But not too soon. He had to stay alive until he had finished his job, so he was extremely careful as he crawled along the top of the car. The Silver Eagle might be a luxury train, but it still swayed and jolted from time to time as it traveled along the steel rails. Noorzai didn't want to slip and fall off.

He only had to make his way over one car before he was able to climb down the ladder at the front and step over to the catwalk that ran along the locomotive's side to the door into the cab. He was careful during that brief journey as well, clinging to the handholds as the wind of the train's passage buffeted him.

Four other members of Lashkar-e-Islami were aboard the train, also posing as employees of the Silver Eagle excursion line. They would step in only if there was trouble, and that wouldn't happen unless the infidels somehow realized that they were on their way to their deaths.

That would only occur if someone noticed that their speed was increasing before they reached the point where the explosives would topple the cars off the track and down the steep side of the gorge. Noorzai didn't want to take any chances. The locomotive had to derail as planned. The added speed was just a precaution to make sure it happened.

He reached the door into the cab. The handle twisted in his hand. He stepped inside and drew his gun as the engineer jumped up from his padded leather seat, yelling, "Hey!" Nobody else was supposed to be in here. There wasn't even a seat for a conductor in this locomotive.

Noorzai lifted the gun and fired a shot, placing it perfectly in the center of the engineer's forehead. The pistol was a small caliber, deadly enough at this range but without the power to pass completely through the man's skull and ricochet around, possibly doing damage to some of the controls.

The engineer's head jerked back under the bullet's impact. He folded up at the knees and collapsed onto the cab's floor. Blood leaked from the wound. Noorzai stepped over the corpse and took his seat, placing the gun on a little shelf where an open soft drink can also sat. The engineer would never finish that drink.

A pair of monitors, along with dials, gauges, and displays for various instruments, filled the control panel that angled around him from the left. On the console directly in front of him were the two big levers for the throttle and the brakes. The view through the windshield was spectacular, but he wasn't at all interested in beautiful mountain scenery. In the distance, at a somewhat lower elevation in a valley, he saw the buildings of Granby, looking a bit like child's toys from here.

The train would be there in fifteen minutes, Noorzai

knew. He wouldn't have wanted to cut it any closer than this.

But now, with approximately forty-five minutes left to live, it felt as if he had all the time in the world. He leaned back in the comfortable seat and grinned in anticipation as the train rumbled along the tracks.

The Granby station manager, whose name was Arvin Jones, switched on the emergency signal and told Jake and Barry, "That'll do it. When the engineer sees that the flag is up, he'll stop to see what's wrong. That's what we use when there's been an avalanche, or a pass is closed by bad weather, or anything like that."

"Do you know who'll be at the controls today?" Barry asked.

"No, sir, I don't. I know all the regular California Zephyr engineers, of course, but that Silver Eagle is different. The people who work on it aren't Amtrak employees."

"But you're confident that whoever it is will stop," Jake said.

"Absolutely. No engineer in his right mind would proceed against an emergency signal like that."

"All right," Barry said. "We appreciate your help, Arvin. But it's time for you to get out of here now. There may be trouble once the train's stopped."

Arvin stood up and squared his shoulders.

"If there's gonna be trouble at this station, then it's my job to be here and keep it contained," he said.

"Not this kind of trouble," Jake said. "Besides, you're hurt."

"I've got to admit, this ol' noggin of mine does ache a mite."

"Go home," Barry said. "It doesn't look to me like that cut needs stitches, so get your wife or somebody to clean it up, and then you rest a while. Then you can let the authorities know that something is going on if they haven't heard about it already."

Arvin frowned and said, "I'm gonna get in trouble for not reporting all this right away, aren't I?"

"More than likely," Jake admitted, "but I also give you my word that you're helping your country right now."

"For some reason, I believe you, son. I'll give you boys the benefit of the doubt . . . for a little while."

"That's all we ask, Mr. Jones."

"Should I wish you good luck?"

"We'll take that, too," Jake said. "We sure will."

Alexander Sherman stood up from the long table and said, "I'm going to make sure that lunch will be ready on schedule. The rest of you continue the excellent work you've been doing, my friends."

The buzz of conversation around the table resumed as Sherman turned toward the door at the front of the car. "Excellent work" was really an exaggeration, he thought. The idiots hadn't accomplished a blasted thing with all their wrangling. Mostly they had argued about who was responsible for the recent attacks. The conservatives all insisted it was Islamic terrorists—which, of course, it actually was. The liberals insisted it was more likely some sort of false-flag operation by the warmongering administration, since Islam was a religion of peace. They had gone around and around the usual tired talking points on both sides.

Sherman was ready for the whole thing to be over. Ready for everything to come crashing down—literally, in the case of the train, and figuratively, in the case of the government—so that things could start anew and be rebuilt into the sort of shining paradise that he knew was waiting . . . if only people would allow him to lead them to it.

He passed through the dining car, nodding to the staff getting ready for lunch, including the new men and women from Saddiq's group who had infiltrated the Silver Eagle's crew. Sherman didn't treat them any differently from the others. Even now, he didn't want any suspicion that something might be wrong.

He entered the vestibule at the front of the dining car and waited there, checking his watch. Three more minutes, and the train would reach Granby. It would stop, and he would step down, and as soon as he waved to the man in the cab, the train would roll on without him. That is, if Saddiq's man had succeeded in eliminating the engineer and taking over the controls.

If not, if the actual engineer was still running the train, Sherman would go inside to check on the "emergency" and then order the man to proceed. He would step onto the train but immediately get off again and hope his departure wasn't noticed.

Sherman didn't believe it would come to that, however. He was confident that Saddiq's man was up there in the cab, running the controls. Despite a few glitches, Saddiq's people really hadn't let him down so far.

Sherman looked at his $25,000 watch again. Soon now. Very soon.

The infidels had tied Tarik's hands and feet and left him on one of the benches in the waiting room. Beni's body was on the floor beside the bench. Tarik had stopped crying and he thought the wound had stopped bleeding, but his shoulder still hurt a lot. Every time he moved even the least little bit, it hurt worse.

But despite that, he writhed slowly, trying to work his legs off the bench so they would swing down to the floor.

His captors—he didn't think of them as Americans since *he* was an American, too, but rather as infidels— must have figured that as badly hurt as he was, he wasn't a threat any longer. And it was true, he couldn't do anything to them, especially tied up the way he was. But maybe he could warn his friends on the train that something was wrong. The train was supposed to stop, but if it did, those two guys would be waiting, and they had lots of guns and were good with them.

So maybe it would be better, Tarik's pain-addled brain decided, if the train just went on instead of stopping. Bandar al-Saddiq, their leader, would go on to martyr-dom instead of living to plot more attacks against the Great Satan, but under the circumstances, Tarik was sure that was what a holy warrior like Saddiq would want.

Pushing the pain to the back of his mind, he got his feet on the floor while the two guys and the station man were inside the office. He struggled to his feet and leaned against the bench to hold himself upright. There was nothing wrong with his legs except being tied up. He could still hop.

Sure, it hurt like the devil when he did, but if he could keep his balance . . .

Closer and closer he moved to the door that led out of the station next to the tracks.

The door opened onto a small concrete porch with steps leading down from both sides to the concrete platform on the same level as the tracks. Tarik's hands were tied behind him. When he reached the door after a few near-falls along the way, he turned his back to it and fumbled for the knob. After a minute or so, during which he nervously watched the office inside the station, thinking the infidels would come out and see him at any second, he got the door open and hung on to the knob as he hopped awkwardly backward.

The steps were more than he could handle. He tried to hop down them but lost his balance and toppled to the platform instead. He almost screamed from the agony in his shoulder, but he held back the cry.

As he lay there on the concrete, he realized he heard the steel rails humming. That meant the train was approaching, didn't it? He rolled and twisted and lifted his head to peer to the east. Yes! There it was!

One of the members of his cell should have taken over the locomotive by now and would be in the cab, looking along the tracks toward the station. Tarik knew that in the shape he was in, and with his hands tied behind his back, he could never stand up and wave to get his friend's attention. There was only one thing he could do.

He drew in a deep, rasping breath and rolled again, off the platform and onto the gravel of the roadbed.

Struggling, gasping with pain and effort, he wriggled like a snake until he was able to heave himself up and over the closest rail. The man in the cab couldn't miss seeing him, lying there across the tracks like that.

The train was closer now, starting to slow down. Tarik stared at the locomotive's nose as it came nearer and nearer, got larger and larger in his pain-blurred vision. He could tell that the train was continuing to slow.

"No, bro," he whispered. "Don't you see me? Don't you know it's gone wrong? You . . . you gotta keep goin', bro . . . Don't stop . . ."

With a sudden, sharply rising roar, the locomotive surged forward again as the man in the cab pushed the throttle forward. A grin stretched from ear to ear across Tarik's pain-wracked face.

CHAPTER 65

Jake came out of the office inside the station and exclaimed, "Damn it! That guy's gone!"

He had been convinced that the wounded man had passed out, but the bench where they'd left him was empty now except for a pool of blood that had leaked from his shoulder wound. More blood led toward the door to the platform. Jake rushed in that direction with Barry following close behind him.

He hadn't realized the train was so close—close enough that it was already slowing to a stop. Jake caught a glimpse of the wounded terrorist lying across the tracks and instantly guessed the man was trying to warn his friends on the train that something was wrong and their great plan was in jeopardy.

The train seemed to leap ahead like a great silver beast.

Jake didn't stop to think about what he was doing. He bounded down to the platform without taking the steps and raced alongside the train as it began to build up speed again. He could no longer see the man he had shot in the shoulder. That man—an American seduced into Islamic terrorism, judging by his accent—had to have perished under the train's wheels by now.

That was all the proof Jake needed that another member of Lashkar-e-Islami was at the locomotive's controls. The regular engineer would have done everything in his power to stop, instead of deliberately plowing right over the poor son of a gun.

That meant somebody had to get to the engine and stop the train—and as he reached out and grabbed the vertical steel bar next to the vestibule door on one of the cars, he figured he was the best one for that job.

Alexander Sherman felt the train slowing and got ready to open the vestibule door so he could step out. Then, with no warning, the floor lurched under his feet as the train surged forward. Instead of slowing, it began to pick up speed.

That was wrong. That was all wrong! Instead of stopping, the man at the controls in the cab sent the train thundering on through Granby.

"You idiot!" Sherman exclaimed aloud, even though he knew the man in the cab couldn't hear him. "I'm still on board!"

Beads of cold sweat popped out on his forehead. He jerked the vestibule door open, knowing that he had to jump—otherwise, he would go crashing down into that gorge along with everyone else. The location that had been carefully picked for the derailment wasn't that far away. Ten minutes or so.

Sherman stood in the open doorway and looked out at the landscape flashing past outside. The train was already back up to a good speed, moving fast enough that if he jumped from it now, he would be seriously injured, at best. More than likely, he would die.

There was still time to stop the train. But to do it, he would have to reach the engine and find out why that lunatic had disobeyed his orders.

Sherman closed the outer door and moved to the one leading into the passage between cars. He reached under his coat and loosened the gun he carried there. He wasn't sure how to operate the train's controls, but the man in the cab would stop the train at gunpoint, if need be. Otherwise, Sherman would shoot him.

Sherman bit back a groan as he realized that the fanatic intended to die shortly, anyway.

As Jake pulled himself up onto the step leading into the vestibule, he glanced back and saw that Barry was following his example on the next car back. The two men, uncle and nephew, paused where they were for a second and exchanged a brief nod along the length of the train car Jake was about to board.

Then Jake twisted the handle on the door and jerked it open. The wind was already tugging at him as the train picked up speed. He hauled himself up into the vestibule and closed the door.

A man stood there staring at him. The guy didn't look like a terrorist, more like a shocked employee of the excursion train, but Jake pulled the Browning from behind his belt anyway and said, "FBI! Don't move, mister!"

The man put up his hands and stammered, "W-What's going on here?"

Jake didn't answer the question. He asked one of his own.

"What car is this?"

"The . . . the dining car."

"How many cars between here and the engine?"

"Th-This one and one more."

"What's in that second one?"

"An office. Storage and supply rooms. Bunks for the staff."

"You can get all the way to the locomotive cab from here?"

"Well, you have to go up the walk on the outside of the locomotive to reach the cab—"

That was all Jake needed to hear. He nodded and said, "Stay here. Don't raise the alarm. That's an order. This train's now under the jurisdiction of the FBI."

The man nodded weakly. Like most people, he would go along with anything that he believed came from an official source.

Jake opened the door into the dining car, which was so luxuriously appointed that it could have been in some fancy, exclusive restaurant in New York or Los Angeles, maybe even London or Paris. The tables were set with expensive china, silver, and crystal for the lunch that was supposed to be served soon. Several neatly uniformed staff members were scattered around the long room. Jake expected them to exclaim in surprise and fear when they saw a man with a gun, but he figured they would get out of his way when he waved them aside.

Instead, two of them, a man and a woman, both dark-complexioned, yanked guns from under their jackets and opened fire on him while the rest screamed and dived for cover.

* * *

Barry had never seen quite this many bigwigs in one room before, and as he looked around, he realized just how brutally effective the plot hatched by Alexander Sherman, Bandar al-Saddiq, and Mitchell Cavanaugh had been. Wipe out all the people in this room, and the American economy would crash, all right, crash like it hadn't in a long time. And people would suffer enough they would turn to Sherman to relieve their pain.

It was the oldest play in the totalitarian playbook. Dictators the world over had used it with smashing success, and U.S. presidents had taken advantage of times of crisis to grab more control for the presidency. And now Alexander Sherman was poised to seize the reins of power and transform America into a true dictatorship.

Barry wasn't going to allow that to happen.

But as soon as he stepped into the car with a gun in his hand, half a dozen men in dark suits standing around the outer edges of the room also pulled their weapons and leveled them at him.

"Drop it!" one of them yelled.

"Down on your belly!" another added.

Well, of course a bunch of rich big shots like this would have security on hand, Barry thought. He was glad they hadn't just opened fire on him. He didn't drop the Colt, but he half-lifted both hands and pointed the .45 at the ceiling.

"Take it easy, boys," he said. "I'm on your side. My name is Barry Rivers."

All but one of the private security contractors didn't look impressed, and he figured they had never heard of him. The oldest one, though, exclaimed, "Dog?"

"That's right," Barry said. "Have we met?" He looked

closer at the guy and went on, "Is that you, Grigsby? How are you doing, George? How are Dolan, Cordie, and Putt?"

Barry had last seen George Grigsby in Malaysia, five years earlier, on a job that had gone south in a hurry and might have proven disastrous except for the four American mercenaries he'd run into. Obviously, Grigsby had semi-retired into executive protection. He said, "The rest of the boys are doing fine, all busy with lucrative jobs."

Barry smiled and said, "I'm glad to hear it." Having friends in lots of low places certainly came in handy in his line of work.

The big shots in the room were all buzzing with outrage and fear. Grigsby lowered his gun and said to his fellow contractors, "This guy is all right. You're all too young to have heard of him, but he's a living legend. They call him Dog."

"I don't care what they call him," one of the executives said. "He can't just come in here waving a gun around."

"What's going on, Barry?" Grigsby asked.

"There's going to be a terrorist attack on this train," Barry replied, setting off even more gasps and curses and questions. He overrode them and went on, "I don't know when, but pretty soon, I'm betting."

Grigsby nodded, clearly knowing that it was best to believe what Barry had to say.

"What can we do to prevent it?"

Barry took a deep breath and said, "Preventing it is up to my partner, but I think I know a way to keep all these folks safe. You'll have to trust me, though."

"Whatever it takes," Grigsby said.

"Is everybody in here who showed up for this summit meeting?"

"Alexander Sherman isn't," one of the female executives replied. "He's gone up to the dining car."

"Then he'll have to look out for himself," Barry said. The plan that had sprung into his mind meant that Jake would be on his own, too, but that couldn't be helped. The fate of the nation depended on saving the people in this car. Barry didn't necessarily *like* any of them. They were arrogant, pretentious stuffed shirts, for the most part, and most of them had way more money than they needed, as well as dubious political beliefs, but the economy, like it or not, still needed them around.

Grigsby put his gun away and motioned for the other contractors to do likewise. He asked Barry, "What are we going to do?"

"We have to cut this train in half," Barry said.

"What in blazes is wrong with you?" Alexander Sherman demanded as he stepped into the locomotive's cab after the nerve-wracking trip along the narrow ledge outside. He cast a distasteful glance toward the bloody, crumpled corpse of the engineer. "You were supposed to stop in Granby!"

The terrorist glanced back over his shoulder at Sherman and replied, "Something was wrong! One of our men was lying on the tracks, wounded. The Americans must have been waiting to ambush us!"

"There was a man on the tracks? What did you do?"

"Ran over him, of course," the terrorist replied. "I'm sure he was trying to tell me to keep going."

Sherman scrubbed a hand over his bulldog face in exasperation. He tried to gather his thoughts, then said, "You were supposed to stop back there so I could get off the train. You'll have to do it now." He didn't like the idea of getting off out here, but he had no choice. "Stop the train."

"I cannot," the man said flatly without turning around. "The infidels may be pursuing us. The plan is in danger, and I must carry out my mission as quickly as possible."

"You're insane!" Sherman burst out. He wracked his memory for the man's name and came up with it. "Look, Noorzai, be reasonable. I have to get off the train in order for the plan to work."

Stubbornly, the terrorist shook his head.

"When all the wealthy, immoral infidels aboard this train die, the Great Satan will collapse no matter what happens to you or me. The death of America is the only death that matters!"

Sherman's jaw tightened. This idiot wasn't giving him any choice. He pulled the gun from under his jacket.

Soon there were going to be two dead men on the floor of this cab.

Chapter 66

Jake kicked one of the beautifully set dining tables over, causing the expensive china and crystal to shatter, and threw himself behind it. Bullets thudded into the table as the two terrorists continued firing at him. He wasn't surprised that some of Saddiq's people had managed to infiltrate the train's service staff. It was the same pattern Lashkar-e-Islami had used in El Paso and Long Island.

He popped up long enough to trigger a shot at his enemies. The man reeled backward and dropped his gun. Blood bubbled from his throat where Jake's bullet had ripped through it. He staggered and went down.

The woman retreated from the dining car into the vestibule at the front, throwing more shots at Jake on the run.

As the door banged shut behind her, he leaped up and called, "FBI! Is anybody hurt?"

A few heads popped up from the places around the car where the actual serving staff had taken cover.

"What's going on?" a man asked. "Are we under attack? Is it those terrorists again?"

"Yeah," Jake replied. That was the short, easy answer, since he didn't have time to go into details.

"We're all going to die!" a woman wailed. "The train is going to crash!"

"No, it's not," Jake said firmly. He pointed to the man he had shot, who had collapsed and was bleeding out, if he wasn't already dead. "That one and the woman, they were new hires, weren't they?"

"Yeah," replied the man who had spoken. "This . . . this was their first trip on the Silver Eagle."

"Anybody else who's new?"

"There are three more of them," the man replied. His voice was a little stronger now, and understanding had dawned on his face. "They're terrorists!"

"More than likely," Jake agreed. "Where are the others?"

The man nodded toward the next car.

"They went up ahead a few minutes ago, where Lilah just went. They were fetching some more things for lunch."

That might be true, or they might have been hatching more trouble, Jake thought. But the important thing now was that there were more enemies between him and the destination he had to reach—the locomotive's cab.

They didn't have to stop him permanently. All they had to do was delay him long enough for the train to reach the point where the attack was supposed to take place. Since Jake didn't know where that was, he had no way of knowing how much time he had. But he was certain he didn't have enough that he could afford to waste any.

But if he couldn't go *through* the next car to get to the engine, he could still go *over* it. He slipped a full magazine into the Browning and stuck the gun behind his belt.

"Go back to the other car where they were having their meeting," he told the people in here. "There's a man back there named Barry. He'll see to it that you're safe."

"What are you going to do?" the man asked.

"Stop those people from wrecking this train."

He went into the vestibule and opened the door to the outside. Holding on and leaning out, he saw the metal rungs attached to the front of the car.

"Up you go," he muttered to himself as he reached around, got hold of one of the rungs, and swung around onto the ladder.

The gap between cars was barely big enough for Jake's brawny form to fit through it. He reached the top, twisted around, and pulled himself onto the top of the car right behind the engine. Wind whipped and battered him as he lay there, stretched out on his belly.

He grimaced as he thought about how many movies he had seen where guys ran around and fought on top of moving trains. They made it look easy. In real life, the thought of even standing up on this one was scary as blazes.

But the train getting blown up or derailed was pretty scary, too. Jake worked his way to the center of the roof, then pushed himself to hands and knees. From there, he made it to his feet and lurched unsteadily toward the front of the train.

A small part of his brain realized how beautiful the scenery was all around. Steep, thickly wooded mountain slopes and deep, rocky gorges, including the one that ran to the left of the railroad tracks, only a short distance away. At the bottom of that gorge, a good-sized stream raced along. That was the Colorado River, Jake recalled from his study of the maps of the area.

He wished he could fish that stream. He bet there were some good trout in it. For a second, he thought about how nice it would be if he and Barry could set up camp and just laze away, spending some time fishing. It would be even better if Gretchen came along, too . . .

A head appeared at the front of the car, followed by a set of broad, powerful shoulders. Almost before Jake realized what was happening, a man had pulled himself on top of the car and was charging toward him.

The terrorists had had the same thought about getting to the engine this way, and they were determined to stop him. Jake grabbed the Browning, figuring he would shoot this guy off the train, but before he could fire, a shot blasted from somewhere else and a bullet ripped along the outside of his right upper arm. The fingers of that hand opened involuntarily, and the 9mm dropped out of his grip to hit the car's roof and fly off into space.

The next second, the big guy lunging at him tackled him and drove him backward off his feet.

Barry stood on the steps just outside the vestibule, which leaned down toward a white-painted metal bar that led into the coupling apparatus between this car and the next one. George Grigsby was just above him, hanging on to his other arm.

"I don't think you can do it, Barry," Grigsby shouted above the train's rumble. "That coupling's got too much weight on it for you to be able to lift the cut bar and disengage it."

"We don't have any choice," Barry replied. "Cutting loose the back half of the train is the only sure way to save all you folks."

He had already tried pulling the emergency chain to engage the air brakes, just in case it worked, but as with the freight train in El Paso, the plotters had taken care of that contingency. Someone must have closed the air cocks in the line before the train left Denver.

With that option gone, Barry had fallen back on his original idea: to uncouple the back half of the train.

He leaned down and wrapped his fingers around the bar. Gritting his teeth, he heaved up on it . . . and the bar didn't move. Grigsby was right. Railyard workers uncoupled cars when they were stationary, or else when the locomotive had bumped the string in the other direction to make sure the pressure was off.

He tried again and failed.

Of course, uncoupling when the train was moving, especially at speed like this, had some inherent dangers of its own. Hydraulic and air pressure lines would rip loose, the brakes wouldn't work, and there was no way of being sure what the suddenly freed cars would do. But it was still the only option Barry could see, and as he hung there with Grigsby holding his arm, another idea occurred to him.

"Pull me in!" he called.

Grigsby did so. Every moment that went by stretched Barry's nerves a little tighter, but he said, "We need some belts we can weave together to make a strap sturdy enough not to break when several of us use it to pull that lever up."

Grigsby nodded, instantly grasping Barry's plan.

Both of them started taking off their own belts. Grigsby turned his head and said to one of the other security contractors, "Don't just stand there. Get a couple more belts for us!"

Within minutes, they had woven the belts together to form a thick strap. Barry fashioned a loop in the end of it and got out onto the step again. He leaned down, dangling the loop and trying to jockey it into position where it would catch the cut bar. Doing that took several tries and cost more precious moments of time, but finally it was in place. Grigsby joined him on the step, which was pretty crowded with two big men on it. Two more of the security contractors were in the doorway. All four men got hold of the strap.

"All right," Barry said. "Heave!"

They pulled up with all the strength they could muster. Through clenched teeth, Grigsby said, "I wish we had . . . Red Dolan here . . . That big Mick . . . is the strongest guy I know."

"Yeah," Barry said, "and my nephew Jake . . . could probably do this by himself. But it's down to us . . . now . . . to get it done!"

Jake undoubtedly had his own problems.

The terrorist's weight coming down on top of him drove the air out of Jake's lungs and half-stunned him, but it also pinned him to the roof of the car. He wouldn't fall off as long as the guy was lying on top of him.

But he wouldn't be able to stop the train, either, so he forced his muscles to work and clapped his open hands against the man's ears as hard as he could.

The guy yelled in pain and jerked back. Jake punched him in the throat. The man started to gag and his eyes bugged out.

"Get out of the way! I'll shoot him!"

That was a woman's voice. Jake realized that the female terrorist had climbed onto the car and winged him from behind, causing him to drop his gun. From the corner of his eye, he saw her move unsteadily forward, her gun held in front of her.

The man who had tackled him was still choking, but he managed to try sledgehammering Jake's head into the car's roof. Jake jerked aside from the fists at the last second. He whipped a punch into the guy's ribs and thought he felt one of them break.

The woman loomed over them, watching for an opening through which to put a bullet in Jake. He grabbed the man's shoulders and heaved, throwing him off to the side. The man hit the woman's legs and got tangled up in them. She screamed as she lost her balance and fell backward.

Both of them went off the side of the car. Jake didn't see what happened to them, but he knew the odds of them surviving such a fall onto rocky ground, from a speeding train, were slim to none. Closer to none.

He rolled onto his belly again, breathing hard as he tried to get enough air back in his lungs. His heart slugged so hard in his chest it felt like it would rip right through his body at any second.

He would have been content to just lie there, but he knew he couldn't. He forced himself up again and moved forward, arms outstretched to help him keep his balance. Assuming that one of the terrorists was in the engine, that left another man unaccounted for. Jake had no idea where the man was, but he had a bad feeling he might find out before he reached the engine.

He made it to the front end of the car without anybody else shooting at him. His guts were shaky as he climbed down the ladder there, but his muscles worked just fine. A narrow walkway led along the side of the locomotive to a door that opened into the cab.

The fourth terrorist was part of the way along that ledge. He twisted around, holding onto a small iron grab bar with one hand while he snarled at Jake and pulled a gun from under his jacket with the other.

Jake didn't have anywhere to go except straight ahead, and he had to do it fast. With every bit of agility he could muster, he ran along the walkway while the wind tried to pluck him off. The terrorist triggered a pair of shots, but both of them went wild.

Then Jake reached him, batted the gun aside, and grabbed the front of the guy's jacket with both hands. He tossed the man right off the train. Shrieking in terror, arms and legs windmilling, the terrorist sailed out over the gorge, closer than ever to the roadbed, and plummeted toward the churning Colorado River almost a hundred feet below.

That was the last Jake saw of him.

The effort almost overbalanced Jake. He grabbed hold of the little support bar and hung on for dear life. When he was steady again, he moved forward to the door into the cab.

Through the window in the door, he saw two men—a man in the uniform of one of the Silver Eagle's serving staff sitting in the engineer's seat, and a bulky older man in an expensive suit holding a gun to the first man's head. Jake had seen enough pictures of Alexander Sherman in the past twenty-four hours to recognize the multibillionaire, but this was the first time he had laid eyes on the true architect of this terror plot in the flesh.

This was no time for big, dramatic statements or witty quips, Jake knew.

He jerked the door open to charge into the cab, raise hell, and get this train stopped.

CHAPTER 67

Sherman heard him come in and started to turn. Jake lowered his shoulder and rammed it into the older man, knocking Sherman forward against the locomotive's control console. The unidentified terrorist whirled around and slashed at Jake, who only realized the guy had a knife when he felt the line of fiery pain cutting across his chest.

Jake grabbed the man's wrist before he could attempt a backhand slash, closing his fingers so hard he felt bones grind together in the man's wrist. The terrorist cried out in pain and punched Jake in the face. It was a good strong blow and landed cleanly, but Jake was too full of adrenaline to feel it much. He hammered a left to the man's jaw and knocked him against one of the big levers sticking up from the console.

The train started to go faster.

Okay, that had to be the throttle, Jake thought as he grappled with the terrorist. That meant the other handle would be the brake. Good to know.

Sherman regained his balance and fired. The gun blast was deafeningly loud in the already noisy cab. Jake felt something warm against his cheek and knew the bullet had missed him by a whisker. He kicked backward at Sherman.

The terrorist headbutted him. Pain made Jake squint, and his eyes watered, further blurring his vision. He twisted at the waist as the man tried to knee him in the groin. The guy's knee thudded against Jake's thigh instead.

Jake got a hand on the man's throat and swung him around just as Sherman triggered another shot. That move wasn't intentional, just something that happened in the heat of battle, but it saved Jake's life anyway. The bullet struck the terrorist in the back of the head and killed him instantly.

Jake shoved the body at Sherman, trying to keep the billionaire distracted for a second. Lunging at the control levers, Jake grabbed the one for the brake and hauled back on it.

"Yes, stop the train, you fool!" Sherman yelled as he shoved the terrorist's corpse aside and leveled the gun at Jake. "We have to stop now!"

The panic in Sherman's voice told Jake they must be almost at the spot where the attack was going to take place, whatever it was. He grinned as he said, "Not going the way you planned, is it, Sherman?"

"Stop the train!"

With a laugh of perverse satisfaction, Jake moved before Sherman could stop him. He shoved the throttle forward again, and the locomotive responded smoothly and instantly, surging ahead.

Jake pointed at what he had just spotted through the window in the cab door.

"Look back there!"

The tracks, following the long curve of the canyon through which they were passing, put the locomotive in a position where Jake and Sherman could look back along the rails and see the rear cars of the train falling farther and farther behind. Barry had cut them loose somehow, Jake knew, freeing them from the threat of whatever was about to happen to the rest of the train. And Jake was sure Sherman's intended victims were back there, too, safe now. He hoped the other innocents on board the train had made it to the rear cars.

"I think you and I are the only ones still alive up here," he said to Sherman, whose face had turned as gray as ashes. He planted himself between the billionaire and the control levers.

"You madman! I'll shoot you!"

"I won't die quick enough for you to get to these controls," Jake told him. "Whatever's going to happen is gonna happen, Sherman, and you'll have a grandstand seat for it."

Sherman's eyes were huge with horror and disbelief. He muttered, "No . . . no . . . it can't end this way. I was going to change the country . . ."

"Not for the better. Not for freedom. You wanted to put your foot on America's throat . . . and you're going to end up like all the other petty, would-be tyrants. This country always finds a way of dealing with guys like you."

Sherman suddenly howled in incoherent rage and jerked the gun up as his finger tightened on the trigger.

Jake dove for him, feeling the sudden shock as a bullet struck him, but his momentum carried him into Sherman. They crashed against the back wall of the cab. They might both die in a matter of minutes in whatever catastrophe Sherman and his allies had planned, but

Jake was damned if he was going to stand there and let the crazy billionaire shoot him.

Jake was bigger and stronger, but Sherman fought with the strength and feverish intensity of a madman. They swayed and staggered back and forth in the cab, tripping over the bodies of the engineer and the terrorist. They lurched against the control panel and shoved the brake handle forward again. The train screeched and shuddered. A second later, their weight shoved the throttle ahead again. They were probably wreaking havoc on the train's gears—not that it mattered at this point.

Jake felt a sudden, hot weakness flowing through him and realized he was losing enough blood to put him on the verge of passing out. Didn't matter, he told himself. Alexander Sherman would never become the dictator of America he so longed to be. That was enough.

The gun boomed again. Jake had lost track of it in the struggle. But it was Sherman who jerked this time, his eyes widening until it seemed they were about to pop out of their sockets. He let go of Jake and slumped back against the rear wall. A large, rapidly spreading blood-stain turned his shirtfront red. Gasping for breath, he slid slowly down the metal wall.

"Not . . . not fair," Sherman rasped.

Jake had to hold on to the back of the engineer's seat to keep himself from falling.

"Seems like it to me," Jake said as his head hung forward in exhaustion. "You were willing to kill this country to get your hands on more power. But it didn't work. America's safe . . . for now. Until some other crazy son of a—"

He stopped short. He was talking to a glassy-eyed dead man.

As soon as the implications of that realization percolated through Jake's brain, he turned and hauled back on the brake lever as hard as he could. But as the train began to slow, he saw a sudden burst of flame from the tracks several hundred yards ahead. He couldn't hear the explosion, but he was sure it shook the earth for miles around.

It took a long distance to stop a train, especially one going this fast. But the Silver Eagle was slowing down now. It wouldn't stop before it reached the site of the blast, but maybe it would slow enough for Jake to steal his life back.

That possibility galvanized his muscles. He threw off the weakness from being shot and the loss of blood. The human body was capable of incredible things with enough willpower and desperation behind it. Leaving the three dead men in the cab, Jake flung the door open and climbed back out onto the walkway.

He threw caution to the wind now. No point in being careful when you had a minute or so to live. He raced along the side of the locomotive and came to the next car. Scrambling up the ladder, he rolled onto its top and pushed himself to his feet. He glanced back over his shoulder, saw the cloud of dust from the explosion coming closer, looming larger and larger. He ran toward the back of the car, and when he got there, he leaped the gap between it and what was now the final car without even slowing down.

He stopped when he came to the end of it and bent over to put his hands on his knees and draw in several huge breaths, gasps that hurt like blazes after being shot in the chest, but he did it anyway. The train had slowed to a pace that was faster than that of a running man, but Jake thought he might survive a leap from it now. That is, if he didn't hit his head on a rock and bust it open, or ram a tree limb all the way through him, or tumble all the way down the side of that gorge and land in the river and drown . . .

But he supposed that was why they called it a leap of faith, he told himself as he gathered himself, bunched his muscles, and jumped, sailing up and out, up and out . . . until the inevitable occurred and he went down and down . . .

And down.

CHAPTER 68

Somebody poked him and said, "Wake up."

"Uhhh," Jake said. "Wha . . ."

"Wake up, I said." This time, he recognized the voice as Gretchen's. "You're dreaming again."

Jake lifted his head a little, rested the balls of both hands against his temples, and rubbed as he yawned. He blinked his eyes open for a second, then closed them again against the hot glare of the sun.

"I dream all the time," he said. "It's a sign of an active brain."

"Yeah, but you were on that train again. I could tell. There's no need to relive that, even in your dreams. It's all over."

"You're right about that," Jake said drowsily. He did most things drowsily these days. How could it be any other way when your only job was to lie around on a beach with a beautiful woman and recuperate from enough injuries to, as Dr. Caleb McIntire put it, "kill half a dozen normal men"?

Jake stretched his legs and wiggled his toes. He was still a little amazed that everything worked after the punishment he had put his body through. Amazed but grateful. And with Gretchen's help during the past six weeks, he had been satisfied that *everything* still worked.

They lay on beach chairs in the sun, with the blue-green waters of the Gulf of Mexico lapping at the sand a few yards away. Jake wore a rather baggy bathing suit, while Gretchen's blue bikini was as small as the law allowed. Not that they had to worry about the law here. Nobody was around except Barry, who at the moment was inside the beach house about fifty yards behind them in the trees.

It was the nicest safe house Jake had ever seen. He sometimes wondered if they could stay here permanently. Jake Rivers, Barry Rivers, and Gretchen Rogers were all dead, after all. Jake and Barry had died in that horrible train wreck in Colorado, and Gretchen had succumbed to injuries suffered in the line of duty as an agent of the Department of Homeland Security.

That was the story, and Jake didn't see any reason they shouldn't stick to it. He had paid for this with scars all over his body, and Gretchen had a scar, too, from that bullet wound, which was clearly visible in the bikini. She didn't try to cover it up. It was a badge of honor, she had explained, earned by helping to save the country from Alexander Sherman, and she would wear it with honor.

Sherman had died in the crash, too, officially. Died a hero trying to stop the terrorists bent on wrecking the train. That was a bitter pill to swallow, but the President had convinced Jake and Barry it was for the best. It helped that Mitchell Cavanaugh had spilled his guts, confessing to every bad thing he had done going back to high school, and dozens of high-ranking officials and bureaucrats in Washington had resigned quietly, then been taken into custody and plea-bargained their way into federal prisons across the country. The ones who hadn't committed suicide, that is. The rat's nest inside the Beltway hadn't been cleaned out completely, by any means . . . but at least there were fewer rats to dirty it up.

The problem was that all the people on the other side didn't know just how much of a maniac their progressive "hero" had been. Even if they *had* known, they wouldn't have really believed it. And if they had been shown incontrovertible proof, they still wouldn't care. They would continue to vote based on their so-called "ideals" without any real understanding of what was actually going on or what the country needed to survive.

America had ways of dealing with would-be tyrants, Jake had told Alexander Sherman . . . but all too often, it was the American people who lifted up those tyrants and invited them to take over.

That was a bigger problem than Jake could deal with today, however. Today, his biggest decision was whether to go swimming, or fishing, or just lie here on the beach with Gretchen and bake away his aches and pains.

Sand crunched behind them. Barry said, "I can see you two are busy, so I hate to interrupt—"

"Then don't," Gretchen said.

Barry chuckled and said, "Sorry. I don't have much choice. I just got off the phone with . . . well, let's just say a certain somebody very high up."

"We're retired," Jake said without opening his eyes.

"It would be nice to think so, wouldn't it?"

Jake sighed, opened his eyes, and sat up, swinging his legs off the beach chair.

"There's a job waiting for us out there?" he asked.

"Yeah. They won't order us to accept it, of course. Technically, we're free agents and can do whatever we want, being, well, dead and all. But . . . the truck's been refurbished and reoutfitted and is ready to go again. There's a problem that it seems we're uniquely suited to deal with."

"All three of us?" Gretchen said.

"If you want."

"We'd be Rig Warriors," she mused. "I kind of like the sound of that."

Jake said, "When's the truck supposed to get here?"

"Somebody will drop it off tomorrow."

Jake put his legs up on the beach chair, stretched out, and closed his eyes again.

"Then we still have today," he said.

He reached out his hand without looking, found Gretchen's outstretched hand, and held it tightly as the sun warmed them and the waves whispered against the sand.

National Bestselling Author
WILLIAM W. JOHNSTONE

RIG WARRIOR

In Vietnam, Barry Rivers learned how to be a hero.
In a busted marriage, he learned how to be a survivor.
And in Washington, he learned how to make big
money, consulting with the U.S. government on
weapons. Then he got a message from home.
Someone had come after his old man—and turned
Barry Rivers into the deadliest enemy of all . . .

Now Rivers is back behind the wheel of a
midnight-blue Kenworth—with a hard-swearing,
hard-driving, tightly packed blonde named Kate
and his dog named Dog by his side. With a few good
trucking friends, Rivers has the firepower to take on
an army. And he'll need it. Because a contract to
haul Safe Secure Transport has plunged him into
a world of betrayal, corruption, and violence that
is killing everyone around him. And the only way
to stop a coming war is to start one first—
behind the barrel of a machine gun.

**Look for RIG WARRIOR,
available exclusively in e-book now!**

Connect with Us

Visit us online at
KensingtonBooks.com
to read more from your favorite authors, see books
by series, view reading group guides, and more.

Join us on social media

for sneak peeks, chances to win books and prize packs,
and to share your thoughts with other readers.

facebook.com/kensingtonpublishing
twitter.com/kensingtonbooks

Tell us what you think!

To share your thoughts, submit a review,
or sign up for our eNewsletters, please visit:
KensingtonBooks.com/TellUs.